DUKYARIAN RECTANGLE

BABS SOARES

Dallas, Texas

DUKYARIAN RECTANGLE

For information contact:

Djarabi Kitabs Publishing

PO BOX 703733

Dallas, TX 75370

https://www.djarabikitabs.com

Cover and jacket design by Lillian…

Library of Congress Control Number: 2018938521

EBook ISBN: 978-1-947148-12-3

Paperback ISBN: 978-1-947148-11-6

First Edition: May 2018

10987654321

ALSO BY BABS SOARES

With This Gun, I Thee Wed

DEDICATION

To the worldwide champions of inter-faith harmony and multi-cultural understanding

Table of Content

Chapter-1

Little guy, big dreams!

LONG BEFORE COMPLETING HIS eight-year course of study at the Markas Islamiyya, or Islamic Center of learning, in Potiskum, Abu Danja Mamba had chosen Maiduguri as the place where he would propagate God's Word. He wasn't going to make a living teaching at an obscure primary school somewhere or eking out a living by officiating at an occasional marriage or naming ceremony. Ever since he was a student at the Dikwa Primary School, he had nourished the dream of becoming one of the Dukyarian society's Big Men. This was a tall ambition for a man of his size. Now, a grown man and standing five foot four, he could hardly pass for a hunk. Whatever he lacked in height, he failed to make up for in body weight. His thin lips left his protruding upper teeth perpetually exposed. His narrow face and deep-sunken eyes completed the picture of a ghost in a human body. A childhood ailment had left him with a speech defect and a bad temper. Neither impediment helped his social networking cause.

On top of the physical and psychosomatic challenges, Abu was born into a *talakawa*. He would have stood no chance of going to school had the government not intervened to relieve his parents of their responsibility for his tuition, clothing, and upkeep. Yet, and unmindful of the formidable obstacles which he faced, he had gone through his adolescence wanting to be like one of the nobility, locally referred to as the *sarauta*. A brilliant pupil, he couldn't see any reason why he should not be able to stand up to his school mates who talked down to him. He considered himself equal to the supercilious Bukar, who always came to school in a flashy, chauffeur-driven

Mercedes, and Zarma, the bully, whose family owned the Maiduguri refinery. He didn't get why the pretty but sharp-tongued Zainab considered him below her, more so since she was an average pupil, while he, Abu, was the top of his class.

As was to be expected, Abu's dream of social advancement remained unfulfilled throughout his sojourn in Dikwa. The dream vanished completely by the time he reached Potiskum. His mallams, or teachers, at the markas were strict, equal-opportunity disciplinarians. They didn't want to know whether one of their wards was from a rich or a poor home. He had to abide by their rules or face the consequences, such as drastic reduction in food ration; curtailment of weekend sight-seeing privileges; or, for serious transgressions, thorough whipping at the hands of heartless enforcers handpicked by the head of the markas security unit. School meals were also far from regular. Even though the markas was subsidized by the government under its nomadic knowledge seekers, otherwise known as the almajir, program, the school administrators still managed to pocket the monies budgeted for food, clothing, and other essential items. It was not unusual for Abu or any of his school mates to ward off starvation by begging for alms, accepting odd jobs in a car wash, or offering to fill potholes on highways in the hope that kind-hearted motorists would drop a few coins in his bowl.

Chapter-2

You are destined to be famous. Trust me, Abu!

PREOCCUPIED WITH HOW TO keep body and soul together, Abu perished the thought of ever joining the ranks of the nobility. Then, something happened to renew his dream and rekindle his ambition. After the weekly Friday prayers at the Potiskum central mosque, his classmate at the markas, Usman Darazo, requested him to accompany him, Darazo, to a mallam who lived close to the city stadium along Maiduguri Road. The gangly, six-foot three Darazo was having problems memorizing the Qur'an. His father had sent him a letter advising him to see Mallam Adamu Alkaleri. The letter assured Usman that he would be gifted with a sharp, photographic memory once he contacted Alkaleri.

To avoid being caught in the rush of worshippers, the two students made for the mosque's north exit as soon as the Friday prayer ended. Too poor to hire a taxi, they trekked all the way to their destination. Leaving the Local Government Secretariat behind, they swung right and headed east.

They soon caught a glimpse of the Potiskum market on their left. Men with garishly painted faces had gathered on a dry, sandy terrain outside the market. It was a familiar sight. Both knew that men seeking the hands of women in marriage would shortly prove their mettle by engaging their rivals in physical contests. The common events were wrestling, kick-boxing, and mutual lashing. Whoever tapped out or somehow succumbed to his opponent's dominance lost not only the contest but also the chance to pick his bride on that occasion.

The vanquished contestant had to wait till the next market day to look for another woman worth exchanging blows over. It was a frivolous pursuit that Mamba and Darazo could do without.

Leaving the prizefighters behind, Mamba and Darazo plodded along the highway until they reached the city stadium. Alkaleri's mud-built, thatch-roofed, unpretentious bungalow sat on a wide expanse of parched land a few meters from the highway. "Salaam alaykum," Darazo announced his presence, tapping the front door gently. A girl, barely seven years old, opened the door, let the visitors in, and pointed to the only seats available, the prayer mats on the bare floor.

Fifteen minutes later, the recluse Alkaleri emerged from one of the rooms. A man of average height with a slim frame and fine features, he looked dignified in his spotlessly white kaftan. He knew, even before the visitor opened his mouth, who Usman was and why he had come. He also knew right away that Usman's buddy, Abu, needed no help with the Qur'an, as he had already committed more than half of the holy book's contents to memory. He wasted no time attending to Usman. The mallam went back into one of the rooms and returned with a bottle filled with a dark brown liquid. Usman was to gulp the bottle's contents down in one go. That should take care of his memory lapses.

As regards Abu Mamba, he needed nothing more than to be prayerful. If his intentions were pure and his prayers were sincere, his light would, in Alkaleri's words, "shine throughout the length and breadth of Dukyaria. You started out in life unknown, but yours will be a face that everyone will recognize and none will ever forget."

Abu took that to mean that he was destined for greatness. That was settled then. It had been "written" in his pre-natal logbook that he would be counted among Dukyaria's people of consequence. Alkaleri was just being overly cautious when he attached two conditions to his forecast—that is, purity of heart and prayerfulness. The anchorite was merely hedging his bet; he didn't want to be called out for false prophesy. He feared that his credibility would suffer irreparable damage should his prediction be proved wrong. The mystic had clearly forgotten that Allah's decrees are precise and absolute, Abu assured himself.

Chapter-3

Abu's all for tolerance, provided you see things his way!

"NO COERCION IN MATTERS OF FAITH, as right and wrong are self-evident. Verily, Allah is with the patient. Repel the bad with the good. I hope that no matter where you are, you will always be guided by these ayahs of the Noble Qur'an." With these words, Mallam Shehu, the rector of Potiskum's Markas Islamiyya, dismissed the graduating class of 2065.

"Allahu Akbar!" A chorus of voices signified their appreciation of Shehu's words of wisdom by acknowledging Allah's unrivalled majesty. The students had reasons to glorify God. Every word coming out of the Rector's mouth was backed with the authority of the Qur'an and was accepted as divinely inspired.

With the ceremony over, the graduating students dispersed. They headed in different directions, determined to spread the word of God. Dawah, or call to salvation, is the name given to the mission they were about to embark on.

Abu recalled Alkaleri's prediction of a bright future. The new markas graduate wasn't taking any chances all the same. He realized that he had to play his own part to ensure that the prediction came to pass. In other words, he, like Alkaleri, saw the need to hedge his bet. He decided to move to a thriving metropolis. Maiduguri was an ancient city with many advantages. First, as a renowned center of learning, it was home to highly venerated mystics who had stayed out of the public eye and were accessible only to a few. The closer he was to these rare gems, the greater would be his opportunity of deepening his knowledge of Sufi metaphysics and acquiring the power he so much craved. Second, since Maiduguri was predominantly Muslim, the population would not only understand what he had to say but would also unreservedly embrace his teachings. Third, Maiduguri was not too far from his own place of birth, Dikwa. With these reasons at the back of his mind, Abu left Potiskum that Monday afternoon, 2 March 2065, and travelled eastwards.

Abu could hardly contain his fury when he caught glimpses of churches along the way. He wondered what the infidels were doing in Ngelzerma, Damaturu, and other towns and villages along the route His rage knew no bounds when his bus slowed down on approaching Maiduguri's western frontier and unfamiliar images appeared before his eyes. The empty space which he remembered leaving behind in the outskirts eight years earlier had now been taken over by the kuffar, non-believers. Various denominations had erected churches all over the place. The most aggressive of these invaders were the Pentecostals. They pitched their tents anywhere: close to residential areas, motor parks, automobile workshops, supermarkets, restaurants, schools, water-logged spots, children's playgrounds. Everywhere!

Anyway, the structures he found revolting were in the periphery, not in the center, Abu consoled himself. His disquiet quickly returned when he sighted, directly in the heart of the city, images which he thought he had left behind in the outskirts. To his dismay, churches, with their unmistakable signs of the crucifix, shot up defiantly at strategic locations throughout the entire city. Most alarming of all, a denomination known as the Prayer Warriors had formed the habit of knocking on the doors of Muslim homes and calling on the inhabitants to believe in three gods all at once, God the Father, the Son, and the Holy Spirit. Another itinerant sect, the Jehovah's Witnesses do not believe in the Trinity. They might as well, since the one God they believe in was, in Abu's view, a human being, Jesus Christ. An anthropomorphic god was, by his own definition, one that had a beginning and an end. This contextual god was different from the absolute and universal Supreme Being he, Abu, had been taught to believe in—meaning, Allah, the First, without a beginning; the Last, without an end; the One without Whom there would be nothing.

His stomach turned each time he reflected on the possibility of co-existing with beliefs alien to his. He could not understand why, on top of the lurid stories he had been told about goings-on in the church—stories of demonic practices perpetrated by cultists under the priests' noses, of celibate priests molesting young children, of lecherous ministers impregnating female worshippers, of monies mysteriously vanishing from caskets, and of shepherds routinely pulling wool in the eyes of their flock—Christian evangelists now had to rub his face in this Trinity or anthropomorphic doctrine! No coercion in matters of faith, as right and wrong are self-evident, he recalled. Verily, Allah is with the patient. Repel the bad with the good. He wondered whether Mallam Shehu really knew what he was talking about. Did the Markas rector himself believe in what he had recited to his graduating class? Maybe he should come over to Maiduguri and reconcile his recitations with the obscenity which was staring Abu in the face. What other name than "coercion" would one give to the Pentecostals' decision to set up shop in the midst of the faithful? Putting up churches right in the center of the city, in Muslim neighborhoods, and close to mosques? And worst of all, shoving the Trinity doctrine down the Muslims' throat? Haram! How long could one remain patient in the face of these provocative acts? And how can the good be expected to repel the bad and still remain good under such circumstances?

The Pentecostals were not the only ones that tried Abu's patience. His own Muslim brethren grated on his nerves. The first thing he did on arrival in Maiduguri was to search for a Sufi master. Alas, he found his Sufi guides particularly insufferable. They never stopped setting him impossible tasks, and he never quit letting them down. And the mystics' teachings? The precepts were too grounded in paradoxes and inexplicable contradictions to be imbibed by a short-tempered person like him. One Sufi master, Sheikh Awwal, even had the temerity to suggest that belief in one universal God was not inconsistent with belief in multiple provincial deities. Shirk! That, as Abu recalled, is the name given under the Sharia to the crime of associating other gods with Allah. To part ways with Shaytan, the Devil, Abu left Sheikh Awwal's madrassa on Mafoni Road to seek knowledge elsewhere. He was sure that even Rector Shehu, in spite of his emphasis on patience, would endorse his decision to move on.

Chapter-5

Where's the future greatness long foretold?

ABU HAD A LONG journey ahead of him. His search led him to Sheikh Sule, in another part of Maiduguri. Abu might have distanced himself from Awwal's sacrilege, but he still had to contend with his new spiritual guide's eccentricity. Sheikh Sule groped women that he sighted on city avenues or in marketplaces; sat by the roadside to eat from the same bowl as persons with psychiatric disorders; and, while clad in a thick woolen robe, stared at the red-hot sun for hours without blinking. Abu overlooked all this. He became one of the Sheikh's disciples. The oddball, Sule, was of inestimable value after all. He was his generation's foremost numerologist. He knew what numbers to combine to get a deed done or to foil the best contrived plot.

Fortunately for Abu, the association with the crank came with benefits, especially of the material kind. As he got close to Sule and gained the master's confidence, Abu, the disciple, served as the intermediary between Sule and the wealthy clients seeking the free-spirit's favors. No client's request for psychic evaluation reached Sule without Abu's knowledge. No algorithm mystically worked out by Sule to solve a problem got to the distressed client without Abu's say-so.

He was generously rewarded for serving as the go-between for the seekers and the expediters of heavenly intercessions. A politician who won a hotly contested election rewarded Abu with a brand-new Toyota Land Cruiser. A contractor who landed a major infrastructure development project built him a six-bedroom bungalow in the choicest part of the city. He promptly let it out to a government agency. Even Zarma had got off his high horse to befriend Abu. Zarma's father, Ngilaruma, was going through a bad patch. Unless Abu got Sule to work one of those miracles, the banks would be all over Ngilaruma's refinery and other prized possessions. Zarma's flashy Mercedes was already gone, auctioned off to settle urgent bills. He pleaded with Abu to do something before he, Zarma, was forced to part with the only ride he had left, a BMW. Abu's spiritual guide, Sule, eventually succeeded in staving off Ngilaruma's creditors, leaving Abu a quarter of a million dollars richer.

Material comfort had its downside. As Abu piled up riches, he wrestled with a growing feeling of personal inadequacy. While rejoicing over the wealth he had accumulated since crossing from Awwal's to Sule's side, he was increasingly tormented by his Sufi master's weird, possibly ungodly, deportment. His teachers at Potiskum had drilled into his head that the timely performance of the five obligatory prayers on a daily basis was one of the main pillars of belief. However, he was yet to see Sule perform the prayers either alone or in the mosque. Abu's problem was how to bring the delicate matter up with the master—a master who was not only highly temperamental but also happened to be his source of wealth.

One bright morning, the opportunity Abu had for long craved finally arrived. The sun shone as it always did, but a cool north-easterly wind tempered Maiduguri's usually sweltering heat. Having noticed that Sule was in a cheery mood, Abu summoned the courage to confront the

master. He wanted to know why, ever since they had met, Sule had not been seen praying alone or with the rest of the faithful. The master's response jolted the underling. Without batting an eye, Sule asserted that his status before God was such that he could afford to dispense with, as he put it, "the ritualistic but largely insincere obeisance to God." Sule didn't see why he had to join hypocritical, hate-spewing, possibly evil-plotting congregations in ostentatious acts of devotion when he had other means of showing his love for the Almighty. What means? Abu had hardly finished framing his sardonic but unspoken question when Sule responded, "I know what you are thinking. You are silently asking about the means at my disposal, and I am telling you, means beyond your comprehension."

Abu wasn't satisfied with his master's explanation for skipping the five daily prayers. However, he had to get a grip on his inner thoughts while he was in the mind reader's presence. As soon as he was alone, he began to ask himself whether moving from Awwal's Mafoni Road commune to Sule's isolated camp along the Konduga Expressway hadn't been a mistake. He had been taught both in Dikwa and Potiskum that no Muslim was higher in the spiritual hierarchy or closer to God Almighty than Prophet Muhammad. And here was Sule, an ordinary human being—and a deranged individual at that—arrogating to himself a status higher than the Prophet's. For what status could be higher than that which exempts you from humbling yourself before the Creator of the heavens and earth? Abu thanked this universal Supreme Being for sending Muhammad, as the Prophet never once considered himself too learned or too important to glorify his Creator and to perform the obligatory prayers either alone or in the company of other worshippers. As the Qur'an says, every object on earth and in the heavens glorifies Allah—whether voluntarily or instinctively. Who was Sule to think that he was any different? Who was he to decide who was sincere and who was hypocritical? Anyway, hypocrisy or not, the five daily prayers were compulsory and non-negotiable. End of discussion!

Abu decided to look for a spiritual guide who combined godliness within with observance of the basic religious injunctions without. He, however, did not decamp without filching a mystical code written by his benefactor on a piece of paper. Sule knew about Abu's obsession with psychic power. He knew that this mysticism fixation would be his discipline's undoing. Yet, the numerologist pretended as if he did not know that the key to invisibility was missing. "Let the Shaytan walk into his own trap," was how Sule left the matter.

Sule did nothing as Abu began his discreet inquiry for a new guide. To Abu's disappointment, the search in Maiduguri and the suburbs yielded no savant whose teachings and practices matched his own orthodoxy. The murshids whom he had heard so much about were beyond his reach; they had completely removed themselves from the public's sight and were not keen on taking on new disciples, least of all someone like Abu, who was more interested in miracles than in meaning.

Unable to find a madrassa to use as a springboard to personal advancement, he travelled back to Potiskum to interest his old classmate, Usman Darazo, in a new project—their own madrassa. Who needs an institutional affiliation when one could be established at the twinkling of an eye? Money would have been a problem. Fortunately, the tidy sum which he had already put aside as the principal go-between in Sule's outfit cleared that obstacle. And with the pliable Darazo as his own sidekick, it was a matter of time before the new madrassa started making waves.

Chapter-6

The call to damnation and hate!

ABU HAD NO PROBLEM convincing Darazo to go along with his plan. Docile as he was, Abu's classmate was finding his unsalaried job as Alkaleri's assistant in Potiskum too uninspiring. He gladly packed his bags and accompanied Abu to Maiduguri. Within three months, they had taken over an empty space along the Maiduguri-Damaturu Road and converted it into Markas Lil-Dawah al-Islamiyya, MDI. Besides running a madrassa that taught street children how to read, write, and memorize the Qur'an, the MDI recruited preachers who, under Abu's leadership, travelled far and wide to give fiery sermons. More often than not, the targets of attack at the public lectures were the Trinity, Jesus's divinity, and polytheism, although not always in that order.

These faith propagation endeavors rarely ended without incidents. Goaded by Abu's incendiary orations, the gatherings of the faithful frequently unleashed vicious attacks on the kuffar, meaning Christians, polytheists, and others that the preachers fingered as 'infidels'.

The hate campaign continued until the local authorities responded with deadly force. As had been the practice, a crowd had formed where the day's lecture was to take place, in front of the Hausari Central Mosque. The lecture, scheduled to commence on Thursday morning, 1 October 2071, was meant to serve a dual purpose. First, taking place on the 111th anniversary of Dukyaria's independence, the occasion provided an opportunity to mobilize the people against plans by the World Government

Organization (WGO) to turn Dukyaria into a Dependent Territory within the new Mali Empire. Second, and more important, the lecture would enable Abu Mamba and his associates to bring an issue which was still being discussed in hushed tones at the WGO headquarters—the legalization of same sex marriage—out in the open.

For a slightly built man, Abu had a remarkable knack for working the crowd into a state of frenzy. As he had done on previous occasions, he waited for the gathering to settle down before making a grand entry. He was flanked on the right by Darazo and on the left by Ghazzali, a tall, lean person who was a rising star in MDI circles. The lesser clerics took the rear. As soon as Abu Mamba appeared with his entourage, one of the madrassa pupils, on cue, hailed him, "The great Khalifah is here! The Sheikh is here! The light is here, let darkness disappear! Those who truly love our faith will join me in welcoming Sheikh Abu Danja Mamba to this august gathering!"

"Sheikh! Sheikh! Sheikh!" The crowd's collective voice rent the air. Men and women elbowed each other to catch a glimpse of their hero.

"Allahu Akbar kabeeran, wal hamdul-Lahi katheeran. We thank Allah Almighty for sending Prophet Muhammad with the message of truth. We also hail the holy Prophet for bringing the message of guidance. Our country is going through momentous changes. At no other time have we so desperately needed a rightly guided and focused leader. We are particularly fortunate to have such a leader, a visionary leader, in the person of Khalifah, Sheikh Abu Danja Mamba. There is no Dukyarian who is not aware of his views and is not impressed with the courage he has shown in expressing those views. He believes, and rightly so, that the kuffar will never stop until they take over and corrupt every aspect of our country's life. It is your duty and mine to stop them. Our esteemed Sheikh will soon show us how to proceed. I therefore have the rare privilege of handing the microphone over to this remarkable leader." It was Ghazzali glorifying God and prepping the crowd for Mamba's address. He promptly handed over the podium to his superior.

"Exactly one hundred and eleven years ago, God, in His infinite mercy, inspired our forefathers to demand and achieve our independence from Great Britain. Open your ears, and open them very well. Listen to every word that comes from my heart and out of my mouth. This independence, which our forefathers fought for and which they rightly earned, is about to be taken away. The illegitimate World Government Organization has carved the world into six spheres of influence, and it has constituted each into a satellite Empire made up of virtually dependent states." Mamba paused for effect. He rolled up the sleeves of his flowing gown and adjusted his zanna bukar cap.

"Honestly, it won't bother me one bit if they create a thousand spurious empires, provided they leave us out of the charade. I won't even mind if each docile empire is made up of a constellation of equally docile states, so long as they leave us out of it. But, no, no, no, letting us be is not part of their plan. Uh-uh," he said, shaking his head. "Rather than leave us alone, they plan to convert our country into a Dependent Territory within the Mali Empire. Can you imagine, a Dependent Territory, after more than a century of independence? And this Mali Empire? Where did they even get this idea that Mali is the empire we want to be grouped with? What is our concern with it? And, if I may ask, what is the legitimacy of the decisions taken by the Emperor, elected or not?"

The thought that poor management of Dukyaria's finances might be largely responsible for the imminent loss of autonomy did cross Mamba's mind, but he promptly erased it before it passed over his tongue. He didn't think that the crowd before him would grasp the intricacies of high finance sufficiently to draw the connection. Besides, his immediate adversary now was the WGO, and not the corrupt Dukyarian politicians. The politicians were a distraction he did not need right now. He had to get rid of the WGO first. The bungling politicians he would fix later, when the time was right.

"Death to the WGO! No to the Empire! God save Dukyaria!" The crowd was up in arms. Mamba's strategy was working. The prospect of losing Dukyaria's sovereignty was too much to bear.

Sensing that he was standing before a captive audience, Mamba stoked the fire before it died out. "Allahu Akbar! Don't get worked up until you hear what else I have to say." The orator didn't mean what he said. Nothing would please him more than to see the crowd perpetually worked up—so long as it remained worked up sufficiently to topple the WGO. "Do you know why they want to deprive us of our freedom?" he asked.

"No!" Abu's reverse psychology proved effective. A chorus of voices answered his question.

"They want to deprive us of our freedom so they can force on us a law permitting men to marry men, and women to marry women. In no time, a father will be able to marry his daughter, a mother will be allowed to marry her son, and a human will be able to take out a license to be joined in unholy matrimony with lower animals like horses, dogs, and pigs!" Mamba knew that same-sex marriage was a serious issue already but saw no reason why he should not inflame passions further by conjuring up other nightmarish images.

The crowd stared at him in disbelief. Totally flustered and livid, the men and the women before him were ready for anything. "The WGO and its subsidiary organs must be dismantled," the cacophony of voices swore. Mamba started by engineering a pandemonium. He ended igniting a mini civil war.

"Homo Haram! Homo Haram! Homo Haram!" Ghazzali prodded the crowd again.

"Homo Haram! Homo Haram! Homo Haram!" The crowd took Ghazzali's bait. It chanted the slogan vociferously and repeatedly. Mamba had at last found not just a cause worth killing or dying for, but also a brand name which would distinguish his from other proselytizing groups.

Noticing that failure to disperse the increasingly restive crowd on time threatened public peace, the police ordered everyone present to vacate the lecture grounds.

"And if we refuse to comply with your instructions, what will you do? Shoot us down one by one?" Mamba had defiantly asked the most senior police officer present, a superintendent.

"We are duly authorized to apply all means necessary to enforce public order. So, in answer to your question, yes, we shall shoot whoever refuses to leave or otherwise stands in our way. We shall apply deadly force to ensure that the WGO's will prevails." The superintendent didn't mince words.

The exchange became so heated that Darazo had to intervene. Moving both hands up and down gently, and invoking the names of Allah and the Prophet, he urged his comrades to leave the police alone, "Don Allah, don annabi, ku kyale su", was how he appealed for calm. Unfortunately for him, instead of brokering peace, he became the first casualty of the undeclared war. A nervous police constable had apparently aimed his gun at a visibly angry preacher. In an attempt at pushing his subordinate out of harm's way, Darazo had caught the impact of what the police in its report termed "accidental discharge."

The first person who "killed for the cause" was Abu Mamba, with his hate-filled sermon of 1 October 2071. However, the first to die for it was his close friend and confidant, the un-obtrusive, mild-mannered lumbering giant, Usman Darazo.

Mamba's right-hand man had hardly hit the ground when all hell broke loose. The crowd descended on the law enforcement agents with unspeakable fury. By the time calm returned, five police constables and thirty rioters had lost their lives. Taking advantage of the confusion, the MDI hate preachers got away in Abu's Toyota Land Cruiser and other vehicles commandeered on the spot. They fled to the snake-infested Gashaka-Mambilla Hill. A sprawling, multi-chamber cave under the hill was to be their place of abode and operational headquarters for a long time. It was from here that Abu Mamba would plot, monitor, and coordinate acts of terror within Dukyaria. He had left Darazo's body lying face down where it had fallen.

Chapter-7

Mutiny in the vicarage?

OKOYE LOOKED WORRIED THIS particular Sunday. He could not understand the sudden change in his catechist's attitude. Brother Emman, as he preferred to be called, had suddenly developed the habits of turning up late for mass, showing little interest in church activities, responding to simple queries rudely, and carrying out the vicar's instructions with a body language signaling gripe mixed with resentment. The vicar had, for a fairly long period, let the catechist's insolence pass unchallenged. He finally decided to summon him to his compact office and find out what his problem was. "I have been watching you for the past few weeks, Mr. Kalu, and honestly, I am not sure I know what is happening." The vicar addressed the catechist formally, but in a soft voice.

"Happening like how, Father Okoye?" Brother Emman dodged the vicar's comment with a bland response and a clueless expression.

"You tell me. After all, you are the one who knows for certain what is going on in your mind. Do you have any problem with me, with any of the vicarage staff, with the parishioners, or with anyone else?" The vicar was determined to get to the bottom of the matter.

"I have no problem with anybody, least of all, the father," Emman answered, the clueless expression still masking his true feelings.

"Then where is all this feeling of animosity coming from? Why have you suddenly become cold and distant to almost everyone, me included?" The vicar saw no point in dilly-dallying. He went straight to the point.

"I am sorry, Father, if it appears that way. But I can assure you that I have no problem with anyone, and certainly not with the local representative of the Holy Father," Emman looked sideways to avoid Okoye penetrating gaze.

"Ok, if you say there is no problem, then there is no problem. We just have to leave it at that." Okoye dismissed Emman with a wave of the right hand, expecting to see the re-emergence of the Kalu he once knew, that is, the gregarious, Bible-quoting, knowledge-sharing Emmanuel Kalu.

That wasn't likely to happen any time soon. In the absence of a miracle, the catechist that Okoye once knew was gone for good.

Chapter-8

Can't they find a less charismatic vicar than this?

EMMAN'S INDIGNATION AT members of his Utako Catholic circle was too deep to allow his old, easygoing self to resurface. For one thing, he had lately developed a strong antipathy towards the vicar. It wasn't as if the local representative of the Holy Father treated him harshly or with needless condescension. If anything, Okoye went out of his way to be accommodating when Emman blundered and was apt to be effusive in his commendation when the catechist did something praiseworthy. Unfortunately, Okoye's efforts were in vain. No matter what the vicar did, Emman could not help feeling like the priest's houseboy at best, and his doormat at worst. As it so happened, he was not keen on being anybody's houseboy or doormat.

The vicar would definitely need to apply extraordinary techniques to get through to the catechist. The tall but skinny Emman had grown up with an inferiority complex. His worst nightmare was being treated as a nobody. The latent feeling of being ignored came to the surface when a new priest arrived at the vicarage. The change of guard triggered alarm signals in the catechist. Of all the priests in the world, the north-central diocese could not find anyone to post to Utako to take over from Father Ignatius Nwuke except fine-boy Okoye! Was the church short of the likes of the outgoing priest, the plain-looking, soft-spoken, and sexually unappealing Nwuke? The church had apparently not looked hard enough for Nwuke's mirror image. What other explanation was there for picking this tall, handsome, self-confident poster boy named Okoye?

Well, let's see how far his good looks will take him, Emman had thought the first day he set his eyes on his new boss.

Emman did not have to wait too long to see how far Okoye's charisma would take him and the church. To the catechist's shock, those lovely ladies who used to gather around him in search of answers to biblical questions had suddenly developed the habit of by-passing him and, what was worse, stumbling over one another to get the new vicar's attention. The ladies had not only ignored Emman but had also rubbed it in by throwing themselves at Okoye. Emman didn't mind the short and plump Bose making a mockery of herself, looking for the slightest excuse to get close to Okoye or an opportunity to unsettle the vicar with her overexposed cleavage.

What Emman couldn't stand was the sight of the comely Catherine Henshaw selling herself short and openly flirting with the vicar. He was disconcerted by the fact that the Catherine behaving like a tart was precisely the beauty that he, Emmanuel, had had his eyes on right from the day she joined the parish. Unfortunately, she wouldn't give him the time of day! She couldn't bear to be in the same room with Emman, much less agree to go out with him. When would Catherine come to her senses and perish this thought of hooking up with Okoye? The quicker she looked beyond the pretty boy's face, the quicker she would realize that he, Emman, was her real soul mate, the one destined to be hers forever. To his dismay, Catherine had no time for the eligible bachelor-catechist, as her mind was still fixated on the pretty face.

As if the humiliation of losing Catherine to Okoye were not enough, the vicarage staff, which had earlier treated Emman as the priest's virtual deputy, abruptly stopped according him the regard befitting a second-in-command. The staff fawned on the vicar but took no notice of the catechist. As the point man for religious education, he still had the attention of the laity. However, parishioners who already had basic knowledge of the Bible and of Catholic practices would rather shove one another aside to get to the vicar than bring themselves to attend the catechist's classes. Even Samuel, the physically impaired choir master, pulled larger crowds than himself.

Chapter-9

The vicarage hates preachers

EMMAN BADE HIS TIME, waiting for an opportunity to pay the Utako parish snobs in their own coin. He soon took to looking through the parishioners, saying and doing the minimum necessary to avoid another Q&A session with the vicar, and maintaining a standoffish attitude in his dealings with the vicarage staff. Even Catherine no longer got as much as a casual nod or a familiar wink. What did she think of herself anyway? She is not the prettiest girl in Dukyaria after all! If she and her likes felt superior, Emman would just have to put them in their place.

The opportunity Emman craved to cut his tormentors down to size came on Monday, 4 May 2071. The entire Utako congregation had decided to watch a live, intercontinental television debate featuring their vicar, leading secularists, and other protagonists of religion from different parts of the globe. The Catholic Events Auditorium was filled to capacity that afternoon. The church elders had occupied the floor-level seats on the front row, leaving the other parishioners to scramble for seats screwed to the upper rungs at the back.

As the one in charge of religious education, the not-so-elderly Emman was entitled to a front-row seat. For no reason whatsoever, he walked past the dignitaries seated in front and made a beeline for an upper-level seat at the back. As he ascended the steps, he noticed a forest of hands waving at him and inviting him to their side. Among the waving hands were those belonging to the buxom Bose; the gaunt, unsmiling Mary; the choirmaster with a humped back; and...wait a second... Catherine in her pristine, angelic, and supremely desirable form. Emman suddenly developed a surreal feeling.

Could he be dreaming? Catherine among his circle of admirers? Impossible! It was only after pinching himself that he considered the probability of a dreamlike situation being real. That sensation, the sensation of seeing without fully believing, left him in a quandary. Should he accept the invitation, or should he retaliate for months of humiliation by playing hard to get? Unaware of what was going on in Emman's brain, the waving hands persisted, getting invigorated by the minute. He had little time left to make up his mind. If the window closed and the "fans" stopped cheering, well, that was it. He decided not to press his luck. An opportunity like that might not come his way again. He promptly trudged to the upper level and took a seat next to Catherine.

The television program was yet to start. The viewers assembled in the auditorium still had a few minutes for chit-chat. Catherine opened the informal discussion with her own expectations. "Our man, Reverend Father Okoye, will teach his fellow debaters a few lessons in faith. He will floor his opponents with his charm and his superior intellect!"

"I won't bet on that," Emman said, cutting Catherine short. "I hear that the Moslem priest, Kamil, or whatever his name is, is as sharp as a razor and as hard as nails. Well, with a PhD from a renowned university, what do you expect?" Emman basically poured cold water on Catherine's fervent and pre-emptive endorsement of the vicar.

"PhD my foot! A PhD from a Moslem university doesn't count! It cannot match our man's Masters from an

American university!" Buxom Bose joined the ad hoc vicar-admiration group which Catherine was intent on founding.

Emman was infuriated "What do any of you know about PhDs or Moslem universities? We may not like the Moslems, but when they engage you in an argument, they don't let go until they fight you to a standstill or subdue you. And each time they make a point, they will back it up with quotations from their book, the Koran. I don't envy Father Okoye at all!"

"Don't tell me you have decamped to the Moslems' side! Anyway, what else is new?" Samuel, the hunchback, responded to Emman irritably. He could not stand Muslims or their admirers. In fact, praising a "Moslem," as Dukyarian Christians pronounce the word, was, in Samuel's eyes, a crime tantamount to treason.

Emman flipped. His fist clenched and the eyes bloodshot, he stood and faced his adversary, "What kind of rubbish is that, Brother Samuel? Have you ever seen me in the company of Moslems before? My point, which I repeat, is that this man Kamil is one to watch. He is no pushover." Had the two not been separated by a few seats, they would have come to blows.

The shorter antagonist, Samuel, was equally spoiling for a fight. With a face misshapen by a scowl and loathing contempt, he rose from his seat and started hurling insults across the buffer seats, the seats separating him from Emman. "Look at this stupid man! Are you implying that rubbish is coming out of my mouth simply because I dare say what others are merely whispering? OK, let me say it loud and clear: your loyalty to the Holy See is doubtful. You need to go for penance and purge yourself of all those subversive and heretical thoughts! See how you have been carrying yourself lately, antagonizing everybody and behaving as if you are the lord and master of this parish! The nonsense has to stop right away!"

Emman, still burning with rage, wanted to respond, but by now the giant screen behind the podium had come alive. The Dukyarian Television Service was about to start transmitting the live debate. The two combatants sank back into their seats, fuming. All eyes focused on the screen, waiting for the debate to commence.

Emman sat through the ninety-minute television debate incensed. On top of calling him stupid, the hunchback had had the guts to challenge him, the taller and presumably more physically intimidating opponent, to a fist fight! What impudence!

Emman was not the only one burning inside. Samuel too remained piqued for as long as the television program lasted. How can a practicing, self-respecting Catholic take a Moslem's side? What do Catholics and the Moslems have in common? Nothing! Even their Allah is different from the good Lord that the Holy See enjoins every Catholic to adore. Samuel recognized no other authority expect that of God the Father, the Son, and the Holy Spirit. No matter how anyone breaks it down for him, Samuel would never understand or accept that his God is the same as the One "the Moslems" call Allah and pray to five times every day.

Ironically, both Emman and Samuel were on the same page on this matter of the Muslim's Allah. Emman might take exception to the pugnacious Samuel's impertinence and, especially, the choir master's frontal attack on the catechist, but the latter saw no reason to disagree with his local Nemesis on the "Moslem God." As Emman saw it, the Arabs wanted to fool the world into worshipping their local god. That was why they coined the word "Allah" and projected Him as the Lord of the Heavens and Earth. Well, let the Arabs keep their Allah. The catechist and his church brethren would stay with God the Father, the Son, and the Holy Spirit.

Chapter-10

Faithless and proud!

BRAD CUNNINGHAM WAS UP early that Monday morning, 4 May 2071. He was billed to participate in an intercontinental television debate on religion. He had spent days reflecting on the topic. As had become his habit when getting ready to face the cameras, Cunningham sized himself up in the mirror. His imposing stature appeared to have been specially built for the dark Franco Fellini suit, the power blue shirt, and the bluish-purple tie with a dimpled knot. The five-foot eleven, blue-eyed, all-American boy liked the image staring back from the mirror. You can't ask for a finer specimen of a man, he assured himself.

His confidence was not totally misplaced. His face had been adequately upgraded. Cosmetic surgery had replaced his crooked nose with a straight one. In fact, with his vibrant and moderately tanned complexion, square jaw, high cheek bones, dimpled cheeks, and deep, commanding voice, he was more likely to be mistaken for a film star than the evolutionary biologist that he was. There was no trace of grey in his hair or of a wrinkle on his face. His teeth were intact and sparkling white. Thanks to the implantation of new cells, the colon cancer that his forefathers had brought from Scotland centuries earlier had left his body for good.

Convinced that he couldn't look or feel any better, Cunningham left his twenty-fifth floor apartment at 20 Waterside Plaza and took an elevator to the lobby. On getting out of the lift, he walked down the Plaza's pavement to FDR Drive. He then took a left to Twenty-third Street, walked past the high-rises on his left and right and continued till he reached First Avenue. He had waited no longer than five minutes when a taxi pulled up directly in front of where he stood. He quickly hopped in and, as directed, the taxi sped to the Avenue of the Americas.

As the taxi looked for crevices to slip into to beat the New York traffic and wended its way to the Global Television Network (GTN) studio, Cunningham cast his mind back to his previous encounters with men and women of faith. The believers, he concluded, were ever eager to make a case, but never ready to back their affirmations with facts or reason. He found their "take-it-or-leave-it" attitude highly exasperating. The believers talk glibly about the afterlife, but they become evasive when you ask them to explain the current and completely meaningless life. If you are going to affirm the existence of something or somebody, you must at least be prepared to come up with a proof. Anyway, the debate coming up within the hour would settle the matter once and for all. The defenders of religion would have to come up with an irrefutable proof of their Supreme Being's existence or forever keep their peace. The viewers won't settle for anything less. He would make sure they didn't take the believers' word at its face value.

A few minutes after leaving First Avenue, the taxi ran into a holdup in a tunnel near Park Avenue. Dammit! The compact, solar-powered, helicabs already competing with regular taxis in other cities were not yet licensed to land and take off in Manhattan. The security-conscious city authorities had to weigh the grave risks that helicabs posed to Manhattan's high-rises. Now blocked from the rear and the front by vehicles standing bumper to bumper, Cunningham's taxi had run out of escape routes. Since the gridlock around the subway area was unlikely to be cleared any time soon, he decided to get out of the taxi and trek the remaining distance to the Avenue of Americas. He wouldn't make his ten o'clock appointment at the GTN studio if he waited for the comatose traffic to regain consciousness and, like a cornered reptile later released, to resume its slither around Manhattan's clogged streets. He quickly settled the taxi bill, adding the customary tip.

It was a bright morning in New York. Cunningham didn't feel the heat as the weather was generally mild. As he and other pedestrians maneuvered their ways out of New York's morning traffic, Cunnigham had enough time to reflect on the trajectory taken by his life. His mother having died the day he was born, he had been raised by a single parent on Staten Island. His father, also a biologist, had shielded him from "unsavory religious influences" in his formative years, preferring that his only son's free time be spent on comics, computer games, and chess. Brad Cunningham remained active in Harvard and Yale sororities as long as "born-again" members kept their views to themselves. As a university professor, he spent his time ripping faiths to shreds, exposing the discord among the believers, and condemning the sanctimonious, self-righteous attitude of the religious establishment. Thanks to the GTN, he was finally getting another opportunity to let the whole world know what he thought of the best organized racket known to man: religion.

Chapter-11

The Holy Father's representative at the debate

CUNNINGHAM WASN'T THE only one with something to say on the subject of meaning or meaninglessness. At about the time he was sauntering to the Avenue of Americas to mount a spirited attack on religion, two clerics were getting ready thousands of miles away in the Union of Dukyaria with their own views on the same subject.

Basil Okoye, an alumnus of the University of Notre Dame, Indiana, and Georgetown University, Washington D.C., was also scheduled to participate in the live television debate. He had to leave his Utako vicarage early if he was to make his 3:00 p.m. (10:00 a.m. New York time) appointment at the Abaji studio of the Dukyarian Television Service, a GTN subsidiary. He feared that unless he gave himself adequate lead time, the clouds gathering overhead might end up depositing huge quantities of rain on the road and, in the process, impede the smooth flow of traffic. It was also a windy afternoon; he had to look out for uprooted trees likely to block the road, or flying objects that might head straight towards, and shatter, his windscreen.

Just as Cunningham's trek to the Avenue of Americas had afforded him an opportunity to connect with his past, the leisurely drive from the vicarage to Abaji enabled Okoye to relive his journey to the priesthood. He had been born into a devout Roman Catholic family in Obiangwu, a small town outside Owerri. His father, a poor farmer, recognized the value of education early. That was how little Basil was exempted from farm duties and allowed to concentrate on his studies.

Fortunately, an Irish priest, Father Cian O'Neil, had taken a liking to him and had offered to pay for his education right to the secondary level. By the time he left the Owerri Grammar School, the now strapping Basil had resolved to follow in Father O'Neil's footsteps. Nothing could make him change his mind—not his interest in politics, philosophy and economics; his graduating at the top of his class at Notre Dame; or his equally impressive scholastic record at Georgetown.

On completing his pastoral training in Rome, he was ordained as a priest and posted to the Utako parish, then part of the north-central diocese. He loved the job, especially the part affording him an opportunity to counsel social deviants and integrate them in society. The only occupational hazard he faced was the adulation of the female members of the congregation; pretty girls who were not particularly religious found time to come to church. It was not clear whether they came to listen to Okoye's sermons or to have him to themselves. If it was the latter, they were wasting their time; Okoye had pledged his life to Christ.

"What a waste! Such a hunky frame doing nothing except preach the gospel!" A frustrated Catherine Henshaw once remarked about Okoye. She wasn't sure what to call him—a heartthrob, a priest, a prude, or all of the above. Inwardly, she wanted him to be nothing but the love of her life.

"This means that anytime you come to church, your design is on this man, and not on the sermon, the sacrament, or the communion!" Theresa Ekpo teased her friend. "Then, why not let the reverend father know how you feel?" Theresa was now dead serious.

"You think I can? Let him know, that is?" Catherine, her eyes squinted and her brow wrinkled, sought her friend's counsel.

45

"Yah, why not? The worst that can happen is the priest will politely say 'no'. It won't matter if he says 'no', so long as he doesn't turn you down in public."

Catherine soon acted on her friend's advice. To keep her pride intact, she took adequate precaution not to hit on the priest in the full view of other congregants. She waited for other parishioners to disperse before walking bashfully to the vicar. She started by asking if the priest did not find his pastoral duties boring.

"Are you kidding? Boring does not come anywhere near describing how I feel about this job." Okoye assured the concerned member of his congregation.

"I am not talking about that kind of boring...."

Catherine was not looking to be reassured that way. She wanted the man's mind to wander from his regular pastoral duties to extracurricular activities, and then leave open the possibility of a liaison with someone, preferably someone like her.

"Then what kind of boring are you talking about?" The priest interrupted her, looking puzzled. The situation was getting awkward for Catherine. The priest's brusque response did not allow the conversation to drag on long enough to be steered down her path, the boy-meets-girl path.

"I thought... I was hoping... Perhaps... Let me put it this way. You won't know what I am talking about unless you and I get to know each other better. The question is whether your job will let that happen." Catherine saw no reason to beat about the bush any longer. She bared her mind and hoped the priest got the message.

Okoye got the message. "You are right; my job leaves no room for activities that are not church-related. Besides, I had sworn to give my life to Christ before taking up the job. You can do that as well, that is, give your life completely to Christ. If you can't, I advise you to give your heart to the right man, a pious, caring, and devoted husband. I am sure you would be baffled when I say that I too find you physically attractive. Don't be baffled. I am as human as any other human. The only difference is I look beyond the flesh. Anyway, if I consider you pretty, you can imagine how many men are pining for your companionship! You just need to be on the alert to ensure that you give your heart to the right man." As Theresa had assumed all along, Okoye said no to Catherine's offer—in private, of course.

"I shouldn't have listened to Theresa. She is the cause of this embarrassment." Catherine held her friend responsible for her own lack of self-control.

"Which Theresa, and what has she got to do with this?" Okoye asked.

"Theresa Ekpo. She was the one who encouraged me to let you know how I feel, or should I say, how I felt." Catherine apprised Okoye not only of the plot she had hatched with Theresa, but also of the designs that other female worshippers had on Okoye. "You had better watch out! Not every girl in the church will give up as easily as I am doing now."

That was how the matter ended.

Okoye snapped out of his nostalgia as soon as he caught a glimpse of the Dukyarian Television Service's massive, grey-coated building. He wondered whether Kamil was already in the studio waiting. He parked his car and walked into the reception.

Chapter-12

The Muslims too have something to say

KAMIL WAS NOT YET in the studio, but he was not far away. He too had set out early. The rain, which started as a drizzle around Okoye's vicarage in Utako, had turned into a deluge in Garki. The Garki downpour actually uprooted trees and sent easily identifiable objects hurtling in all directions. Kamil didn't take any chances; rather than drive his SUV himself, he sat back and left the task of navigating the pockmarked, waterlogged Garki-Abaji road to Lawan, his full-time chauffeur. Relieved of the obligation of driving in stormy weather, he had enough time to reflect not only on the past, but also the present, especially the imminent television debate.

His trip down memory lane brought flashes of his youth. He had started out in a village outside Hadejia, where he helped his father watch over the family's livestock. He really loved cattle rearing. He felt truly emancipated as he roamed the wild and gazed endlessly at the blue sky, his two hands clutching the fodder stick to brace the shoulder blades and the neck. He never stopped glancing admiringly at the swath of virgin, unspoiled, boundless territory and the columns of undulating mountains.

As it turned out, his cattle rearing days were numbered. His wealthy uncle, Alhaji Ali Kamil, had prevailed upon the father to send young Salim to him in Kano to acquire western and Islamic religious education simultaneously.

Salim proved to be a fast learner. After completing his secondary education at the Union Government College in Kano, he proceeded to Cambridge to earn a degree in philosophy. Fluent in Arabic, he subsequently enrolled on Al-

Azhar's post-graduate program in Islamic philosophy. His command of Arabic often left his Al-Azhar professors as well as his classmates spellbound. They frequently wondered whether he was not a native Arabic speaker disguised as an ajamyy, a non-Arab. His doctoral thesis written in Arabic was published virtually unedited by Al-Qairah Press. He turned down a teaching position at Al-Azhar because a wealthy financier had asked him to return home and join a team to establish an Islamic university. Noticing the dithering on the part of the university's sponsors on his return to Dukyaria, and bothered by the financier's poorly disguised political ambitions, Kamil decided to establish his own non-governmental organization devoted to the propagation of Islamic teachings.

Kamil was no stranger to adversity. As his SUV sped past the Kwali cemetery, his mind drifted back to Armya'u, his first son who had died mere days to his eighth birthday. As the eldest male child, Armiya'u was Kamil's khalifa, that is, the heir apparent. Kamil and his wife, Amina, doted on the cute and precocious little boy. Then, without warning, death took Armiya'u away, leaving his three younger sisters. Two years later, Amina gave birth to another son, Abdullah. The family's joy was short-lived. Abdullah, the new heir apparent, suddenly came down with a rare bone disease. "Fibrous dysplasia; that is the medical term for your son's condition," the orthopedic surgeon handling the case coldly passed the bad news to a distraught Kamil. Where did this fibrous dysplasia come from? It certainly cannot be traced to my or Amina's DNA. Kamil had struggled with the diagnosis, trying in vain to make sense of it. As he pondered the mystery surrounding Abdullah's bone disorder, Kamil became increasingly frantic about the upcoming medical bills and the unending visits to the Hayat Hospital's pediatric ward. He quickly dismissed Abdullah's fate and his own worries from his mind, confident that Allah, Who knew about this problem, would guide him to the solution. With his mind back in neutral, Kamil shifted his attention to the intercontinental debate.

Kamil never expected the Dukyarian Television Service to invite him to participate in the television debate. He suspected that his frequent face-offs with Okoye must have influenced the studio managers' decision. Whatever was behind the decision to invite him, he would, in-sha-Allah, Allah willing, try to live up to their expectations. He would give it his all.

His SUV finally reached the Dukyarian Television Service's flower-bedecked compound. Kamil got out of the vehicle and, silently admiring the scentless roses and carnations adorning the surroundings, headed straight to the reception desk. The lady attendant promptly ushered him to a spacious, air-conditioned lounge where Okoye was already seated. He shook hands with Okoye and took a seat next to his Catholic counterpart. Both remained mute.

Chapter-13

Let's get camera-ready

A FEW MINUTES AFTER Kamil's arrival in Abaji, the lady attendant reappeared to take the two guests to the brightly illuminated studio. Now seated a few yards away from Okoye, Kamil politely but persistently turned down the make-up artist's repeated offer of assistance. Even though he was rarely conscious of the fact, he was not a bad-looking bloke. Anyway, since when did looking glamorous become a qualification for those in the service of God? Attractive or not, the face would just have to stay the way it was, without make-up. The lady beautician should particularly forget about trimming the long beard or tilting the cap towards a new, camera-friendly angle. It didn't matter if touching up their guests here and there had become standard practice at the studio. No one was touching him up, least of all a woman to whom he was not married.

Okoye watched with tacit amusement as Kamil ducked and wriggled to foil the beautician's determined efforts to spruce up his bearded face. When it came to his turn, Okoye sat still and upright as the beautician carried out her tasks. He only drew the line when it came to the zucchetto, his skullcap, and the cassock, his robe. "Both stay as they are." He was firm but polite.

Cunningham had no objection to his face being made camera-ready in New York. He submitted completely to the GTN make-up artists' dictates. So did Luiz-Fernando in Salvador, Beaumont in Paris, and Harelal in New Delhi, so long as the local studio left his ascetic, Gandhi-like look basically intact.

With camera one focused on him, Gavin Stokes, the GTN anchorman, finally flagged off the big event, "To our viewers in different parts of the globe, I say, 'Good morning, good afternoon, good evening' at one and the same time. As I speak, it is 10:00 a.m. in New York, 11:00 a.m. in Salvador, 3:00 p.m. in Abaji, 4:00 p.m. in Paris, and 7:30 p.m. in New Delhi. We haven't got much time, so let me get to it right away. GTN, your number one stop for news and entertainment, is again going where no other station has gone before. It has assembled the best brains on the planet to discuss a matter of importance to humanity: the need for and the place of religion in contemporary life. In the studio with me here in New York is Dr. Brad Cunningham, a foremost evolutionary biologist currently teaching at New York University." The camera shifted from Stokes and zoomed in on the beaming Cunningham.

"The other participants are Reverend Father Basil Okoye and Dr. Sheikh Salim Kamil, both leading clerics in the Union of Dukyaria." The New York camera took a break, allowing the spotlight to fall on the two debaters standing by in Abaji. Okoye's photogenic face glowed with delight. Kamil, beard and all, smiled for the camera as well.

"Also joining us today are Swami Krishna Harelal at our studio in New Delhi," the New Delhi-based camera picked Harelal's youthful, harmony-radiating face; "Monsieur François Beaumont in Paris," the Paris camera got the hint and captured Beaumont's grin; "and finally, the only lady participant, Iyalawo Luiz-Fernando, in Salvador, State of

Bahia, Brazil." Luiz-Fernando waved and smiled simultaneously to Salvador's camera.

"To make the best of today's opportunity, we have divided the ninety-minute program into three segments. The first segment will allow each participant to spend ten minutes stating his or her case uninterrupted—I repeat: un-inter-rup-ted! I hope we all got that. In the second segment, I, the moderator, will ask each participant a question which he will spend no longer than two minutes answering. A panelist who still has a few minutes left in his or her account after answering my question is at liberty to spend the balance restating his case or picking holes in another debater's argument. The third segment will last no longer than twenty minutes, during which I shall take comments from our viewers. Now over to you, Dr. Cunningham; your ten minutes start right now!"

Chapter-14

Belief in reason, that's my religion

THE OPERATING CAMERA IMMEDIATELY settled on the first debater's face. Cunningham went on the offensive.

"Thanks, Gavin. Religion, as I see it, is founded on this fallacious assumption that there is a Supreme Being somewhere watching over us, happy when we toe the path of righteousness, and livid when we do one tiny wrong. Dammit, when the body dies, everything dies with it. So, I won't stand for anyone giving me this crap about life after death. By the way, who and where is this Supreme Being that the believers are ever eager to kill and die for? Haven't we looked long and hard enough for proof of his existence? What did we get for our efforts? Absolutely nothing! We looked everywhere on earth. We didn't find him. We went to space; we came back empty-handed. Even the believers have not reached an agreement on a uniform, precise, and categorical definition of God. There are as many definitions of this made-up being as there are believers! Anyway, I personally don't see the need for an external, all-knowing, all-caring God. How can any right-thinking individual reconcile the idea of a benevolent God with all the unpleasant occurrences in our world? How can anyone reconcile our meaningless world with the idea of an all-knowing and meaningful God? Fortunately, reason has begotten science. Science has, in turn, exposed the absurdity of belief in superstitions and of the neurotic dependence on miracles. The human race has evolved sufficiently to clone itself and live forever. If our cells burn out or somehow become diseased, they can be replaced at the nearest human genome store. Like your average iPad or laptop, bodies that

54

age can be sent to bio-technology labs for upgrades. We can even train monkeys to play Beethoven. A reluctant male can go under the knife and, after a simple procedure, step out a sexy female. A man or a woman doesn't need an invisible God to choose his or her gender. A black man got to be president of a world power earlier this century, and he didn't need a capricious god to make this happen! In fact, as a candidate for the top job, he fired his church minister for sermonizing instead of encouraging studied application of the intellect as demanded by the challenges at hand! Should I continue?"

Cunningham went on to remind the viewers about man's evolution. He spoke with passion about man's capacity to create and mold his own destiny. He saw awe-inspiring but largely beneficial technological innovations in man's future. Cunningham wanted to continue, but time, or specifically, its keeper, wouldn't let him. Stokes pressed a button on his right, and his executive producer cleared the airwaves for the transmission from New Delhi.

Chapter-15

God is neither a verifiable hypothesis nor a researchable subject

WITH THE STUDIO CAMERA peering at him, Swami Krishna Harelal began with a rebuttal to Cunningham.

"I beg to disagree with Dr. Cunningham. That you have not seen God does not mean He is not in or around you. Belief, after all, is not what you can put under the microscope. You can't analyze it; neither can you affirm nor deny the logic underpinning it. Those of us who subscribe to the Hindu philosophy believe in a Supreme Being along with the other gods and goddesses. Belief in multiple deities is not inconsistent with reason, particularly, as it allows everyone to experience the divine in more ways than one. Among the Hindu gods and goddesses are Vishnu, Shiva, Hanuman, Durga, Krishna, Lakshmi, Annapurna, Ganesha, Brahma, Saraswati, and Buddha. You don't have to see any of these gods. All you need is to feel connected to them. This is the essence of meditation—that is, the essence of going outside the body to be connected to infinite possibilities, and to experience what lies beyond the finite, empirically verifiable world. And by the way, if seeing is a condition precedent to believing, Dr. Cunningham and other sceptics are welcome to visit us in India. On arrival in India, he would witness the futility of explaining reality 'scientifically,' the plain absurdity of applying standard measures to plot movements in space and time, and the insuperable obstacles to attempts at naming the unnamable. Regardless of whether or not he visits us, I do not see why somebody else's belief should be a non- believer's problem. Faith is, after all, something personal. If one person chooses to have faith, another is free to live without it. We would not be human if we all feel, think, talk, and act the same way! If lower animals disagree among themselves most of the time, why would human beings, with all their mental endowments and their varied, mostly unique, experiences, agree on anything, least of all, on matters of faith?" Harelal summed up with a poser.

Chapter 16

Body may be enslaved; the spirit's free!

IT WAS NOW UP to Salvador's studio camera to pick up from where its New Delhi equivalent had paused. The local GTN camera promptly settled on Luiz-Fernando's ageing face. Thanks to the wonders of simultaneous interpretation, the views she expressed in Portuguese were transmitted live to English-speaking viewers, including the deaf and the visually impaired.

"I agree with Swami Krishna's views on faith. You cannot force your faith or lack of it on another person. I am one of the high priestesses of the Ogun shrine here in Bahia, Salvador. Ogun is the god of iron, the god whose name is invoked to come to the rescue of the unjustly oppressed and visit unspeakable wrath on devils incarnate. Our forefathers brought the religion from the Odu ethnic group of south-western Dukyaria. Although they came to Brazil from Africa as slaves, they jealously guarded the freedom that mattered most, the freedom to worship the gods they could rightly and proudly call theirs. They came to Brazil with their hands and feet manacled, but their spirit remained free. There was nothing the slave owners didn't do to deprive us of this vital freedom and make us bow before their own god, a god that our forefathers considered oppressive. Our forefathers would never worship a god that looked the other way when they were being carted off as slaves to distant lands. They would never recognize the authority of such an unfair and uncaring god."

Luiz-Fernando took a sip from the glass of water in front of her before continuing. "I expect Dr. Cunningham to respond by saying that belief in an ancestral god is stupid, especially as there is no proof that such a god exists, or if it exists, that it has the power to make those things happen which we wish to see happen and to foreclose occurrences we find distasteful. You want proof. Here is a proof: There are instances of persons who die violently before their time. How come? One may ask. Those who die violently had committed one crime or another but tried to cover their tracks by proclaiming their innocence and invoking Ogun's name in support of their plea. In other words, they called on Ogun to bear witness to their treacherous acts as well as to their claim of innocence! Ogun will do no such thing. It will not pronounce the guilty innocent or vice versa. It has sufficiently demonstrated its commitment to justice and fairness to make people believe in its unfailing law, the law of retribution. Simply put, the law states that if you do a wrong and hide behind Ogun, you will sooner or later get run over by an object made of iron, be this a train, a motor vehicle, or a common bicycle. The result is that even the modern elite would rather swear in the name of Jesus than that of Ogun. Where Jesus is slow to act, and is generally forbearing, Ogun's retribution is swift and inescapable! Let me sum up by commenting on Dr. Cunningham's denial of God based on the bad things happening in the world today. Honestly, I find this logic totally irrational. I just cannot understand how a scientist who prides himself on his grasp of reason can hide behind hypotheses that are founded on sentiments and emotions. Good and bad coexist; so do joy and sadness, and bitter and sweet, as well as all flavors in between. Diversity, be it of language, color, or emotion, further points to infinite possibilities in human life. That is the reality of our existence. You cannot grasp that reality if your mind is focused exclusively on the observable world." Luiz-Fernando ended by defending her faith and questioning the logic underpinning the denial of God's existence.

Chapter-17

A secular intolerance manifesto

"**GOOD MORNING, GAVIN. GOOD** morning Brad," Beaumont joined the discussion from Paris.

Though fluent in English, he couldn't make his case without the French lilt getting in the way. "I have no problem whatsoever with rheligion. I would even go to any length to affirm and defend the individual's right to freedom of rheligion. As Swami Krishna eloquently stated before, we cannot all feel, think, talk, or act the same way. Yes, we all belong to the human familie. Yes, we have many attrhibutes in common. Yes, we all believe in one thing or the other. However, each and every one of us lives in a world unique to him or herself. And this is the crux of the mattaar—belief is a personal, not a public mattaar. This is why I would vehemently oppose having rheligion or any of its manifestations in the publique space. The burqa, the veil, the yarmulke, the zucchetto, the turban, the monk's civara, and the crucifix— these and other rheligious symbols must not be allowed in publique places. The secularism that we favor in France has no place for these symbols." Beaumont was brief and to the point.

Chapter-18

Freedom is not having to leave your identity at home or your faith in the closet!

"THAT IS ODD. ARTICLE 10 of the French Declaration of Rights of Man and of the Citizen categorically states that 'No one shall be disquieted on account of his opinions, including his religious views, provided their manifestation does not disturb the public order established by law.' The question is: since when did France, the land of liberty, equality, and fraternity, become so paranoid to deem public manifestation of faith a threat?" The GTN camera in Abaji came alive to capture Reverend Father Okoye's opening argument, basically a question presaging other questions. "If an individual's right to freedom of belief is fully acknowledged, and the individual is a member of a public somewhere, why should he leave his faith behind any time he steps outside his home? This question cries for an answer, more so as faith is inseparable from one's very identity. If secularism is an article of faith, as Mr. Beaumont insists, that makes it a religion of sorts. What then are we going to do with secularism's symbols, which we see every day and everywhere? Is it asking too much to expect our tolerance of secularism's idols to be extended to our own religious beliefs and symbolisms? That is just by the way. In my view, a matter of far graver importance than symbolism is freedom of religion along with what I perceive as an impending and well-orchestrated attack on that freedom. While I don't see myself worshipping the Hindu gods and goddesses mentioned by Swami Harelal, I fully acknowledge any other person's right to do what I have resolved not to do. I also wish to underscore a point that Swami Harelal made— that is, regarding the connection which a believer feels towards the deity or deities of his own choosing. Those not brought up under the Roman Catholic Christian tradition will not understand the doctrine of the Trinity. I do not expect them to. However, I expect them to recognize my right to believe in God the Father, the Son, and the Holy Spirit. Belief in any deity is an enigma that science can neither comprehend nor resolve to everyone's satisfaction."

The Reverend paused briefly to clear his throat. He continued, "I am really intrigued by the references that Dr. Cunningham made to human progress. I hope he is not implying that because the West already controls technology, it has now become the god before whom we should all bow and whose moral laws supersede the ecclesiastical ones. The West may master modern technology. It may have the capacity to manipulate public opinion through its exclusive control of the communication media and of information flow. It may dictate whatever is uttered or heard, whatever is written or read, and whatever is thought or felt. It may even continue to take all the big monetary and economic decisions that shape our world. None of these powers would ever make the West the real or the surrogate God. It will only remain a self-designated god, one that can easily be toppled either by its own arrogance or by its rivals' scheming. The real God, by contrast, lives forever." Wrapping up his contribution with quotations from the Bible, Father Okoye provided a long list of civilizations which had defied God and paid dearly for their arrogance and rebellion.

Chapter-19

.In the mysteries of the universe lies the very essence of belief!

THE STUDIO CAMERA AND the lights instantly veered towards the last participant in the debate, Sheikh Salim Kamil. Cunningham got Kamil's attention. With his son, Abdullah, fighting for his life, why would Kamil not be captivated by someone hyping the wonders of science and, in particular, the promises of biotechnology? But then the last debater remembered the verses of the Qu'ran that portray earthly life as an illusion.

Convinced that Allah is the source of all knowledge, Kamil promptly took science's spokesman to task: "Let me start with a question posed by Dr. Cunningham. How can any rational mind reconcile the idea of a benevolent God with the disorder prevailing in the contemporary world? The only way to answer that question is by asking another: will our denial of God's existence make all those things that we detest, all those calamities befalling our world, disappear? Have we considered the possibility of the free will, which we exercise as human beings, causing or aggravating our predicament? Haven't we in fact contributed our fair share to the prevailing feeling of meaninglessness and absurdity? How can we declare our independence of God and still hold Him responsible for the detestable happenings around us? Now back to the substance of the atheists' case against God. If I may paraphrase a maxim once popularized by the school of names in Chinese philosophy, a god whose behavior can be observed, measured, or predicted is no god. So, with due respect to Dr.

Cunningham, the very absence of a definition, precise or otherwise, is a plus for the believers, not a minus. God Almighty, which in Arabic comes out as 'Allah', is too profound and too intriguing to be grasped by an ordinary human mind—a supremely arrogant mind, a mind with an overblown sense of its own importance. Let me state upfront that a god with a date of birth and a place of death is no god. The thought of God that comes to a Muslim's mind is of the First without a beginning, the Last without an end, and the One in Whose absence there is absolutely nothing. Now, when I say, 'One', don't get me wrong. God's oneness is unique; it is not the 'one' that you often come across in the system of numbers. It is 'One' that has no parallel and has no number before or after Him. It is 'One' that encompasses and accounts for all values, finite and infinite.

"Let me now return to humankind, which often, out of ignorance, puts itself on par with, or as an alternative to, God Almighty. If you want to know how insignificant the human race is vis-à-vis the rest of God's creation, just look at one of those sweeping and dramatic images of the cosmos regularly beamed by NASA from outer space to the world. When placed within the context of the observable universe, we, the members of the human race, are a mere tiny dot, possibly a dot tinier than a mustard seed.

"Yet, mesmerized by its own discoveries and inventions, the human race suddenly declares God redundant. I am rather amused by all the "achievements" that Dr. Cunningham attributed to man, including the nature-defying "achievements" that the Qur'an already anticipated in the chapter titled Al-Nisa, verse one hundred and nineteen. Many of the so-called achievements are clear evidence of the Satan's plot to pump man with pride when the going is good and laugh in man's face when human action backfires. The conceited human forgets that God, Who is capable of creating, is also capable of destroying. The human being is created to be religious, but his or her rebellious, satanic spirit keeps inflating his or her ego. Allah already anticipated the arrogant streak in the human being. This is how He puts it in the chapter titled Al-A'araf, verse one hundred and forty-six: 'I shall (let them) turn away from my signs those who behave arrogantly on earth without any justification. Even if they see all the proofs (pointing to Allah's existence) in the world, they will not believe in them. If they see the path of righteousness, they will not follow it. However, if they see the path of error that is the path they will find alluring. That is because they have rejected our ayahs (proof, evidence, laws, and principles) and remain obstinate in their rejection.'

"Dr. Cunningham categorically denies the reality of life after death. That is his privilege. However, I wish to ask him one simple question: what is exactly the part he played in his own creation? If Dr. Cunningham had no hand in decisions that brought him to this planet, and probably had no idea that he was about to join the brutal, absurd, "meaningless" earthly beings, what guarantee does he have that he will not find himself on another plane of existence when his sojourn on earth ends? If we are here involuntarily, what guarantee do we have that we will not end up somewhere else involuntarily? Allah Almighty neither asked for our permission to create us nor sought our assistance when He set the creation and procreation processes in motion."

Kamil took a deep breath and then continued, "Are we surprised that man continues to shoot himself in the foot? He who was nothing in the beginning, and will end up as nothing, suddenly gets it into his head that he is everything! It is undeniable that we played virtually no part in the mating, genotype construction, conception, delivery, and social interaction processes preceding our births. Show me the role you played in your preconception days, and I would unhesitatingly agree that you know or can determine your last stop! It is not your science that placed you in the white race with all the positives and the negatives. It is not my wisdom or lack of it that made me a citizen of Dukyaria, with all the advantages and the disadvantages. It is, in both cases, the will of our Creator that brings meaning to an otherwise meaningless, and perhaps pointless, existence!

"Mind you, I am not arguing that man has no choice. If I may paraphrase a famous thinker—Albert Camus—an individual that finds the world absurd has three choices, namely, self-annihilation, self-indulgence, and self-discovery. Self-annihilation becomes an option when the human being sees no point in living. The self-indulgent individual acknowledges the imperfections of life but chooses to make the best of what he has. The only string which he attaches to his compromise with life is the freedom to do as he pleases. Of course, this unrestrained exercise of freedom has adverse side effects: it lures the individual into believing in his own omnipotence. That is why the self-indulgent individual makes his own rules. In his arrogance, he takes decisions that may later backfire, the decisions which promote precisely what he detests, that is, a sense of meaninglessness and absurdity. The third option, which is to embark on a journey—the journey of self-discovery—warrants that the individual step or migrate out of himself to know who he really is. The search for meaning is the essence of faith in the unseen. And by the way, if what we are seeing around us is all there is to life, I mean, if there is no life different from this, then consciousness has definitely been overrated.

"Dr. Cunningham searched everywhere but couldn't find God. Really? If he did not find God, it is because he has refused to ponder the significance of what science has so far revealed—especially, the configuration of planets, galaxies, clusters, and superclusters. These and other awe-inspiring objects are God's own indisputable signatures. They together constitute the irrefutable proof of God's existence." The Muslim cleric finished with almost no minutes left to spare.

Chapter-20

How can your right justifiably obliterate mine?

AS SOON AS KAMIL wrapped up, the spotlight returned to New York in readiness for the second segment of the debate. Stokes lost no time in firing off the first question. "Since you started this debate, Brad, you have to go first. My question to you is 'why bother about somebody else's belief when your right not to believe is not threatened?'"

"Religion is like a pandemic. If you don't quickly track and quarantine those who catch the bug, the health of the community is likely to be endangered. Quite apart from the fact that religious superstitions may hinder or halt human progress, the acrimony among the believers constitutes a threat to public peace. Now, let me quickly return to a few issues raised by other panelists. Krishna talks about multiple gods. Doesn't that raise the question whose authority will prevail in the event of conflict? To which of the several gods would a believer be loyal at any point in time? Luiz-Fernando talks about the ancestral gods. I am still trying to wrap my head around the idea of a person long-dead resurfacing on earth to mete out punishment to criminals. I didn't realize that Brazil has aliens from outer space. I thought these creatures exist only in sci-fi thrillers! I must of course thank François for advocating the confinement of religion to private places. I am surprised, however, that he said nothing about Okoye's cassock or Kamil's provocatively long beard. When I saw Okoye in his get-up, I asked myself: what fashion statement is this guy trying to make with his cassock, skull cap and all! And

Kamil's beard? Boy, does it make this handsome man look aggressive!"

Stokes cut Cunningham short. "Brad, let's not get personal. Besides, your time is up." The matter was far from resolved, of course. Kamil had prevailed upon the Abaji studio to let him have his right of reply. Abaji in turn had sought New York's clearance to proceed to air Kamil's rebuttal. "This is unusual, but dammit, let the Abaji camera start rolling." Stokes was inwardly pleased that a boring debate was about to turn lively. His ratings would shoot to the sky after this.

"Thanks, Mr. Stokes. I have no problem whatsoever with what Dr. Cunningham said about my beard. In fact, it brings to mind one challenge that I face every day in my country here, Dukyaria—that is, getting illiterate peasants to see the world in more ways than one. If Dr. Cunningham were to walk into my village dressed the way he is, two things are likely to happen, neither of them pleasant. The villagers would, in all probability, have confused the tie fastened on his neck with a rope and would instantly have mistaken him for a sheep or a goat—since only sheep and goats have ropes fastened on their necks. Alternatively, the villagers may recognize the tie and the suit as a mode of dressing, but since that is the type of get-up which is generally associated with the so-called infidels, the villagers would treat him like a leper. They wouldn't want to be in his company let alone have anything to do with him. If the illiterate community in my country can find foreign modes of dressing odd or offensive, well, yes, I can understand why illiterates in other parts of the world would see red anytime I show up with my beard and flowing gown!" Kamil laughed at himself, thus triggering equally jolly reactions in different parts of the world. Only Cunningham wore a sore look. How could anyone mistake a Harvard and Yale alumnus like himself for an illiterate? He silently blamed himself for dragging Kamil's beard into the discussion.

69

"Ok. Let's now return to the substantive program. My next question is for Swami Harelal. If Hinduism acknowledges the possibility of experiencing the divine in a unique, and as you implied, entirely personal way, how come you and the Muslims rarely get along?" Stokes yielded the camera and lights to New Delhi for the response.

"Hinduism is a peaceful way of life. I believe that Islam is also a peaceful religion. Commenting on Islam, Mahatma Gandhi said, and I quote: 'I became convinced that it was not the sword that won a place for Islam in those days in the scheme of life. It was the rigid simplicity, the utter self-effacement of the Prophet, the scrupulous regard for pledges his absolute trust in God and in his own mission.' Of course, when extremists on both sides are calling the shots, you cannot rule out conflict. This is probably as good a time as any to respond to Dr Cunningham's point about multiplicity of gods. It is only in the eyes of an outsider like him that loyalties conflict. The believer knows the deity to whom he or she is connected at any one time." Harelal killed two birds with one stone and handed over the outstanding airtime to New York.

"Madame Luiz-Fernando, it is now your turn. Dr. Cunningham already beat me to the questions on my mind. How can the living rely on guardian-angels that are long dead? What is the basis of this faith in your ancestors?" Stokes framed Cunningham's skepticism as a question.

"If you ask me to supply a scientific proof of the ancestors' power to do and undo, I must respectfully decline. I simply can't do that. I can't establish a causal link between the will of the ancestors and changes in the conditions of those they left behind. However, I can supply proof of the ancestors' hold on our mind. I already told you that when modern, educated members of our community commit a crime and are asked to swear in Ogun's name, they refuse to do so. They will sooner swear in Jesus's name than invoke Ogun's to settle a disputed matter. They know from experience that whoever lies and tries to bury the lie under Ogun's name will die a horrible death. Come to think of it, no proof is more empirically verifiable and 'scientific' than that!" She giggled for the camera.

"Let's go back to you, François. You want to see religion confined to private quarters. What is your reaction to what Reverend Father Okoye said about Article 10 of the French Declaration of Rights?"

"I don't see any inconsistency between what I said and Article 10 of the Declaration of Rights. Remember, there is a reference to public order in the Declaration. If a religious symbol constitutes a serious threat to public order, the right of the public must supersede that of the individual." François found the question awkward, but he managed to wriggle out of it.

"Let me get this clear, François. Are you implying that the crucifix; the skullcap, or hijab; and other symbols pose a threat to public order?" Stokes sent a new question back to Paris.

"I am not implying. I am convinced that they are threats to public order and should therefore be banned."

"Umm! That's interesting! Anyway, my next question is for you, Reverend Father Okoye. Christianity is supposed to be a monotheistic religion like Judaism and Islam. What is the origin of this Trinity you mentioned, the Trinity that has room for God the Father, the Son, and the Holy Spirit? Please, explain to our viewers as you would to a seven-year-old just starting out to learn about God." Stokes was being deliberately provocative. His mind was still on the ratings.

Okoye squirmed in his seat. He had no problem grasping the concept of the Trinity. He could clearly visualize it in his mind. His problem was how to break the concept down sufficiently to make it intelligible to a seven-year-old. There is a limit to which a complex problem could be simplified without losing its essence. Still, he would give this his best shot. "Of course, Christianity is monotheistic. Just as Judaism rests on the doctrine of Shema, and Islam on Tawhid, Christians firmly believe in One God. One Corinthians 8:6 categorically states as follows: 'There is but One God, the Father.' Deuteronomy 6:4 says basically the same thing: 'Hear, O Israel, the LORD your God is One.' This is confirmed by Isaiah 43:10, 11 which says, 'Know and believe me, and understand that I am he: before me there was no God formed, neither shall there be after me. I, even I, am the LORD.' However, while the Trinity is not expressly mentioned in the Bible, Matthew 28:19 provides an authority that the doctrine's advocates frequently invoke: 'Go therefore and make disciples of all nations, baptizing them in the name of the Father, the Son, and the Holy Spirit.' Even then, the Trinity was not accorded any canonical recognition until 325 A.D., when Emperor Constantine, in an attempt at mediating the conflict between the advocates of the Trinity and the Arian Unitarians, got an ecumenical council to put its weight behind the Trinity. Simply put, the Trinity is One God with three attributes, those of the Father, the Son, and the Holy Spirit. I acknowledge the fact that the doctrine is still hotly contested by a number of Christians. That notwithstanding, those of us brought up to accept the Trinity as part of the Gospel have no reason to contest it."

Kamil looked at his compatriot with squinted eyes as the latter made a spirited effort to define and justify the doctrine of the Trinity. Kamil didn't see any difference between Okoye and the animists whose only excuse for their belief was staying faithful to the 'way of the ancestors'. Kamil forgot about the Trinity the moment Stokes mentioned his name. The anchor-man was not beyond ambushing ill-prepared panelists with awkward questions. Kamil had to be ready and fully attentive. As expected, Stokes fired off his question, "A prominent Congressman recently declared that Islam is a cult, not a religion. What are your views on that?"

The question left Kamil in stitches. His convulsive laughter must have been infectious, as fellow debaters and viewers watching thousands of miles away soon joined in the hilarity. Kamil quickly got a grip on himself. Wiping his moist eyes, he looked directly at the studio camera and responded, "Forgive me, Mr. Stokes for my inexcusable behavior. It is not your question I was laughing at. It was this Congressman whose ignorance I found at once weird, pathetic, and comical. I have heard many unflattering statements about Islam, but none of them beats this in inanity. Some of Islam's detractors have worked tirelessly, though largely in vain, to pin the terrorism label on the faith. Others accuse Islam of being patriarchal and anti-women, even when they know it is neither. Yet others dismiss it as an Arab religion—another kite that will never fly. Fortunately, the more viciously Islam is attacked, the wider it spreads. You can say that Islam's best PR agents are its enemies. They say about Islam things that even the faith's most hardnosed opponents would find whacky and incredible. Islam, a cult? A cult that has existed for one thousand five hundred years and has a membership of close to two billion must have something which its adherents find appealing. A cult that has a clear and easily comprehensible definition of its doctrine must be one that educates rather than brainwashes. A cult that established one of the oldest universities in the world,

Al-Azhar, and has contributed to the advancement of knowledge in various fields must have blown its cover and opened itself up to rigorous examination. What is a religion, anyway? Isn't it a set of beliefs about the divine; about thinking out of the body; about humankind's obligations to itself, to its environment, and to its Creator; and about the link between earthly life and accountability in the life hereafter? I think the Congressman should stick to law-making and leave a subject that he knows nothing about well alone."

Chapter-21

The jury is out!

AS SOON AS KAMIL rounded up, Stokes announced the commencement of the third and final leg of the program. Already, several viewers had signaled their intentions to weigh in with comments or questions. Time would not permit Stokes to take all.

"I thank GTN for this vital public service. I've learned more about religion today than I ever knew before. I am particularly intrigued by the contributions on Hinduism, Ogun, and Islam. I wonder if there are websites on which I could learn more about the three," Damon Sedgwick asked, phoning in from Phoenix.

On cue from Stokes, Krishna, Luiz-Fernando, and Kamil dictated their web addresses, which immediately appeared on the screen. Brad Cunningham, meanwhile, fidgeted in his seat. The program was not taking the shape he had in mind. Still, anything could happen before the day was over.

"I agree with François Beaumont. Religion is a private affair. I don't want to see those scarves and those beards in my backyard!" Brigitte Benoit called from Quebec. Since hers was a comment rather than a question, Stokes moved on to the next caller.

"I find Kamil's contribution highly enlightening. I never expected to hear a cleric try to clarify religious dogmas or affirm positions that could be readily verified. Yet, the Sheikh presented the Koranic doctrine and the associated concepts in a lucid and coherent manner. My question to him, was he a full-time scientist before he crossed over to his present job? I must also commend Madame Luiz-Fernando. She demonstrated a clear and easy-to-follow link between faith and day-to-day experience." That was Alistair David from Manchester, England.

Kamil responded to David's question with a no; he was not a scientist. He only studied philosophy in Cambridge and went on to do his post-graduate study in Islamic philosophy at Al-Azhar.

Cunningham was now getting really frustrated. Not one question had been directed at him. It was as if he had not participated in the debate. He had never been so humiliated in his life.

"Isn't it true, as Dr. Cunningham brilliantly argued, that man has advanced sufficiently to conquer any challenge without relying on any god, be it Kamil's Allah, Okoye's three-in-one contraption, Harelal's numerous deities, or Luiz-Fernando's vengeful Ogun? Any of you guys can answer." Jude Montgomery, a renowned Australian atheist, gave Cunningham the long-awaited break.

One by one, the panelists restated their positions, taking the opportunity to clarify moot points and to attack views contrary to theirs. It was time to wind up. The debate was over. Stokes, beaming glowingly, thanked the contributors and the viewers. He didn't have to wait too long for a ratings update. The debate had clearly shot the GTN ratings into the stratosphere. He was ecstatic reading the following day's newspaper coverage of the event. With the possible exception of Thinkers Daily, an atheist mouthpiece which dismissed the debate as a pointless exercise, newspaper editorials saw the event in a positive light. Stokes didn't even object to the Thinkers Daily labelling him a "crusader" masquerading as a television anchor. That just gave him the cover he needed to air anti-religious views on his program in the future without triggering any backlash. Judging by the smiles on their faces, the debaters were also delighted with the outcome. Only Cunningham looked crestfallen. He had reasons to be. With headlines like "HARVARD ILLITERATE: Cambridge alumnus berates Cunningham!" "THE BOUNDS OF REASON," and "THE BRAINY BEARD," newspapers in different parts of the world dumped a heavy burden on the leading secularist's mind.

Chapter-22

The catechist falls for reason

CONSOLED BY THE BELIEF that despite their differences on Kamil, he and Samuel had one God in common, Emman instantly downplayed the choir master's insolence, sat upright, and, like the rest of the viewers, gazed expectantly at the cinema screen in front. He had heard a lot about Cunningham and his irreverent views on religion. As catechist, it was his duty to note all of the atheist's gaffes and seize upon them when conducting his Bible classes in the vicarage. He had come with a notepad and three ballpoint pens, two of which were held as backup, in case one suddenly went dry. He readied one pen and the jotter for the task ahead. Those sitting close to him eyed him, occasionally wondering what he was up to. He noticed but ignored their furtive glances. He had not come to entertain or be entertained. He had come to learn. After all, the catechist's job description required him to instruct those preparing for sacraments of penance and reconciliation, first Holy Communion, confirmation, and initiation into Catholic beliefs and practices. The debate would not only expose the flaws in rival religious teachings but also reinforce his own Catholic belief and enhance his skills as a religious instructor.

He scribbled briskly as Cunningham started making his points, "Blunder No. 1: He wants to see God before he believes! Is this man serious? How can an arrogant, pompous, 'know-all' mind see God? You remain blind until you open your inner eyes!" The notetaking began with two queries and an observation.

"Blunder No. 2: Life after death. He believes in life, but not in after-life consequences. He wants to eat his cake and have it! Well, as it was in the beginning, so it shall be in the end. In the beginning, he came to this world, not of his own volition, but as divinely decreed. In the end, he will return to another world, again, not on his own terms, but as the good Lord decides." The second note was more copious than the first.

"Additional Comment on Blunder No. 2: Reason and human progress. The man seems to have a point here. Don't see any difference between what he's saying, i.e., man's salvation lies in his own hands, and what the scriptures teach us, i.e., heaven helps those who help themselves. Ref. 2 Thessalonians 3:10, FOR EVEN WHEN WE WERE WITH YOU, WE GAVE YOU THIS RULE: 'THE ONE WHO IS UNWILLING TO WORK SHALL NOT EAT." The third note started hoping to find faults but ended concurring with Cunningham's observations on the role of reason in human progress.

"Blunder No. 3 (replacement for deleted blunder 3): Nonsense! Science has not rendered faith in God superfluous, as argued by the debater. This is not an either-or issue. Human initiative and belief in God are mutually compatible, not contradictory." The fourth note entertained the possibility of reason and faith converging at one point.

Emman didn't find anything to comment on when Harelal took over. He tersely dismissed the Swami's faith as "pure idolatry." According to Emman's notes, Harelal was "nothing but an idol worshipper." Other jottings on the note pad are "Origins of Harelal's multiple gods?" "Is faith divisible, such that the believer will be loyal to one god one minute, and to another the next?" The catechist didn't see any discrepancy between his rejection of multiple gods and his staunch defense of the Trinity.

In his reaction to Luiz-Fernando's contribution, Emman's notes implied that the Odus were given to idolatry: "Odus not satisfied with worshipping the gods of their ancestors at home decided to export one of the gods, Ogun, to Brazil! Anyway, comparing Jesus with Ogun, both insulting and sacrilegious! Must emphasize this at next bible lesson for Odu-speaking converts! No room for Ogun in the scripture!"

It was now time to pick holes in the next debater's argument. "Bowman (that's how the notes spelt Beaumont) is right re-Moslem beards and scarves. Can't stand excessively long beards or veiled women myself. But he's dead wrong on the cassock and the skull cap! These are insignias of clerical office, insignias carrying the authority of the Holy Father." That was all the notes had to say on Beaumont's advocacy of the banishment of religion from the public space.

Okoye was the next to speak. Silence descended on the auditorium the moment the handsome face appeared on the screen. Then, suddenly, someone at the back started to applaud. Within a few seconds, most of the viewers had been conscripted into Catherine Henshaw's pro-vicar cheering squad. Moved by the crowd's adulation of her man, Catherine's heartbeat increased. She imagined Okoye's tongue locking in with hers and his strong hands gently stroking her back before working their way down her midsection and then up to caress her firm breasts. Bose, unaware of what was going on inside Catherine's brain, imagined the vicar's touch in the sensitive regions of her own body—the massive boobs, the round and protruding buttocks, the narrow forehead, the short but straight nose, the thin lips, the slightly curved chin, even her ear lobes.

All the female viewers in the auditorium practically swooned when the vicar opened his argument. They greeted each point he made with thunderous applause. The hand clapping got so loud and so persistent that a church elder had to appeal for calm. "We shall not be able to follow what the Reverend Father is saying unless we remain quiet. I therefore urge each and every one of us to hold his or her show of approval until the end," Chief Andrew Njemanze, standing up and facing the crowd, peremptorily ordered everybody to be quiet.

The crowd heard the corpulent Njemanze but decided not to obey. The wealthy Chief's writ might run in his chain of companies, but not here in the church. The cheering squad did what it knew best how to do—cheer Okoye vociferously any time he opened his mouth and regardless of what he said or how he said it.

The only exception was Emman. He greeted Okoye's contributions and the unending rounds of applause with feigned boredom and a prolonged yawn. He hissed loudly as Okoye struggled with a question on the Trinity. "Just look at him! This is a question that can be answered by the laity effortlessly," he murmured to himself. As it so happened, the din in the auditorium rendered his derogatory remarks inaudible. He jotted his unfavorable rating on his notepad all the same.

Then came Kamil's turn. Emman's pen scribbled furiously when the Muslim cleric started to speak. The catechist was ready to call him out if Kamil stumbled, as

Emman was sure the cleric would. The pen soon went back to work on the notepad:

"Comment 1. Allah! Allah! Allah! The Arabs have brainwashed this Kamil. He knows no other name except his Allah! Is the word 'God' so difficult for him to remember or pronounce?"

"Comment 2. Strange! Who taught this man the self-evident truth? Amazing, the Moslems too agree that as it is in the beginning, so it will be in the end. Checkmate, Cunningham! Hallelujah!" Emman wasn't sure the Bible categorically affirmed, as Kamil did, that human existence was God's unilateral decision. Emman needed to reassure himself that, contrary to Samuel's allegation, he was not a Kamil fan. He continued to search for ways to prove the choir master wrong by minimizing the Muslim debater's contribution.

"Comment 3. White or black, rich or poor, pretty or ugly—doesn't matter; we are from one source: God. Can't quarrel with that! The man must have copied it from the Bible!" To belittle Kamil's contribution again, the note continued attributing the knowledge of the human being's involuntary existence exclusively to the Bible.

The catechist had no other bone to pick with Kamil except to wonder why the Muslim cleric's expression changed at the mention of the Trinity. Emman's notes summed up his own reactions as follows: "Kamil's grimace at the mention of the Trinity totally uncalled for! Still, don't blame him. Blame our incoherent vicar." Emman knew in his heart of hearts that Okoye was anything but incoherent, but then how could he find anything nice to say about a person he envied so much?

The ninety-minute program came and went reinforcing Emman's faith. Despite Cunningham's heroic efforts, the catechist saw nothing appealing in atheism. There was also nothing in Harelal's and Luiz-Fernando's doctrines that would make the catechist renounce his allegiance to God the Father, the Son, and the Holy Spirit. As for Beaumont, Emman found the French debater's views on Kamil's beard and the Moslem scarf apropos, but wrong when it came to the cassock and the skull cap.

Chapter23

Reason's winning! Faith's incorporated!

EMMAN WAS ABOUT TO dismiss the intercontinental debate as a complete waste of time when memories of the issues raised by the debaters came flooding back into his brain. He had by then taken leave of other television viewers to return to his one-bedroom apartment on Ekuninam Street. As he trudged towards his destination, he began to turn the bones of contention over in his mind. No panelist fascinated him more than Cunningham. "The man certainly has a point regarding the role of reason in human progress. Surely, God's abounding grace does not exclude or forbid personal initiative! Isn't that the essence of that crucial verse in Thessalonians 3:10? Is there any harm in seeking the kingdom of the earth simultaneously with the kingdom of heaven? Since wealth is created by God, would He object to us humans working hard for its possession? 'He that shalt not work shalt not eat!' Is that not what the Bible says?" Emman continued to ruminate on his way home. Cunningham might have failed to convert him to atheism, but the evolutionary biologist had somehow managed to start an uprising in the catechist's head.

The self-questioning continued long after the live television debate had ended. No matter where he was or what he was doing, Emman would ask why he should be condemned to an ascetic life. It was all well and good for Father Okoye to swear an oath of poverty; what did the vicar need money for anyway? The church took care of his basic needs. The girls flocking around him would gladly elope with him and not care where the next meal would come from—

were it not for his vow of celibacy, of course. The parishioners would move mountains for him in a heartbeat without counting the costs. Okoye, after all, had the only thing his admirers cared about and cherished: his gorgeous personality. What did he, the catechist, have? Nothing—except possibly a penniless, purposeless, and loveless life. Virtually living from hand to mouth, he could hardly contemplate starting a family. Seven years after leaving university with an award as the Most Promising Information Science Graduate, he could not nail down a decent job. The catechist's job might be prestigious, but it was not exactly a goldmine.

Emman's failure to find a job was not due to lack of trying. He responded to every vacancy announcement, sent out countless unsolicited resumes, and, when he was lucky enough to be invited, showed up at job interviews. All the job-search efforts yielded nothing.

As vehicles sped past him and other pedestrians on Ekuninam Street, he cast his mind back to a particular job-hunting experience. He and Akin Mosafejo had just come out of an interview. Fate, or, to be specific, the hostile economic and employment conditions, had brought the two together. Both graduates were among the five thousand that had applied for ten vacancies at the Environmental Sanitation Agency. Both were among the unsuccessful applicants. Although they were meeting for the first time, their membership of the virtual Association of the Long-term Unemployed had provided both a justification to feel bonded to, and make common cause with, each other. Akin spoke first, not minding that he was about to spill an intimate family secret to a total stranger.

"My uncle is a disgrace to the family and to his class." Akin looked gloomily at his worn shoes before waving a bulky folder in Emman's face. "What kind of 'big man' finds it so difficult to place his nephew in a good job in Abuja?" The pain of endless job hunting was finally beginning to tell. Akin had been at it for eight years. Every time he thought his chance had come, the job would go to somebody else. The recruiting bodies were never short of excuses. If his second-class lower-division degree in business administration did not render him "over-qualified" for a vacancy, his "lack of cognate experience" was likely to stand between him and the dream job. He was either too fat for one job or too skinny for another. He might be eligible for consideration for yet another position alright, but, alas, his state or district of origin had exhausted its employment quota.

"And you know what is funny? I have met many who had the same qualifications and 'disqualifications' as me but who somehow managed to get the job! It all boils down to connections. Yes, connections!" Akin moaned, and then quickly turned his face skywards, "I know, God Almighty, that You hear every word I am uttering. I also know that You will not come down to personally find me a job. But what choice do I have? The uncle that You left me with is useless. No, he is worse than useless!" Akin's increasingly bleary eyes shifted from the sky back to Emman.

"You are lucky that you have a big man in your family. I have none." It was Emman's turn to lament his fate.

He too had been at it, the full-time job of job hunting, for six years.

"You don't know how lucky you are. At least, you know why things haven't gone your way. You can always take comfort in the fact that you have found no job because you have no big man holding your hand and walking you to powerful people's homes and offices. Instead of overworking yourself praying to man and God at one and the same time, you have only to turn in one direction, that is, to God. You have only the Almighty to beseech, not pin your hopes on worthless uncles." Akin tried to console Emman.

"This uncle of yours, how big is he? And I am not talking about his height or weight. I am talking about his position in society." Emman was curious about Akin's uncle. He couldn't imagine why a truly big man would neglect his basic family responsibility.

"Trust me, he is big—and I am not referring to his physique." Akin answered ambiguously.

"Is he a party elder or godfather?" Emman was interested in specifics.

"No." Akin remained cryptic.

"Is he a Permanent Secretary?" Emman tried again.

"No."

"Is he an honorable member of the House of Representatives?" Emman wondered what queer pleasure the stranger derived from prolonging the conversation. Well, that's what joblessness does to people, he thought to himself.
"No."

"Is he a senator of the Union of Dukyarian Nationalities?" Emman persisted.

"Definitely not!"

"Is he a state governor?"

"No."

"Is he a cabinet minister and member of the Union Executive Council?"

"No."

"Is he the Speaker of the House of Representatives or President of the Senate?"

"No."

"Is he the President of the Court of Appeal or Chief Justice of the Union?"

"No."

"I am sure if I ask if your uncle is the President, your answer will be, 'No.' So, if he, your uncle, is none of the above, who or what exactly is he?" Emman was tired of fencing with his new acquaintance.

"He is a university professor." To show Emman how "big" his uncle was, Akin quickly summarized the professor's credentials. "He has written several books. He has also won many international awards in his field of specialization, social psychology. I know because I have seen the testimonials prominently displayed on his sitting room wall. I have also seen copies of his books all over the place. Are you satisfied?"

"Not quite. When you approached him for assistance, what did he say?" Emman drew Akin out further.

"He gave me the usual nonsense—about how unfair it is for him to exert undue influence on public recruitment process and deny other applicants full and fair consideration. He even had the guts to tell me to name anyone who got jobs by the backdoor so he could take the matter up with the Civil Service Recruitment Office! Can you imagine? He expects me to betray my friends! If I mention their names, they will not only lose their jobs, but they may also be handed over to the police! Olo'un maje! God forbid. I shall not be the downfall of my friends and relatives!" As he often did when symbolically warding off bad omens and dismissing evil thoughts, Akin made the sign of a ring around his head with his left hand and snapped his fingers. Barely audible, he continued whining about his uncle, "He keeps talking about reform, as if reform were what I need to put food on my table."

"And you think that your uncle is wrong and you are right?" Emman looked at Akin wide-eyed.

"I certainly do! What is my concern with civil service reform? I am not a politician or a high-ranking government official. I am an ordinary citizen looking for my daily bread.

Who cares about reform when he cannot find one lousy job? Na reform we go chop?" Akin avoided Emman's piercing while he underscored his contempt for reform by switching to Pidgin English, the Ndis' alternative lingua franca. He couldn't think of a better way to get his message across to Emman, a Ndi.

"Yours is the uncle that I wish God had given me— an uncle who would be far more interested in changing things for the better than in getting a disproportionate share of the unjustly sliced cake. And I have news for you. There are grades of 'big men' in Dukyaria. Thank heavens; your uncle does not belong under any category. Our 'big men' have no time to read, let alone learn from, the books that your uncle writes. They haven't the slightest idea what 'international recognition' means. They have no plan to reform anything— at least, not when the reform brings no personal and immediate gain. Their overriding interest is how to confiscate power, and with the power in hand, gratify their basest desires. Do you see my point?"

"I don't. If your point makes sense to you, good for you! See you at the next interview and the numerous ones after. And here is my own newsflash for you: If the system continues like this, revolution is just around the corner! The meek won't wait indefinitely to 'inherit' the earth! The meek will shake the earth to its foundation and grab whatever they can salvage!" Akin turned his back on Emman, highly irritated by his friend's naïveté.

"Bye for now." Emman waved back and headed in a different direction. Since he had no uncle to turn to, he decided there and then to accept Akin's unsolicited advice. He took his grievances to God and became an active member of the Utako

Catholic community. However, when he thought that his faith in Christ was unshakable, a guy called Cunningham had now given him a lot to mull over.

With one side of his mind leaning towards conformity and the other plotting an insurrection, Emman resolved to table the matter before God. First, however, he had to get supper. He quickly whipped up his favorite dish, a mélange of fried plantain, steamed rice, and smoked fish stew, all washed down with a sachet of "pure water," the poor person's substitute for real, potable water. As had been his habit after supper, he thought of going to the room directly opposite his to watch the evening news on his co-tenant's television set. He quickly changed his mind. The news would be about nothing other than the intercontinental debate, and there was nothing the news would carry about the debate that he did not already know.

Instead of listening to the evening news, he went straight to the matter on his mind, the matter for which he needed the Almighty's backing in order to resolve it. However, try as he might, he did not know from where to start and how to frame his prayer. He did not know whether to beseech God for His abiding grace, whatever that meant; repeat his long-standing but yet-to-be-granted entreaty for a well-paying job; or get straight to the point and ask for divine guidance on an idea which he had repeatedly dismissed as preposterous—the idea of breaking away from the Catholic fold and establishing his own church. Thanks to Cunningham's spirited defense of reason, the idea long rejected had suddenly become not only appealing but also inexorable. If he was to be honest, this was the project that his mind leaned towards. He could do with heavenly support on how to make it a reality. Still unsure which way to turn, Emman threw everything that bothered him in his supplications. He was confident that the All-seeing and All hearing God would take his long shopping list into consideration and grant his urgent request.

After his prayers, he grabbed a copy of Chinua Achebe's Anthills of the Savannah, lay face up on the bed, and read himself to sleep. Curiously, the only image that kept popping up in his dream was that of a church—a church of which he was the proprietor, general overseer, and lead evangelist. The only things missing were the church's name and his title. Neither should be a problem. He woke up the following morning convinced that the dream was a "vision," specifically, an unambiguous instruction to establish his own church and deliver the message from on high.

He promptly called Akin on his mobile number. Akin, who had by then squeezed himself into a dead-end job as a fuel pump attendant somewhere along Herbert Macaulay Way, didn't think twice before accepting Emman's invitation to participate in the establishment of Abounding Grace Ministries Inc. Emman, in turn, instantly arranged a meeting with his new associate. This was where both would agree on how to translate Emman's dream into reality.

Wearing a brown, weather-beaten French suit, Akin was the first to arrive at the venue of the meeting; a quiet, largely vacant, wing of Sheraton Abuja Hotel's guest lounge. Emman joined him shortly thereafter, his long-sleeve white shirt tucked loosely into a pair of faded blue Levi pants. Unperturbed by the piercing and unflattering stares of bystanders, Emman had kept the appointment with his bathroom slippers announcing every step he took in the plod to the rendezvous.

Akin was particularly delighted that someone finally recognized the worth of his business administration training. He quickly set about drawing up a business plan. The plan showed Abounding Graze Ministries starting modestly on a vacant plot as an open-air church and then generating resources from tithes and endowments to put up a permanent structure. To attract hordes of worshippers to the new church, the plan envisaged co-opting individuals skilled in the art of miracle-making. It didn't matter whether the miracles were real or faked. What mattered was finding someone with the ability to take total control of the congregation members' mind. If that could be accomplished by hook, fine. But if crook was what was needed to make miracles happen, well, the end justifies the means.

"How about schools and universities? I understand there is a lot of money to be made from this peculiarly Dukyarian obsession with paper qualifications!" Emman, excited by Akin's plan, threw in his own ideas.

"That will come much later. For now, we should not get ahead of ourselves. Remember that schools and universities are capital-intensive. Since we are just starting out, we're unlikely to find the kind of money needed to build and run schools and universities right away." Akin's words dampened Emman's enthusiasm.

"OK, but there is another project we can start to implement right away." Emman persisted.

"And what is that?"

"Funeral homes. Have you seen how impressive Gwagwalada Funeral Home's building is from the outside?

Wait until you get inside. You will think that you are in an upper-scale luxury suite downtown. I was there with Father Okoye a few months back. I asked the manager how come their building outshone the most magnificent corporate headquarters in Abuja. You know what he told me? He said, and I quote, 'With the multiple hazards contemporary humans face every day, no business is as lucrative as the business of dying.' So, as you can see my friend, the business of dying is going to be alive and well for the foreseeable future." Emman laughed raucously, a cynical look darting across his eyes.

Meanwhile, Cunningham sank into his swivel chair in the Department of Biological Sciences of New York University, brooding. He concluded that if he were to be given another chance, he would do things differently. If only he knew what he had already accomplished, he wouldn't contemplate changing his strategy. His debating style, warts and all, had had an immediate and dramatic impact. The Abounding Grace Ministries had not only become a done deal, but the pastor and lead evangelist, Emmanuel Kalu, looked like he would be upstaging Reverend Father Okoye. It didn't matter that the Ministries' tendency to mix faith with fortune handed Cunningham and other secularists the ammunition they needed to fight not only "religious racketeering" but also all manners of believers, especially, adherents of various religious traditions and practices.

Chapter-24

The terrorist in our dragnet

KAMIL ARRIVED AT THE airport sweating profusely. His chauffeur, Lawan, had left him at the check-in counter and returned with the SUV to Garki. Unfortunately, the airport cooling system had broken down at precisely the time Abuja inhabitants would give anything to have relief from the sun's oppressive heat and the metropolis's constantly high humidity. Hoping that the inside temperature would be cooler, he promptly completed the check-in process and proceeded to the passengers' lounge.

The flight to Jos was not due to depart for another two hours. Instead of sitting idly in the lounge, he decided to move to an isolated spot in the lounge and perform the second obligatory prayer for the day, Zhur. As a traveler, he was allowed to perform the third obligatory prayer, Asr, ahead of the scheduled time, that is, to combine the third with the second obligatory prayer.

Zhur over, he rose to his feet to take advantage of the special dispensation. Before he completed the iqamah, signaling suspension of worldly activity to commune with the worlds infinite, seven other passengers whom he had never met before trooped to the impromptu praying ground and lined up horizontally behind him, following his lead. The Sheikh thus became the de facto Imam, or leader of the devotees, for the Asr congregational prayer.

The seven congregation members were obviously on a different flight. The prayer had hardly ended when they proceeded to the boarding gate as instructed by the airport's public address system. They left Kamil on the bare floor, holding both palms below his face, silently reciting verses of the Qur'an, and inaudibly praying for the safety of departing and arriving passengers at all airports. He ended his supplications by beseeching Allah to ensure Abdullah's quick recovery.

Kamil remained the object of fellow passengers' attention for as long as the obligatory and supplementary prayers lasted. Two elderly women stared rudely at him and cackled. The onlookers were probably amused by Kamil's long beard, and most certainly perplexed by his curious decision to torture himself. How else could they explain Kamil's act of intermittently standing up straight, prostrating, and then head-butting the snow-white ceramic floor? A young, well-dressed man nudged the lady sitting next to him, whispered into her ears, gestured towards Kamil, and grimaced. He wondered what had gotten into the man. Why would he, or anyone, stand up straight at one time, crouch at another, and then rise again, only to knock his forehead on the floor repeatedly? Only someone seeing things—someone who has gone around the bend—behaves in such a bizarre manner! And to imagine that it was not just one person, but eight, who went mad at one and the same time! The compilers of the Seven Wonders of the World should think of adding this odd behavior as the Eighth! The couple, like many others present, found Kamil's behavior weird and entertaining. Fortunately, none yet knew about Kamil's personal anguish—the anguish over Abdullah's ill-health.

It wouldn't have bothered Kamil if others had known about his son's health status, ready to gloat and wonder derisively why his prayers for his son's full recovery had so far gone unanswered. He was already used to non-Muslims scoffing at Muslims, particularly at their call to prayer, their mode of worship, and even their sartorial style. As he had done on previous occasions, he ignored his fellow passengers' disapproving glances and barely disguised mockery.

After his prayers, he walked across to where the passengers were seated and took a seat next to one of them. Out of his briefcase, he produced a copy of Imam Al-Ghazzali's Ihya Uloom al-Deen, which roughly translates into The Renaissance of the Sciences of Religion, a philosophical tract written in Arabic. Engrossed in the Ihya's metaphysical discourse, he paid no heed to the characters or happenings around him.

He was on the book's eleventh page when a man in his mid-thirties rose from his seat and made as if heading towards the washroom. He soon made a U-turn and melted into the airport's boisterous crowd before ambling towards one of the offices. He returned about fifteen minutes later to find Kamil still on the Ihya. He sank back into his seat, an expressionless look on his face.

Kamil glanced at his watch. It was two fifteen in the afternoon. The flight would take off in less than an hour. He wondered what kept Okoye. Since he and Kamil were headed in the same direction, he, Okoye, ought to have checked in with him or shortly thereafter. Unknown to Kamil, the reverend father had taken an earlier flight. Pastor Emman Kalu, who had been invited to the Jos meeting despite Okoye's objections, had also boarded the same earlier flight. Kamil knew that a prominent dibea, medicine man, was coming from Okigwe, and a voodoo priest was expected from Badagry to represent the polytheists at the Inter-Faith meeting, but Kamil did not know how both planned to get to Jos. He could only hope that all the parties would show up. The stakes were too high for any delegate to skip such a meeting.

As he waited for Okoye to appear and for his flight's departure to be announced, Kamil reflected on the agenda of the Jos meeting. The letter of invitation which he had received from the Inter-Faith Secretariat of the Union President's Office indicated that the delegates would deliberate on three issues, all of them grave. First, after receiving an update on the security challenges facing Dukyaria, the meeting would advise the government on the measures it should adopt in order to defeat or appease the arrowhead of terrorism, Abu Danja Mamba. The second item on the meeting's agenda was equally weighty—the impending transformation of Dukyaria into a Dependent Territory in the wake of the World Bank's decision to impound the Union's Deeds of Sovereignty/DoS as collateral for outstanding debt. The third and final agenda item was basically a fishing expedition, since nobody had the facts needed to take a reasoned position on the topic. Although newspapers were awash with stories of an American-European initiative to abolish the United Nations and replace it with a full-blown World Government Organization, details of the initiative had not yet been made public.

Kamil was still wondering what business religious leaders had dabbling in state matters when the public-address system suddenly crackled into life. The lady announcer, with a sweet voice, politely requested passengers on flight DK 758 to proceed to the boarding gate. Kamil knew that possession of a boarding pass did not guarantee a seat on any of

Dukyaria Airline's flights. He hurriedly grabbed his hand luggage and readied himself for the upcoming stampede in the boarding area. Making it to the front of the queue this afternoon required that the passenger be not only fit but also fast. As the passengers subsequently learnt, the airline was no longer going by the seat numbers appearing on their boarding passes. The bigger plane originally assigned to the flight, they were told, had been commandeered at the last minute by the President's Office to take the First Lady to a family friend's wedding in Las Palmas, in the Canary Islands. The airline regretted the inconvenience which the substitute plane's free-seating arrangement would cause. That was all the passengers needed to be told. Every passenger naturally anticipated that the sudden change would set off a rout at the boarding gate, with the strong muscling their way to the front to make sure they would not be left behind.

Kamil, no weakling himself, raced to the front. He was beaten to the third position in the line by only two passengers, who had strategically placed themselves close to the boarding gate beforehand. At least, as the third passenger waiting to board, he was assured of a seat on the 50-seater plane. He looked at the long line at the back and lamented the fate of close to twenty passengers who were likely to be "off-loaded." No other thought came to his mind then except gratitude to Allah for giving him the strength to make it to the front. In-sha-Allah, he would be on the flight and make it to his destination.

He was still treasuring his vantage position on the queue when three tall, muscular men in uniform marched to the boarding area. Armed with automatic weapons, the uniformed men started, from the bottom end of the queue, scrutinizing each passenger from head to toe. Each time the most senior officer, a non-commissioned officer, concluded that a passenger was not a person of interest, he would shake his head, and his subordinates would, on cue, do likewise. Then the search party would move to the next passenger. The routine continued until the officers of the law got to Kamil. "That's him! Tall, yes! Handsome, yes! Bushy beard, yes! Flowing gown, definitely! I don't see anybody else that fits this description. Sir, I am afraid you will have to come with us!" The most senior, the NCO, insisted, although he went out of his way to be polite.

"Go with you where? You must have got me mixed up with somebody else!" Kamil could not believe his ears or eyes.

"I am sorry, Sir, I haven't done that Sir, that is, get you mixed up with somebody else. My instructions are specific: I am to ensure that you accompany me and my men to our boss." The senior officer was unyielding.

"Who is that boss of yours?" Kamil wanted to know.

"Sir, you will find out when you get to our office," the officer persisted.

"What do you want me for in your office?"

"Sir, I can't answer that question. You will find out when you get to our office." The officer wouldn't say more than he had been programed to say.

"This is unbelievable! What kind of nonsense is this? What exactly am I supposed to do in your office?" Kamil was on the verge of exploding.

"Sir, I can't answer that question. You will find out when you get to our office."

"OK, let's go. I hope you are aware that my flight is taking off in a few minutes."

"I can't comment on that, Sir. My instructions are specific...."

"Never mind; we know how unspecific your specific instructions really are! Let's go!"

"After you, Sir." The NCO motioned with his right hand.

"Are you kidding? How can I be in front when I haven't the slightest idea where we are going?" Kamil laughed at the stupidity of the officer's suggestion.

"Sorry, Sir! Aziz, lead the way! Big Boss will follow, and the two of us will be right behind him," the senior officer realized and quickly corrected his mistake. With Kamil in the middle, the party headed towards an office tucked behind the airport check-in counters. The sign on the door was intimidating, identifying the office Kamil was about to enter as the Directorate of National Security/DNS. Aziz rapped on the door three times before opening it. He shouldn't have bothered. The colleague he had left behind had strolled out to get a pack of cigarettes. Now inside the first office, the senior officer politely waved Kamil to one of the vacant seats. With two armed men standing guard and fixing their piercing gaze on their guest, the NCO walked into an inner office. He had to let his boss, the Assistant Station Director for National Security, know that his instructions had been carried out to the letter.

"Good. I already called the Station Director. Until the Director arrives, go back to where you left the accused, and don't let him out of your sight even for one second. Is that clear?" The Assistant Director dismissed his subordinate with a bored look and a languid wave of the hand. He returned to glaring at his desktop's illuminated screen.

"Yes, Sir!" The NCO stood upright, pounded both feet on the office floor, and saluted his boss as members of disciplined forces were trained to do. He turned 180 degrees and marched back to the detention room.

Like his two subordinates, the NCO fixed his eyes on Kamil. Inwardly, he was delighted to be the one to bring Kamil in. His name would be in all the following day's papers. He might even be invited to speak on television about his role in capturing Dukyaria's most dangerous criminal. Meanwhile, two hours after being held against his will, Kamil had no idea what the Directorate of National Security wanted from him.

The Station Director finally arrived. Since he had to pass by the outer office to get to his own inner office, there was no way he would not notice Kamil's presence in their midst. On sighting Kamil, the Director, Brigadier Anas-Adamu Girei, quickly warmed up to him, "Sheikh, Salaam alaykum! What brought you here? Aha! News travel fast! You've heard about the terrorist who walked into our dragnet! I am sure you will laugh in his face and say, 'I told you so,' that is, before we put the fear of God in him!" The Director extended his right hand to Kamil, not realizing that the person whose hand was locked in his was the "terrorist" he had dropped everything to see. Kamil, without disclosing what was going on in his mind, shook the Director's hand vigorously.

The three stern-looking soldiers froze in military salute on sighting their boss. With a casual wave of the hand, Girei signaled that it was ok for his subordinates to stand at ease. However, instead of relaxing, the soldiers were jolted by the Station Director's weird behavior. How could the boss fraternize with Dukyaria's Enemy Number One? Their astonishment turned into apprehension when the boss and the accused walked side by side to the most prestigious office at the airport, the boss's own office. They stared with their mouths agape as the two chatted with each other along the way.

The Assistant Director was next to be perturbed. His boss had started by asking why the Assistant Director had kept Kamil in the detention room instead of inviting him to wait in his office. The subordinate knew there and then that he had got the wrong man. No outsider was in the detention room except Kamil. And like his boss, the Assistant Director already knew and instantly recognized the cleric. He could not believe that the man he had held without charge was none other than the famous Salim Kamil, the one whose face was a permanent fixture on television and in mainstream newspapers. "Oh! My God, what have I done now!" The Assistant Director realized only too late that he should have ascertained the identity of the arrested. He blamed himself for relying on tips from an informant like Kennedy Ossas, Emmanuel Kalu's head of security!

It was Ossas who had fingered a passenger as a terrorist, a terrorist who posed real and present danger to passengers travelling to Jos, Ossas included. Unfortunately, the

103

self-appointed informant didn't mention the terrorist's name and, to make matters worse, the Assistant Director didn't ask. Kalu's head of security had obviously taken undue advantage of his position as a former DNS agent to gain the Assistant Director's confidence. Now, how would he, the Assistant Director, explain to his boss's satisfaction, not one, not two, but a litany of monumental errors? He decided to act normal and see where that would lead him, "Good afternoon, Sir!" He backed his act with a voice. He kept mute on the intelligence he had relied on to place Kamil in DNS custody.

"Good afternoon, Olufemi. You can now brief me about our latest victory in the war on terror. I am sure the Sheikh here will be interested in the progress we have made," the Director said, meaning every word. Brigadier Anas-Adamu had talked to Kamil on several occasions, and he knew that the cleric found that the terrorists were doing incalculable damage to his religious constituency's reputation. What better way to convince him that the DNS was more than equal to the challenge than by parading a terrorist in the Directorate's custody?

Kamil sat patiently. There was no point saying anything until the Colonel who signed his detention warrant either showed cause or owned up to his error and tendered an unreserved apology. Like the Director, he focused his gaze on Colonel Gideon Olufemi and waited for the Colonel's update on the war on terror.

Olufemi avoided his boss's gaze, preferring to stare blankly at the wall behind the boss.

"Well, I am waiting!" The Director nudged him for a response.

"I am sorry, Sir, there has been a terrible mistake. This is clearly a case of mistaken identity. We received and acted upon tips that we considered credible. We were told that a terrorist was among the passengers flying to Jos. We learnt that this terrorist was murmuring something which our informant suspected to be incantations, incantations meant to mysteriously whisk him off the plane just in time to save him from the impact of an explosion that he himself masterminded...."

"You keep saying 'we.' Who are the 'we'? And precisely what is the name of this terrorist with extraordinary powers, the terrorist who has the power to set off an explosion on a plane flying at high altitude, the power to bail out of the fire-consumed plane, and the power to land on his feet thousands of feet below, without a parachute, and unharmed? Alu-fe-mi! Are you listening to yourself?" The Director scowled at his subordinate. He had tried for five years to pronounce 'Olufemi' but gave up when his tongue found the Odu name impossible to master.

"Sir, my boys acted on the description that I was given. That's why I can't blame them, Sir. As to the person unfairly accused of being a terrorist, I must apologize to our highly regarded Sheikh. I should have come over when my boys brought him in to confirm that we had the right man. I couldn't at the time because I was busy analyzing the data on outward- and inward-bound passengers. I was particularly after the drug baron flying to Laguna. We already knew that he was planning to sneak out of the country. I had to make sure that he was apprehended by my boys and handed over to our sister Directorate, the Directorate for the Control of Narcotics and Psychogenic Drugs."

"And who is this informant of yours, the one on whose intelligence you relied before ordering my detention?" Kamil was curious.

"I am afraid we can't answer that question, Sheikh," Girei quickly cut in. "You see, everything we do or say here is governed by the Official Secrets Act. The law setting up our Directorate also requires us to protect the identity of informants, regardless of whether they are trustworthy or disreputable. In fact, as far as the law is concerned, you are not here and you and I have never met. As for you, Alufemi, you have really disappointed me. Your explanation is not good enough! It is watery and despicable! An officer of your caliber ought to check the reliability of the inform brought to his attention before acting on it. You not only failed to check the fact at your disposal, but you proceeded with unseemly haste to act on it! You also failed to supervise your subordinates and ensure that they acted within the confines of the law. You didn't even bother to check the identity of the person whose detention you ordered. That of course is not my immediate concern. My concern right now is how to get the Sheikh to Jos for the important meeting starting tomorrow. The flight he was to board must have landed in Jos by now. Can you call the Dukyarian Airlines to check if they can find a seat on the five o'clock flight? What am I even talking about? Just tell the Station Manager that the exigency of national security demands that a seat be made available on the flight leaving for Jos at five o'clock. Do you think you can handle that?"

"Consider it done, Sir! I shall personally accompany the Sheikh to the boarding gate and get him a front-row seat!" Olufemi, looking contrite, assured his boss.

"You do that! And while at it, make sure you don't arrest the airline's ground staff. You know, the staff that we see every day as peace-loving Dukyarians and not as terrorists? I can't believe that he would make me drive all the way from DNS headquarters in Asokoro to watch all this! How embarrassing! I must apologize to our esteemed Sheikh. I am sure you must be ravenous by now. I shall order my men to get you anything you want from Nando's," the Director alternated between rebuking his subordinate and talking to himself, before finally apologizing to Kamil. Kamil was not particularly happy that someone might have to be "off-loaded" to make room for him on the five o'clock flight. He did not contradict the Director of DNS in his subordinate's presence, but there was no way he would agree to board the five o'clock flight if that meant taking another passenger's slot. For him, getting to Jos was not a do-or-die matter, and it was certainly not worth depriving another passenger of his or her right. If it was the will of Allah, in-sha-Allah, he would be on the flight. He would not travel unless and until everyone with 'ok' reservations got on the flight.

Kamil soon discovered that his fear of shortchanging a fellow passenger was unfounded. The five o'clock flight that he expected to be full was anything but. He and other passengers got their boarding passes with the seats clearly indicated. The First Lady might have commandeered one aircraft, but she couldn't, in far-away Las Palmas, eye the roomy and spotlessly clean 737 taking the five o'clock passengers to Jos. It didn't harm in the least that Colonel Olufemi redeemed himself by assisting Kamil with the boarding process. The Colonel carried the two pieces of hand luggage, accompanied the accused-turned-VIP onto the plane, and made sure that both the bag and the owner had settled in their appropriate places comfortably before take-off. As Kamil reckoned, it was Allah's will that he would be on the five o'clock rather than on an earlier flight.

Chapter 25

Jos, here we come

KAMIL DID NOT GET to his hotel until eight thirty that night. Contrary to the information supplied on its website, Ambassador Hotel turned out to be a seedy joint with sparse facilities. The previous occupants of Kamil's room must have been habitual smokers, and slobs to boot. They left behind a strong whiff of nicotine which compelled the new guest to hold his nostrils on opening the door.

The room itself was in terrible shape. The lighting was too dim for guests interested in reading at night. The rug must have seen better days, with blotches around the edges and clouds of dust all over left un-vacuumed. The television channels carried nothing but pornographic images. The tap was liable to be dry for hours and to flood the room when water unexpectedly started to flow and nobody was around to turn it off. The leakage in the bathroom was by itself a clear testimony to poor plumbing and shoddy workmanship.

Most disturbing of all, the past occupant had left used condoms in the toilet without flushing them down. Kamil murmured something in Arabic as Muslims were wont to do when expressing their revulsion at behavior they deemed indecent, decadent, or profane. He opened the refrigerator and shut it back the instant he caught a glimpse of whisky, vodka, and cognac. The Inter-Faith Secretariat had definitely booked him into the wrong hotel.

It was certainly too late to start looking for alternative accommodation. He took his mind off the room's shortcomings and called housekeeping. He needed the staff to bring him two buckets of water. He had to perform his nightly, Maghrib and Isha'a, prayers and then take a shower.

The obligatory prayers and the shower over, he decided to order room service but immediately reconsidered. Since room service was notoriously slow, it was better that he went downstairs to have his meal. Surprisingly, the elevator was in good working condition. He spent less than ten minutes in front of the shaft before the car rolled up and took him to the ground level.

He was surprised to find Okoye seated in one corner of the poorly lit restaurant and Emman in another. He suspected that other delegates he could not place must be scattered all over the spacious dining hall. He made a beehive for Okoye's table. Okoye was glad to see him, "What happened to you Salim? I thought you were booked on the two forty-five flight. I was surprised that you were not on the bus which brought the other delegates to the hotel at four thirty-five!"

"That's a long story. And what happened to you too? Weren't you supposed to check in at the same time as I did?"

"My staff at the vicarage called the airline at nine in the morning to find out if the flight that you and I were booked on would be departing on time. The airline not only confirmed the departure time but also asked whether I would be willing to be on an earlier flight since the one on which I was booked was full. You can imagine my shock to discover my ticket was 'ok' one minute but 'request' the next! Still, I should have asked my staff to pass the information about the sudden change to you. I am sorry for the omission."

"No harm done, Basil. You wanted to know why I was not on the two forty-five flight; here is what happened." Kamil gave a mystified Okoye a blow-by-blow account of his experience at the hands of Olufemi's "boys."

"That's most uncivilized, most barbaric, and definitely most unacceptable! What kind of training does the DNS give its staff, especially, staff operating in the senior cadre?" Okoye wondered.

"Are you sure the problem starts or ends with training? The method by which candidates get selected for sensitive posts in the public service is really where the problem lies. For all you know, Olufemi might have been nominated by a political godfather, or pushed on the DNS to fill a particular geo-political zone's slot in the civil service! Unfortunately, the civil service is filled with people like him," Kamil said, venting his own grievances against the professional civil service.

"You have a point there. I can't understand how the government misses the connection between the steady erosion of our sovereignty and the ineptitude of people in key positions! How can our officials match their foreign counterparts vision for vision, brain for brain, and grit for grit?"

Okoye had barely finished making his point when the steward brought the main course: marinated chicken and French fries for him, and tuwon shinkafa with alayyaho and smoked fish for Kamil. The reverend father said grace, crossed his heart and went to work on the chicken. The Muslim cleric recited Bismillahi ar-Rahman ar-Raheem, and from then on maintained radio silence. He nodded or shook his head depending on the response he considered appropriate to Okoye's remarks. Kamil never uttered a word until he was done with the tuwon shinkafa and showed his gratitude to God by uttering Alhamdulillah Rabbi-l-aalameen!

Absorbed in conversation at their own end, Emman and his large entourage gave no thought to Okoye or Kamil. The General Overseer had, at his church's expense, come with Akin Mosafejo (Deputy General Overseer), Amos Benjamin (Emman's personal assistant), Kennedy Ossas (the head of church security), Willy Osaretin (Online Services Manager), and three female members of the congregation (Amaka, Ngozi, and Doreen). At the end of their sumptuous meals, the General Overseer's underlings followed protocol by escorting their boss to his suite before dispersing to their rooms.

As mutually agreed, Amaka, the prettiest of the ladies, tiptoed from her own room and sneaked back into the General Overseer's suite when the others had hopefully tucked in for the night. She needed not worry about being caught red-handed. Akin Mosafejo, an Okoye look-alike, had planned his own tryst with the well-endowed Ngozi. The head of security would not be in his job for long if irregular movements or activities passed him by unnoticed. Fully aware of all the philandering in the church, he made the best of the latest situation by "camping" Doreen, a nymphomaniac unrestrained by marriage or the thought of her two adolescent children. Only the General Overseer's personal assistant and the Online ServicesManager were left out of the nocturnal carryings-on. With nothing to do, both hit the sack early, ready to face the challenges of the morrow.

Chapter 26

Let's pray! Yes, but in what language and to which deity?

AS ARRANGED, THE DELEGATES to the Inter-Faith meeting turned up promptly at the Ambassador Hotel's banquet hall the following morning. Kamil barely recognized many of the faces in the large and duly festooned hall. However, the large frame hunched on a chair not too far from the chairman was unmistakable. It was that of Ambassador Liswaniso Mulenga, the head of the United Nations office in Dukyaria. As Kamil was to learn later, Ambassador Mulenga had attended the meeting to update them on the proposal to transform the UN into a full-fledged World Government Organization. In fact, it was to allow him to return to Abuja early that the organizers had agreed to tweak the agenda substantially by taking the second item first, the third item second, and the first item last.

The hotel staff had spent the greater part of the night before preparing a large conference table and arranging high-backed chairs around it. They covered the table with a white cloth and planted vases of flowers on the high table, the table reserved for the chairman and the august Ambassador Mulenga. Bottles of Eva water and assorted soft drinks were also placed directly in front of each delegate's seat. Banners announcing the event to the world adorned the conference hall's entrance and the inner walls.

Kamil checked his watch. It read fifteen past ten. Okoye sat across the table, opposite him. To get his attention,

Kamil waved, and when their eyes met, he signaled by tapping his watch with the right index finger. When Okoye looked puzzled by the sign language, Kamil followed up with a whisper across the table, "Weren't we supposed to start at ten?" His voice was barely audible.

Okoye glanced at his timepiece. He whispered back to Kamil, "You are right. It is already a quarter past ten! I hope we start the meeting and get it over with on time. I have to return to Abuja no later than tomorrow afternoon."

The meeting's host and chairman, His Eminence, Bishop Mathias Jengre, must have sensed the disquiet around the table over the late commencement of the proceedings. "Gentlemen," he began, "I must apologize for taking so long to begin the meeting. We are still waiting for our secretary to get here. The Executive Secretary of the Inter-Faith Secretariat assured me as recently as yesterday that his deputy would be with us to cover our deliberations and settle your hotel expenses."

The Anglican Bishop had hardly completed the last sentence when the secretary walked in, looking dapper in his Hugo Boss suit. Samuel Akerele informed the meeting that he was staying at the InterContinental "at the far end of the city." He would have arrived early, but he had been held up in Jos traffic. If he was sorry for the uncharacteristic bad timekeeping, he did not say as much. He took his seat on the chairman's right, sweeping the hall with condescending eyes.

Civil servants! They have no regard for anybody except their political masters! Okoye thought to himself. Still, he was glad that Secretary Samuel Akerele managed to squeeze the event into his crowded agenda. At least, the meeting was now cleared to proceed.

However, substantive discussions could not commence, as the delegates were bogged down by controversy over a minor procedural issue. The bones of contention were who should be given the honor of invoking heavenly blessings on the gathering and how the supplications should be framed. The chairman had called on Father Okoye to give the opening prayers when Emman lodged a formal and loud protest, "Point of order, Your Eminence!" Emman wanted to know first and foremost the criteria applied by the chair in nominating the Roman Catholic priest for the task. Had the meeting forgotten that not every Christian was a Roman Catholic? Yes, he was once, but now he had been 'born again' and had seen the light. Besides, as General Overseer of a fast-growing church, he had greater claim to the honor of leading the prayer than "a mere parish priest." He forgot to mention that the "mere parish priest" was once his boss.

Okoye, not interested in making a mountain out of a molehill, had graciously conceded to his antagonist the right to be the gathering's intercessor before the Almighty. "I have no objection to the 'born again' Pastor leading us in prayers. We just have to be attentive, lest he sneaks in mumbo jumbo that only he understands!" Okoye could not resist the temptation to take a jibe at the Abounding Grace ministers' tendency to "speak in tongues" and bamboozle their audience.

Now given the floor, Emman ignored his opponent's sarcastic remark. He closed his eyes, placed his right palm on his chest, and started to pray, "Holy Father, we come before you—"

"Stop right there! What Holy Father are you sending our prayers to? I don't recall any of us designating you as our emissary to any father, holy or not. The chairman told you to pray, and the best you can do is invoke the name of a father?" Ahmed Onitira, a teacher of Arabic and Islamic studies from Abeokuta, was livid.

"I have no problem with a heavenly father. We too have our own heavenly fathers, our ancestors. We invoke their names and pray to them all the time! Carry on Pastor! Don't mind these Moslem fundamentalists!" Babalawo Kaka from Ado-Odo interjected, a wreath of red beads encircling his neck, and ostrich feathers shooting out defiantly atop his cowrie-adorned hat.

"Who are the Moslem fundamentalists? We must watch our language. That is no way to talk about adherents of rival faiths." Kamil could not restrain himself.

"So, you object to being labelled a Muslim fundamentalist! Huh? Where were you when your brother was making jest of the Holy Father?" Okoye suddenly found himself on Emman's side.

It took the chairman's swift intervention to stop a minor disagreement turning into an all-out war. "Gentlemen, gentlemen, let's get a hold of ourselves. Incidentally, why don't we have a single lady in our midst? This is a serious omission that we must rectify before our next meeting. I am sure that if we have women at our meeting, they will walk us through our disagreements before things get out of hand. They are always a voice of reason. Women would not be at one another's throats over a simple matter like this. I have a compromise

115

proposal. We should allow Pastor Kalu to complete his prayers. When he is done, the Moslems can frame their own prayers as they wish."

"How about us, followers of the ways of our ancestors? Don't we get to say something to our own gods too?" Kaka wouldn't allow his faith to be belittled or swept under the carpet.

"And how many personal gods do we have time to beseech today?" Onitira took another swipe, this time, at the polytheists.

"As many as are represented at this meeting!" Kaka was insistent, his dilated eyes betraying surging rage.

The chairman intervened again, "You know what, let's break for ten minutes and iron this out informally. Since we have agreed that the Christians and the Moslems would pray at this meeting, it is only fair that adherents of the traditional religions meet among themselves and decide who among them would pray on their behalf. Is that agreed?"

"Agreed!" The voice vote unanimously approved the chairman's proposal.

The chairman slammed his cudgel on the table. The meeting immediately went into a ten-minute recess. When it reconvened, Emman prayed the way he understood. The Muslims held their peace. They of course refused to say Amen when the supplicant rounded up with "...in the name of our Lord, the Father, the Son, and the Holy Spirit."

116

The chair then turned to Kamil. The Muslim cleric promptly delegated Onitira to offer the Muslim prayers. Onitira did as he was told, "BismilLah ar-Rahman ar-Raheem, wa-s-salat wa-s-salaam alaa say-yedina, wa maolaa na, Muhammad…."

That's it! The mere mention of "Muhammad" got the Christians kicking and screaming. They promptly weighed in with their veto. Onitira could not continue praying in a language the intended beneficiaries did not understand, neither could he invoke a name they did not believe in. What do these Mohammedans think of themselves? How can they come here and be praying in a foreign language? For all we know, they might be building a case for themselves and invoking the wrath of God on those who don't share their belief! "Bismilai!" What does that mean? There is no room for any "bismi" here. It is just not happening. The Christians put their feet down. The polytheists nodded approvingly. The Christians and the polytheists suddenly and effectively entered into a bilateral alliance against the Muslims.

The Muslims, feeling isolated and unfairly targeted, saw no point in continuing. They decided to walk out of the meeting. With Kamil in front, the fifteen Muslim delegates from different parts of Dukyaria gathered their papers and headed for the exit. They had nearly made it to the door when Bishop Jengre, a good-natured man in his late sixties, left his own seat to prevail upon the Muslims to return.

"We shall return on two conditions. One, the Christians will let us explain our prayer formula. Two, whether or not they accept our explanation, they will allow us to pray our own way, as they did theirs. Well?" Kamil looked at Jengre expectantly.

"Done! Both conditions seem reasonable enough. Now, let's get back to business."

To ensure that his prayers were not interrupted by hisses or outright objections, Onitira went out of his way to translate the words and phrases uttered in Arabic. "Bismillah ar-Rahman ar-Raheem," he explained to the non-Muslim delegates, stands for "In the name of God, the Merciful, the Beneficent." The second part of the opening prayer merely invoked the Merciful and Beneficent God's blessings on Prophet Mohammad, he added.

The non-Muslims stayed mute as Onitira took them through the opening part of the Muslim's prayer. Before he proceeded to the next segment of his prayer, one delegate requested a minor clarification, "You mean that your Muhammad too needs the blessings of God? We thought that you, his followers, regard him as your god, the dispenser of blessings and favors. When we see you turn towards Mecca during prayers, we were under the impression that you were praying to, not for Muhammad and yourselves. That is why we assume that you Muslims are 'Muhammedans', meaning, worshippers of Muhammad." Maxwell Efanga, a delegate from Abak, gave his own understanding of the Muslims and their faith.

"It's not Mecca. It's Makkah. In addition, we are no worshippers of Muhammad. Yes, we are his followers. Yes, we regard him as a prophet. Yes, we believe that he was sent to confirm the message with which other prophets had been sent in the past—that no deity deserves to be worshipped except Allah, the Lord of the heavens and earth. But read my lips: we are no 'Muhammedans'. We are believers in God Almighty, the

Creator of the heavens and earth, and in the prophetic mission of Muhammad, may the peace and blessings of Allah be on him," Onitira veered from his original terms of reference to enlighten the non-Muslims about the fundamentals of Islam.

If that was all the recitations meant, the non-Muslims asked rhetorically, then why didn't Onitira say so in a language everyone understood, English? Why did he have to turn a simple, easy-to-grasp idea into rocket science? Anyway, if he had to pray in Arabic, he might as well continue. But could he get it over with quickly? The non-Muslims could not wait to put the Muslim mode of prayer behind them.

Onitira wouldn't be hurried. He took his time to recite verses from the Qur'an and sealed the prayer by asking fellow Muslims to join him in the recitation of the first chapter, Surah al-Fatihah. They readily complied, rubbing their faces with both prayer-sanctified palms to signal the end of the supplication.

It was now up to Babalawo Kaka to pray on behalf of the polytheists. "Eledua, Oba Oga Ogo, Oba t'ojoba lo, Obatala, Obatakuntakun…."

"What is this man talking about? I thought when we asked him to represent us, the understanding was that he would frame his prayers in English. I am Ndi. I don't speak a word of Odu. How can I say Amen to a prayer whose meaning, purpose and intent I don't understand? Why do our people find thinking and praying in English so difficult?" It was Dibea Umezuruike from Ahiara, registering his opposition to a fellow polytheist's prayer formula.

Babalawo Kaka was livid. "Thinking and praying in English? Why not sleep and dream in English? Tell me, Umezurike or whatever your name is; is English your mother tongue? Aren't you ashamed to think and pray, and possibly dream, in a foreign language? Just a few minutes ago, we accused the Moslems of praying in Arabic, a non-Dukyarian language. Now you are insisting that I should pray in another foreign language. Olo'un maje! God forbid! I will never talk to my God except in the language He put on my tongue!" Kaka snapped his left fingers and circled his head as Odus often did to symbolize the resolve to thwart an evil omen.

"Then we have a problem! You won't pray in English. And I won't say Amen to your Odu prayer." Umezuruike was equally adamant.

The Muslims and the Christians watched as the two polytheists squabbled on the language in which to communicate their entreaties to the Almighty. They wondered how the chairman planned to de-escalate tension and break the deadlock. Another recess was definitely out of the question.

Bishop Jengre, with the episcopal insight and Solomon's wisdom, came up with yet another compromise proposal. If the meeting had no objection, the time allocated for traditional religious prayers would not exceed ten minutes. Kaka would pray in any language of his choice so long as he took no longer than five minutes. The remaining five minutes would be expended by Umezuruike to pray as he saw fit. The two allies turned antagonists bowed to the chair's will. Both wrapped up their differently structured prayers within the allotted time. Neither polytheist dignified the other's prayer with an Amen.

Chapter 27

Render unto Caesar the things which are Caesar's

THE DIAL ON KAMIL's watch put the time at twelve thirty in the afternoon. Lunch was approaching, but the meeting had yet to get to just one substantive item on its agenda. Not to take chances with time management, the chair proposed, and the delegates agreed, that the meeting should take the first item on the revised agenda—the religious community's reactions to speculations about the replacement of Dukyaria's sovereign status with a dependent one.

Before the topic was thrown open for discussion, Sam, the Secretary, presented the president office's view of how things were shaping up. "The presidency needs the religious leaders to be fervent in their prayers so that the independence we achieved over a century ago will not be taken away by our enemies," he started. "Dukyaria's foreign enemies have conspired to cripple our country's economy as a first step towards reversing our sovereign gains and re-imposing foreign colonial rule. They told us to privatize. We privatized. They told us to deregulate the economy. We deregulated. They told us to reduce government expenditure and balance the budget. We reduced government expenditure and made super-human efforts to balance the budget. They told us to devalue our currency. We devalued our currency. They told us to liberalize our economy. We removed tariff and non-tariff barriers and went a step further by allowing the free flow of foreign products. We have done practically everything they asked us to do. Yet they are not satisfied.

They want to seize our Deeds of Sovereignty and turn us into a Dependent Territory within the proposed Mali Empire. Can you believe that? By a stroke of the pen, they want to demolish what took our forefathers centuries to build!"

"Mr. Akerele, I am sure that even you should be ashamed of what you have just told us. 'They told us to do this. We did this. They told us to do that. We did that.' I wish you could play yourself back and listen to the words coming out of your mouth. If foreign powers told you to do something, and you blindly obeyed, you have none but yourself to blame. You have, by your thoughtlessness, proven that you are incapable of discharging the responsibility that comes with independence! In other words, you lost your independence not now, but right from the time you waited to be instructed on what to do to earn and preserve that independence. You lost your sovereignty when you allowed corruption to fester, and nepotism to flourish. You lost your independence the day you thumped your nose at superior intellect and promoted mediocre performers to strategic positions." Okoye did not spare the government or its messenger.

"Is the government serious? It wants us to be 'fervent in our prayers,' but it does little to give the prayers any chance of being accepted by the Almighty. As the Qur'an says, the supplications of non-believers are null and of no effect. There is no day Muslims do not pray for this country. I am sure that such is also the case with the Christians and the members of traditional religious orders. But the government keeps making wrong choices. This then is what I think you should do, Mr. Akerale. Did I get your name right?" He did not. He did not even notice Akerele's raised hand signaling an attempt to correct the error. Kamil was far more interested in passing a message to the government than worry about the pronunciation of the messenger's name. "You should return to those who sent you here, Mr. Akerale, and tell them to step up. When they take the business of governing seriously, they will see the effect of our collective prayers."

Emman saw the matter differently. "The Bible says, 'Render unto Caesar the things which are Caesar's and unto Jesus the things that are Jesus's.' As I understand the situation before us, Caesar knows his limitations and has had the good sense to come to Jesus for guidance. Mr. Akerele, I want to assure you that our church, the Abounding Grace Ministries, will not shut its doors to anyone looking for salvation. Tell your superiors that we are ready and willing to help in any way we can. Our prayer warriors will beseech the Holy Father to deliver Dukyaria from the claws of its foreign enemies. My personal assistant is here to exchange phone numbers with you. You can talk to him after this meeting. His name is Amos Benjamin, and he is seated right behind me." Emman gestured to his personal assistant, who promptly stood to be recognized. Emman practically turned Okoye's and Kamil's misgivings about Dukyaria's future into a business opportunity.

Okoye and Kamil were speechless. Neither knew what to say. Both only knew that they would never swallow their words. They had qualms about their government's policies; they were not ready to hold out the hope that the policies could be rescued with prayers. Besides, to counter Emman's offer of assistance would portray them as opportunists who were more interested in squabbling over market share than in ministering to the souls of their congregations.

Regardless of what anyone might think or say, Emman had effectively brought discussions on the first agenda item to an abrupt end. He had relieved the meeting of the responsibility for pleading Dukyaria's case, hopeless as the case might appear to some, before the Almighty. With that delicate matter out of the way, the chairman quickly steered the meeting to the next topic—the plan to transform the UN into the WGO. He gave the floor to Ambassador Mulenga.

Chapter-28

The special envoy presents his compliments!

AMBASSADOR MULENGA CAME TO Jos prepared. The gangling and extraordinarily bulky frame rose from his seat and snapped his fingers to get his subordinate's attention; the subordinate, having positioned the overhead projector for the task ahead, readied himself for the task of flipping the power point presentation's slides. Mulenga dazzled the delegates with statistics, pie charts, and multi-colored diagrams on global political developments, and in particular, the sundry threats to public order within and across countries. The United States, Ambassador Mulenga noted, was getting war weary. The superpower no longer enjoyed the reputation of a state given to militarism, a nation that whipped up military coalitions at the drop of a hat and risked its own soldiers' lives defending the freedoms of peoples in distant lands—peoples who probably showed no appreciation for the huge sacrifice. Since terrorism was now a global threat, the United States would gladly welcome the opportunity to hand over the war on terror and the attendant headaches to a world body. Unfortunately, the United Nations, as then structured, was too weak to perform this critical role. This was why the General Assembly resolved to start the process of investing the UN with sovereign supranational powers. Ambassador Mulenga made his point with cold hard facts, and within the allotted thirty minutes. He then fielded questions.

Many hands shot up simultaneously. The chair recognized Okoye.

"Thank you, Ambassador Mulenga, for this lucid presentation. I have only one question: Are you sure this project is not dead even before it is conceived? It is bad enough for us to lose our independence. It will be a disaster if our loss turns out to be a distant bureaucracy's gain! I don't see an electorate trooping out to elect the movers and shakers of the new World Government. What I see is a global bureaucracy ordering us around and taking decisions that are far out of proportion to its legitimacy."

Mulenga noted Okoye's question and comment.

The chair gave the floor to Babalawo Kaka.

"I have no problem with the proposed World Government Organization so long as it does not come between me and my Obatala, the god of my ancestors." Kaka was brief and to the point. Mulenga noted that as well.

Kamil silently wondered if there was anything Kaka had a problem with, except possibly, Umezuruike's opposition to prayers offered in Odu language. He could stand just about anything, except anyone demurring to his communing with his ancestors in his mother tongue, Odu.

The chairman noted that one delegate had persistently raised two hands, even going as far as standing, to be noticed.

"I hope we can rely on the new World Government Organization for financial assistance. We don't need technical assistance since we have qualified manpower. What we need is a massive infusion of funds," Chief Olowolaiyemo, a Sango worshipper from Ode Remo, lived up to his name. Olowolaiyemo in Odu means 'it is only the affluent that the world knows and acclaims'.

Kamil could not believe that Olowolaiyemo would be that naïve. He raised his hand, and, with a nod, the chairman gave him the go-ahead.

"Thank you, Sir. With the exception of a few, those present in this hall have yet to grasp the significance of what the Honorable Ambassador has just told us. This much I can say: if the next session of the General Assembly makes the mistake of endorsing this outrageous proposal, freedom as we know it will cease to exist. The right to freedom of expression, belief, and association, or to any freedom that makes us human, will vanish. We will not have the right to elect our leaders or to throw them out if we find them wanting. A proconsul appointed by the WGO will continue to order us around, and the president or prime minister elected by us will remain mere figureheads. Our finance, defense, internal security, and in fact all cabinet-rank, ministers will be imposed by the WGO and will become nothing more than mid-ranking officials of the world organization. If at all we are allowed to go to the polls, we will accomplish nothing except to rubber stamp decisions taken over our heads by the WGO or by of any of its affiliates like the World Bank or World Trade Organization. Mr. Ambassador, Sir, I can assure you here and now that we Dukyarians will not stand for this flagrant disregard for individual freedom! We shall fight the World Government Organization with every bone in our body!" Kamil's bloodshot eyes revealed the depth of his anger. Try as he might to suppress it, the memory of his son lying critically ill at Hayat welled up, shaping not just his feelings but also the force with which they were expressed.

Kamil's speech went down well with the delegates. It was greeted with uproarious applause. The chairman had to call the rowdy house to order. "Alright, gentlemen, you've made your point. Let us have His Excellency Ambassador Mulenga's reactions to the issues so far raised."

Mulenga, a quintessential diplomat, realized that the greatest mistake a bearer of bad news could ever make was to go on and on, oblivious to his listener's preference for blissful ignorance. Even if his memory had failed him and he had been about to proceed pigheadedly with delivering the rest of the unpalatable message, Kamil's harsh comments and the clamorous applause they had generated gave the UN envoy pause. He deftly parried all the comments and the questions. "I must thank you all for your observations. I find them pertinent. Since the questions are not the type that I can answer at my level, I have noted them for the attention of Headquarters."

Mulenga was not completely upfront with the meeting participants. He noted their observations alright, but not because he found them pertinent. He had no intention of allowing the reservations expressed by Okoye and Kamil to change anything, least of all, his superiors' stand on the WGO. Fortunately, before coming to Jos, he had met and obtained the endorsement of other "stakeholders," individuals and groups whose backing the UN needed to turn a bureaucratic initiative into a program of action. As his counterparts in other parts of the world did, he had practically sold the world government idea to political actors, captains of industry, newspaper editors, television anchors, leading academics, civic leaders, and trade unionists. Now, a bunch of Dukyarian clerics were proving difficult. He knew how to fix them, these members of the Kamil-led resistance movement. He would appear to go along with their objections but actually exploit the internal discord that was clearly on display before the meeting went into substantive business. His report to Headquarters would accordingly start with the wrangle between and among the religious leaders. The secularists in the UN Secretariat would be thrilled to no end to hear that the believers could not agree on a single subject, not even on the language to use to communicate their entreaties to the Almighty! Anyway, Kamil could fume all he wanted, and his rivals-turned-admirers might clap as vociferously as they liked. The World Government Organization was a done deal. He took leave of the meeting, satisfied that his wishy-washy response to the participants' questions had gotten him off the hook. He was ready to file his latest Stakeholders Meeting Report to his superiors at Headquarters.

Mulenga did not know whether his job would survive under the proposed arrangement. He was sure of one thing, though: dithering was costly in a period of rapid transition. He knew he had to move fast and make the right move. He had to ingratiate himself with individuals having the clout to advance his career. Even though Brad Cunningham had not yet gotten the job, he was widely believed to be the next High Commissioner for Secularism if and when the WGO took off. Mulenga decided that it would not be a bad idea to send a "blind" copy of his Inter-Faith report to the sworn enemy of religion and prospective holder of a powerful WGO post.

As Mulenga expected, Cunningham liked the report, especially the sections confirming his own long-held views on the faiths' irreconcilable differences.

Chapter-29

Any ideas on how to handle Abu Mamba, the terrorist?

THE UN ENVOY'S departure afforded Bishop Jengre an opportunity to close the morning session. After lunch, the meeting reconvened to take the third and last item on its agenda—the threat posed by Abu Mamba to Dukyaria's security. The question before the meeting was how best to end the insurgency in parts of Dukyaria. Should the government launch an all-out war on Abu Mamba and his associates, or invite the group to the negotiation table?

"You can only negotiate with people who are reasonable. Since terrorism and reason don't mix, there is no way the government can even think of negotiating with Mamba. You don't negotiate with terrorists. You crush them and wipe them off the face of the earth!" Emman was for a military response to the threat, not diplomacy.

"Much as I hate to be perceived as a warmonger, I am afraid I would have to support the Pastor on this one. Mamba and his gang are not even interested in dialogue. They are interested in applying terrorist tactics to Islamize Dukyaria and impose Sharia law on us Christians," Okoye said, virtually endorsing military action.

"Wait a minute. Did I just hear Reverend Father Okoye associate Islam with terrorism?" Onitira, fuming, scowled at Okoye from across the table.

"If Islamists are not behind the insurgency in Dukyaria, tell me exactly who are! Have you heard of Christian terrorists?" Okoye stood his ground.

"You are right, Reverend Father. We don't have Sango terrorists either. It is these Moslems that are giving us sleepless nights." There were other things Babalawo Kaka had a problem with after all. The "Moslems" had obviously made the list of those likely to tick him off.

"Baba Kaka, watch your language." Kamil protested.

"And if I don't? What will you do? Will you call your brother, Mamba, to come here with his gang of killers? They can't do anything to me, not when the gods of my ancestors are wide awake!" Kaka dipped into his flowing gown's pocket and took out a talisman, the horn of an antelope stuffed with rock-solid black soap.

"And you think that that puny little object in your hand will avail you against Allah's decree? All it takes to render it impotent is a combination of numerical codes from the Qur'an. I advise you to control your tongue and yourself before you say or do what you will forever regret." Kamil remained calm despite the provocation.

"Mr. Chairman, did you hear him? He is threatening me! If anything happens to me here or on my way back, you all heard him. He is the one to hold responsible!" Kaka appealed for the chair's protection. The chairman immediately intervened. "I don't think this is getting us anywhere. Instead of attacking one another, let us put heads together and attack our common enemy, terrorism. I need concrete ideas on what to do. If we think that military action is the answer, the government is already doing something along that line. What it hasn't done is to explore alternative methods of resolving the conflict." The chairman wanted cool heads and sound logic to prevail at the meeting.

Kamil raised his hand, and the chairman promptly gave him the floor.

"My advice is that we stop seeing terrorism as part of the Muslims' mission to, as they say, 'Islamize' Dukyaria. It would be foolish of Muslims to rely on terrorism to propagate their faith. By the same token, it is bad strategy for non-Muslims to portray the terrorist Mamba as the defender of Islam, especially since doing that is likely to assist Mamba in recruiting illiterate Muslims to his cause! Let me give you another reason why faith profiling is at best, counter-productive, at worst, dangerous." Kamil then narrated his experience at the hands of the DNS at the Abuja airport. This was presented by the DNS as a case of mistaken identity, but it had the potential of pushing moderate Muslims into the arms of terrorists. Ossas's heart skipped a beat the moment Kamil mentioned the DNS. Emman's head of security hoped that no-one connected him with the sordid affair.

Ossas had nothing to worry about. Kamil was too busy trying to sway the Jos meeting towards a new anti-terrorism strategy to think about who was behind his ordeal at the Abuja airport. Terrorism, he argued passionately, has no religious affiliation. There are terrorists among Christians, Muslims, Jews, Hindus, and Buddhists. Terrorism is a weapon of choice among political extremists and drug cartels, Kamil reminded the delegates. Despite his persuasive argument, the meeting was unable to agree on his 'peace plan', or any plan for that matter. The meeting ended as it had begun— polarized along religious; sectarian; and, particularly as regards the Kaka-Umezuruike face-off, ethnic and linguistic lines. With Emman's well-timed pro-Christian utterances pulling Okoye to the right and Mamba's terrorist acts forcefully dragging Kamil to the left, the believers' camp promised to be rowdy for the foreseeable future. None was as happy about this turn of events as Brad Cunningham.

Chapter-30

Enough of this political correctness!

THE FALL SESSION OF the General Assembly was unusually rowdy. It had started with a strong statement from Carl Henderson, President of the United States, urging member-nations to relieve his country of the heavy burden of policing the world. Henderson had won the presidential election on the platform of the American Progressive Party. His party, the APP, and the rival American Homeland Party/AHP had emerged in response to public angst at the cynicism and the corruption in the two political parties that had alternately ruled America for centuries, the Democratic and the Republican parties.

With the two traditional parties constantly shifting their positions on issues to gain maximum political advantage, the electorate could hardly distinguish between one and the other. The voters initially registered their protest with low turn-out at the polls. When this changed nothing, two political novices, Carl Henderson and Gary Landon, led revolts in their respective political parties. Henderson spearheaded the formation of the progressive wing in the Democratic Party. It was a matter of time before the progressive wing transformed itself into APP and displaced the parent party. The story was the same in the Republican Party. What started off under Landon's leadership as the American Era movement soon resulted in the birth of the American Homeland Party/AHP and the Republican Party's demise.

With the emergence of the APP and the AHP, the American electorate now had a clear choice. Where the APP presented itself as a secular party with global ambitions, the AHP trusted in God, and looking out for America's interest in a hostile world was its sole mission. The electorate clearly preferred this neat arrangement. It also preferred the APP's hedonistic, secular thrusts to the AHP's stiff-necked puritanism. That was how Henderson got to be the first president elected on APP's ticket. With the active support of Brad Cunningham, Henderson had made a strong case for global secularism.

The address to the UN was the first chance Henderson had to bring the world up to speed on America's role in the world. America, he noted, had shouldered a disproportionate degree of responsibility for securing the world against terrorism. He reeled off statistics on the number of American service men and women killed or wounded in foreign wars, the number and cost of military jets brought down by hostile fire, the ratio of military outlay to total expenditure, and the impact of his country's growing deficit on domestic and global economic health. President Henderson noted that to keep the world safe, the American taxpayer was called upon to forego his own pleasures and bear other people's burdens. The people of the United States, the president informed the gathering, were no longer willing to be taxed to death to keep their foreign counterparts alive. Americans had started saying, 'enough is enough'.

The President added, "An economically prosperous America is the world's best news. When our economy thrives, it keeps economic engines in other countries running at full capacity. Yet, we cannot prosper, and the world economy cannot perform at optimum capacity, if we continue to allocate huge proportions of our resources to military expeditions in different parts of the world. Our commitments in different parts of the world have deprived us of the resources needed to power our industries and create jobs. We expended huge amounts of resources in Afghanistan, Pakistan, and Iraq, to mention but a few. Iraq's case is particularly troubling. When we thought that we had fully liberated that country from Al-Qaida's brutal grip, a murderous gang going by the name ISIS moved in rapidly and seized swaths of Iraqi and Syrian territory. As I speak, ISIS has its design on Turkey and on countries lying along the Gulf and the Arabian Peninsula.

"In Africa, terrorists affiliated to Al-Qaida and ISIS are active in Libya, Algeria, Egypt, Mali, and Dukyaria. My latest intelligence briefing indicates that a comic character with an equally funny name, Abu Danja Mamba, has seized half of Dukyarian territory and is poised to impose his own brand of Sharia rule over the entire country. America will naturally not stand for this. We won't fold our arms and watch a bunch of lunatics take over the world. Just as we resolutely dealt with the genocide masterminds in Somalia, Rwanda, Central African Republic, Liberia, and Sierra Leone, among others, we shall leave nothing undone to make the African continent and the world safe for democracy. This is the reason we are throwing our weight behind a new body in place of the United Nations. I wish to assure the distinguished heads of state and government attending the current session of the General Assembly of the United States' unqualified support at this critical juncture. In collaboration with all member states, we shall invest the proposed World

Government Organization with the authority, and endow it with the resources, it needs to enforce public order in any part of the world."

Following President Henderson's example, other world leaders signified their support for the new world body.

The only hold-out was the President of the Russian Federation. President Mikhail Yevgeny Bogdanov had threatened to derail Henderson's plan with a veto. Bogdanov changed his mind when America prevailed upon the World Trade Organization not to approve Russia's membership application until that country dropped its opposition to the World Government Organization. For its own part, the World Bank was to suspend action on the Russian request for a new structural adjustment loan until America's rival came to its senses and joined the WGO bandwagon. Neither arm-twisting tactic worked. The Russian Federation would have remained adamant in its opposition to the WGO but for the Chechen brigades' frequent attacks on its interests in the Caucasus. This, more than any other factor, influenced Bogdanov's decision to soften his stand. Even then, he did not give up without a fight. The Russian Federation, he warned, would watch every move the WGO made. The Federation would respond decisively if the new world body threatened its geo-political interests.

It was now up to the ordinary member states either to toe the super-powers' line or assert their independence. Nevertheless, what they decided wouldn't matter in the least. Although they were in the majority, none of them wielded the veto needed to delay or stop the WGO train's departure. All the same, they did not give up without a fight. They exercised their right to be heard. Countries like Brazil, India, South

Africa, Bolivia, Cuba, and Venezuela made loud noises. The Secretariat staff duly 'noted' their reservations and went further to assure them that their sovereign rights would be preserved under the new dispensation.

It was a different matter entirely for the least developed member states. Their request for the unconditional guarantee of their sovereign rights fell on deaf ears. "We shall review the issue of state sovereignty on a case-by-case basis," was all the assurance Arabia's Permanent Representative and presumptive Commissioner-General of the proposed body was prepared to give when Dukyaria contributed to the debate on the WGO. And, in case Dukyaria gave as much as a thought to an insurrection against the new body, it should remember that the World Bank had not yet decided what to do about its Deeds of Sovereignty. Unless Dukyaria paid its debt in full and on time, that precious document was likely to be impounded by the Bank. In other words, that country was not in a position to say anything about sovereignty, least of all, its own.

Chapter-31

You won't see reason, wise guy? OK, see this!

THE US AND THE other powers behind the WGO initiative left nothing to chance. They promised top officials in UN member states prestigious positions in the WGO and twisted the arms of country permanent missions to the UN. As a recalcitrant Dukyarian diplomat soon found out, no method was beneath the dignity of WGO backers. Suave Biyi Idris was his country's Permanent Representative to the UN. He was preparing for a meeting of the Africa Group when his phone rang. "Am I talking to His Excellency, Ambassador Idris?" the female voice at the other end asked.

"Yes, you are. Can I help you?"

"Please hold while I transfer you to the US Permanent Representative."

Idris heard the phone click, and within seconds, a male voice was on the line. "How are you today, your Excellency, Mr. Ambassador? Forgive this intrusion. There is one little matter I need to discuss with you. It's rather urgent, and I hope you will make time so we can get the matter settled quickly," Travis Berger said, cutting to the chase.

"That's mysterious! Can your Excellency give me an idea what this is about?"

"It is not a subject that we should discuss over the phone. How does 10:30 sound? My Head of Chancery will be downstairs to receive you." Berger hung up, leaving no room for negotiation.

Idris's mind raced as he walked from his Second Avenue office on 44th Street across to 45th and then down to First Avenue. What could be so urgent to require his presence at the US Permanent Mission? He could not explain the feeling, but a voice inside him told him that the meeting was unlikely to proceed or end pleasantly. Regardless of whatever came up at the unscheduled encounter, he hoped it would be disposed of in time for him to address his colleagues in the Africa Group. Africa must speak with one voice and let the world know that the continent would never accept the WGO and its multi-lateral colonialist designs.

The US was not unaware of the Dukyarian Permanent Representative's misgivings on the WGO. Berger had tried several times to make him see "the big picture," but Idris's eyes were on another picture—the imminent loss of his country's sovereignty. If Berger was still counting on his support for the WGO and had decided that summoning him to his office was the way to go about it, he was wasting his time. Idris was resolute.

He arrived at the US Permanent Mission at 10:25. As agreed, the Head of Chancery was at the reception, ready to usher Idris to Berger's twenty-eighth-floor office. Berger cut the diplomatic smile archived in his brain and pasted it on his aging but well-chiseled countenance. "I don't have to ask how you are doing, Mr. Ambassador. You are in top form! Must be the regular exercise! I understand that Dukyarians love to exercise regularly. Anyway, I shouldn't take too much of your time. Let's sit somewhere comfortable," Berger waved Idris to one of the leather seats arranged around a large coffee table. He took the most prominent and strategically placed one.

"Well? Didn't your Excellency say over the phone that there is a matter we need to discuss?" Idris, though inwardly edgy, sounded as casual as he could manage.

"I sure did!" Berger responded heartily, reaching for a file on the coffee table. The room light bounced gracefully off his graying but thick hair. "Let me get right to the point. It is this little matter of the WGO," Berger continued, his eyes on the file. "The Government of the United States of America would really appreciate having an important country like the Union of Dukyaria on its side with respect to the WGO. All the countries that matter are already on board. My government sees no reason why Dukyaria would be an exception." Berger made his point while at the same time flipping through the pages of his file. The cut-and-paste smile was still switched on.

"Haven't we discussed this issue several times in the past? And haven't I made our position clear? My country's position remains unchanged. My government sees no reason to support a project that will further erode its sovereignty. We are not even sure that the little autonomy we have left will not soon be confiscated by the World Bank." Idris reiterated his government's position.

"Let me get this straight. Dukyaria will not support the transformation of the UN into the WGO? Are you sure there is nothing you can do personally to get your government to see reason?" Berger, having failed to get Idris to 'see the big picture' came up with another object worth seeing, 'reason'. A cynical grin began to form on his face.

"You are right on both counts. My government won't budge, and there is nothing I or anyone can do to change the government's stand." Idris's frigid countenance signified tenacity.

"Are you sure about that—about you not being able to advise your government to change its mind and cast its lot with the WGO?" Berger's cynical grin was now all over the face.

"Positive!" Idris ignored the grin. He remained grim-faced. He got up, fuming. He was ready to leave, but Berger wouldn't let him.

"I think you'll want to sit down when you hear what I am about to say. You told me that you couldn't do anything to change your government's position on the WGO. Right? Now, let's see whether this will help change your own as well as your government's mind," Berger pulled out seven high-resolution snapshots from an envelope lodged in the file and handed them over to Idris.

The Dukyarian Permanent Representative's countenance changed the instant he saw the first picture. How had Berger obtained this? He asked himself the same about the other pictures as well. Each was as unsettling as the others.

"How did you get these pictures?" Idris finally regained his voice, both hands suspended mid-air, his eyes cloudy, his brow wrinkled, and his entire body quivering. He suddenly realized that Berger's earlier seemingly innocuous observation about the Dukyarians' love of physical exercise was in fact a combination of sarcasm and an ominous signal.

"Just let me know if you are now ready to play ball or whether I should simply pouch these exhibits to our Ambassador in Dukyaria for onward transmission to your President!" Berger showed what he meant by 'reason'. Reason was not the 'big picture' Idris had all along refused to see; rather, it consisted of small snapshots with the potential to cause maximum damage.

"You wouldn't descend so low!" Idris protested, the scowl on the face pronounced.

"Then you don't know me, and you don't know how determined we are to put down whoever stands in our way!" Berger's grin developed into mocking and uproarious laughter.

The US Permanent Representative knew he had Idris where he wanted him. Berger's determination to control Idris started the very month the latter assumed duty as his country's Permanent Representative to the UN. The CIA followed him everywhere—to restaurants, the Empire State Building, the Yankee Stadium, WWE tournaments, the Museum of Modern Art, theatres on Broadway, the Statue of Liberty and Ellis Island, the Waldorf Astoria, and the Islamic Cultural Center.

The CIA surveillance camera trailed Idris for months without capturing anything interesting. Then Ekineta Blankson came to town, and everything changed. Ekineta was never short of pretexts to travel to New York. If she was not a member of her country's delegation to the UN General Assembly, she would be at the head of the delegation to the annual conference on the Advancement of the Status of

Women. At one time, she was vacationing in New Jersey, at another she was shopping at Macy's.

Ekineta, after all, was no ordinary person. She was the President's concubine. That was precisely Idris's problem. He couldn't take his eyes off Ekineta, his boss's girl. She was the type capable of making a man do what he might live to regret. She was the perfect temptress—with her vibrant, brown skin; high cheek bones, big, round eyes; straight nose; sparkling white teeth; curvaceous body; sweet, confident voice; and sharp intellect, not to mention her extraordinary ability to shift effortlessly from humor to serious conversation.

Idris knew that it was injurious to his personal and career health to sidestep the president and carry off the big man's lady. As he told himself, Ekineta was the forbidden fruit, or what his Odu ethnic group termed eran agba, meaning the meat that was off-limits to a child having been set aside by the gods for the elders. No matter how he felt about Ekineta, he was determined not to tempt fate by grabbing and running away with the forbidden fruit. For crying out loud, the lady whose affection tore at his heart was in the same category as the First Lady. The only difference was that the real First Lady stayed in the palace full-time with all the paraphernalia of office while her rival held court outside the palace where she ministered to the king's regular and after-hour needs. In fact, if the title of First Girl Friend existed, Ekineta would be the one to hold it.

Idris would have succeeded in banishing Ekineta from his mind if the latter had let him be. Being who she was, Ekineta passed up no opportunity to come onto the lithe, smartly dressed Idris, calling him at odd hours, sending unmistakable signals, and all but challenging the Permanent Representative's prowess and masculinity. Idris eventually succumbed to Ekineta's charm. He threw caution to the wind, set protocol aside, and started bedding the First Girl Friend. What you don't know won't hurt. He was probably right. In faraway Abuja, the President could hardly be expected to know everything going on in New York.

Unfortunately, the CIA knew Idris's comings and goings, particularly, with Ekineta in the picture. The cameras recorded all the sensuous moments, including moments when the couple swiftly and impulsively yanked off their clothes, locked tongues, caressed each other's sensitive spots, and, having been duly primed, went all the way, taking each other to the summit of sensuous delight.

The rapturous encounters happened several times and at different spots. The cameras recorded every scene—Idris's fingers on the firm, round breasts, Ekineta's hands wrapped tenderly around the broad shoulders, and the couple's romps under the bedspread. If those sizzling snapshots landed on President Isaac Ugochukwu's desk, Idris was as good as dead. For a start, he would be recalled and served a letter of dismissal. His problem would not be over until he landed in jail. Since bedding the President's woman was technically not a criminal offense, the highly inventive Dukyarian police could be trusted to pin an offense on Idris for which there would be no bail. Before he knew what hit him, he would find himself in a rat-infested wing of Snake Island prison.

"How do I know that all this will go away if I do your bidding?" Idris was now sober.

"You don't. But I give you my word that the photos will disappear as soon as you get your government to fall in line. While we're at it, I understand that you are addressing a meeting of the Africa Group later today. I suggest you rewrite your speech. Better still, read no speech. Just tell your colleagues to conduct themselves properly. We don't need any embarrassing noise from the Group. Do we have a deal?" Berger, cynical grin and all, extended his right hand.

"We do." Idris reluctantly shook his adversary's hand.

Idris did as he was told. He called home to say that the WGO resolution was "a forgone conclusion." It would pass with or without Dukyaria's support. The forces behind it were too formidable to be challenged. It was therefore "in the national interest to be on the winning side." He did not even bother to read his address to the Africa Group. To the consternation of the small states looking up to Dukyaria for leadership, Idris virtually told the anti-WGO troops within the Africa Group to stand down. The battle was lost. He told them point-blank. There was no point expending more ammunition or putting life at risk.

Berger too kept his word. Or so it would seem. At least, the snapshots in his possession never made it to President Ugochukwu's desk. Having come in handy at a time when profiting from Idris's indiscretions appeared to be the only option, the not-so-big pictures, the 'pictures of reason', had served their purpose. They stayed locked up in Berger's safe. He hoped he wouldn't have cause to pull them out again.

Chapter-32

Say Bye to insanity! Hail World Government!

MEANWHILE, THE GENERAL ASSEMBLY moved expeditiously to rubber-stamp the WGO resolution. The passage of the resolution was a mere formality. The UN was sure to be transformed into the WGO so long as Berger and other foot soldiers did what they were supposed to—that is, co-opt, or failing that, neutralize, the opposition. When the votes were tallied, the 'Ayes' had it by a wide margin. Africa kept its peace. So did the Middle East, Central and Eastern Europe, the Baltic States, and the Asia-Pacific region.

Having got the member states' signatures on the WGO Treaty, its sponsors dismissed other expressions of dissent with a wave of the hand. Watching live coverage of street demonstrations across the world—New Delhi, Abuja, Riyadh, Cairo, Teheran, Ankara, Kuala Lumpur, Rawalpindi, Kathmandu, Lhasa, and El-Salvador—Berger and Cunningham laughed at the WGO opponents' naiveté.

Berger and Cunningham had a point. The WGO train had left. It was too late to try and stop it. The world had been transformed into a confederation of Empires, even if some Empires were more equal than others. The Great American, the Russia-Ottoman, the New Mongolia, and the New European Empires were basically free to act as they pleased, so long as they did nothing to challenge the WGO's dominant doctrines. By contrast, the Pan Arabia and the Mali Empires acted under the general oversight of the Global

Guidance Council/GGC and were subject to directives issued from time to time by the General-Commissariat.

As provided for in the WGO Treaty, the General Assembly was reconstituted into the Assembly of Nations/AN, and the Secretariat of the defunct United Nations became the Commissariat-General. The Commissariats under the Commissariat-General were to enforce basically three Global Directives: Secularism, Capitalism, and Militarism.

The Global Directive on Secularism, the mandate of the High Commissariat for the Triumph of Secularism, categorically denied the existence of God and forbade any reference to Him in public. It further criminalized any open display of religious symbols. There would be no room for the yarmulke, the cross, minarets, the cassock, skull caps, turbans, female headscarves, and what the High Commissioner termed "provocatively long beards." The Empires were to promulgate decrees deleting Yom Kippur, Hanukkah, Christmas, Eid, Diwali, and other religious festivals from their calendars. The celebration of the events should cease forthwith. In any case, the Gregorian calendar was thenceforth the only measure of time recognized by the world authority. All other culture- or faith-based calendars were proscribed with immediate effect. Above all, the Secularism Directive required that all places of worship be converted into re-education centers. From then on, all puzzling questions were to be directed to, and answered by, science. The religious instructors were given a twelve-month deadline to close their establishments down and look for alternative, preferably, gainful and visible means of livelihood.

The High Commissariat for the Advancement of Capitalism was obliged to enforce the Capitalism Directive which substituted the profit motive for the timeworn moral and religious precepts. The Directive was founded on the premise that whatever yielded a high rate of return was, ipso facto, good and desirable, and what didn't was bad and objectionable. A good battle would naturally end with a high-kill ratio, meaning, with maximum body count for minimum expenditure of time and munitions.

The Militarism Directive, within its own High Commissariat, authorized the application of maximum force to suppress insurrections in any part of the world, and to uphold the New Global Order. The militarist agenda accorded rather well with the WGO's underlying doctrines of faithlessness and capitalist accumulation.

Chapter-33

WGO's movers and shakers

ANYONE INTERESTED IN HOW the WGO operated in real time would need to go beyond formal stipulations. Her Excellency, Madame Siriwangi Warioba, the first Chairperson of the Assembly of Nations and titular head of the World Government had no power to act independently of the Global Guidance Council. She said nothing which the WGO bureaucracy did not whisper in her ears or did not jot on a piece of paper. In fact, she did nothing that the Commissariats considered "beneath her dignity"—which was practically every deed the bureaucrats arrogated to themselves. Warioba had no problem with this arrangement. A pretty and fashionable woman from the Bukoba Republic of the Mali Empire, she enjoyed smiling for the cameras.

The Committees that were established to proffer solutions to designated problems merely ratified the reports and recommendations submitted by the Commissariat officials. The Committee Chairpersons, drawn from the Sovereign States and a sprinkling of Dependent Territories, were mere figure heads whose only chance of being noticed was when declaring high-profile conferences open or representing the Commissioner-General at other events covered by the media.

The real movers and shakers of WGO were the Special Consuls appointed by the six Empires to serve on the Global Guidance Council. These are the Greater America, New

Europe, New Mongolia, Pan-Arab, Russian-Ottoman, and Mali Empires. Headed by a rotational and elected

Emperor, each Empire was fully mandated to maintain law and order within its federating States and Dependent Territories. Delegates from Dependent Territories and Satellite States were duly screened by their Emperors before taking their seats in an enlarged body, the Assembly of Nations/AN.

The Global Security Council exercised general oversight over the Empires. It also kept a political eye on the WGO bureaucracy through the office of the Commissioner-General. Otherwise, it gave the Commissioner-General and his High Commissioners much leeway in running the WGO.

The WGO organogram placed Khaled Bin-Sayed El-Maktoum, an Arabian national from the Pan-Arab Empire, as the Commissioner-General and Head of the Commissariat-General. It also purportedly empowered El-Maktoum to supervise the activities of the three Commissariats—notably, the Secularism, Capitalism and Militarism Commissariats.

However, what appeared on paper was one thing, what happened in real life was another. For one, the mild-mannered El-Maktoum was no match for the abrasive Brad Cunningham, the High Commissioner for the Triumph of Secularism. Popularly referred to as the Secularism Supremo, Cunningham's American nationality helped in no small measure to invest him with the power and influence that were out of proportion to his official status in the WGO.

Wang Xiao-Ping's strength lay in his sharp intellect and his uncanny ability to construct highly complex econometric models. It was thus not surprising that the Commissioner-

General El-Maktoum relied on the counsel of the Harvard Business School alumni and Chinese national from the Mongolian Empire as the WGO High Commissioner for Capitalism.

Marshall Grigori Popov, WGO Commissioner for Militarism always got what he wanted because of his forbidding mien. Only a few relished the prospect of engaging the imposing, taciturn, and unsmiling Russian in regular conversation much less a prolonged debate.

One exception was the fearless Evangelista Torres. A strong-willed, strikingly-pretty Nicaraguan, Torres melted Popov's steely heart with the sheer force of her personality. She was one of the few Commissariat employees not intimidated by Cunningham. She was well-positioned to stand up to the Secularism Supremo. As one of the senior staffers inherited from the UN Secretariat, she knew the inner workings of supranational bureaucracies in general and the one just taking shape in particular. This was more than could be said for Cunningham, who came from the academic world.

Uncomfortable with situations he could not control or manipulate, Cunningham tried every trick to get Torres out of the way, including cooking up restructuring and downsizing plans targeted at her post. Each plot failed. For one thing, the Developing Countries Bloc in the Assembly of Nations would never permit the removal of one of their own from the strategic post of Chief of Staff to WGO Commissioner-General. For another, the soft-spoken El-Maktoum valued her intellect, her insight, her superb communication skills, and above all, her courage. The Commissariat staffers adored her, simply because she was the exact opposite of Warioba. With the Treaty duly signed, a new structure created in place of the old one, and key officials appointed and invested with varying degrees of authority, the WGO was set to accomplish its mission. Okoye watched the GTN's live coverage of the momentous events. So did Kamil, Emman Kalu, Swami Harelal, and Abu Danja Mamba. Each pondered the next line of action. With the exception of Mamba, none yet knew exactly what to do to respond to the new threat.

Chapter-34

WGO's Triumph as Freedom Lovers' Nightmare!

KAMIL SAT IN HIS living room for hours wondering how to react to the birth of the WGO. Although he already knew that a government with global authority posed a grave threat to freedom, he did not expect that the WGO would go this far. As he heard on television, the new body had a clear secularization agenda. That agenda had no place for religion or for anything remotely suggesting allegiance to an authority higher than the WGO. In plain language, the WGO had constituted itself into a god in place of the Supreme Being worshipped by the believers. Science had become the new scripture. Scientists had replaced the long line of prophets.

"This is pure nonsense, and they know it!" Kamil screamed out loud to no one in particular. "The WGO can and will never take the place of Allah. Even if they succeed in banishing faith in public squares, they will never succeed in wiping the memory of Allah from our hearts and minds! Thank God, I already archived the entire Qur'an in my brain!" The harder he tried to console himself, the more agitated he became.

Okoye was equally distressed. He had given his entire life to Christ. He had never dreamt of honor, fame, or riches. He had even passed up the opportunity to be joined in holy matrimony with a woman, or to gratify momentary urges for sensual delight. Now these clowns just told him that his sacrifices were in vain, and that he was insane to place his trust in the Lord the Father, the Son, and the Holy Spirit.

"No, it is they who are truly insane! This project they have just embarked on will not succeed. How I wish all the worlds' faiths would come together and confront the monstrosity they call the WGO," the reverend father thought to himself as he paced the compact living room of his Utako vicarage. He was in the middle of the introspection when the Dukyarian Television Service interrupted its program with breaking news.

"Following the breakdown of negotiations with the World Bank, the Union of Dukyaria has been declared an incurably indebted nation. Its Deeds of Sovereignty will now stay with the Bank as collateral for the settlement of the outstanding debt and the extension of an additional line of credit." Garba Kubwa, the newscaster brought his listeners up to speed. Emmanuel Kalu's Save-our-Sovereignty prayers were either not properly framed, or they had not been dispatched fast enough to heavens on high to forestall the disaster.

Thousands of miles away, Swami Krishna Harelal sat cross-legged in his Haridwar-Rishikesh Ashram outside Delhi. He was in the middle of meditation when one of the disciples rushed in. "Sahab, you have a visitor. Should I bring him here, or shall I ask him to wait until you are ready to join him?" Navin Pandey bowed as he awaited the master's response.

"Bring him right away," the master instructed Pandey.

"Namaste, Sahab!" The visitor, with both palms pressed together and held close to a bowing face, greeted his host respectfully. Lal Kapoor was a ranking member of the

155

Vishwa Hindu Parishad, an Indian nationalist group committed to the preservation of the Hindu way of life against corrupting external influences. Since Kapoor knew that Harelal rarely watched television, he, Kapoor, had taken it upon himself to alert the guru to the changes taking place outside the Ashram.

"Is that all?" Harelal asked, unperturbed by the message or by the messenger's visage.

"That's all, Sahab. But the leaders of the Vishwa believe that we should not take the matter lightly. We should move and move decisively. That is why I was delegated to see you and ask for your blessings." Kapoor, still fuming, bared his mind to his guru.

"No. That would be a mistake. You remember how Gandhi defeated the powerful British without firing a single shot? He applied patience to overwhelm superior forces and bring them to heel. That's exactly what you are going to do— at least, as your immediate response. If the situation calls for review, we will know what to do. For now, do nothing. Just watch. Watch as greed dissipates its energy and impatience exhausts its options. Remember, the conquest of the universe lies in doing nothing."

"Are you sure, Sahab? These mad people are serious. I don't mind what they plan to do to advance the cause of capitalism. I don't even mind what they do to militarize the world. What I mind is their frontal attack on the right to freedom of belief!" Kapoor was for immediate response to the new threat.

156

"I knew all along that it would come to this. Right from the day we had that intercontinental debate on religion, I knew that a plan like this was in the offing. I knew that a shadowy group was determined to impose secularism on the world and was just using the television debate as a cover for its grand design. Cunningham realized that his argument did not hold water. Yet, instead of giving up gracefully, he persisted in his efforts at elevating secularism to the status of a religion. With him as the High Commissioner for the Triumph of Secularism, he hopes to ride on the back of the WGO and promote his doctrine of faithlessness. But mark my word, the secularization plan will fail. Oh yes, I saw Cunningham on television laughing triumphantly when the WGO Treaty took effect. However, his joy of today will be his grief of tomorrow. Go back and tell your people not to lose hope. There is light at the end of the tunnel." Harelal pacified Kapoor and the Vishwa.

Harelal went back to his meditation. Completely detached from the world, he was oblivious to the changes taking place around him. One change that he did not quickly notice was the decision by the WGO to legalize same-sex marriage throughout the world. The resolution permitting persons of the same gender to marry one another was sponsored by the Great American Empire and was passed unanimously by the Assembly of Nations. Dissenters knew the risks they ran, including risks similar to the one that Idris had, to his own detriment, overlooked. They abstained rather than be hounded for opposing the WGO's first major initiative.

Chapter-35

Stop whining, comrade! Fight for your freedom!

THE ASSEMBLY OF NATIONS' delegates having been stampeded into adopting the same-sex resolution, the way was now clear for the Empires to "domesticate" the resolution and enforce the law. Emperor Kambumba of the Mali Empire was set to proceed along this line when he encountered stiff opposition in, of all places, the Dependent Territory of Dukyaria. The very act of legalizing the illegal, as Kamil famously put it, helped unite otherwise dissimilar minds against the new world body and against its same-sex marriage plan. Christians, Muslims, and polytheists—all stood together to block the implementation of the new policy in Dukyaria, and if possible, to plot the gradual dismantling of the WGO structure itself.

"Have you heard the latest? You should be ready to pronounce man husband of man, and woman wife of another woman! How about that?" Kamil asked Okoye over the phone.

"I heard quite alright, but I wait to see that happen here in Dukyaria. One thing is certain; the Holy Father will not sanction an unholy matrimony," Okoye responded.

Deciding to overlook his doctrinal differences with Okoye and to focus on the upcoming challenge, Kamil replied, "So, what does the Catholic Church plan to do about this—the latest unwarranted attack on believing men and women?"

"I don't follow you."

"You mean you will just fold your arms and do nothing? Well, if nothing is what you plan to do, I hope you will not be one of those calling me names when I respond to this affront the only way I know—through direct action."

"Don't tell me you and your men have decided to take up arms and join Abu Danja Mamba in his Gashaka-Mambilla cave!" Okoye could not conceal his feeling of apprehension. He might not be particularly fond of Kamil, but Okoye would not like to see such an intelligent character in bad company. Kamil should, as the reverend father reckoned, put his intellect to good use instead of teaming up with despicable characters like Mamba.

"So, you now label me a terrorist simply because I will not acquiesce to such blatant sacrilege as same-sex marriage? And without even hearing me out?"

"Sorry. But 'direct action' sounds very much like a phrase from Mamba's terrorist handbook! If your own 'direct action' doesn't include killing people and destroying property, what exactly does it entail?"

"Now you are asking the right question. By direct action, I mean mobilizing our followers and getting them to participate in peaceful demonstrations. If we sit in our homes moaning, the WGO will assume that we accept its same-sex arrangement. Silence, they say, implies consent. And I know that this same-sex idea doesn't have your Church's backing. The question is whether you are willing to reinforce your

159

dissent with action—direct, but completely non-violent, action. As for us Muslims, we are planning a series of demonstrations in Abuja and other major cities to register our opposition. Are you with us on this or not? There is no sitting on the fence! Are you in, or are you out? It is as simple as that."

"Of course, I am in. If that is what you mean by 'direct action,' what reasonable person would be against it?" Then, unsure how "direct action" would be viewed by their opponents, he asked Kamil to clarify a few nagging issues: "You realize that you and I take exception to the secularists' dogmatic position on religion. In other words, our case against radical secularism is that it is intolerant of worldviews different from its own. How can we defend ourselves if the same secularists turn around to accuse us of being intolerant of gays and lesbians?" Okoye paused, waiting for Kamil's response.

"That is one question that I have turned over in my mind several times. On the one hand, we want to be tolerated (even if not accepted) by non-believers. On the other, we, the adherents of the various religions, can't stand gays and lesbians in our midst. Isn't that a contradiction? I don't think so. It would have been a contradiction—and a glaring one at that—had our opposition to same-sex marriage been inconsistent with our sovereign culture's stand on the subject, or if it had been directed ultimately at the elimination of a group advocating a lifestyle that is alien to our culture. Am I making sense so far?" It was Kamil's turn to pause and wait for Okoye's reactions.

"What do you mean by 'culture,' particularly, alien culture and lifestyle? We must take nothing for granted. We must anticipate every question our opponents will raise." Okoye responded.

"In my humble opinion, a people's culture is not just a guide to right and wrong but also a compass they rely upon to navigate their ways out of complex challenges. Anything alien to the culture adds a new layer to the existing challenges, blurs a people's vision of their willed future, lowers their self-esteem, and threatens their way of life. Just imagine, for a moment, the consequences of grafting the Communist central planning model and mindset onto a free-market, capitalist economy—"

"What if we are told that cultures thrive or decay depending on their capacity to learn from others and to evolve accordingly?" Okoye interrupted Kamil.

"In that case, in order to 'thrive' and 'evolve,' the Americans ought to have installed certified communists in key government positions at the height of the Cold War. Succeeding US Administrations should have copied the British Labor Party's nationalization policy in meeting the post-World War II's challenges! If we must learn from other cultures, why should other cultures not learn from ours? Or are we implying that one culture is, in every sense, superior to another? I have nothing against learning and evolving. But then, let me ask you a few simple questions. What specific lessons can Dukyaria learn from same-sex marriage, and how will imbibing these lessons serve our overriding national interest? Come to think of it, what is there to learn about sex—whether of the heterosexual or the homosexual kind? No matter how you look at it, sex is nothing but the gratification of cravings for ephemeral pleasure, intimacy, or companionship. Unless Plato is wrong to argue that 'the body is the prison of the soul,' this excessive yearning for sensual gratification is precisely what stands between the average human and the knowledge of the good. Regardless of whether Plato was right or wrong, we Dukyarians can never develop if we sit on our hands and wait

161

indefinitely for foreigners to show us how to live as human beings, or better still, expect them to give us handouts, otherwise, but inappropriately, termed 'financial or technical assistance.' We cannot regain our freedom, or stay free, unless we first get a grip on our longings—especially, longings for wealth, fame, and, yes, sex. Remember, our people were sold into slavery by greedy tribal elders who had been enticed, not with a progress blueprint or knowledge, but with cheap items like cigarettes, liquor, sugar, and exotic fabrics." Kamil paused again, not sure whether he was cleared to continue.

"Are you still there? Carry on." Okoye noticed the hesitation.

"I am! As I was saying, intolerance becomes stark, absolute and, if I may add, totally unacceptable, where it starts with hate and ends with the desire for total elimination of dissent. This, as far as I know, is our grievance against Homo Haram. The terrorist group simply does not want to see any practice or person on the face of the earth that does not fully embody its ideals. Homo Haram would rather annihilate than educate its opponents. Now, that is one type of intolerance none can defend."

"If I may paraphrase your argument, there is a difference between pure bigotry on the one hand, and objection dictated by conscience or belief on the other, just as there is between blind rage and righteous indignation."

"I can't think of a better or more accurate summary, Basil. There is no human being who does not judge what he sees, hears, smells, or feels. You cannot be truly human if you can't separate 'right' from 'wrong', 'good' from 'bad', 'praiseworthy' from 'reprehensible', or 'just' from 'unjust'. The right to distinguish between good and bad is integral to the exercise of other rights, especially the right to freedom of belief, conscience, and expression. Of course, what is right or wrong tends to be situationally determined. The contextual and relativist nature of value judgements is what makes mutual accommodation necessary, and intolerance condemnable. It would be the height of injustice to choose a lifestyle and, in the same breath, deny an advocate of a contrary lifestyle an equivalent and proportionate right.

"Fortunately, our position on same-sex marriage is not of the hateful, dogmatic, exclusivist kind. It leaves room for dialogue and dissent. Our advocacy of heterosexual marriage allows dissent and presupposes inclusiveness. It is not the same as the WGO's rabid intolerance of religion. Our principled, conscience-dictated objection to same-sex marriage, to borrow your phrase, is not in the same category as Homo Haram's pure, undiluted, bigotry." Kamil stopped and waited for Okoye's reactions.

"I am glad we are having this conversation. Without it, we may never know when we have crossed that delicate line— the one separating legitimate dissent from terrorism." Okoye summed it up the best way he could.

The leaders of the two rival faiths agreed on a platform of action to reclaim Dukyaria's freedom in a peaceful manner. Both had barely ended their telephone conversation when Mamba registered his opposition to non-violence and re-defined "direct action" his own way. He started by mounting commando-like raids on banks, government ordnance depots, police stations, and army barracks. He then proceeded to attack WGO offices within and across the Union of Dukyaria. To replenish his treasury, he soon branched out to kidnapping for ransom, treating un-ransomed hostages as slaves, and selling them to the highest bidder. Mamba's followers were implicated in criminal acts like cattle rustling, highway robbery, as well as siphoning off unrefined crude oil and bartering the proceeds for sophisticated weapons.

The passage of the same-sex resolution gave Mamba the perfect ammunition to deploy against the WGO. To rally the faithful against the world organization, he promptly renamed his hitherto loosely organized group 'Homo Haram', meaning: homosexuality and lesbianism are, under the Sharia, illegal, forbidden, impious. Although he inwardly believed that every individual had a right to choose his or her sexual partner, he deemed it expedient to use homosexuals and lesbians as pawns in his quest for power. He saw nothing wrong or cynical about this; he told himself that even right-wing conservatives seized upon and gladly embraced ideas they did not really believe in so long as such "pragmatism" assured them maximum political advantage. He flatly rejected the suggestion that pragmatism and hypocrisy were inseparable, or that 'pragmatic hypocrisy' was the reason the

American public turned against the Democratic and the Republican Parties.

Based on their own understanding of direct action, Okoye and Kamil had successfully mobilized their followers and had organized peaceful demonstrations across the length and breadth of Dukyaria. Mamba watched as Okoye and Kamil moved from one city to another addressing increasingly dense crowds on why the Mali Emperor, Odhambo Kambumba, should not make the mistake of promulgating an Imperial

Decree legalizing the co-habitation of same gender couples, let alone same-sex marriage. Kamil was often tempted to take a harder line than his Catholic counterpart. "Hell is the destination of men who marry men, and of women who marry women. They will be heralded into jahannam by the priests or individuals who officiate at such un-Godly events," Kamil repeatedly warned his listeners, ignoring the discomfiture on Okoye's face.

Then, without warning, Mamba and his men showed up in Abuja at the venue of a street protest against same-sex marriage. The terrorists came fully armed. Unfortunately, neither Kamil nor Okoye was present to control the crowd massed in front of the WGO office that Saturday morning, the 22nd of August 2085. The demonstrators were led by the two clerics' lieutenants.

"Homo Haram! Homo Haram! Homo Haram!" One of Mamba's men had shouted at the top of his voice.

Within seconds, men and women suspected of being gays and lesbians were hauled before a wildly cheering crowd. The lynch mob punched the luckless individuals repeatedly, inflicting serious injuries on some and beating others to death. In other parts of the city, squads of Homo Haram terrorists lobbed bombs at houses, petrol stations, and WGO offices.

From the look of things, Dukyaria faced bumpy rides ahead. So did the WGO. Cunningham couldn't wait to have Mulenga by his side in New York. The in-coming Director of Political Affairs knew Dukyaria inside-out. His counsel would be priceless at a time like this.

Chapter-36

Run for your life!

FATHER OKOYE WAS IN the shower when a deafening sound shattered the morning's peace. A powerful explosion from a place he was yet to establish shook the vicarage. He made the crucifix sign, dried himself with a blue towel, and then cast quick glances around the building. Fortunately, the structure was solid enough to withstand the blast, if in fact it was a blast. The Catholic priest reckoned that the reverberating sound must have come from afar, even if he couldn't say exactly where. He promptly got into his faded blue jeans, tucked in his checked white shirt, laced his sneakers, and rushed out of the vicarage. He wanted to find out what was afoot in or around his Utako neighborhood.

It was unusual for the sun to appear that early or beam so radiantly at that time of the year, the height of the rainy season. Okoye took no notice of the sunny sky, however. He was focused on the strange activity occurring not too far away. Shaken by the first deafening sound, men and women, adults and adolescents, and toddlers and their nannies had trooped out of their houses and started scurrying in different directions, mostly towards the Turkish International University on the airport road. Each time they felt secure enough to pause and catch their breath, another explosion would go off, increasing their panic and prolonging their distress.

Okoye moved a bit closer towards the restive crowd. He wanted to get to the root of the pandemonium. However, everyone around was too preoccupied with staying alive to have time to answer anybody else's questions. It was a miracle that he was not thrown off balance in the rout and trampled under insensitive feet. Throngs of disoriented persons elbowed him out of the way without caring how he felt.

Well, if the crowd would rather run helter-skelter than satisfy his curiosity, Okoye would just have to stand aside and watch the madness from a distance. Dodging and meandering to survive the shoves and the pushes, he maneuvered himself out of the stampede and took a position by the curb. As he pondered the next line of action, he caught a glimpse of vehicles speeding towards him. What a relief! Here, finally, was an opportunity to find out what was going on. However, any hope of flagging the vehicles down and getting his questions answered was soon dashed. The drivers obviously took him for another passerby itching to escape the horror which appeared to be spreading from the city center to the outlying districts. The drivers were naturally more interested in putting a distance between themselves and trouble than ferrying another terrified bystander to a safe haven.

Certain that nothing would come out of the wait except further disappointment, Okoye made as if heading back to the vicarage. He had not walked more than ten yards when he heard a loud voice call out to him. "Oga Sah! Master, Sir!" It was the voice of a minivan's driver. James had pulled up by the roadside close to where Okoye had stood a few seconds earlier. The wiry looking driver, in his early twenties, had to lean across the passenger side of his vehicle and holler to get Okoye's attention. "A beg Sah, I dey look for the road to Hayatu Hospital. The people in my car don hurt very bad! They need dokta quick!" James pointed to his passengers.

Chapter-37

You don't believe in hell? How 'bout this?

"WHAT HAPPENED TO THESE people?" Okoye asked as he peeked through the van's window. "Anyway, the place you want is Hayat, not Hayatu, Hospital. This is how to get there. Drive straight on but stay on the right lane. When you reach the overpass, drive under it and immediately swing right. Drive straight on, leaving the Abuja International Market on the left. By now, you are ready to hit an intersection. Wait until the traffic police clears you to proceed. As soon as you are cleared by the police to proceed, drive straight until you arrive at a point where the highway forks to the right. In other words, make a right to Michael Okpara Street and proceed for about fifty yards. Look for the Hayat Hospital sign on the right side of the street. That is where you want to take your passengers. Hayat Hospital! You got that? Is this clear, or would you rather take me to my vicarage so I can take my car and lead the way?" Okoye must have caught the perplexed look on James's countenance.

"Oga Sah, I think that is more beta, Sah!"

"Which is better? Finding space for me in your van till I get to my own car, or following the directions that I have just given you and going by yourself?"

"I think the first one, Sah. Oga can manage with the only passenger in front and we can all go Oga house to collect him car. Oga can then go in front, and we can come in the back. I think that is more beta and more easy than if I go by myself. Oga's English too big and Abuja road too difficult for a village boy like me!" James embraced his modest education sufficiently to quip about, and even celebrate, it.

"Aren't we all village boys? OK, make room in front and let's go!" Okoye squeezed himself into what remained of the front passenger's seat.

On their way to the vicarage, and leaving the explosions behind, the driver introduced his passengers and narrated their ordeal.

Auta, the only front-seat passenger, had had both eyes gouged out. He would surely bleed to death if he made the mistake of taking his hands off the swath that the Red Crescent medic had supplied to plug the hollow sockets and stop the hemorrhage. Even then, his survival was not guaranteed unless he received immediate specialist attention in a well-equipped trauma center. There was no point worrying about Auta's male friend, Audu. The minivan had to leave his lifeless body behind in the Central District where he had been set upon and butchered by a pack of youths screaming "Homo Haram!" After years of living on the edge, Audu had finally found peace, James consoled himself.

If Helen and Suzie, two rear-seat passengers and intimate companions, lived to recall their nightmare, they were unlikely to find peace for a very long time. Their faces had been beaten in and disfigured by blunt but sturdy objects. They too stemmed excessive bleeding by keeping wads of cloth pressed firmly on their wounds. The pain was excruciating; but what choice did they have other than writhe and wail? The Central

169

District lynch mob had unleashed its fury on the elegant ladies and had treated them worse than it would common punching bags.

Hassan's predicament was not easy to explain. He was an innocent bystander caught in the middle of a squabble. He was on his way to his uncle's house when he noticed a crowd pursuing two young men, Dodo and Jerry. The lovers might run, but they weren't going anywhere. The crowd eventually caught up with both and was about to constitute itself into a law court, "pass judgment," and mete out the appropriate punishment when Hassan intervened. Hassan did not condone the male couple's lifestyle, but he was vehemently opposed to a kangaroo court summarily charging both with "crime against nature," finding both guilty, and then sentencing them to death.

"So, we are now a kangaroo court?" Tijjani, the ringleader, caressed his club with the left hand. The look in his eyes was ominous. It was quickly replaced with a sarcastic grin and melodramatic gestures, "That's ok. We shall show you what this kangaroo court can do to unrepentant sinners like these two, and to a jobless 'lawyer' like you! By the way, in which law school were you trained? You argued your case well! That in fact is why we are not going to kill you and your clients. That is the good news. The bad news is that by the time we finish with all of you, you will wish this court had put you out of your misery." Tijjani then turned to one of his minions with precise instructions, "Bahago, sharpen your scalpel blades. You, Rapper Boy, and Charlie have three emergency operations to perform!"

As ordered by Tijjani, the lynch mob "commuted" the gay couple's death sentence to grievous bodily harm.

Over Hassan's objections, the mob delegated the unsmiling, left-handed Bahago, the mean-looking Rapper Boy, and the rotund Charlie to carry out an unusual surgical operation— using machetes, they amputated every finger on the two primary accused persons' hands. Hassan, the "advocate" and secondary accused, lost only the fingers on his left hand. This was, in Tijjani's words, "To teach you, Mr. Advocate, two lessons: mind your own business, and desist from condoning blasphemy."

Okoye listened patiently as James provided the gory details. Although inwardly disturbed, he managed to retain his composure. As soon as James had finished his narrative, the priest said something which a powerful blast rendered totally inaudible. He waited for the boom to taper off before making another attempt to be heard, "Are you saying that Homo Haram is behind all this?" He repeated his question, this time raising his voice before another bomb went off.

"Yes, Oga! We pray to God to help us defeat this Homo Haram people!"

"Umm," Okoye, striking his left palm with the clenched right fist, took a deep breath. His mind immediately went to Sheikh Salim Kamil, his Muslim counterpart noted for his strident attacks on Dukyaria's gays and lesbians.

On arrival at the vicarage, Okoye asked James and his passengers to bear with him as he changed his clothes. It was when he reappeared five minutes later that James realized that the devilishly handsome man he had been talking to all along was a Roman Catholic priest. Okoye was now decked in an off-white cassock with a black zucchetto to match. With his rosary dangling from the right hand, the six-foot two hunk of a priest eased himself into the driver's seat of his Honda Civic sedan. The journey to Hayat had begun.

Chapter-38

Off to Garki, to scold intolerance's icon!

FOR OKOYE, HAYAT WAS just a transit stop. His destination after taking James's traumatized passengers to the hospital's emergency ward was Salim Kamil's house in Garki, which, strange as it might sound, was not too far from the trouble spot which sane persons were fleeing from. If he was right, the explosions originated from somewhere in or around the Central District. Garki was the southern tip of the Central District.

Okoye believed that, subject to canonical injunctions, every individual was free to live as he chose. No matter what, he would look Kamil in the eyes and tell the Muslim fundamentalist to go to hell with his anti-gay rhetoric. He was not going to be deterred by bomb explosions or other frightful incidents. Kamil's sharp tongue would not prevent Okoye from facing his former adversary and condemning his covert support for Homo Haram. Why did he even agree to patch up his differences with this Kamil in the first place? To hell with the lunatic and his fellow terrorists! The hateful thoughts had darted across Okoye's mind again. He immediately realized he needed to control himself. He penitently made a sign of the crucifix. He vowed silently not to allow such thoughts to pass through his mind again.

As he drove down Herbert Macaulay Way, he cringed at the sight of bodies left unattended on both sides of the boulevard. He wondered how many innocent souls had perished along with the fuel stations and the shopping complexes that had been reduced to ashes by unguided rockets or by plain acts of sabotage. Filled with grief, Okoye continued his mission to Garki. He wiped his sweaty face as he drove uphill and then down the valley. On reaching the top of another gradient, he saw the extent of the damage wrought by the arsonists for the first time. The smoke that appeared to billow mildly from afar when he was in Utako had now, at close range, revealed itself as a full-blown firestorm. The skyscrapers which once gave the Abuja skyline a unique character had been brought down, likely by rocket fire.

Although the organizers of the civil strife took many innocent lives and destroyed many impressive structures, the World Government Organization was their primary target. Other casualties and assets were either victims of collateral damage or secondary targets taken out on the way to the primary one, the WGO. The Organization's offices in the Central District were levelled to the ground. It was a miracle that the majority of the Organization's staffers survived the well-coordinated attack.

This won't end well, Okoye thought to himself on sighting the wreckage that was once the WGO's nerve center in Dukyaria. As he drove towards the International Conference Center, he ran into a roadblock erected by stern-looking officers and men of the Dukyarian Army. To give the Bomb Disposal Squad of the Army the space it needed to clear the rubble left by hand-propelled grenades, heavily armed troops cordoned off the Conference Center and diverted traffic to Moshood Abiola Way. A few headstrong motorists drove on only to be turned back by stern-looking soldiers. The hot wind brought passersby a whiff of the Center's smoldering remains.

Rather than drive straight on, Okoye saved himself the embarrassment of being turned back. He immediately took a detour to the right. No sooner had he driven across Moshood

Abiola Way, down Muhammadu Buhari Boulevard, than he was pulled over by a pack of rampaging youths. Armed with clubs, machetes, and other dangerous weapons, the youths wanted to know precisely what brought him to Garki. "What is the purpose of your mission in Garki?" Maigari, one of the rioters, peremptorily demanded an answer.

"I am going to Sheikh Salim Kamil's house. You know the Sheikh, tall like me, but with a long, well-combed beard." The priest, gesticulating with both hands, answered confidently.

"You are going to the Imam dressed like this?" Maigari surveyed Okoye from head to toe, disbelief and contempt intermittently darting across the angular face.

"I did not know one needs a special to see his friend," Okoye said, trying humor to de-escalate the looming tension. Why pick a quarrel with street urchins when the person you want to wrestle is elsewhere?

"What's up, guys? What is the padre doing here?" Joseph, who had been relieving himself by the roadside, returned just then.

"Perfect timing, Joseph! Your man here is going to Imam Kamil dressed like this, and we were wondering what to do with him." The angular face brought Joseph up to speed.

"You Moslems! What is so strange about the way the Reverend Father is dressed? Your Imam goes about in flowing gowns, matching turbans, and a long beard. The priest here

175

decides to wear his own priestly clothes. Where is the problem in that? It would be a different matter if he was gay. But a priest? He is not the one we are looking for. Let him go!" Joseph relieved Okoye of any further obligation to defend himself.

Okoye might have been comforted by Joseph's timely intervention, but he was mystified by the experience. He could not understand how this God-sent advocate, a Christian, could be in the midst of a gang baying for human blood. The padre understandably kept his thoughts to himself. He risked being set upon if he lectured Joseph in the presence of the unruly bunch. Still, Okoye could not help wondering how many Josephs were out there. If there were more like him, then the church's message of tolerance was clearly not getting across. In that case, the clergy had to step up and make sure that the laity imbibed the spirit of love and tolerance. While homosexual tendencies stood condemned under canonical law, the same law guaranteed individual right to life. Thou shalt not kill. That is a Biblical commandment. Nothing should be done to abridge, circumscribe, or extinguish this fundamental right— the right to life. That was the Catholic Church's position. It was the position that he intended to reaffirm whenever he met Kamil face to face.

As he approached Kamil's house, Okoye cast his mind back to the duo's squabbling days. Both clerics had disagreed on practically everything. Kamil considered Okoye's belief in the Trinity misguided, and his tendency to liken Jesus Christ to God as blasphemy. Okoye, never one to roll over and play dead, often fired back by accusing Kamil of being a "Muslim fundamentalist" and closet supporter of the terrorist "Homo Haram." They had to close ranks so as to face a new threat— the secularization agenda of the new World Government Organization.

Now, when the two should be working together, Kamil had gone back to his bad old ways. He had reneged on the pledge he signed at the last meeting of the Inter-Faith Council—that is, to condemn same-sex unions as ungodly but to refrain from harassing gays and lesbians. What could be wrong with Kamil's head? He was not the only one opposed to the WGO-backed proclamation signed by Emperor Odhambo Kambumba legalizing same-sex marriage throughout the Mali Empire. All the faith groups had reaffirmed their determination to resist the enforcement of the law in the Empire's Dependent Territory of Dukyaria. Okoye recalled that at his urging, the Inter-Faith Council had agreed to rely on a combination of dialogue and peaceful protests to achieve its objective. Kamil, the hothead, appeared to go along with the other members of the Council, but his body language betrayed his preference for direct action, which Okoye could not help interpreting as recourse to violence. Maybe it was time to revoke the peace agreement with the fundamentalist and confront the WGO his own way.

Okoye was still fuming when he alighted from his weather-beaten Honda Civic. He walked briskly past the gate to the shabby-looking bungalow's entrance. He tapped the door gently. Hamza, one of the madrassa pupils, got the door and let the reverend father in.

Chapter-39

You irredeemable bigot!

OKOYE LOST NO TIME confronting Kamil. "Salim, you finally did it! When will you accept that violence solves nothing? As soon as I heard what was going on, I knew that you are behind it. You put your followers up to it. Now, you must be ready to face the consequences." Okoye, still incensed, pointed an accusing finger at his suspect but stopped short of revealing the nature of the presumed offender's misdeed.

Kamil's phone rang at precisely that moment. He signaled to Okoye to wait until he had answered it. The call was from Hayat Hospital. Kamil's presence was urgently needed at the hospital's pediatric ward. He there and then suspected that the hospital had bad news about Abdullah but didn't know how to pass it on over the phone. Kamil prepared himself for the worst, dropped the phone, and faced Okoye. "I don't know what you are talking about, Basil. But whatever it is, take your seat first and allow me to host you properly. Would you like tea or Coke? I know you don't take coffee, and you already know that beer isn't part of the deal. Ha! Ha! Ha!" Kamil expected to disarm his guest with a joke. The premonition of Abdullah's physical deterioration or imminent death did not show on his face. In fact, were he to lose the shaggy beard, he would have matched, and probably exceeded, Okoye's charm and film star looks. He was of the same height, six-foot two.

"This is no laughing matter, and it is certainly not a social call. I am here because the seeds which you sowed have germinated. The only snag is that the crops you are about to reap are nothing but sharp, poisonous, unforgiving thorns!"

"You keep talking in riddles. What is this thing that I have put my followers up to? You also said something like violence not solving a problem. What problem are we talking about here, and who is employing violence to solve it? And the seeds, the crops, and the thorns? Honestly, I am lost!" Kamil remained calm. It was very much unlike him to be calm, sitting face to face or standing head to head with an aggressor. In his own house, of all places! Still, before he proceeded to put the uninvited guest in his place, he needed to know precisely the crime which he, the host, had committed. When the charge was duly and clearly framed, Kamil would know how to mount a robust defense—that is, if any defense was necessary at all.

"Don't patronize me, Kamil. You can't deny being the brain behind the orgy of violence currently directed at gays and lesbians as well as on WGO assets and personnel in Dukyaria! While you and I agree that same-sex marriage should not be legalized, you have always outflanked me by advocating violence against homosexuals. Weren't you the one who publicly insisted that those who doubt the existence of hell in the hereafter would get a taste of it here on earth? Congratulations! You have brought hell to the doorsteps of the gays and lesbians. Your men and women have turned Dukyaria into one gigantic killing field! Turn your TV on to get the full picture on GTN." Okoye saw no reason to hold anything back any longer. He decided to come out and repeat what he had thought all along—that Kamil was and would ever remain a closet supporter of the Homo Haram terrorist group.

Chapter-40

The charges against you? Aiding and abetting terrorism!

"**HAVE YOU FINISHED, OR** do you have anything to add?" Kamil remained unperturbed.

"Have you been listening to what I've been saying? Isn't the atrocity that I just described grave enough? Do you have in reserve any punishment harsher than the one you have so far inflicted on homosexuals and their sympathizers?" Okoye was furious. The scowl didn't tally with his well-sculptured countenance or with his image as a man of God.

"Have I been listening? Let's see." Kamil gently tapped his temple with the right index finger. "You started with a problem that violence could not solve. You then went on to ramble about gays, lesbians, transgenders, hell, and my previous statements on these topics. I was hoping you would stop where you quoted me as predicting a taste of earthly hell for impenitent homosexuals. However, instead of stopping there, you went beyond the bound of reason to assume that I gave my own prediction a helping hand. You allowed your unverified assumptions, or should I say, suspicions, to cloud your judgment. In none of my sermons did I advocate violence against gays, lesbians, or their sympathizers. You can check the recordings at any time."

"You do understand if I don't believe you?" Waving his left hand contemptuously, Okoye dismissed his host's plea of innocence.

"That's your privilege. This may come to you as a surprise, but 'thou shalt not kill' is as much a Qur'anic injunction as it is a Biblical one. I am sure you will remind me of the Homo Haram squads that kill and plunder while claiming to be acting on Allah's instructions. If you choose to believe that lie, the blatant lie that Homo Haram is executing God's command, then that, again, is your privilege! Don't take my word for it. Here is the exact translation of what Allah Almighty says in ayah twenty-eight of surah seven, al-A'raf, about the tendency to portray human desires as God's will: 'When they perpetrate an atrocity, they say we found our forefathers doing it, and Allah commanded us to do exactly the same thing. Tell them: No, Allah never commands what is atrocious, indecent, or unjust. Do you attribute to Allah what you know not?' That is not all. In surah thirteen, al-Ra'd, of the Holy Qur'an, as in many other ayahs, God Almighty explicitly confines the Prophet and his followers to the delivery of His message, and reserves for Himself the prerogative to punish or to forgive trespasses against His commandments. Since you don't understand Arabic, here again, in English, is how the Qur'an puts it: 'No matter whether We allow you to witness (while you are still alive) part of the punishment We promise the transgressors or We take your soul (before they are punished), your own duty is to deliver the message. It is up to Us, Allah, (not you, the messenger) to hold them to account.' Lasta alayhim bi mussaytir, meaning watching over them isn't your responsibility, is how another ayah of the Qur'an cautions a prophet or a priest against micromanaging his followers. The point here is that the messenger's job is done once he delivers the message. He cannot take it upon himself to kill, maim, terrorize, or torment those who reject the message.

"This implies that every human being must be careful not to confuse his own pet desires with the Will of God or to substitute his own law for Allah's Decree. To rationalize a personal will as the Divine Plan is to look for a pretext to play

God and to suppress rival human wills. This is no different from the secularists making choices that interfere with the natural evolutionary process.

"The name which I give to that folly, that folly with horrendous consequences, is 'inverse evolution.' Evolution in reverse mode is change for the sake of self-glorification. It is representing your personal urges and emotions as reason, and your fabrication of reality as the truth. It is what you do when you want to get a kick out of playing God and making others do your bidding, no matter how preposterous or despicable that might be. Inverse evolution is that queer idea of 'reason' which leads a tin-pot dictator to make and unmake rules at the twinkling of the eye. In contra-evolution's world, pedophilia would be considered the height of depravity one minute, and legalized the next, especially, when the dictator decrees, in the name of freedom, that toddlers be exposed to sex education. Under inverse evolution, wrong and right are interchangeable, leaving everyone to decide what is permissible. Wealth or power serves as the tiebreaker, the force that determines in what direction a society is headed. In inverse evolution's amoral universe, the rich and powerful will always be 'right.' His poor and defenseless counterpart will always be 'wrong.' As it is with individuals, so it is with nations. In such a manmade world, the strong will almost invariably decide what is moral and legal and expect the weak to accept its dictate without question. Of course, no matter how hard it tries, inverse evolution will never succeed in changing the ultimate reality, the reality that nothing evolves outside the evolutionary process itself. None plays God or creates and controls the evolutionary process except the Almighty Himself." Kamil concluded the lengthy but impromptu tafsir.

"Kamil, it is all well and good quoting the Koran and sermonizing. But you still have not explained your role in the massacre of innocent souls and in the wanton destruction of property," Okoye said, still skeptical.

"I knew you would say that. If you are ready to accompany me, I shall explain my role."

"To where should I accompany you?" Okoye glared at Kamil.

"Don't be afraid. My men and women will not carve you up and share out the pieces over a cannibals' fest. Ha! Ha! Ha! I shall lead the way. You just get into your car and drive closely behind me."

Chapter-41

Back to Hayat for rapprochement and rededication!

THIRTY MINUTES LATER, KAMIL and Okoye reached their destination. The Catholic priest got out of his car wondering what stunt his Muslim counterpart was trying to pull. Why did the man make him drive all the way back to Hayat Hospital, a place he, Okoye, left not long ago? He would just have to wait and find out.

Leaving their cars in the space reserved for visitors, both Kamil and Okoye walked up the stairs of Hayat's elevated pavement. They headed straight to the pediatric ward. As they approached the ward, Kamil looked tense. The cheery expression which he had earlier put on to calm a livid Okoye at Garki had suddenly turned sullen. He wiped his eyes to suppress tears. The thought of losing another son was too much to bear. Okoye was perplexed. He could not understand why his friend's mood suddenly changed, and, by the way, what brought them to the pediatric ward.

"Sorry about the last frantic call, Sheikh. Abdullah gave us a fright after taking his medication. Fortunately, his condition has since stabilized. Anyway, now that you are here, you might as well see for yourself how he is doing." The orthopedic surgeon calmed Kamil's nerves. Okoye looked even more perplexed. That was the first time he heard about Abdullah's condition. While he sympathized with his friend, Okoye was still anxious to know the part Kamil played in the attacks on gays and lesbians.

Satisfied that Abdullah was out of danger, Kamil led Okoye to the emergency ward. The men of God were instantly recognized by the duty nurse at the reception. Bypassing the hospital protocol, Nurse Grace cleared the august visitors for immediate and unrestricted access to the ward.

Hayat lived up to its reputation as the finest and best-equipped medical facility in Dukyaria. It had no equal even in the sovereign Dominions of the Mali Empire. The paint on the wall was easy on the eyes. The floor glistened as light bounced off it—a clear testimony to constant scrubbing and diligent varnishing. The corridors were wide, leaving enough room for time-conscious staff to move briskly from one spot to another without colliding with distraught, absent-minded visitors. If the emergency ward was anything to go by, admission into Hayat must feel like a sojourn at an expensive vacation home rather than a confinement to a dreary recuperation center. The beds were fitted with mosquito nets. Wide-screen television sets were screwed to stands at strategic places, thus keeping the patients duly entertained and abreast of developments in the world.

Hayat might rival any world-class hospital, but it would need more than that enviable standing to nurse the newly admitted patients back to sound health. One was Ahmad, Kamil's trusted lieutenant. With his head heavily bandaged, and one leg suspended from a rectangular bar soldered to the bed, Ahmad hardly stirred when the two important visitors came to inquire about his progress. He lay still as Kamil narrated the patient's ordeal.

Kamil started by telling Okoye how Ahmad had stood in for him, Kamil, at a rally planned to start in the early hours of the morning. Present at the gathering were Muslims,

Christians belonging to various denominations, and adherents of traditional religions. They had converged in front of the WGO field office to register their protest at the legalization of same-sex marriage in Dukyaria. Things were going well at first. The protesters exchanged jokes, went out of their way to be courteous to one another, and resolved not to harass anyone or give the law enforcement agents an excuse to disband the gathering.

Then, suddenly, the peaceful protest turned violent. What started the melee was the arrival of a group that called itself Homo Hunters. The group had launched a witch hunt, ending it with gays and lesbians being frog-marched to the venue of the protest. Each time the agent provocateurs chanted "Homo Haram!" they would mete out a punishment they considered fitting—an amputation, a stoning to death, a pounding, or whatever came to their mind. Not long thereafter, motor cyclists materialized from God knows where and started lobbing hand grenades at the WGO office. This was when Ahmad decided to call Kamil on his cell phone. Within minutes, Kamil was at the venue of the protest, rescuing victims of the attack, arranging the evacuation of the wounded to Hayat, and mobilizing his own supporters against the Homo Hunters.

Although Homo Haram was behind it all, its leader, Abu Danja Mamba, was nowhere in sight. He was believed to be in his hideout in Mambilla Hills planning further raids and coordinating attacks on innocent souls as well as WGO installations in Dukyaria. Kamil believed that for Mamba, the same-sex marriage proclamation was a means to an end. The law helped his membership recruitment and fund-raising efforts. It also served a larger political cause—mobilization of support for the disbandment of the WGO with all its trappings, and the declaration of Dukyaria as a sovereign state headed by no less a person than the Homo Haram boss himself. It was therefore not in Mamba's interest that the same-sex controversy be expeditiously resolved. The terrorist was basically milking the controversy generated by the proclamation for his own gain. The longer the widely detested law stayed on the statute book, the greater the opportunity Mamba had to subvert the WGO and seize control of Dukyaria. This, Kamil reminded Okoye, was clearly at odds with the goal they had both set for themselves. Both clerics wanted a quick but peaceful resolution of the WGO impasse. The terrorist saw his interest as lying in a bloody and protracted war.

Okoye listened to his Muslim counterpart, unable to connect him with rational discourse or any good deed. A fire-spitting Muslim fundamentalist and an act of compassion? The two didn't go together. Kamil and logic? Nope! Anyway, if the man had seen the errors of his ways, who was Okoye to doubt human capacity for redemption?

The Catholic priest kept turning the matter over in his head when it occurred to him to check on the condition of James's patients. He had left the van driver and his battered passengers at the Hayat reception in the rush to get to Kamil's house and give him a piece of his mind. Now that he was back at the hospital with a "new and improved Kamil," he might as well find out how the other patients were doing.

"Good job, Kamil. But now, it is my turn to lead the way while you follow closely behind me."

"I should follow you where?" Kamil asked.

"Are you afraid that I shall carve you up and roast the pieces for dinner? Follow me and find out where we are headed." Okoye got his own opportunity to crack a morbid joke at Kamil's expense.

Okoye suddenly caught a glimpse of Hassan at the far end of the emergency ward. For reasons no one understood, the medication had failed to sedate the peacemaker turned patient. Strong as a bull—that was a fitting description for Hassan. Though slightly off-color, and still feeling throbbing pains in the left hand, he recognized Okoye. More surprising, the patient recalled the bearded face next to Okoye's. "Reverend Father, this is the man who rescued us from the hands of Homo Haram. He and his men risked their lives to save ours. We cannot thank him enough." Hassan recalled Kamil struggling to retrieve him from his assailant's claws and instructing one of his men to look for taxis and minivans to ferry the wounded to the hospital.

For the first time, Okoye allowed the possibility of compassion and Kamil coexisting. He there and then extended his right hand to Kamil. They shook each other's hand vigorously and patted each other on the back repeatedly. "You are a good man! Don't let that beard of yours tell you or anybody otherwise." The Catholic priest's smile was warm and genuine.

"You are not so bad yourself—even in that cassock and skull cap! Of course, you and I still have our fundamental differences. I believe in one God. You believe in three! You are not ready to merge your three gods into One, and I am not ready to split mine into three! You see the problem?" Kamil alternated between staying nice and reinforcing the doctrinal wall separating him from his Catholic friend.

"I see the problem quite alright. The question is whether we can get past the problem and work together to confront our common adversaries, especially, the atheist Cunningham, the prosperity preacher in my vicarage, and the terrorist who claims to be a Muslim." Okoye responded, carefully choosing his words.

"I have a solution. We should refrain from bringing up issues likely to set us against each other. We should reserve our ammunitions for the enemy. You have any problem with that?" Kamil concluded, looking expectantly at his friend.

"I am all for tolerance. Incidentally, why did you keep your son's condition secret? Don't you trust me? Whether you realize it or not, your pain is mine, and mine is yours. That is the meaning of friendship." Okoye reminded his friend.

"I did not want to saddle you with my personal worries. Thanks for the empathy all the same." Kamil replied.

Chapter-42

Corruption and our country's health

ALTHOUGH THE TWO CLERICS had seen the patients at their bedsides and had even talked to a few, neither knew precisely if and when the victims of the unprovoked attack would be discharged. Both headed straight to the Medical Director's office located in another wing of the hospital. Only he was capable of providing a reliable prognosis on the trauma patients' recovery.

As far as Helen and Suzie were concerned, the chief medic, Dr. Kola Awise, had nothing but good news. Both ladies would come out of their traumatic experience more attractive than they had ever been. He assured the clerics that Hayat had the equipment, the specialists, and the resources to undertake the necessary reconstructive surgery. Besides, the WGO had a special fund for women's health. The fund was meant for the likes of Helen and Suzie. Awise was not totally sure about 'defense counsel' Hassan and his two 'clients'. The three victims of attack could be temporarily patched up, but the prosthetic fingers which they needed to get on with their lives and perform basic tasks did not come cheap. Unfortunately, the WGO did not have any provision for the replacement of nicked fingers in its budget. Neither did the government of Dukyaria. Awise quoted the hospital administration as saying that global recession was to blame for the widening fiscal and economic deficits as well as the government's inability to meet urgent expenses.

"Hold it right there, Doctor," Kamil interrupted, raising his right hand. "It goes without saying that corruption is behind Dukyaria's recurring budget deficits and economic decline. I read a WGO report indicating that half of the Territory's budget is routinely skimmed off by corrupt politicians and by, to quote the report, 'light-fingered civil servants.' I am sure the report doesn't have dedicated civil servants like you in mind."

"Thanks for the vote of confidence, but —" Dr Awise wanted to respond.

Okoye quickly interrupted the chief medic, "It may go, and we may leave it, unsaid, but we all know that Dukyaria lost its sovereign status because of corruption. Do you know, Doc, that over a century ago, Queen Elizabeth the Second signed and gave us a document formally releasing us from colonial bondage and certifying our freedom?"

"No, Father. You can't expect a medic like me to know about our history," the chief medic responded calmly.

"Yes, we received that document called DoS, meaning Deeds of Sovereignty. Do you know where that document, that important national treasure, is right now? Never mind. I will tell you. It is lying in the vaults of the World Bank in Washington D.C. as we speak. What is it doing there? The Bank demanded it as a collateral for our unpaid debt. Our leaders gladly parted with it so we could be granted a moratorium on debt amortization along with an extended line of credit. The document, the DoS, will of course not be released until we pay off our debt. And does anyone see us doing that in the near future?" Okoye rounded off his mini sermon with a rhetorical question. Kamil was at once bored by the subject, frustrated by his country's failure to find a cure for a malady which had set it back decades, and intrigued by Okoye's familiarity with the technical jargons.

"You are both probably right," the Doc saw an opportunity to respond to Kamil's and Okoye's concerns simultaneously, "but as a career civil servant, I am not at liberty to make comments of a political or quasi-political nature. The Civil Service Rules require me to keep my mouth shut and my views to myself. Anyway, back to the issue of direct interest to you, I can say without any fear of contradiction that Hayat has no provision for cybernetic eyes or prosthetic fingers in its budget. We simply can't cover that type of expense." He left no room for further dialogue or negotiations.

This wasn't going to be music to Auta's ears. The ears were still intact, but another part of the body needed urgent medical attention. Auta had been rendered eyeless by the Homo Haram mob, and he would give anything to have his sight back. The problem was finding the wherewithal. Although biotechnology had by then advanced sufficiently to enable him to plug in a new pair of made-to-specification eyes, Auta's family was too poor to contemplate placing an order with the overseas suppliers, CyberVision Inc., or even to get a cheap, over-the-counter substitute at a local pharmacy.

Dr. Awise summed up his prognosis by accentuating the positive. Leaning backwards in his swivel chair, he reminded his visitors that Hayat had at least succeeded in keeping the traumatized patients alive. That was worth celebrating. Didn't he hear that one of the victims didn't make it, having been killed on the spot by a lynch mob? He was referring to Audu, the one who, according to James, had found peace in death. The clerics were speechless. Having checked on the condition of all the patients that had arrived in James's van, the two men got off their seats, took leave of the Medical Director, and lumbered to the car park.

On their way down the hospital pavement's stairs, Kamil pulled Okoye aside and muttered, "Lest I forget, we should no longer leave our lieutenants to their own devices on important matters like the organization of rallies. We should be present at future rallies to make sure that no charlatan hijacks them to advance his own agenda."

"I agree with you one hundred percent. Our presence should be enough to keep trouble at bay! Of course, there is still this other matter of how to handle Brad Cunningham. You remember the war he waged on believers before he became the WGO High Commissioner for Secularism? You can then imagine what havoc he can commit now that he is in that powerful position—a position that carries the intimidating authority of the WGO itself," Okoye responded, hoping that his Muslim counterpart would forget neither the battles of the past nor the tough challenges ahead.

"How can I forget Cunningham? No day passes when I do not think about what he did in the past and what he is capable of doing today and tomorrow. As I think about him, I think about our own countryman, Abu Mamba. I don't even know who constitutes a greater threat to religion—Brad Cunningham, the atheist, or Mamba, the self-seeking politician masquerading as an ambassador of the faithful."

"I can always trust you to sum things up quickly and, when you are not ticked off, admirably. The question then is how we can successfully manage the likes of Cunningham and Mamba. I also have a Mamba counterpart in my vicarage. His name is Emmanuel Kalu. I don't know what he wants— to remain in the service of the Holy Father or to become a full-time worshipper of riches and fame," Okoye observed as he and Kamil walked towards their vehicles.

"Then we have a problem. If those expected to be with us are neither with us nor with our opponents, how do we classify or relate to them?" Kamil asked Okoye.

"As 'prontagonists'! There is no other name for those who are neither with us nor with our antagonists," Okoye responded humorously.

"That is apt, Basil. This is how I see it: if we remain focused on our struggle for Dukyarian sovereignty while, at the same time, preaching tolerance among our followers, we can fix a thousand Cunninghams and a thousand 'prontagonists' like Mamba and Kalu!" Kamil summed up as he reached for his car key and walked towards his RAV4 Toyota SUV.

Chapter-43

Abu Mamba strikes again!

Cunningham was presiding over the weekly session of his Commissariat's top executives when his secretary called him on the intercom to bring him up to speed on happenings in Dukyaria. "What the hell is going on in Abuja? Get me the Dukyarian Chief Minister right away! Use Skype and pass the call to me here. I like to see his face as he answers my queries!"

"The Chief Minister is now online, Mr. Cunningham!" The secretary reported. The High Commissioner could never get used to the highly hierarchical organization's phony embrace of egalitarianism. Mr. Cunningham! Happily, that was as far as classlessness went in the WGO, the Secularism Supremo thought to himself.

"Yes, Chief Minister. What time is it over there, so I know how to frame my salutation?" Cunningham went out of his way to be courteous. He wanted the Chief Minister to feel secure enough to let his guard down. He wasn't going to pounce until the Chief Minister felt most secure against, and least prepared for, an attack.

"It is ten thirty p.m., Your Excellency." Chief Minister Ugochukwu was fast asleep when the call came through. He rubbed his sticky eyes to stay awake.

"So, good evening is about right. It is still afternoon here in New York. But don't let me deprive you of your well-earned rest. Let me cut the crap and get to the purpose of this phone call. I have just heard that a bunch of lunatics went from place to place killing law-abiding citizens, destroying property, and attacking WGO personnel in Dukyaria. I hope this isn't so! Tell me that it is all a fabrication. Tell me that none of these happened on your watch, or that if they did, you at least have a good explanation for the slip-up!" Cunningham enjoyed making Ugochukwu squirm and sweat. He raised his voice each time he got to a new sentence.

Ugochukwu, squirming on the other end of the video telephone, but not yet sweating, became defensive, "Your Excellency, we are doing our utmost to arrest the situation..."

"You gotta be kidding, Chief Minister!" Cunningham interrupted Ugochukwu mid-sentence. "Your utmost is not producing the required result. Your utmost has not fully grasped the situation, much less 'ar-rested' it." Cunningham used air quotes to mock the chief minister.

"We are trying our level best to get the situation under control. I have already issued a warrant for the arrest of Abu Mamba, the leader of the terrorist Homo Haram group. Our efforts will soon start bearing fruit, I assure His Excellency."

"How many times have you issued warrants for the arrest of Mamba? Several, as I recall. And how many times has he eluded the police dragnet? Every time. In fact, I am beginning to think that the man is a myth. If he is not a ghost cooked up by Dukyaria to extort money from the WGO, why has he not been captured?"

Good question, Ugochukwu thought to himself. The answer he voiced was totally different from the one lodged in his chest. "We nearly got him last week. He escaped as our

196

troops approached his safe house here in Abuja. Only God knows who tipped him off."

"Did I just hear you mention God? Now, what has God to do with the matter on the table? The longer I listen to you, Chief Minister, the more convinced I am that we made a mistake allowing you to remain in office as Chief Minister after your country became a Dependent Territory. We should have allowed your term as President and Head of State to lapse with the revocation of Dukyaria's Deeds of Sovereignty!"

"I assure His Excellency that I am equal to the challenge. Besides issuing a warrant for Mamba's arrest, we have captured many of his lieutenants. These criminals are talking to the Directorate of National Security as we speak. The DNS will not relent until it extracts valuable intelligence from the scoundrels." Ugochukwu tried to convince Cunningham that the WGO made no mistake letting him stay on as Chief Minister.

"Your DNS is a joke. It is so inept it can't tell the difference between an anthill and a beehive! You have to convince me that you are on top of the situation. Of course, you are at liberty to say so if the job is beyond your capacity. We will find a replacement without effort. All it takes is one phone call to Emperor Kambumba, and before you know it, you are out." Cunningham brusquely dismissed Ugochukwu by ending the video conference. "Is anyone here surprised that Ugochukwu's hired hand was smooching the Chief Minister's second wife under his very nose? A weak, indecisive, and bumbling character like him would always be outfoxed by smart ladies." He laughed hysterically. His subordinates, embarrassed as they were, joined in the hilarity.

Chapter-44

Immunity from sudden death

MEANWHILE, DUKYARIA WAS STILL on the boil. Cunningham arrived at his office the following morning when he was informed that his incoming Director of Political Affairs had died in a bomb blast at Abuja airport. Ambassador Mulenga had bid his staff goodbye a day earlier. His stint as head of the WGO office in Dukyaria had ended with his elevation to the headship of the Department of Political Affairs, which was then part of the Secularism Commissariat.

Mulenga didn't have to come highly recommended. Cunningham had penciled him down for a big post the day Mulenga started filing reports to the UN Headquarters and sending blind copies to Professor Cunningham. By sharing privileged information with an outsider, one that the rules lumped with "bodies external to the UN," Mulenga had not only violated the rules but had also betrayed his superiors' trust. This had not bothered the ambitious career official. His last communication, as the UN Ambassador, was addressed to Cunningham and marked "for your (the addressee's) eye only." The memo painted a grim picture of Dukyaria. The politicians were corrupt, the civil servants were even worse, and the ordinary man in the street didn't care, so long as his or her tribesman was the one presiding over the mess. "Dukyaria will be easy picking for the WGO when (not if) it is established. The country does not have what it takes to stay independent and united."

Cunningham loved Mulenga's writing style. What he loved even more was Mulenga's contempt for his fellow Africans.

The prospective Director of Political Affairs had left his posh six-bedroom villa at Maitama three hours prior to his flight's departure. As a diplomat of standing, he did not have to leave so early. His staff was there to relieve him of the headache of checking in his baggage, declaring the contents of his checked-in luggage, filling the departure form, having his passport stamped, and submitting himself to invasive body checks. He didn't even have to mingle with the crowd at the departure lounge. VIPs like him were entitled to rub shoulders with presidents and prime ministers in a spacious, well-appointed salon in an exclusive wing of the departure terminal.

Mulenga must have had other reasons for hurrying to the airport. One possible explanation was that he had had enough of the increasingly insecure Dukyaria environment and couldn't wait to leave it all behind. Another was the thrill that comes with relocating to the civilized First World environment.

As the black Mercedes pulled out of the fenced-off compound, he cast the last long glance at a house he had called home for the previous four years. He had entertained friends, mostly fellow diplomats and high-ranking government officials, in that mansion. He would surely miss it—with its lush, flower-studded grounds, its impressive exterior, its tastefully furnished interior, and its isolation from Abuja's densely populated and crime-prone quarters. How about the domestic staff ever ready to minister to his every need? And

Maxwell, his dutiful chauffeur? Mulenga would forever treasure the memory of his interactions with these happy-go-lucky people. A remarkable people! No matter the weight dumped on their backs or the worries they carry around in their heads, Dukyarians would always go about with smiles on their faces.

Still, before nostalgia got the better of him, Mulenga shifted his attention to the future, his upcoming trip to and happy sojourn in New York. New Yorkers might not be as carefree as Dukyarians, but he wouldn't mind keeping their company for as long as the WGO would let him. As his driver stepped on the gas and the Mercedes sped towards the airport, he savored the prospect of living in the Big Apple.

He was received at the VIP foyer by the WGO Protocol Officer and Head of the Travel Unit, Augustine Duru. Both instantly sauntered to the VIP lounge. A junior member of the Travel Unit staff followed closely behind, clutching the boss's two pieces of hand luggage.

On getting to the lounge with his superiors, the junior staffer deposited the hand luggage close to the seat that the Protocol Officer had reserved for Mulenga. Liman, the junior staffer, quickly departed. As soon as he exited the lounge and found a secure spot, he took out his mobile phone and dialed a number, "He is there. You are good to go!"

"You mean you've checked him in?" the voice at the other end asked in Kasaranci, the language spoken throughout the phone conversation.

"You know these guys with their diplomatic passports and diplomatic immunity; it doesn't take long to get their exit visas stamped!" Liman assured his mysterious listener.

"Immunity my foot! Let's see whether his immunity covers sudden death."

"It's good we got his exit visa duly stamped. At least, he will have something to present to the border guards on reaching the other side—the other side of existence, that is!" Liman didn't find his own joke funny. He scowled as he reeled off his response. He immediately switched his phone off and headed back to the WGO office in town.

It took the suicide bomber less than ten minutes to flush his own SIM card down the toilet, dump his clothes, strap on the instrument of mass destruction, and slip on the lounge attendant's uniform that he had purchased from one of the airport managers. Mulenga and the Protocol Officer were on their second bottle of beer when the suicide bomber lumbered towards them, making as if trying to clear the side tables. Without warning, he set off a deafening explosion. Not one of the forty-five occupants of the lounge survived the blast. Mulenga's massive frame lay sprawled on the blood-soaked rug.

Cunningham promptly called Emperor Kambumba. "Heads must roll this time. I want to be able to report to the Commissioner-General that those behind the latest atrocity have been apprehended and brought to justice. If they have the urge to explode, we shall show them the determination to contain! And lest I forget, Ugochukwu must be replaced immediately. We need someone we can trust to run the place properly and turn it around!"

Mamba sat back leisurely in his armchair as his spy briefed him on the outcome of the latest raid. The terrorist was delighted to hear that the raid had not only plunged families into sorrow but had also rattled the WGO and its Dukyarian proxies. Mamba did not see how Kamil and Okoye could sustain their peaceful struggle after this. With Mulenga's assassination, the WGO would be in no mood to tolerate civil disobedience. It would spare no effort to outlaw Kamil's and Okoye's street protests and, if possible, clamp the two principal organizers in jail. Homo Haram would thenceforth be the only anti-WGO force left standing.

But Mamba miscalculated. Kamil and Okoye had other plans to keep their street protests alive.

Chapter-45

Enter the Martial Law Administrator

EMPEROR KAMBUMBA DID AS he was told. He fired Ugochukwu and appointed General Homkwap Hilary Homkwap, a soldier, as Martial Law Administrator. The new military ruler wasn't taking any chances. Aware of Ugochukwu's reputation for political intrigue and his legendary mischief-making capacity, Homkwap clamped the former Chief Minister and top members of his government in detention. Dukyarian Ambassadors accredited to the WGO and to foreign countries were not spared in the crackdown on the old order. That was how Idris came to share a cell with his former boss and rival for Ekineta's affection.

With the competition safely behind bars, Homkwap did not have to pursue Ekineta. She came over by herself. This time, however, she was not going to play second fiddle to anybody. She would be the undisputed First Lady. On Ekineta's say-so, Homkwap banished his first wife to his village.

Power produced other effects besides the aphrodisiac. Ugochukwu's former adulating crowd quickly switched sides and started cheering the new strongman. Even the Head of the General Services Office, who a day earlier had groveled before the now ousted Chief Minister, made a show of personally leading his staff to government offices to take down Ugochukwu's official portrait and replace it with Homkwap's. To show Emperor Kambumba and the WGO that he meant business, Homkwap himself ordered the indiscriminate arrest of persons suspected to be behind the previous and the latest terrorist attacks. On his instructions, the DNS sent squads to different parts of Dukyaria to fish out the troublemakers. Unfortunately, the hot pursuits persistently missed the primary target, Mamba. None of those that fell into the DNS's hands remotely resembled the WGO's Enemy Number One. He remained elusive.

Homkwap's immediate reaction to the street protests was to order the detention of Kamil and Okoye. Sam Akerele, a member of the new regime's transition team, counselled against such a rash action. "Instead of throwing the two popular clerics in jail, I advise His Excellency to invite them for a face-to-face dialogue," Sam advised his boss.

"Go ahead! What do I have to lose?" Homkwap accepted Sam's recommendation.

The two clerics accepted the Administrator's invitation to a dialogue. Both pledged their allegiance to Homkwap's government. Both dissociated themselves from Mamba's recourse to violence. However, that was as far as they were prepared to go. They weren't yielding on their opposition to same-sex marriage, and they wouldn't give an undertaking to suspend their street protests. The dialogue ended with the two sides agreeing to disagree.

This notwithstanding, Kamil and Okoye left Homkwap's office believing that the military strongman was one they could work, or at least dialogue, with. Neither saw on the horizon a matter so contentious as to widen the gulf between them and the Martial Law Administrator. How wrong the two arrowheads of civil disobedience were! They did not have to wait too long to find out. The Martial Law Administrator's next move soon revealed the magnitude of the challenge ahead of Kamil and Okoye. It wouldn't be long before tension escalated to fever pitch in Dukyaria.

Chapter-46

Start to re-educate, now!

WITH BOTH HANDS CLASPED behind his back, Homkwap marched up and down his spacious office. He did that anytime he was infuriated. And he was more than infuriated this morning. He had many reasons to be enraged. First, he had just learnt that Mamba had not only routed the highly trained squad sent to capture him, but had also inflicted heavy casualties on the better-armed service men. When Homkwap thought that he had enough problems to last him a lifetime, his subordinates brought him other unpleasant news: Okoye and Kamil had flatly refused to comply with the Administrator's very first directive, the one on the conversion of places of worship into re-education centers. This was over and above the two clerics' persistent habit of inciting the masses against the same-sex bill then before Dukyaria's National Guidance Council. The NGC, as the press called it, was the highest decision-making body made up of the military top brass and a few hand-picked civilians. It was presided over by Homkwap, and in his absence, by his lookalike deputy, AZ.

"Who do these two rabble-rousers think they are? Weren't these the same people who looked me in the eye in my office a few weeks ago and pledged loyalty to my government? Is this their idea of loyalty? Is this what they meant by total renunciation of violence and respect for constituted authority? How dare they turn around and act contrary to my instructions, even when it is clear that those instructions have the backing of the Emperor and of the

World Government Organization? We will see who's boss around here!" Homkwap abruptly stopped pacing the room and reached for the intercom, "Get me Sam. I want him in my office right now!" He barked an order to his secretary, Kike.

When he got the message, Samuel Akerele immediately dropped the file that he'd spent the greater part of the morning poring over. He raced down the corridor and, on reaching the elevator, went up to the interim head of government's office on the third floor. He stood with his hands folded behind his back, wondering why the imposing Homkwap had summoned him. "Sir, I understand that my presence is required here urgently."

"Yes! In the first briefing that I received from you and your colleagues, you mentioned one Catholic reverend and one Moslem cleric both of whom, according to you, you regularly interacted with. Or should I say that your department, the International Faith Department—or what was the name again? —regularly interacted with."

"The department is the Inter-Faith Secretariat, Sir. His Excellency must be referring to Reverend Father Basil Okoye and Sheikh Salim Kamil."

"That's right! Inter-Faith Secretariat. Yes! Okoye. Kamil." Homkwap gently rapped his temple with the right index finger. "Now, where was I? Yes, you've been dealing with these characters for quite some time. Yet, you have not been able to drum my message into their thick heads! I told the religious zealots that we don't want to see their places of worship continue to poison our people's minds, putting wrong ideas into their heads and making them promises of heavenly bliss—promises they know full well they can't keep. I told them to evolve into re-education centers failing which I would be forced to shut them down. Instead of teaching the Old and the New Testaments, or the Koran, they should devote their time to extending the frontiers of knowledge in areas directly beneficial to the human race. Who wants to know who begat whom, who turned water into wine, or to which line of Abraham's family tree one prophet or the other belongs? We are interested in knowledge that is critical to the survival and advancement of the human race! Is it that my message is not clear enough, or it is these religious fanatics who are hard of hearing? Tell me, Sam!"

"I too have been wondering, Sir!" Sam was caught off guard. He knew he had to say something. The snag was he didn't know precisely what the intimidating figure before him wanted to hear. He decided to say what first came to his mind.

Chapter-47

Position vacant: One memo-writing and faith-regulating wizard!

"IS THAT WHAT YOU are paid to do: wonder? Where does your wondering lead us? I need concrete ideas on how to enforce the special proclamation on the conversion of places of worship to re-education centers. You heard that? Re-education centers!" Homkwap tugged at his own right ear. Short of pulling Sam by the ear, there was no better way to drum the need for attentiveness into the civil servant.

"Sorry, Sir. I did not realize that His Excellency was waiting for my own position on the subject. As far as I know, Sir, these religious leaders are too set in their ways. They will not change unless we force them to. They simply won't evolve on their own. We have to act proactively and push them in the right direction. We have to hold their hands and guide them to the path of steady evolution. I call this 'helping serial change resisters along the change trajectory.'"

"That sounds interesting, but what you still haven't told me is exactly how we are going to do that, that is, 'help them along' the evolutionary path. Are we going to fasten ropes to their necks and pull them in a direction we deem appropriate?"

"Not exactly, Sir, but it might well come to that. For now, helping the believers along the evolutionary path requires the government laying down the law, monitoring compliance, and hanging tough on penalties for infractions. This may entail rethinking the abolition of the Inter-Faith

Secretariat. Sir, monitoring compliance with the letter and spirit of the latest proclamation at least warrants recruiting a corps of inspectors and empowering them to audit, and report on, the activities of the re-education centers. Members of the inspectorate cadre will move from one place of worship to another to determine the extent of compliance with the re-education proclamation and to seal any premises breaking the law. If His Excellency signs off on this plan, it will be necessary to expand the mandate and increase the staff complements of the Inter-Faith Secretariat. Of course, the Secretariat would have to be suitably renamed. If His Excellency approves, I think that something like Re-education Monitoring Secretariat or Re-education Enforcement Agency is worth considering." In one fell swoop, Sam managed to put a smile on Homkwap's face, stave off the abolition of his department, and keep his job, possibly at an enhanced level.

"That sounds sensible." The soldier-statesman's frigid countenance mellowed. "Send me a one-page memo outlining the next plan of action and indicating briefly how much it will cost. The memo must be on my desk by two o'clock this afternoon. I have had more than I can take from these bloody civilians!"

Sam pretended not to hear the disparaging remark. Even though he too was a civilian, he could not look the boss in the eye and ask why he had seen it fit to label him and others in his class 'bloody'. Sam had no other job. Besides, there was a more appealing job that he would require Homkwap's backing to get: that of Permanent Secretary. He was not about to spoil his chances by grumbling over a harmless slur.

The first thing Sam did on returning to his office on the ground floor was to lock himself in. He neither needed nor wanted any distractions. Taking advantage of the serenity that came with his self-imposed lockdown, he set to work. However, preparing a readable and 'actionable' memorandum proved more difficult than he had imagined. His problem was how to organize the numerous, sometimes discordant, ideas floating around in his head logically and sequentially while at the same time squeezing them into one page. He wrote and discarded one draft after the other. Finally, he produced something which he was proud of, something which the NGC would peruse once and approve without hesitation. The memo made it to Homkwap's in tray by one forty-five p.m., fifteen minutes ahead of the deadline. It hadn't been so hard after all.

Since he was already privy to the matter raised in the memo, Homkwap lost no time ordering that it be placed before the following day's meeting of the NGC. He also faced no resistance getting his NGC colleagues to endorse the plan to transform the Inter-Faith Secretariat into the Re-education Monitoring Agency and to appoint a cadre of inspectors to enforce the directive on the conversion of places of worship into re-education centers.

Chapter-48

Faith inspectors swing into action!

UNDER SAMUEL AKERELE, NOW Executive Secretary of the Re-education Monitoring Agency/RMA, inspectors were recruited to enforce the WGO's re-education policy. The enforcers were mostly clones who worked virtually gratis. They and their conventionally procreated counterparts travelled the length and breadth of Dukyaria, peering into secret compartments and under beds and tables looking for hints or relics of spirituality.

To earn their keep, the inspectors started with the earliest, easy-to-spot contenders for human souls—the traditional religious shrines with their massive blood-drenched, oil-oozing, scary-looking idols. The inspectors made bonfires of the ancient temples and the inert gods displayed therein. What contribution to knowledge could one expect from carved images—or from objects like hides and skeletons of wild animals, talismans for political charisma, money potions, fertility gourds, hypnosis-inducing horns, and evil-dispelling cowries and fly whisks?

Only Dibea Nwogugu's idols in the heart of Okigwe forest resisted the field inspectors' attack. The carved images kept coming back and tormenting their enemies. Each time the inspectors set the medicine man's shrine ablaze, the idols would mysteriously resurface. They would then wait until the inspectors were fast asleep before encircling the inspectors' houses and keeping them and their families awake with grating, unceasing howls. After several sleepless nights, Sam's inspectors left Nwogugu alone and directed their fury at the less hostile targets.

Having finished off the first line of resistance to secularism, the inspectors next set their sights on the organized religions. They shifted their attention to mosques, churches, and 'revival' grounds. Unknown to the overzealous Agency officials, the Christians and the Muslims were ready with a surprise. Long before Sam switched sides and took the erstwhile Inter-Faith Secretariat along with him, Okoye and Kamil had obtained inside knowledge of how the Martial Administrator's Office planned to deal with places of worship which failed to comply with the directive to 'evolve'. Both knew what to do to 'evolve' and, at the same time, preserve the integrity of their missions. Programed to think and act rationally, the inspectors were scarcely aware of plots that irrational, often self-contradicting, human minds were capable of hatching.

Knowing how headstrong Kamil was, the inspectors had seen him as an easy target, one that would leave his weakness out there in the open and dare his opponent to move in for the kill. Two inspectors promptly headed in the direction of his Dawah Center at Garki. As they suspected all along, the aggressively long beard was still there, unshaved and untrimmed. The inspectors started with that. "Mr. Kamil, we don't understand why you are still keeping this beard of yours. It is in clear violation of the imperial proclamation banning the display of religious symbols and identities in public places. Aren't you aware that the international proclamation became law in Dukyaria the very minute it was 'domesticated' and ratified by the Martial Law Administrator? What do you have to say in your defense?" The shorter and senior inspector, a human, peremptorily demanded an answer.

"That's odd! You are on private property, not a public place. Besides, I need you to educate me on precisely how a personal decision to spot a beard translates into a display of religious symbol. The last time I checked, Christians, Muslims, animists, and atheists were free to keep their beards. Are you implying that the proclamation has confiscated this basic right? Can you show me the law that says a person is now prohibited from existing unless and until he is clean-shaven?"

The two inspectors exchanged quick glances. They were dumbfounded by Kamil's response. They didn't give up. They changed tactics. They were determined to nail the smart Alec.

"Where is your mosque?"

"I thought you people have banned salah. My mosque has moved to where it can't be banned."

"Meaning what?"

"Meaning exactly that."

"What answer is that?"

"What question is yours?"

"Are you making a mockery of this exercise? Are you aware that this is an exercise personally sanctioned by the

Martial Law Administrator?" The senior inspector asked, eyes dilated, irritation written all over his face.

"Who am I to defy the almighty Administrator? You asked me a question; I answered it as best as I could. If my answer is not adequate, your question must have been imprecise. Do you want to try again?"

The senior inspector could swear he spotted a mocking grin on the bearded face. He ignored the face but not the matter on his mind. "Where is your mosque? Don't worry whether we are able to ban it or not. Just tell us where it is and leave the rest to us!"

"Why didn't you say so before? My mosque is in my mind, my heart, and my soul." Kamil gestured with his right index finger to identify the parts of his anatomy in which his mosque was lodged.

The two inspectors again exchanged quick glances. This man was proving more difficult than they had anticipated. Still, no man is invincible. They would vanquish this difficult Kamil one way or the other.

"Ok. We understand that you run classes within the premises. Where are your students?"

"I will be delighted to lead you to them, if you would be so kind as to follow me!"

With Kamil in front, the two inspectors trudged from one class to another, looking for clues of defiance. They found none. What they found were students struggling with algebraic equations, geography, physics, biology, and environmental hygiene. The closest they came to seeing the hands of religion was when one of the classes got to world history. The teacher, having been duly coached ahead of the inspectors' arrival, made only passing references to Islamic contribution to world civilization, skipping the parts where Muslims practically invented algebra and led in other areas of human endeavor. The teacher knew but cleverly omitted the fact that the pioneer in the development of algorithm was a Muslim by the name of Abu Abdullah Muhammad ibn Musa al-Khwarizmi. The teacher remained completely, and for understandable reasons, silent on the pathbreaking contributions of Islamic philosophers like Abu Nasr al-Farabi, Ibn Sina (Avicenna), Ibn Rushd, Mulla Sadra, Muhammad ibn Zakariya al-Razi, Ibn al-Arabi, Muhammad al-Ghazzali, and Jalal ad-Din Muhammad Rumi.

The inspectors left Garki unable to find any evidence to justify shutting down Kamil's center or helping it along the path of 'evolution'. They had hardly left when the students returned to their regular syllabus, which included the study of the Qur'an, the Hadiths, as well as subjects that the inspectors would definitely approve: science, mathematics, economics, and the like.

The inspectors did not realize that they had been had. Thinking that the curricula in Kamil's school excluded the study of religion, they hurried to their next destination, Okoye's Utako vicarage. The sign they saw on their arrival at the front gate of the Utako vicarage had by now changed from 'Utako Catholic Church' to 'Utako Continuing Education Center'. Mr. Basil Okoye's collar had mysteriously disappeared; so also had the carved and the drawn images of Christ, the cross, the pulpit, the curtain separating the parishioner from the priest at confessionals, and all object which the inspectors might use as a pretext to close down the premises.

The parish was not singing the song of praise, nor was the priest administering the sacrament when the inspectors arrived. Every parishioner had been instructed on how to conduct him- or herself. Each was to stick to his scripted role.

"Where is your church?" The senior inspector fired off the first question. The second one, a clone, scribbled on his notepad as instructed.

"This used to be a church, but in compliance with the directives of the government, we have decided to turn it into, as you can see from the signs outside, a continuing education center. An adult education center is more to the point." Okoye responded with a straight face. He inwardly made a sign of the crucifix, hoping that his premeditated lie would be forgiven.

Not knowing what was going on in their host's mind, the two inspectors exchanged their usual glances. This time, both followed up the exchange of glances with approving nods. This one won't give us any hard time. Besides, he does not need any help complying with the re-education order. He is already doing everything by the book. They thought.

"What do you teach in your adult education class?" The senior enforcer threw in another question.

"Oh, it varies depending on the age and the vocational interests of each student." Okoye perfected his lie.

"You mean you have a class for each student?" The junior inspector, the clone, felt he had kept quiet long enough. He too had to put in a word.

"Not really. Perhaps I should have made myself clearer. Although we group our students by age and vocational interest, we pay particular attention to the jobs they have or are interested in, as well as the skills they need to excel at their jobs." Okoye had definitely rehearsed his part well. This was not surprising. He was the show's producer, director, and lead actor.

"That's splendid, commendable in fact. We should remember to take special note of this in our report. Can we see the classes in session?" The senior inspector again nodded approvingly, and the clone followed suit.

"Certainly; I would have been disappointed if you had left without seeing for yourself the progress we've made within such a short time. Please, come with me." Okoye confidently led the inspectors to the adult education classes, chatting with both along the way.

The first course that the inspectors saw in session was for roadside mechanics. The teacher, a middle-aged man, was just starting to take the students through the intricacies of automobile maintenance and repair, the planning and layout of mechanical workshops, and the application of 'scientific management', including time and motion techniques to the allocation of human, material, and financial resources. "You must remember that time is money. Unless you make the best use of time, you are bound to lose money," the teacher warned his students. "When you scatter your tools all over the place and have to spend hours remembering where they are, you have lost the time needed to produce concrete outputs and to make money."

The inspectors apparently found scientific management boring. They moved to the next class. It was for students in the construction industry. The teacher was just warming up to the money to be made in the sector. "The jobs that Dukyarians underrate are precisely those which bring tremendous fortune. Take bricklaying for instance. This is a highly skilled job, one that calls for competencies in masonry, plastering, and finishing, competencies that are perpetually in short supply."

Time and motion study must be a staple on the adult education curriculum. It came up again in the construction class. "Building contractors anxious to make a killing will simply cash in on the shortage of skills by extracting maximum productivity from each laborer. That is why it is important to master the technique of time and motion study and its application to all the critical operations, ranging from site clearing and excavation, through masonry, to plastering and finishing," the instructor went on enthusiastically.

The inspectors were, however, not interested in scientific management, least of all, the application of time and motion knowhow to bricklaying. Even the slides that the instructor pulled out of his brief case to illustrate his points could not persuade them to stay.

Hoping to find what they were actually looking for— signs of resistance to the government's re-education policy— they moved to the next class, the one for garment manufacturing. They were sorely disappointed. The garment manufacturing instructor went on and on describing the processes of fashion design, measurement standardization, stitching, hemming, embroidering, labelling, warehousing, supply chain management, marketing, and distribution. If he knew anything about the Ten Commandments or the Acts of the Apostles, he never for a split second weaved either into his tactfully boring lecture. He never strayed from the scientific management script.

The inspectors left Utako convinced that the government's re-education plan was on course. As soon as the lookout stationed for the purpose informed Okoye over his mobile phone that the coast was clear and that the inspectors had left, the vicarage went back to its normal business. The parishioners, now assembled in the events hall, welcomed the return to normalcy with a hearty rendition of 'Onward, Christian Soldiers, marching as to war...'

Blissfully ignorant of Kamil's and Okoye's well thought-out and brilliantly executed plan, the inspectors returned to base with a glowing report of compliance. The places of worship had, the report noted, voluntarily 'evolved'.

"But then, Sir, one can never be sure what those two clerics are up to. Maybe instead of auditing places of worship here in Abuja, we should extend our dragnet to towns and villages in other parts of the country. I am sure that the people running the places of worship in rural communities are not smart enough to pull the wool over our eyes. The carved images that we set on fire in the first phase of the re-education campaign were located in rural areas." The senior inspector, standing at attention in front of Sam's desk, summarized the report's contents while adding his own recommendation. His mind was on the money to be made from the generous "transport and travelling" allowances normally paid to peripatetic officials. Sam, himself an experienced civil servant, knew this. He acknowledged his subordinate's suggestion with a cynical nod.

"I think that is worth considering, Sir," the other inspector, encouraged by Sam's nod but ignoring the straight face, seconded his immediate supervisor's motion. The clone was not so much interested in the money to be made from official travel as in getting the job done. He had been programed to enforce an order. Meeting his superiors' target was his sole motivation.

"I agree with you in principle. The only snag is the budget. The Finance and Accounts Department warned me a few days ago that our transport and travel budget was almost depleted. Besides, the government is under strict instructions from the World Bank to implement cost-cutting measures. In fact, it is a miracle that we found a budget line to accommodate the recruitment of inspectors, particularly those of you earning monthly salaries. So, I am afraid, we have to confine our operations to Abuja and the environs until the next fiscal year." Sam dashed the senior inspector's money-making, and the clone's mission accomplishment, hopes.

Anyway, lack of money was the least of the Re-education Monitoring Agency's problems. Even if the inspectors had decided to comb every nook and cranny of Abuja, their search would still have been in vain. Kamil and Okoye had seen to it that nobody left any clue that might lead the Agency staff to the actual goings-on in the places of worship. Madrassas knew they would be easy to spot. They promptly hung 'Under new management' signs at their front gates before migrating in droves to the hinterland, far from the prying eyes of Sam's inspectors. The churches did likewise. They took the precautions necessary to escape involuntary 'evolution' or precipitous shutdown.

Only the Abounding Grace Ministries continued business as usual, and in the full view of the Re-education Monitoring Agency. A courageous Agency staffer drew Sam's attention to the anomaly:

"Sir, my understanding is that all places of worship should either transform themselves into re-education centers or cease to operate. But there is this stubborn Pastor called Emmanuel Kalu. He has refused to rename his 'Abounding Grace Ministries' or start the process of re-educating his followers. Shouldn't we go and seal his premises up immediately?" The punctilious inspector, a clone, asked his boss, Executive Secretary Sam.

"No, you can't do that! We are not to touch the Pastor or his church. Do you hear me? Don't go anywhere near the church! I don't know what His Excellency has in store for the Pastor, but I suspect he wants to make an example of pig-headed characters like him. You just watch. By the time we are through with him, even his bitterest enemy would pity his condition. So, run along. Forget about the Abounding Grace Ministries." Sam dismissed the finicky official, scoffing at the clone's impertinence. He couldn't believe his ears! A rookie teaching him to do his job! Anyway, what do you expect of clones? They are too full of themselves!

Chapter-49

Faith inspection hits a speed bump

SAM HAD HARDLY FINISHED ruminating over his subordinate's effrontery when news filtered through the television channels that one Jonas Temidire Temileke, "a concerned citizen of Dukyaria" and prominent member of

Okoye's congregation, had filed a suit at the Abuja High

Court praying the Court to declare places of worship private dominions not covered by the provisions of the imperial proclamation on conversion of places of worship to re- education centers. The plaintiff also pleaded with the court to rule that sending inspectors to these private dominions constituted 'home invasion' and was thus in clear violation of the Criminal Code that the government, on its own accord, enacted, as well as the Universal Declaration of Individual and Civil Rights. The Court duly received the petition, entered it on its calendar, and then adjourned to allow the parties to file their submissions.

Sam was lost for words. He rose from his seat and moved close to the television set directly opposite. He stared blankly at the screen for minutes, unable to decide what to do next. A sudden blip on the screen soon reawakened his senses. So, this is the trick the religious fundamentalists are banking on to get out of our grip? They don't know how determined we are! He thought to himself. He quickly rushed out of his own office to Homkwap's on the third floor. He was sure that His Excellency had already heard about the 'frivolous' suit. After all, there were no less than four liquid crystal display television sets in the Number One office.

Therefore, if Sam was in the office, it was not to bring the interim head of government up to date on the news, but to obtain his permission to mount a robust defense of the re-education decree through the Legal Counsel's Office.

"Certainly! You have my permission to work with the Legal Counsel and have the case thrown out immediately. Do you want that in writing? I don't have to type it. I shall hand it over to you in my beautiful cursive. How about that?" Homkwap made light of a serious matter.

Homkwap could do with comic relief this particular afternoon. Not only had a nonentity shown contempt for his office by dragging him to court, but Mamba had plainly refused to give up his habit of sacking police stations, raiding banks, kidnapping women, and dispatching suicide bombers to government and WGO offices. As Homkwap learnt, Mamba's Homo Haram commandos had just blown up an ordnance depot and made away with heavy ammo. They had carted off lethal weapons such as rocket launchers, AK-47 assault rifles, GPMGs, BMGs, RPG7s, and, most frightening of all, anti-aircraft guns!

Chapter-50

Come rain or shine, His Excellency must hear this!

AS HE OFTEN DID when seeking an appointment with the Martial Law Administrator, Sam had left his home in Karu early that morning, at eight o'clock instead of eight-thirty. As he drove towards Mararaba, he ran into a gridlock. There was nothing unusual about this. Getting caught in the eight o'clock traffic jam was the price motorists had to pay for trying too hard to escape the eight-thirty holdup and the attendant inconvenience.

How did Karu inhabitants leave home early but arrive at their destinations late? There is a simple explanation for the paradox. Local commuters had got it into their heads that the only hope of avoiding the early morning gridlock was to leave home early, which the majority soon interpreted as 'eight o'clock' in the morning. To wait until eight thirty, they thought, was to risk missing appointments or reporting late for work.

What the early risers did not realize was that their pack mentality had got everyone or almost everyone leaving home at eight o'clock instead of eight thirty, thus effectively moving the rush hour thirty minutes earlier. Anyway, leaving home 'early', at eight, had been deeply engrained in the average motorist's mind. Only a few civil servants subsequently took time to check what difference leaving home at any particular time of any day would have on traffic flow. The 'peak hour' sketched on the majority's brain was eight thirty, the time when it was insane to set out from home. Strangely, it wouldn't have mattered one way or the other what time Sam left home this particular morning. The pileup on the Karu-Mararaba highway was, as he soon discovered, not caused by the early morning commuters hurrying to their places of work at eight o'clock but by a head-on collision involving a heavily laden trailer and a fuel tanker filled with gasoline. The accident had plunged the whole neighborhood into confusion. It had started with a deafening explosion. Within minutes, the fire that ignited on impact had not only set the two vehicles ablaze but had also threatened to engulf adjacent buildings.

Sam glanced at his watch. It was eight twenty. The dreaded 'peak hour' was only ten minutes away. He quickly backed up and, in flagrant violation of the Highway Code, steered his vehicle contrariwise and drove against oncoming traffic. As soon as he sighted a fuel station, he swerved and looked for a suitable parking spot. The car pulled to a stop, he cut the engine, alighted, and quickly beckoned to a female fuel station attendant. When she came close, he asked whether she would be willing to earn herself five thousand Dukyarian dollars.

"You won' make I kill somebody? I go do am for five thousand!" The attendant responded enthusiastically.

"No, I don't want you to kill anybody. I just need you to look after this car until I come back. Can you also find me an okada motor cyclist to take me to the Union Secretariat? By the way, what is your name?"

"My name be Jane Bayode. No problem, Sir. A go woch di car well well! You get phone, Sir? I won' call my broda to come pick you go Sekiteriat fast." Jane could not stop giggling. Five thousand dollars for doing practically nothing! May this gridlock happen every day! Jane prayed silently.

Sam handed her his mobile phone. Jane dialed her adopted brother's number. Within five minutes, Olu was at the station ready to zoom to the Secretariat. Sam instantly perched on the seat behind Olu. The okada motor cyclist knew the neighborhood like the back of his hand. He bypassed the traffic congestion on Mararaba road, along with the vehicles' mangled parts and the individuals that perished in the accident. He also took shortcuts hitherto unknown to Sam.

By nine o'clock, Sam was behind his desk. He smiled wryly when he glanced at the two phone numbers Olu gave him before zooming back to Karu. The first was Olu's and the other was Jane's. If Jane had a phone, why did she ask for his own to dial and get hold of Olu? It suddenly hit Sam: Jane didn't relish the idea of precious airtime eating into the cool five thousand dollars she just made. Smart girl! Sam stored the two numbers on his phone. At least, there would be no problem reaching Olu anytime Sam was ready to return to his car.

A few minutes on arrival at his office, Sam headed to the men's room. Facing a large mirror, he sized himself up. He wanted to look his best ahead of his meeting with His Excellency. He liked what he saw. The designer black suit and the purple shirt remained unruffled, despite the bumpy motorbike ride. The hair was tidy, and the face brought out the best of the olive complexion. Only the tie needed slight adjusting, the knot having shifted as he bounced up and down on the rear seat of Olu's motorbike. The shine on the shoes was all Sam needed to know that his domestic help did put the black Kiwi polish to good use. He was now ready to meet his own boss. He was ready to table a delicate matter—a matter that had been on his mind for quite some time.

Chapter-51

And by their prophecies ye shalt know them!

SAM HAD STARTED AS a sceptic, but his previous hunch and current developments had finally merged to turn him into a believer of sorts. He still had doubts about the mixed messages he was getting from Kamil and Okoye. Until the two patched up whatever differences they had over Allah and the Trinity, Sam decided to cast his lot with the two clerics' implacable opponent, Emman.

Sam had initially rejected the idea of working with this pastor. How could he associate himself with, let alone trust, someone who, at their very first encounter, had hit him with the demand for payment for services not yet rendered? When they had met in Jos, it was the pastor who, without being contracted, had offered to invoke divine intervention to fend off a looming disaster, specifically, the planned annulment of Dukyaria's sovereignty consequent on the country's failure to honor its debt obligations. However, Emman soon spoilt things by attaching a string to the commencement of earnest supplications—a down payment of half a million Dukyarian dollars. Sam there and then dismissed the pastor as a swindler.

Still, not to be blamed by his superiors for failing to bring such a matter to their attention, he had included, at the tail end of his back-to-office report, Emman's offer of spiritual support, as well as the amount of money needed "to ensure that the prayer warriors get to work quickly and beseech heavens on high to preserve our independence." Sam had done his bit and left it at that. He did not expect anything to come out of his terse reference to Emman's offer of spiritual assistance and his own weak recommendation for the release of the consulting psychic's fees.

As he stood facing his office television screen that morning, he wished he had been "more proactive" in his recommendation. The pastor that he had ridiculed as an impostor was gradually turning out to be anything but. No quack would have such an uncanny ability to see that far into the future. Hadn't Emman accurately foretold the loss of Dukyaria's sovereignty if money was not released fast? Hadn't the pastor assured Sam that, on receipt of the down payment, the prayer warriors would beat back the disaster with everything in their spiritual arsenal? Why would anyone be surprised that Dukyaria lost its independence as predicted when money did not change hands as expected? And, while on this subject, hadn't the pastor also predicted the "change of guard" at the highest level of government and the summary dismissal of Ugochukwu as Chief Minister? Was Ugochukwu not subsequently removed by Emperor Kambumba? Hadn't the pastor foreseen the ascendancy of an army Lieutenant General to power? Who didn't know that the General that the pastor fell short of mentioning by name was the one now holding the top job, meaning Homkwap Hilary Homkwap?

Even on the assumption that all that Dukyaria had witnessed in recent months was a string of coincidences, how about the situation now unfolding in the Dependent Territory? Was it a mere coincidence that Temileke, out of the blue, had decided to join a long line of disaffected elements hell-bent on toppling Homkwap's regime? Didn't the pastor see turbulent days ahead for whoever took over from Ugochukwu? And this was precisely where Sam was going with his musings. What the pastor saw coming had finally happened. The witch howled yesterday; the baby dies today. Who doesn't know that it was yesterday's witch who killed today's baby? Sam immediately drew a parallel between that Odu proverb and the drama unfolding in Dukyaria. Pastor Kalu, the witch, cried turbulence yesterday, and, unless someone intervened, Homkwap's 'baby' government would be strangled by forces opposed to it today. Sam had to alert the boss fast!

He called Homkwap's secretary again, the third time in one hour, to check if the boss was ready to grant him an audience. Sam was anxious to get the matter off his chest. Alas, the boss had just rushed to an emergency meeting of the NGC. Sam regretted having inconvenienced himself by hitching a motorbike ride to the office. He should have waited in line on the traffic congested Mararaba road. He realized that the issues before the morning's meeting of the NGC were unlikely to be settled any time soon. How could the issues be expeditiously resolved when no Council member knew exactly what those issues were? For a start, the whereabouts of the man giving them headache at that moment was unknown. Even if Abu Mamba seemed close to being captured, he had a knack for outfoxing his trackers and vanishing into thin air.

Sam realized he had a long wait ahead of him. He had no choice but to sit tight till the NGC agreed on how to cage Abu, or, in the alternative, adjourned to give exhausted Council members the respite they needed to come up with a watertight, failsafe, strategy. As he sat glumly waiting to be called upstairs, he cast his mind back to his meeting with Emman in Jos. Not content with merely talking to, or exchanging phone numbers with, Personal Assistant Amos, Sam had insisted on a face-to-face discussion with the General Overseer himself.

With everything that had happened since their Jos encounter, Sam could not stop wishing that the President's Office, as it then was, had released the funds requested by

Pastor Emmanuel. Sam was the only one to blame for not making a strong case for the down payment needed to set the prayer war in motion. He ought to have impressed upon his superiors the necessity to get the money out on time. If the funds had been handed over to the Abounding Grace Ministries, the prayer warriors would have gone to work right away and Dukyaria would not have been downgraded to a Dependent Territory. Besides, Ugochukwu would have continued as President instead of coming down to the level of Chief Minister. Now, even the post of Chief Minister had been snatched from his trembling hands—as foretold by Emman!

But wait a minute; wasn't he being too hard on himself? It suddenly occurred to Sam to shift the blame for the non-release of funds to others. Why, he asked himself, didn't his superiors act on his recommendation, weak as it might appear? Couldn't they read between the lines, or better still, take a giant leap of faith? After all, the amount requested to get Emman's prayer warriors to start beseeching heavens on high was paltry. How much was half a million dollars compared to what was at stake, Dukyaria's independence? Now, the office hierarchy's failure to act on his, albeit tepid, recommendation had cost the nation dearly. Dukyaria's foreign enemies had succeeded in confiscating the country's Deeds of Sovereignty! Kai! O ma se O! What a pity! Sam, looking rueful, alternated between biting his right index finger and biting his lower lip.

The situation was not totally hopeless, however. And if it was too late for Dukyaria to retain its independence, it wasn't for Sam to turn his country's predicament to his own advantage. He simply had to act in accord with the prevailing orthodoxy—that is, "evolve." Everybody else is evolving—from the interim head of government, through his new First Lady, to the military's top brass on the National Guidance Council. Even the clerical establishment is on board the evolution train. The seekers of the heavenly kingdom were acutely aware of the fact that the alternative to self-reinvention on earth was to be left behind by a fast-moving train. It was his moral duty to be one of the evolving, outward-bound, go-getting passengers.

Instead of agonizing over what might have been, Sam thus decided to leave the past where it belonged. He engaged his mind's forward gear. As he took off to an imaginary future, he thanked his stars that he was a career civil servant. His job was safe. He was spared the fate that had befallen not just the former Chief Minister and members of his entourage, but also ambassadors and high-ranking government officials. Permanent Secretaries had been relieved of their responsibilities. Ambassadors like Idris had been recalled and served termination notices. Even his immediate boss, the Executive Secretary, was not spared. As it so happened, these individuals' misfortune had turned out to be a blessing. Many key positions fell vacant when Homkwap decided to reshuffle the top political and civil service cadres. The constitution of a new team then was the opportunity he had been waiting for all along. This was the time to make his move. He had to obtain the post of Permanent Secretary. His mission in life would not be complete until he reached the zenith of his career. He had to become a Permanent Secretary and Chief Accounting Officer of a Ministry—either in the Cabinet Secretariat of the Martial Law Administrator's Office or in another arm of the civil service. Luckily, pastor Emman had shown him just how to go about realizing his dream.

Sam waited the whole day, hoping to meet Homkwap. He left his office at nine o'clock at night when it became clear that the NGC had neither concluded nor adjourned its deliberations. Well, the members could sit all they wanted. After all, they were not short of food to eat or beverages to slake their thirst. What was more, they had the kitchen staff to wait on them round the clock. He, by contrast, had had nothing to eat all day except the roasted plantains and ground nuts which he sent his messenger to buy at a kiosk across the road. He promptly headed home, confident that by the time he arrived, dinner would be ready.

Sam did not have to endure hunger for long. By the time he got home, the table was already set, with the yam pounded to a fine paste, the aroma of spicy vegetable and chicken stew wafting across the room, and a goblet of cool water planted within reach. The famished Sam wolfed down the food and retired for the night.

Chapter-52

Try selling religion to a cloned atheist!

THE FOLLOWING DAY, SAM didn't bother to call Homkwap's office or wait for the secretary's confirmation of audience with the big boss. If the NGC finished very late the previous night, as he thought was most likely, it would be unrealistic to expect its chair or any of its members to report for work early the following morning. As Sam assumed, whoever worked uninterrupted into the wee hours of the morning needed to power down and recharge his battery.

So, instead of staring at his wristwatch and at the intercom on the desk as he had done the previous day, Sam went back to his normal routine—wading through the files stacked in his in tray, scribbling in the margin which actions should be taken and by whom, summoning office staff to answer routine questions, and issuing instructions as appropriate. As he wondered when he would be done with the humdrum paperwork, he stumbled on a monitoring team's recommendation prescribing stiff penalties for the mounting of religious or sectarian billboards in public places, especially, along the highways. He didn't know what to make of the recommendation. "Now how do these nincompoops expect to catch anyone red-handed mounting offensive billboards in broad daylight, especially if the culprit already knows that getting caught means going to jail?" He ended his monologue but not without leaving his impression in writing, "Inspector Tanko, this half-baked idea should not have made it to my desk! You and your team can do better than this!" He was about to sign off on his rude assessment of his subordinates and fling the file in the out tray when his phone rang. "His

235

Excellency is now free to see you, Sir." Secretary Kike's sleepy voice didn't belong in a bustling nerve center like the Martial Law Administrator's Office. Yet, that was the voice that had consistently relayed the messages of the occupants of the Number One office—from Presidents to the Chief Minister and now the Martial Law Administrator. Each incoming head of state or government must have found the reserved and shy Kike somehow indispensable.

"Am on my way!" Sam forgot about the files on his desk and rushed to the third floor. He could not imagine His Excellency finding the strength to report for work so early in the morning, especially considering the toll taken by the marathon session of the NGC. As he learnt from a colleague on getting to the office that morning, the high-level meeting had lasted all night. Did the meeting find a solution to the Mamba problem? Sam's informant was "not at liberty" to answer that question. Anyway, the answer could wait. The boss on the third floor could not be kept waiting.

He spent less than five minutes in the anteroom when Kike signaled that His Excellency was ready to receive him. He walked briskly to the inner room, the seat of power. His eyes alternating between Homkwap's official portrait staring down the back of the throne and the watercolor painting of Ekineta mounted on the left side of the throne, Sam stood as he often did when in front of the interim head of government; upright, with his hands folded behind his back. In keeping with the standard rule that the first and the last words belonged to His Excellency, the civil servant kept mute.

"My secretary informed me that you waited the whole of yesterday hoping to see me. Do you know when we left the Cabinet Room yesterday?" His Excellency asked.

"No, Your Excellency," Sam lied. He didn't want to be suspected of keeping tabs on the NGC. To know when it adjourned was a mere heartbeat from knowing what it discussed. His security clearance was not such as would allow him access to sensitive subjects like the NGC working hours or deliberations.

Sam tried but almost in vain to keep his composure every time he was in the Martial Administrator's office. It did not matter how many times he had entered the spacious office in the past, he always felt as if he was visiting it for the first time. True, the large oval desk remained where it had always been, planted in the center, not too far from the wall directly behind Homkwap's throne. The throne, a leather swivel chair, was where it was supposed to be, behind the oval desk. The LCD television sets stayed in their usual spots—with the screens appearing as if following His Excellency's all-too-frequent paces across the room. However, and with the exception of the throne itself, other seats were liable to be shuffled around. New artefacts kept showing up either on the large oval desk or around the expansive room. One week, it was an Adam Smith figurine presented by an Edo sculptor amid flashes of photographers' lights and spontaneous applause. Another week, it was an ancient sword left behind by the Paramount Ruler of Mzzagbala Kingdom to mark the end of his solidarity visit to His Excellency. And this particular morning, two Homkwaps materialized in the office in place of one—the real Homkwap sitting on the throne, and his clone standing with the right hand resting on the throne.

Sam found the sight creepy. Although he had heard about the resemblance between the Martial Law Administrator and his Deputy, he had never once met this particular clone face-to-face, or indeed any person that looked so interchangeable with another.

"This is AZ, my Deputy. What do you think of the resemblance? Striking, huh? The Atlantis Genetics is the one to thank for the miracle." The real and sitting Homkwap cast an impish glance at his unsmiling double.

Sam was in a quandary. He hadn't reckoned with AZ's presence. He was counting on having a one-on-one with His Excellency. How could he talk religion in the presence of an irredeemable atheist, a virtual robot at that? He had to change his tactics. "Yes, Your Excellency. The resemblance is uncanny. Where would we be without science?" He had to show he was on the side of reason—at least, with AZ present and fully attentive.

AZ was not one to be fooled. He immediately saw through Sam. "What do you know about science? Are you a scientist?" he asked, his face still expressionless.

"Not really, Sir."

"What exactly does 'not really, Sir' mean?" AZ was insistent.

"Sir, I studied political science, which, strictly speaking, could hardly be called science. That's what I meant by 'not really, Sir.'" Sam was desperate to wriggle out of AZ's hold. He regretted bringing this upon himself. He should have left science well alone and out of the discussion.

"Let's leave science aside for a moment. What is it you wanted to discuss with me?" Homkwap came to the increasingly clammy Sam's rescue.

"Your Excellency, I have been thinking about the challenge posed by those religious fanatics. I think I might have a solution."

"Well, what is stopping you? I am all ears." Homkwap, with hands flung open, signaled that Sam was cleared to clue him and AZ in.

"Your Excellency must have heard about the Bermuda Triangle. What we have here is not a triangle, but a rectangle, the Dukyarian Rectangle, to be precise. On the top left of the rectangle, point A, is Kamil, and directly below it is point B, Abu Danja Mamba, the terrorist. On the top right of the same rectangle is point C, Okoye, and below it is point D, the business-savvy pastor Emman. All the four points of the rectangle would first appear to be against us. However, if we are able to stoke the embers of discord between and among the four points of anti-government resistance, all we need do is sit back and watch them destroy one another. I know for certain that there is no love lost between Kamil and Okoye, or between the two and their implacable enemies, meaning Mamba and Emman." Sam quickly evolved. He radically modified the strategy he had perfected before AZ entered the equation.

Before AZ showed up and spoilt his original plan, he had rehearsed several times what he was going to tell Homkwap and how he would deliver his lines: "Sir, don't misunderstand what I am about to tell you. Nothing happens without a purpose. The higher purpose that your appointment serves is to get Dukyaria back on track. And I know a man who can help you do this. Sir, it is the same man who, unknown to you, had foretold your ascendancy to the office of head of government. His name is Emmanuel Kalu. He is the Pastor

239

and General Overseer of Abounding Grace Ministries. I met him in Jos, a few weeks to the revocation of our Deeds of Sovereignty." Sam had intended not only to take the Martial Law Administrator through the discussions Sam had had with Emman, but also to over-blow the pastor's psychic credentials. He was going to embellish the story with the pastor's prophesy of the exact date of Ugochukwu's dismissal and of the name of the man 'destined' to succeed the Chief Minister. How could Homkwap hear that Emman knew of his coming and not be moved?

Sam had reckoned that the catalogue of Emman's surefire predictions in the past would persuade Homkwap to retain the pastor's services. As a government insider, Emman, the prophet, could be relied on to wage a spiritual war on the enemies of Dukyaria and on those who were after the downfall of the Homkwap regime.

Now that he knew AZ would be privy to any discussion he had with Homkwap, Sam realized that it would be sheer folly, in fact, suicidal, to go ahead with his original plan, a plan that AZ would immediately have dismissed as irrational, anti-WGO, and treasonable! He had to come up with and defend a new plan, one meant to sow seeds of discord between and among the believers.

"What do you think of that, AZ?" Homkwap turned to his clone that had stood motionless, without even blinking, for close to fifteen minutes.

"I do not see how it is scientifically possible to turn one man against the other, except of course, if you were to apply the latest mind control technique, but I haven't yet heard about any reference to it."

"Trust me, AZ, there is nothing we humans aren't capable of if we set our mind to it. What we need to hear from this man is precisely how we are going to set one point of the rectangle against the other. You get my point, Sam?" Homkwap encouraged Sam to continue.

"I was at the Inter-Faith meeting in Jos where Okoye and Kamil held sharply divergent views on the Trinity doctrine. To keep the antagonism alive, we need to insert provocative articles in the newspapers igniting the Trinity debate. Both Okoye and Kamil do not hate each other as they do Emman and Mamba. The converse is also the case. Since Mamba is out of our reach, we can secretly bring Emman to our side and encourage him to make provocative statements about Kamil's Koran, about Okoye's interpretation of the Bible, and most of all, about Mamba's acts of terrorism. If I have His Excellency's permission, it is something I can easily handle from my office."

"What do you think, AZ?" Homkwap cast one of his frequent sideways glances at his lookalike.

"If you trust this guy, then, by all means, allow him to proceed. We just have to inform the NGC when we reconvene tomorrow." AZ signified his support for Sam's Dukyarian Rectangle plan.

Chapter-53

Your country needs your services, Pastor!

ASSURED OF HOMKWAP'S backing as well as AZ's tacit support, Sam proceeded to implement his plan. Although he had not deleted Emman's name from his phone contact list, Sam could not call the pastor from his own office. He had to wait until he reached the privacy of his own home. Walls, especially office walls, have ears. The people sitting or standing next door did not have to eavesdrop to make sense of his phone conversation, more so as he might have to raise his voice once in a while to overcome network glitches. Since it was virtually impossible to know who the spies were among the unwitting listeners and the habitual eavesdroppers, Sam thought that waiting a few hours to place his call wouldn't do any harm.

On getting home at night, he scrolled down his phone's contact list. As soon as Kalu's name appeared, Sam dialed the pastor's number. The phone's face instantly lit up, bringing out both the name and the number.

"This is Amos. May I know who's on the line?" Emman's personal assistant answered the phone. Amos was in Emman's large sitting room waiting to find out if the boss's rumbling stomach had quieted down. He did not expect to hear from Sam. In fact, since Sam had refused to call after the Jos meeting, the efficient personal assistant had gone ahead to delete his name from the General Overseer's contacts. Amos reserved the contacts app strictly for serious-minded clients.

242

He couldn't think of a better way to put the burner and out of style phone's limited memory to optimum use.

"Amos! It's nice talking to you! How are you and how's life treating you?" Sam, as demanded by the Dukyarian custom, placed courtesy ahead of substantive business.

"I am in excellent health. My God is good! How are you doing yourself?" Amos butted in before the business-like Sam had any opportunity of getting to the substantive point. As dictated by the Dukyarian culture of reciprocity, the personal assistant felt the need to respond positively when a total stranger was kind enough to ask after his health. To keep mute in such circumstances would be considered rude, and to state candidly that things aren't going your way would be un-Dukyarian.

"Good. Could you please put the General Overseer on the line? There is a matter of grave national importance that I need to discuss with him," Sam had decided that the only way to get Amos's or his boss's attention was to hint at the possibility of someone with the wherewithal urgently requiring the Abounding Grace Ministries' services. Who had greater access to Dukyaria's finances than the government or, to be precise, those running the government?

"I am sorry; the General Overseer is not here right now. However, you can leave a message with me, and I shall make sure that he attends to it immediately upon his return." Amos, his pen and notepad ever ready, waited to take down Sam's message.

"When is he expected back home?" Sam was not ready to leave a matter of grave national importance in the hands of a third party, especially a low-ranking church official. He wanted to talk directly to the boss himself.

"Not until tomorrow morning, I am afraid. You are sure you don't want to leave a message?"

"Don't worry, I shall call back tomorrow. About the same time ok?"

"Since you can get him in the morning, why wait till so late? I am sure that he will be back by ten o'clock tomorrow morning." Amos couldn't understand why the man would neither talk business with him right away, nor make time to meet his boss early the following morning. Didn't he realize that time is money? The sooner the interested parties got cracking, the better.

Sam's mind was already made up. He was talking to nobody except the head of the church himself. If pastor Emman was not free that night, the matter would have to wait till the following night. Calling the pastor in the morning was out of the question since Sam would be in the office at that time. No one in his right mind would expect him to sit in his office and announce to his colleagues that he was contemplating an alliance of sorts with men of God. If it came to light that he was consorting with the individuals that the WGO was determined to put out of business, not just his career, but his whole life would be finished.

Convinced that nothing would come out of the first attempt at reestablishing links with pastor Emman, Sam switched off his phone and went to bed. He lay on his back for hours, wondering where on earth pastor Emman was at that time of night.

Amos knew where the pastor was, but he was not about to tell. What he didn't mind doing was restoring Sam's name to the list of the General Overseer's contacts.

Excited to have Sam back in the fold and on speed dial, Amos scampered from the sitting room to Emman's bedroom. On approaching the door, he knocked gently. The pastor was apparently in the washroom. It was Catherine who got the door. She opened the door a crack. She flung it ajar on seeing Amos. "It's you. Come in," she nodded before shutting the door. "I think the pastor's running stomach is getting worse. He has been to the loo more than four times. I asked him to give me his doctor's number so I could call him, but he plainly refused. He assured me that it wasn't anything serious. Maybe you want to talk to him yourself."

"It must be the mango he took after dinner. His bowel can't hold mangoes down, but his eyes just won't let go."

"I heard that, Amos!" The pastor, two hands clutching his abdomen, emerged from the washroom, wobbling.

"Yes, my blessed Pastor. You heard me right. But you know what I said is true. This is not the first time this has happened. You have gnawed at mangoes voraciously many times before and paid with frequent visits to the toilet. I wish my job description would include placing my boss on a diet and vetoing the consumption of foods or fruits deemed injurious to his health! What do you think, Sister Catherine? Shouldn't a personal assistant be responsible for his boss's health?" Amos, his eyes alternately scanning Emman's and Catherine's faces, grinned light-heartedly.

Catherine thought and said nothing. All she did was acknowledge Amos's joke with convulsive giggles. Emman would have loved to participate in the skit but for the ongoing insurrection in his belly. He raced to the loo for the umpteenth time. He went back and forth until he was too weak to continue. Then, totally dehydrated, he staggered to his bed and went to sleep. His loud snore signaled that the uprising in the stomach had finally been put down.

Amos realized that he would have to wait till the following day to brief his boss about Sam's telephone call. With nothing left to do, he took Catherine's leave, ready to return to the living room and, ultimately, to his own apartment down the road. Catherine, however, had a different idea. The personal assistant, who was already familiar with the health issues associated with his boss's eating habits, should stay behind and play the doctor. She, a total stranger to the experience, would then return to her house. She inwardly imagined the morning newspapers' headlines if the pastor gave up the ghost in middle of the night and in the presence of a pretty woman at that! God forbid! She would not be linked to any scandal, least of all, one involving a man of God. Amos had come to check on his boss's health at the right time. He might as well take over from there.

"Just tell the pastor that I had to return as I have an early morning appointment tomorrow. I shall call to check on his health later in the afternoon."

Chapter-54

A slight complication in the rectangular plan

CATHERINE WAS SURPRISED TO find a taxi so quickly at that time of night. Seated directly behind the driver, she was spared the ordeal of listening to the cabbie's endless prattling. In her serene and secure position at the back, she reflected on the miracle behind her resumption of fraternal relations with Emman. What spell did the pastor cast on her to let bygones be bygones and to accept Emman even as a token friend? Although he kept insisting that the friendship was platonic—and thank God, nothing had yet happened to disprove that claim—she feared that the sneaky Emman would not hesitate to take the friendship to the next level if she for one second let her guard down. She had had to fend off his unwanted advances in the past. There was nothing to show that he had given up. In fact, had the upset stomach not sabotaged his plan, he would have steered their conversation down the erotic lane and would have tried to plunge his hands where they didn't belong.

As her mind went back to how they reconnected, her phone rang. "Don't worry, I am on my way. See you in ten minutes," she answered, before switching the phone off and returning to the subject of her inexplicable relationship with Emman. They had met at the height of the uproar set off by the issuance of the Imperial proclamation on same-sex marriage. She and her friends were among those present at an Inter-Faith gathering which Kamil and Okoye had convoked to mobilize fellow Dukyarians against the proclamation. As one of the speakers at the event, Emman had conducted himself with dignity.

Catherine had expected that the irrepressible Emman would use the occasion for grandstanding. However, instead of promoting his Abounding Grace Ministries, he had been magnanimous enough to acknowledge the need for rival faiths to work together. The challenge facing Dukyaria, he noted, required that all faiths and ethnic nationalities bury their differences and work together to defend their freedom. "Freedom is no freedom unless it is so acknowledged and vigorously defended by the individual. The appropriate name for whatever is externally bestowed and forcefully imposed is colonization, not freedom. To the extent that we never once asked for the freedom for one man to marry another and for two women to be joined together in unholy matrimony, to that would we feel justified to reject the same-sex proclamation. On this I stand. To reclaim our freedom, I am willing to work with my brother in Christ, Reverend Basil Okoye, and my brother in the struggle for freedom, Sheikh Salim Kamil," Emman intoned to the dense crowd's tumultuous applause.

Listening to Emman, Catherine could easily understand why Abounding Grace Ministries had attracted and continued to attract hordes of worshippers. The pastor had certainly come a long way. He had changed from a wooden, dreary, and self-conceited individual to a populist, perhaps a demagogue.

At the end of the open-air meeting, Catherine instinctively walked over to Emman's corner to congratulate him on his brilliant performance. "I didn't know you have such fire in you!"

"There are many things in me you don't know I have," Emman responded playfully.

The pastor did not come to the event alone. Apart from the bevy of Abounding Grace beauties duly coached to shout "Hallelujah" on cue when Emman mounted the rostrum, the church elders, mostly financiers, were present. So were Amos, the personal assistant, and Akin, the Deputy General Overseer and de facto business strategist.

Of all the members of Emman's entourage, it was Akin who fascinated Catherine. With squinted eyes, she surveyed the Deputy General Overseer from head to toe. To be sure about the identity of the person directly facing her, she craned her neck and scanned the spot where she last saw Okoye. The Catholic priest had by then moved elsewhere, but not too far from where Catherine could pick out his handsome face from the teeming crowd. She rubbed her eyes. She cast another look at Akin, and then at Okoye. Both looked exactly the same—or almost the same. "Are you and Father Okoye related?" She could not hold the question back any longer.

"You mean the one who addressed the gathering a few minutes ago? The one standing over there?" Akin pointed in Okoye's direction.

"Yes." Catherine nodded.

"I don't believe he and I are related. As you can see, he is Ndi, and I am Odu through and through. Why do you ask?"

"You mean you haven't noticed the resemblance between you two? Go and stand by his side, and people will assume that you are twins or that one is a clone of the other," Catherine exclaimed.

"I never thought of that. Let's ask Pastor Emman here. What do you think Pastor?"

"Think about what?" The pastor was either paying no attention or he wasn't interested in the topic.

"Never mind. And what is your name if I may ask?"

"Catherine. Catherine Henshaw. And yours?"

"Akin. Akin Mosafejo."

The two left the matter there. They did not exchange phone numbers or other personal details. However, both felt a spark—a spark that instantly lit two hearts and increased their yearnings for a physical and emotional connection.

Emman abruptly asked if Catherine cared to visit his church. Catherine accepted without hesitation. "Why not? After all, Abounding Grace Ministries is the only church left standing. The others have to operate under the radar. Which reminds me, how did you manage to exist without falling under the Re-education Monitoring Agency's axe?" Catherine had asked, an awkward smile on the face.

"The secret lies in our name, Abounding Grace. God Almighty is always with us," Emman answered, his face avoiding hers.

"Are you suggesting that we should all change our churches' names to Abounding Grace?" Catherine asked humorously.

"That is one question only you can answer."

At the end of the banter, Emman and Catherine exchanged phone numbers. From then on, they stayed in touch by phone and any time Catherine was free to visit Emman's church adjoining his villa. However, no matter what trick Emman came up with and tried on her, the friendship never went beyond the platonic level. The man whom Catherine had been after was not Emman but Okoye. Now that Okoye was clearly beyond her reach, fortuity had handed her a consolation prize in the form of Akin, the Okoye lookalike.

"Thanks. Am getting down here." She promptly got out of the cab, paid the fare, and alighted. Akin was already outside his apartment, waiting. As soon as Catherine sighted him, she raced into his arms. As the couple had done many times in the past, they started kissing passionately even before entering the apartment and shutting the door. Once inside, it was action all the way. They slid under the sheets and continued the display of affection—kissing, playful nibbling, mutual groping, and all. They didn't stop until they took each other to the peak of sensual delight.

The love birds took special precaution to keep their trysts secret. They knew that if the General Overseer or any of his lackeys got as much as a hint of any romantic link between his dream girl and his deputy, Emman would not hesitate to bring the whole house down, along with everybody in it.

251

It was, however, only a matter of time before Emman figured out that something was going on between Akin and Catherine. What gave the game away was Akin's mobile phone, or to be specific, the mysterious appearance of Catherine's name on the phone. Akin had left his phone on Emman's desk to xerox a document when Catherine's call came in. Emman saw the name on the phone, but he did not do anything. So Akin would not to suspect that Emman knew who had called, the General Overseer had thereafter left his office. Akin returned only to find Emman's seat empty and a missed call waiting. "Phew! That was close! Thank God that he wasn't around to answer the phone!" Akin was glad that Emman's absence had saved him the trouble of explaining what he and Catherine had in common and why they phoned each other.

Unknown to Akin, Emman now knew what his trusted associate had been trying to conceal. The problem was how to bring the matter out in the open. He finally concocted a plan. The plan took the form of a make-believe stomach bug. The frequent rush to the loo was a script written, produced, and directed with consummate skill by Emman and, with Amos's foreknowledge, unwittingly enacted by the two love birds.

Amos's readiness to relieve Catherine of the bedside duties was part of the act. Before Catherine flagged down a taxi, Amos too had left the villa to wait in his own car. When the taxi rolled out, Amos followed from a discrete distance.

He trailed Catherine's taxi all the way to Akin's house. From inside his own car, Amos saw both embrace, caress, and kiss each other. Emman's special assistant watched the erotic display, imagining what had gone down in Akin's apartment on previous occasions. With the way these two are carrying on with each other out there in the open, Amos mused, it should not be difficult figuring out how far they had gone in the privacy of Akin's bedroom. Amos promptly drove back to Emman's villa and filed his report.

The morning's newspaper headlines jolted Sam: "PASTOR KALU FIRES DEPUTY: Accuses Mosafejo of pocketing church funds and mismanaging resources."

This is not good. How will I explain the crisis in Emman's church to His Excellency? Thank God, money hasn't changed hands. I just have to come up with another plan. Sam, clutching the newspaper with his left hand and cupping his chin with his right, stared at the ceiling as if looking for answers to his problems.

Chapter-55

On top of it all, tension at Headquarters!

ON THE INSTRUCTIONS OF the Commissioner-General, Chief of Staff Evangelista Torres summoned an emergency meeting of the WGO Commissariat's top executives. By ten o'clock all the Organization's big wigs had assembled in the Commissioner-General's Operations Room on the forty-seventh floor.

Khaled Bin-Sayed El-Maktoum took his usual place at the far end of the oval-shaped boardroom table. On his right sat Brad Cunningham. Since military matters might come up in the course of deliberations, Marshall Grigori Popov, the Militarism High Commissioner, sat to El-Maktoum's immediate left. Chief of Staff Torres occupied the seat next to Popov's while Wang Xiao-Ping, the Commissioner for Capitalism, sat on Cunningham's right, and by implication, El-Maktoum's far right. The lesser officials, mostly Deputy and Assistant Commissioners, Directors of Divisions, and Chiefs of Sections, occupied the remaining seats. Even among the lesser officials, hierarchy prevailed. No Director would think of sitting closer to the top management than an Assistant Commissioner, and no Assistant Commissioner would breach protocol by taking a seat reserved for a Deputy Commissioner.

"As you can see from the notice of meeting sent out by my Chief of Staff, reports coming out lately from Dukyaria are disturbing. We hear of some Muslim and Christian clerics joining hands to fight the WGO. Then there is the guy called Abu Danja Mamba —"

"What kind of name is that? Is he a reptile or something?" Only Cunningham had, not necessarily the rank, but the temerity, to interrupt the Commissioner-General.

"Brad, you should know better than to do what you have just done. Don't you realize that it is the height of disrespect to cut in before the head of the Organization makes his point? If you can speak out of turns in the university, you can't do that here. You have to abide by the protocol embodying the principles by which international organizations are run," Torres, the keeper of the Organization's conscience called Cunningham out.

"Ms. Torres! You're out of line! How dare you lecture me on how to conduct myself? Mr. Commissioner-General, I take strong exception to your Chief of Staff's impertinence! Goddamit! I'll take no shit from anybody!" Cunningham was hopping mad. His heavy, intermittent breathing and glower said it all.

"Nyet! That is not right, Brad. You should have allowed the Commissioner-General to conclude before making any comment." Popov jumped in headfirst, the r rolling with the heavy Russian accent.

"Is the Commissioner-General calling this meeting to order, or do I assume that I have wasted my time coming here?" Cunningham made as if stacking the papers before him, ready to leave. The sullen look was still on.

"You see what I mean? He is even giving the Commissioner-General an ultimatum. Who does he think he is?" Torres held her ground.

"Ladies and gentlemen, we came here to solve a problem. Don't let us spend the little time at our disposal creating more problems. Everyone has made his or her point. Now, let's move on to substantive discussions. Can I now call on Brad to update us on the situation in Dukyaria?" El-Maktoum might be easy-going, but he was inwardly glad that someone had put the cocky Cunningham in his place.

"The situation is not as bad as the press would make us believe. I spoke to the Acting Resident Representative only yesterday, and he assured me that everything is under control. Mamba is on the run. His ragtag army is no match for our fighting machines. As for the Moslems and the Christians, they are too busy fighting one another to have time for us. Besides, the military strongman, Homkwap, has been consistent in his zero-tolerance of religion. He has closed down virtually all the places of worship which failed to evolve into re-education centers. Any questions?" Cunningham looked round the table for raised hands.

"Yes, I have a question for you, Brad. Are you sure about the facts which you have placed before us? Let me put it more graphically: is the intelligence in your possession up-to-date and credible? I am asking because what we are hearing about Dukyaria is totally different from what you have just described." Torres seemed determined to rile and humiliate Cunningham. She was unlikely to forget how determined the Secularism Supremo was to get her out of the office of WGO Chief of Staff and to install a pliant replacement. One of her Nicaraguan compatriots at their WGO Permanent Mission had reported persistent but clandestine moves by Cunningham to "restructure" her office and declare her post redundant. Had the Developing Countries Bloc not stood firm behind one of their own, Cunningham would have succeeded in kicking Torres out of the WGO.

His efforts stymied by Torres's constituency, Cunningham had resorted to internal bureaucratic intrigue as a way of finishing off his rival. However, unable to reconcile Cunningham's adverse comments on Torres with the Chief of Staff's exemplary qualities, El-Maktoum had pointedly asked if Torres knew exactly what she might have done to tick the Secularism High Commissioner off. "I already ruled out spurned love advances as the cause of the cold war between you two. After all, Brad is gay, while you are not. So, it must be something else. The question is exactly what that something else is, that something that never fails to set you two against each other." El-Maktoum had teased Torres.

What El-Maktoum didn't realize was that one did not have to do anything to set Cunningham off. He was born that way: self-assured, inflexible, and unapologetically arrogant. To him, the world was either black or white—there were no shades in between. Unfortunately, Torres, his nemesis, was equally strong-willed. The only difference was that while Torres was capable of being swayed by logic and facts, nothing ever succeeded in moving Cunningham. Once science taught him one "truth," nothing could persuade him to see the world differently.

Chapter-56

Their rag-tag army against our fighting machines? You gotta be kidding!

"WHAT KIND OF QUESTION is this, for crying out loud?" Cunningham asked irritably. He could not understand why Torres would doubt the reliability of his information.

"The kind that needs a straight answer!" Torres fired back.

"Ok, you want a straight answer; I shall give you a straight answer. There is a revolt in Dukyaria, and we are more than capable of containing it. Those clowns calling themselves clerics will soon get tired of leading street protests. And as I said earlier, Mamba is more of a nuisance than a threat. He does not have a strategy or the resources to constitute a credible threat. He is not an adversary worth losing sleep over."

"Grigori, since military questions have somehow crept into the debate, can we have your assessment?" Al-Maktoum, deliberately ignoring Torres's raised hand, turned to the stern looking, bemedaled Field Marshall.

"Da, nyet, naverno. Maybe Brad is right. Maybe he is wrong. Who knows?" Popov threw both arms up. "He is the one who knows what goes on in Dukyaria. However, if you ask me, I will say that the most dangerous military adversary is the weak, unarmed, ration-deprived, loosely organized, but highly motivated one. Look at how the belittled Vietcong dealt with the better-armed, better-equipped, and hierarchically organized American military in

Vietnam. Look at how the Taliban, with nothing but their belief in Allah, routed the Soviet Army and humiliated the intimidating Union of Soviet Socialist Republics. At any rate, history and my professional training teach me not to underrate the enemy."

Torres nodded approvingly from her seat. Let's see how Cunningham gets out of this one, she thought to herself. The gloating on her face must have been palpable. Cunningham looked indignant when his eyes met hers.

"I doubt if we have reached that stage yet, the stage at which to begin to consider military options. We don't want to dignify Mamba's theatrics with a forceful, but largely ham-fisted, response. It's like treating a comic-book display as a real-life, full-scale war. A tempest in a teacup; that's what it seems to me." Cunningham was confident he could handle the Homo Haram terrorists his own way.

Torres disagreed. "Honestly, militarizing Dukyaria is the last thing I would recommend. As a matter of fact, I am against war in general, and war on Muslim extremists in particular. The whole purpose of war is to dangle the fear of death before the enemy's eyes, but how do you intend to drive the fear of death into the heart of someone who is eager to die anyway, someone who values no life, least of all his own? All the same, we need to watch the Dukyarian situation closely. I have here satellite photos of the raids recently carried out with lightning speed and pin-point precision by Homo Haram squads." Torres pulled out her iPad from her briefcase and connected it to the large LCD screen in the operations room.

"As you can see, the seemingly undisciplined, loosely organized, 'rag-tag' army has taken out entire military formations, seized control of ammunition depots, and imposed Sharia rule over swaths of Dukyaria's territory. Happily, it hasn't yet started amputating thieving hands, branding liars' foreheads with hot iron, or stoning adulterers to death." Torres ran the commentary as she flipped from one high-resolution photo to another and clinched her argument with caustic remarks.

"Before we reach for the stick, can we think of any carrot options, say, options of an economic type? Wang, this question is for you." El-Maktoum turned the economic question over to the capitalism czar.

"Dukyaria is a basket case, pure and simple, but that is not the point. The point, and a serious one, is that it is a leaking basket. Even if we whip up an economic aid package and pump all the world's resources into Dukyaria to facilitate the implementation of the package, government officials will end up diverting the funds into their own personal accounts. Monies meant to build factories will suddenly show up in private accounts in Swiss banks or be laundered to finance condos and yachts in the Riviera. Every Dukyarian, from the Big Man to the lowliest citizen, knows this, but none will talk about it in public. Corruption is a way of life. The average Dukyarian sees nothing wrong with it. He complains only when he or she is not the beneficiary of rule-bending and rent-seeking practices. So long as that culture, the 'Chop-I-Chop' culture as they locally call it, persists, no amount of foreign aid will make any difference. The figures recently compiled by our economists indicate that Dukyaria's fiscal and macroeconomic deficits will widen rather than narrow in the coming months. I don't see them paying off their debt and regaining their independence anytime soon." The Capitalism High Commissioner's assessment was blunt and unsparing.

"So much for the carrot option. We are back to the stick. How about the cloned soldiers we sent at the MLA's request? Surely, they ought to have made a difference. Did they—make a difference?" El-Maktoum directed the military query to Popov.

"The Martial Law Administrator spoke glowingly about the clones' military and enforcement capability. He particularly liked the one we sent as his Deputy. However, since the cloned soldiers are programed to fight disciplined troops and to obey precise commands, they could not adapt to the guerrilla tactics applied by the enemy, in this case, Homo Haram. The binary logic that the clone soldiers understand led many to their premature end. How many of them walked into enemy fire before realizing that the plain field ahead which looked secure was anything but? We either have to replace some cells in their brains or send them for training in guerrilla warfare before they are deployed for tours of duty in Dukyaria. I wish to assure the Commissioner-General that our scientists are up to the challenge. They are working on new clone prototypes, the types that are capable of putting down insurrections in any part of the world. Each clone will be linked to a computer located in the Militarism High Commissariat. That way, we would be able to monitor his or her performance on the battlefield. Defective soldier clones will be decommissioned and culled the instant their flaws pop up on our computer." Popov's response was not particularly reassuring, at least not as far as the problem on the table was concerned.

The meeting's chair saw one raised hand, and he instantly cleared the owner to speak.

"Marshall Popov, I think the purpose of today's meeting is to find a solution to the problem we are facing right now, and not to speculate about the future. As my boss, Professor Cunningham, rightly observed, the situation in Dukyaria has not reached the stage where we would be talking clones, soldiers, guns, and all." Mesfin Kidane, a director in the Secularism Commissariat and unabashed Cunningham lackey, took the opportunity to redeem his master's image while at the same time minimizing an adversary's contribution.

"So, precisely what should we be talking?" Torres could hardly contain her rage. If Mesfin craved the post of Assistant Secularism High Commissioner, he should at least wait until he reached the privacy of their office before licking his boss's boots. Why should he behave so obsequiously in public? Bloody, tail-wagging sycophant! The Chief of Staff muttered under her breath.

"We shouldn't turn this into another round of sharp exchanges. We should instead focus on what needs to be done immediately to contain the situation in Dukyaria. I fear the onset of the domino effect here. If we are unable to maintain law and order in Dukyaria, you can bet that dependent territories in all the six Empires will see that as a signal to rise and fight the WGO. Anyway, I have a meeting with the Chairperson of the Assembly of Nations, Madam

Warioba, later this afternoon. After obtaining her reactions to the impasse, I shall present my own recommendation to the GGC/Global Guidance Council. Don't worry; I shall present the conflicting views expressed at this meeting to the GGC before giving my own take on the subject. So, unless anyone has something else to add, the meeting is adjourned." El-Maktoum, using his knuckle in the place of a gavel, rapped the table thrice and rose.

As demanded by protocol, the other attendees stood up and waited for the Commissioner-General to return to his office before dispersing.

Chapter-57

You see discord, I see unanimity!

EL-MAKTOUM'S MEETING with Madam Warioba was brief and to the point. The titular head of the world government concurred with practically all, but otherwise irreconcilable, recommendations on how to contain Dukyaria's increasingly volatile situation and prevent it from spreading to other parts of the globe. As she told El-Maktoum, anyone in her position should learn to rely on the judgment of the experts. To be on the safe side, she asked El-Maktoum, "What is Cunningham's view on the subject?"

"Brad is against militarizing the situation," the Commissioner-General reported.

"That makes sense," Warioba nodded.

"But Evangelista, who's here with me, thinks we cannot just fold our arms and do nothing." El-Maktoum added, expecting the titular head of government to take a stand.

"She has a point. Have you obtained Popov's assessment of the military options?" The nonaligned Warioba agreed with Torres also.

"Yes. Popov thinks that the answer lies in redesigning the soldier clones and programing them to adapt to unpredictable military circumstances, the type of circumstances created or preferred by the Homo Haram guerrillas."

"I have no reason to disagree with him." Warioba stuck to her right to concur. Being a realist, she did not expect, in her titular position, to make any waves or rock any boat. She, without any reservations, left the make-or-break decisions in the hands of the Proconsuls serving on the Global Guidance Council.

Chapter-58

There's no place for your 'live-and-let-live' nonsense here! Got that?

EL-MAKTOUM EXITED WARIOBA's office as he had entered it—unsure where the titular head of world government stood on an important matter like what to do to contain threats to Dukyaria's stability and, considering disorder's domino effect, to global security. The ball was back in the Commissioner-General's court. He had to decide what to recommend to the GGC.

Realizing that he was now on his own, the Commissioner-General thought of a plan likely to be acceptable to both the hawks and the doves on the Global Guidance Council. Like Cunningham, El-Maktoum ruled out a full-scale military operation. The "soft" option favored by the Secularism Commissariat would stay until it exhausted its momentum and proved no longer effective. At the same time, however, he would, as advised by Torres, propose a review of the re-education proclamation. Although the matter was still before a High Court judge, El-Maktoum would further recommend that the WGO's highest decision-making body brace itself for one eventuality—allowing the unyielding clerics to run their places of worship as they saw fit so long as they did not challenge the foundation on which the WGO rested.

He knew that selling the proposal wouldn't be easy. Already, hawks on the GGC had berated him and his Chief of Staff for being soft on religious fanatics. One Council member had even pointedly accused El-Maktoum of being a "closet

266

Muslim"—running with the secularists in daytime but, at night and in a secluded part of his home, praying fervently to Allah for forgiveness, hoping that Allah would understand his predicament. He was shocked that the accuser, the New Europe Empire's Special Consul, knew him inside out. Still, he put on a bold face, going as far as to swear on the WGO Treaty to clear himself of the "malicious accusation."

El-Maktoum knew what to do. He would get Torres to prepare, and if possible, present the GGC memorandum. Fortunately, no one had yet accused her of being a closet anything. Although she was raised a Catholic, she had learnt early to leave her faith at home if she was to survive in the multi-cultural environment of international organizations. She thus had no problem adjusting to the defunct United Nations' post-modern flirtation with secularism or the successor WGO's open declaration of war on believers. She worshipped her God at home, alone. She also gave her colleagues at the office the space they needed to chase their dream of a godless existence. Her policy was live and let live.

Of course, Torres would never for once think of sending a live-and-let-live memorandum to the GGC. She was acutely aware of the fact that under the new order, you had to live according to the dictates of the world government. As Torres reckoned, a behemoth like the WGO takes; it doesn't give. She therefore decided to exercise the utmost restraint in carrying out her boss's instructions. The memorandum which she drafted for El-Maktoum had started by cataloguing the achievements of the WGO. The Organization, the memo noted, had made "tremendous progress" implementing the Secularism, Capitalism and Militarism Directives. The write-up opportunistically blew up

Popov's update on his scientists' mass-produced combatants. "In the not so distant feature, the WGO will be able to deploy soldier clones at short notice to trouble-spots in any part of the world. These soldiers will behave like their fully human counterparts, and even better, since their brains will be wired in such a way as to anticipate guerrilla forces' hitherto erratic moves." Until that happened, until the clones had mastered guerrilla tactics, the WGO would need to tread softly in Dukyaria. Those religious fanatics were determined to fight the WGO to a standstill. The best strategy was to meet them halfway. By meeting them halfway, the memo meant "standing firm on the principle of secularism while at the same time allowing the places of worship to operate without let or hindrance but under close surveillance."

The GGC took one look at the memorandum and swiftly tossed it out. The hawks were having none of the bureaucratic double-talk. They didn't see any difference between the memo and the live-and-let-live idea that they had previously and firmly rejected. Cunningham's "soft" option was not even given a chance to exhaust its momentum; it was unceremoniously shunted aside by the GGC. Since Wang's carrot wasn't likely to make any difference anyway, the Special Consults decided it was time to wield the big stick. Popov and his scientists had to double up their efforts. The drones and the stealth bombers had to be ready to go into action.

Chapter-59

In the matter of Temileke versus the Martial Law Administrator

IT WAS A PARTICULARLY windy morning in Abuja. As he drove from Garki along Ahmadu Bello Way, Lawan had to endure the grating sound of the SUV's wiper blades as they swept both sides of the dry windscreen, blowing away leaves that had fallen off trees and flying particles looking for a place to settle. Fortunately, his employer, Kamil, had, after much procrastination, released the money needed to procure gas and fix the SUV's faulty air-conditioning system. Both drove along the dusty road to the Abuja High Court with the windows and the side vents firmly shut.

Father Okoye's case was different. His car did not come with an air conditioner. He drove slowly from Utako to the High Court on Ibrahim Babangida Way, his windscreen wiper blades sweeping away leaves coming off trees and the debris which the gust wafted in all directions. With his mind focused on the case coming up that morning, he bore the morning heat's torment in silence. He also ignored the speeding motorists who seemed to get a kick out of hooting loudly and leaving behind clouds of dust on the windswept highway.

"Court! The High Court is now in session, with Justice Ganiyu Philips presiding," the court orderly announced as the judge entered. The spectators instantly jumped to their feet. They sat only after the bailiff signaled that they were free to do so.

"Now that we've heard the two counsels' opening arguments, can I now ask if the witnesses for the plaintiff are here in court?" Judge Ganiyu Philips turned to Temileke's counsel.

"They are, my Lord!" Alex Stanley assured the judge.

"In that case, you may call your first witness," Justice Philips ordered.

Temileke stepped forward, and the court orderly led him to the witness box.

"As provided for under Article 2 of the revised Evidence Act and Article 2 (a) (iii) of the Civil Procedure Rules, you are to repeat after me: 'I, Temidire Temileke, hereby swear in the name of the World Government Organization to speak the truth, only the truth, and nothing but the truth. I swear this oath knowing that I am liable to be sent to prison for six months and fined a sum of one hundred thousand Dukyarian dollars if it comes to light that any part of my testimony is false, so help me WGO!'" The court clerk took Temileke through the oath swearing routine, pausing at intervals to allow the witness to repeat what he heard.

The record duly showed that Temileke not only swore in WGO's name but was also warned that perjury, which the merciful God had overlooked, would be met with instant and severe punishment by the unforgiving WGO.

"Can you please tell this court your name in full?" Barrister Alex Stanley spoke as if he had never met Temileke, his client, before.

"My name is Jonas Temidire Temileke."

"What is your age?"

"I am forty-five years old."

"Where do you live?"

"I live at 2570 Manzini Street, Gwagwalada."

"Are you married, single, divorced, or widowed?"

"I am married with four children."

"What is your profession?"

"I am a general contractor."

"In other words, you are a responsible citizen of Dukyaria?"

"Objection, my Lord? If my learned colleague is taking us on a fishing expedition, he should at least let us know in advance what we are likely to catch." The respondent's counsel didn't see what the plaintiff's social standing had to do with the case.

"Sustained! Will the counsel stick to the matter before this court and refrain from introducing extraneous matters?"

"Withdrawn. I apologize, my Lord. What is your interest in this case, Mr. Temileke?"

"I am the plaintiff."

"That's all from the plaintiff, my Lord." Stanley concluded his direct examination.

The judge asked if the defense had any questions for the witness before he was discharged.

"We have my Lord." Wole Thomas stepped forward. Even without his impressive array of university degrees, his sharp, legal mind, and his reputation for winning every single case he prosecuted or defended, Thomas cut an intimidating figure. Standing six-foot eight, he towered above every one present in the court—in fact, anyone Temileke had so far come across. His robes and wig further projected an aura of invincibility. The thought of withdrawing the case fleetingly crossed the plaintiff's mind. His fear increased as the giant advanced towards him.

"Mr. Jonas Temidire Temileke. That's your name. Right?" Thomas's cross-examination started with the obvious. The faint smile betrayed no emotion, at least, not of antagonism.

"Yes, that is right." Temileke answered confidently.

This wasn't going to be so hard after all.

"Are you a Christian or a Moslem?"

"I am a Christian."

"Are you a priest in your church? Just answer Yes or No!" Thomas's smile abruptly vanished.

"No."

"Are you a Moslem learned man? Yes or No." The state's advocate locked his increasingly hostile eyes with Temidire's.

"Objection. My client already told this honorable court that he is a Christian, not a Moslem." Stanley prayed the court to veto the defense counsel's question and order that the question be deleted from the record.

"Overruled. The witness will answer the question."

"No." Temileke and his counsel exchanged glances. Both wondered whether they would ever get a fair deal from this judge.

"Are you a native medicine man?"

"Objection, my Lord!"

"Overruled. The witness will answer the question.

"No."

"Do you own a place of worship which you are legally obliged to convert into a re-education center? Yes or No will suffice."

"Objection, my Lord!"

"Overruled."

"No."

"If you are none of the above, then precisely what is your interest in this case?" Thomas was looking for a quick end to the case. If he could prove that the person who brought it had no locus standi or a legal right at stake, there would be no need to go into the merits of the case. Thomas would simply move for summary dismissal. That would be a major setback to places of worship as the courts would be reluctant to entertain another round of litigation on a case already settled. Once the court threw Temileke's case out, the government would no longer have to worry about further litigation. The doctrine of res judicata would instantly take over and bar anybody from bringing another cause of action challenging the re-education policy!

"As a freeborn citizen of Dukyaria, I have a right to congregate with other Dukyarians without let or hindrance insofar as our activities are restricted to non-public domains. The Imperial Proclamation on places of worship seeks to extinguish that right."

"I have no further questions." Thomas ended his cross-examination.

"Do you have other witnesses, Stanley?" The judge asked.

"Yes, we do, my Lord. I call on Reverend Father Basil Okoye as our second witness."

Father Okoye rose from his seat and proceeded to the witness stand. As advised by the court clerk, he repeated the oath of affirmation, but he demurred when he got to the part requiring him to swear "in the name of the World Government Organization."

"Isn't the World Government Organization taking itself too seriously? Does it for a moment think that it could take the place of God?" Okoye sneered at the court clerk.

"Permission to approach the bench!" Thomas requested a meeting with the judge. "My Lord, my learned colleague needs to advise his witness to conduct himself properly. He is in a court of law. If he has anything against the WGO, he should take his grievances to the appropriate quarters, far away from this court."

"Did you hear that Stanley? Warn your witness, or I shall hold him to be in contempt of this court. If he as much as makes any speech, he will find himself behind bars." Judge Philips glared in Okoye's direction so he would know that the conclave was all about him and his impertinence.

"I apologize, my Lord."

With what he just heard from the judge, and to save his witness the embarrassment of being charged with contempt, Stanley walked towards Okoye and whispered into his ears. Okoye apparently got the message. He repeated every word uttered by the court clerk. He was ready to be examined by the counsel for the plaintiff.

"What is your name in full?" Alex Stanley started examining his witness.

"Basil Okoye."

"What is your age?"

"I am thirty-seven years old."

"What is your religion?"

"Christianity."

"What is your address?"

"Utako Re-education Center. You can't miss it. It's the only one in the neighborhood. It was formerly known as Utako Catholic Church."

"What is your profession?"

"I was a priest until an Imperial Proclamation unilaterally turned me into a 're-education center' supervisor or whatever. If I may be honest, I don't know what my title is. I am still trying to figure it out." Okoye shrugged his shoulders. The audience laughed uncontrollably. Judge Philips restored order and decorum by rapping his desk with his gavel.

"Are you married?" Stanley resumed his examination.

"No."

"We are done with this witness, for now, my Lord."

Like a lion after his prey, Thomas rushed towards Okoye. The priest remained calm. He didn't bat an eye. "So, you are a re-education center supervisor or whatever. Can you please tell this court what you mean by that?" Thomas baited the witness.

"It means exactly what it says: re-education center supervisor or whatever."

"In other words, you don't even have the slightest idea about the mandate of the re-education center that you are supposed to supervise. Do you?"

"I know about the mandate of the Catholic mission…."

"Yah, but this is not the Catholic mission. It is, by your own testimony, the re-education center, isn't it?" Thomas mockingly tilted his head left and right and, for added effect, gesticulated with outstretched hands.

"My Lord, I have to object. This line of questioning serves no clear purpose. Besides, Mr. Basil Okoye is not on trial here. He is only a witness."

"Overruled! The witness must answer the question." Judge Philips was adamant.

"The re-education center is a recent creation whose goal and mission we are still trying to understand." Okoye's nebulous response allowed him to sidestep the landmine planted by Thomas.

"In answer to my learned colleague's question on religion, you mentioned Christianity. Do you stick by that affirmation?"

"Yes."

"Are you aware that identification with a religious order or sect is an offense punishable under the law?"

"Yes."

"Do you run or manage a place of worship? Answer Yes or No."

"No, unless you call the re-education center 'a place of worship.'"

"I did not ask you to qualify your response. My Lord, I move that the latter part, the unsolicited part of the response be struck from the record."

"Sustained!"

"If you do not run or manage a place of worship, what is your interest in this case?"

"I am not only a witness, but also a party. You can ask the Chief Registrar. Sheikh Salim Kamil and I have filed an application praying this honorable court to join us as parties to this case."

"My Lord, this is most unbecoming of my learned colleague. If he knew that an application for joinder was already before this court, he ought to have brought this to my attention. The defense feels thoroughly blindsided by the plaintiff and is therefore compelled to request an adjournment."

"Hearing adjourned till the two parties resolve the matter of joinder and agree on a date for resumption of proceedings."

"Court!" the court bailiff yelled, as the judge rose and returned to his chambers. The spectators instantly jumped to their feet. They trooped out of the building once the judged had left.

The court could not have picked a better time to adjourn. Thirty minutes after the crowd dispersed, a bomb tore through the windows of a duplex not far from the High Court. The duplex was obviously another case of collateral damage. The real target was the police post located about half a kilometer away from the High Court. Homo Haram was determined to take out the corrupt police officials and bring the entire building down on their carcasses. The terrorists did not mind that their bomb simultaneously drove fear into the hearts of the inhabitants of houses or offices in the vicinity. Homo Haram considered it a bonus if its acts caused abrupt changes in court calendars and unsettled court officials, especially judges.

Judge Philips and his colleagues could not but feel vulnerable. The High Court was not only a crucial arm of the government; it was also increasingly perceived by Dukyarians as a symbol of WGO's meddlesomeness.

Chapter-60

Faith's witness becomes a party in the conscience eradication case

THE HIGH COURT DID not feel secure enough to resume proceedings in the Temileke case until six weeks after its first adjournment. By then, Homo Haram had shifted its attention from the national capital to the outlying districts. The opposing parties had also resolved their differences. Kamil and Okoye were duly listed as parties to the Temileke case. That brought a new complexion to the case. It also warranted stepping up Okoye's cross-examination. After all, he was no longer a mere witness; he was a party with an interest to defend.

"Mr. Okoye, you told this court at its last sitting that you ran no place of worship. Is that right? Just Yes or No!" Thomas pounced as soon as Okoye returned to the witness stand.

"Yes."

"Has something changed since then?"

"Like what? I can't answer Yes or No to a question which is vague." Okoye responded as coached by his counsel.

"Have you started running a place of worship since the last court hearing?" Thomas left Okoye in a dilemma. If he said

"Yes," he would be guilty of violating an existing law prohibiting the maintenance of places of worship and prejudging the court's opinion on the law's validity. If he answered "No," the present case was as good as lost. If he ran no place of worship, he had no right to defend, as none was under attack.

"No, but…"

"No buts! My Lord, the defense requests that the record show that the witness's answer is No."

"Objection, my Lord! If the cause of justice is to be served in this case, my client should not be censored by my learned colleague or stampeded into giving false testimony. We would not be party to any attempt at misleading this honorable court."

"That's preposterous!" Thomas responded indignantly.

"Nothing is more preposterous than someone taking on a task he is not delegated or paid to do. Rather than allow my client to plead his case, my learned colleague is literally dictating the answers my client should give to his questions!" Rasheed Williams, Okoye's counsel, lashed back.

"Can the two counsels approach the bench?" Judge Philips saw a fire and moved quickly to douse it. He beckoned to Thomas and Williams. The two counsels instantly complied with the judge's order. It was time for both to plead their cases quietly in front of the judge, leaving the public to wonder what either was saying. Rasheed didn't care whether the public heard him or not. He was more interested in getting Judge Philips's attention and favorable ruling. Speaking softly and carrying himself in a way calculated to impress Judge Philips, Rasheed Williams stood his ground: "My argument, my Lord, is that my client at no time retained the services of the defense counsel to plead his case. My learned colleague therefore cannot coach or advise my client as to how to answer a particular question! I am the one paid to do that."

"My Lord, I don't see any cause for this hairsplitting. The court has its own procedure. To save time and money, it decided that Yes or No would suffice as answers to properly framed questions." Thomas whispered his response.

"I must thank my learned colleague. He took the words right out of my mouth: 'properly framed questions.' The questions that my distinguished senior at the bar constantly puts to my client are anything but properly framed. The Civil Procedure Rules that the defense counsel alluded to specifically provide in Article 5, section 3 (b) that where elucidation would serve the cause of justice, a witness is at liberty to go beyond answering Yes or No to a question. My Lord, the matter at hand is delicate. If it is not properly and transparently resolved, it may set the nation ablaze. That is why, my Lord, I pray this court to err on the side of caution. I earnestly request that witnesses called to testify be allowed to throw whatever light they believe is necessary to settle the highly complex and multisided matter before this honorable court. A binary approach simply won't do. It will leave many important questions unanswered!" Rasheed Williams basically mixed politics with the law to get the judge on his side.

"I don't…"

"I have heard enough." The judge stopped the altercation with a stern look and a languid wave of his right hand. He decided it was time the curious spectators knew what the whispers were all about. "This is my decision: witnesses will be allowed to provide any elucidation they believe will help this court sort out the tangled issues. However, I shall not tolerate grandstanding or longwinded speechmaking. I shall guillotine any 'elucidation' that serves no purpose except turn my court into a theatre. Is this clear to both parties? If your witness wanders off the track, I shall summarily whip him back into line! Now, go back to where we were before we got distracted." Judge Philips' ruling stopped the bickering. Williams beamed. Thomas bristled. But then, the judge had spoken.

"Let me rephrase my earlier question: Are you running a place of worship right now?" Thomas was determined to throw Okoye off-balance.

"No! I cannot until this honorable court hears my plea and upholds my right to do so," Okoye replied, sidestepping another landmine.

"And what right might that be specifically?"

"The right to self-determination; the right to be me; the right to freedom of belief and conscience; the right to adore my God in my heart and in my private domain."

"Do you consider a church having devotees from all sections of the Dukyarian society a 'private domain'?"

"Yes. It is private so long as the devotees come there with their eyes open and of their own volition. It will be another matter entirely if I go around forcing people to come to the church, the house of the Lord. In that case, I would have moved from a private to a public domain. My right is private insofar as it does not interfere with, or obliterate, other rights."

"Interesting. Are you sure that what you do or say in this your house of the Lord does not interfere with, or does not seek to, obliterate what is being said or done in rival houses of the same or a rival Lord, as in mosques, synagogues, ashrams, and shrines, for instance?"

"I am positive that in the circumstances you just mentioned, no right excludes the other. The church congregation members and I call on the Lord the way we understand. The Moslems go to their own mosques and call on the same Lord in the language and manner they understand. The same applies to adherents of traditional religions. Different paths lead to the same destination, that is, to God Almighty."

"And this—your—God is the same for everybody?"

"I can't answer on everybody's behalf. However, from where I stand, the God we all worship is One and the same. It is the language that we employ to describe Him and the practices we have developed to acknowledge His existence which vary."

"Really? This isn't what I hear about the various religions. I hear that the Moslems have one God, Allah, and you Christians have three. Correct me if I am wrong, but isn't the name you've given your own God the Father, the Son, and the Holy Spirit? Does everyone accept this arbitrarily created and historically determined triumvirate as their definitive, incontestable God?"

"I do not expect everyone to so accept! Human beings are created to be contentious. Conscience pulls every person in different directions and eventually pushes him or her to take a stand on what she or he sees, hears, or feels. If I can doubt the wisdom of my own choices, that is, disagree with myself, who am I to think that everyone will always agree with me or my notion of God?"

"So, the long and short of it is that the jury is still out on who or what God is!"

"I am not aware that any jury has been constituted. What I know for certain is that my God lives. He is eternal and omnipresent...."

"Thank you; don't let's turn this into Scripture 101. Let us stick to the matter before this court. Are you aware that the conflict between and among the rival faiths threatens not only the unity of our country but also risks slowing down the pace of our development?" Thomas changed his tactics.

"We should not be too quick to blame our country's ills on religion. The politicians do not need any help from religion to set one race against the other or to divert the monies needed for capital formation to foreign private accounts. Have you read the latest report from the World Bank which indicates the percentage of the annual budget routinely skimmed off by corrupt politicians and civil servants? I did not see any reference to religion in that report. How about the study carried out by the New Europe Bank?..."

"Thank you. You may step down." Thomas had never cross-examined a more astute witness. He was glad to be rid of Okoye.

It was Kamil's turn to testify. He gladly swore 'in the name of the WGO.' He was certain that the oath meant nothing. With or without it, he was going to give the court a piece of his mind.

As he did when Okoye entered the witness box, Barrister Williams asked for and Kamil supplied all the necessary biographical details. He then handed his witness over to Thomas.

If Thomas had counted on destabilizing Kamil, he miscalculated. Having duly rehearsed with Williams and Okoye how questions were to be answered, Kamil confidently handled every question put to him. Only the one on the Trinity nearly tripped him up. Aware of the long-running battle over the Trinity, Thomas had pointedly asked if Okoye's God the Father, the Son, and the Holy Spirit was the same as the one that Kamil understood as Allah.

"I have nothing to add to what the previous witness said on this subject. If I recall correctly, he told this court that Christians follow their path, while the Muslims follow theirs. It is as if the reverend father was quoting directly from a surah in the Qur'an, that is, the surah in which Allah says (and I reproduce in a language we all understand): '(Muhammad) Say as follows: Oh! Ye non-believers, I worship not that which you worship. You worship not that which I worship. I shall not worship that which you worship and you will not worship that which I worship. To you your way, to me mine.'"

"Spare me! Where is the proof that Allah exists, let alone said all those things attributed to Him?"

"Where is the proof that beauty is truly, absolutely, and universally beautiful? Is that kind of beauty tangible let alone observable? How about our concepts of good, decency, fairness, etc.?"

"My Lord, the witness is asking questions rather than answering the one put to him." Thomas protested, facing the judge.

"The witness will simply answer the question," the judge ruled.

"The God that Okoye and I speak of is above His Throne, everywhere, inside and outside us. He comprehends us but we can never comprehend Him. As a matter of fact, no mind can comprehend Him. When compared to other units of creation, man is too insignificant to demand proof of God's existence. As the author of moral, ecclesiastical, and rational scientific laws, God makes those things happen that He decrees to happen and vetoes any occurrence contrary to His intention. He controls the forces of the universe. He plots the trajectory along which all celestial objects move without colliding with one another or getting in one another's way. When we begin to wonder where God is, He shows up where we least expect—in ourselves, in others known or unknown to us, and in the horizon, far and near. On one side, He unleashes forces that trigger snowstorms, mudslides, earthquakes, and internecine wars. On the other, He endows us with intellect, enriches us with bountiful harvests, and makes sure that comets and meteorites hurtling across space do not collide with our planet and smash us to smithereens. He makes us whole when we are sick and consoles us when we are sad. He comes to our rescue when all hope is lost. With Him in control, the sky stays suspended without pillars or scaffolding. He…"

"Ok, that's enough! Let's move to something else. Does the counsel have any other question for the witness?" Judge Philips guillotined Kamil's tafsir disguised as a response.

"I do, my Lord." Thomas bowed slightly towards the judge before facing Kamil to continue the cross-examination. "You have told us about your own conception of God, but do you think everyone agrees with you?" Thomas looked for a way to divide the opposition.

"No, and I don't expect others to. After all, God Almighty Himself says in the Qur'an…"

"Not another Koranic quotation! I need a straightforward answer to my question, and you have already provided it. What else do you want to add to your 'No'?" Thomas was indignant.

"A lot that will throw light on the case before this honorable court," Kamil answered calmly.

"My Lord, I would have to object! The witness is looking for an opportunity to promote his faith, not to 'throw light' on the case!" Thomas used air quotes to question Kamil's "light-throwing" motive, at the same time fortifying his own point.

"I will decide when he crosses the red line. For now, he is free to, as he said, throw light on the matter before this court," Judge Philips said, clearing Kamil to continue.

"Quite apart from the fact that the Qur'an specifically forbids the application of force in matters of faith, it unequivocally states that if it were the will of Allah, everyone would be a believer. After all, He is the creator of both the believer and the non-believer. My Lord, the first written constitution in the history of human civilization is The Covenant of Madinah. This document not only recognized individual citizen rights but also went on to provide for equal rights for adherents of what we now term rival faiths. Article 25 of the Covenant, for instance, provides as follows: 'And that the Jews of Banu Awf are (an autonomous) community alongside the committed Muslims, the Jews having their deen/faith and the Muslims having their deen. This applies to their dependents and their own selves, except for the unjust or the criminal who do harm to none other than themselves and their clan.' So, my Lord, he is not a Muslim who takes it upon himself to perform a task that is exclusively Allah's, that is, the task of putting faith in people's hearts."

"Are you then saying that the fanatics don't speak for you?"

"That's exactly what I am saying. I am also saying they do not and cannot speak for God."

"My Lord, I am done with this witness. However, I would like to recall the first witness to the stand."

"Objection, my Lord. This is a most unusual request." Temileke's counsel, Stanley, objected.

"The two of you must approach the bench." Philips was not in the mood for another verbal tug of war. "Thomas, what do you need the first witness for?" The judge asked calmly when the three counsels stood directly before him.

"My Lord, when I cross-examined the first witness, this court had not granted the two other witnesses' application for a joinder. Also, the court had not admitted testimonies given in an open-ended format. These developments have brought a totally new complexion to the case. Questions which I would never have dreamt of have now arisen as a result of the new developments." Thomas made a passionate case for Temileke's return to the witness stand.

"And of course, the defense will rather keep these questions to its chest than share them with the plaintiff!" Stanley sneered. Williams, standing by, looked expressionless.

"That is our right under the Civil Procedure Rules, section…" Thomas insisted. He was going to cite the section of the rules in his favor, but the judge, the right hand flailing, stopped him.

"Application to recall Temileke is granted." The judge ruled in Thomas's favor. It was the defense counsel's turn to beam and the plaintiffs' advocates to bristle.

Chapter-61

Faith ordered back to the witness stand

TEMILEKE, BACK IN THE witness box, was jittery. He did not know why the aggressive Thomas wanted him back. Could it be the defense counsel knew about the allegation levied by a rival contractor, to wit, the allegation of offering kickbacks to land a road maintenance contract? Or was it his shoddy implementation of the last road contract? Under the contract's terms, he was to rehabilitate the five-kilometer stretch with four layers of asphalt. However, to pay his church dues and at the same time grease the right palms in the Agency for Public Works Administration, he had left the supposedly revamped motorway with only one layer of asphalt. This was how he allocated twenty percent of the contract cost to the job and split the remaining eighty percent among other interested parties. How was he to explain the discrepancy between the contract and its execution? Jesus! Whom had he offended to be in this kind of hot water? Anyway, his living God would not let him down—not when he had spent part of his hard-earned money championing His cause in a court of law! God forbid! No weapon fashioned against him shall prosper!

"Mr. Temidire Temileke! It's nice to have your back! I am sure you are wondering why we want you back." Thomas looked directly in the witness's eyes. He saw panic's unmistakable signs. That was good. It was a sign that he was right to recall the original plaintiff. A wicked smile played on Thomas's pudgy face. Temileke shrugged his shoulders. The panic in the eyes refused to go away.

"Mr. Temileke, do you believe in God?"

"What a strange question! Of course, I do!" If this was why they wanted him back in the witness stand, he had nothing to worry about. He could even afford to be cocky and assertive.

"The God you believe in, does He approve of lying?"

"Certainly not!" The witness still had no idea where Thomas was going with the question.

"So, your God is happy when you tell the truth, and possibly peeved when you lie. Does that about sum it all up correctly?"

"Yes."

"If that is the case, why did you lie on oath?"

"I don't understand." Temileke was now really scared. He wished he had been allowed to swear in his God's name. At least that God is forbearing, as the WGO was not. If he was found guilty of fudging some facts, he was sure to go to jail. He would also be set back a whole one hundred thousand Dukyarian dollars! Christ!

"Did you tell this court that you had four children?"

"Yes, so what?"

"I put it to you that you have five other children by different women outside your matrimonial home."

"Err, umm, but…"

"I also put it to you that of the four children you call your own, only two are truly, that is, going by DNA results, yours; the other two being products of your wife's indiscretions."

"How did you know that? The information is privileged! We settled that a long time ago!" Temileke protested.

"You told this court that you are a contractor. I further put it to you that a petition is now with the anti-corruption branch of my ministry. In that petition, you are accused of bribing government officials and failing to comply with the work specifications annexed to your contract!" Thomas looked the witness straight in the eyes, watching the latter's reactions.

"Objection, my Lord! Since the allegations against my client are yet to be proved, they cannot be relied on in the proceedings before this court. I therefore move that reference to the allegations be struck from the record." Stanley came to his client's rescue.

"Objection sustained. And by the way, apart from questioning the witness's character, I fail to see the relevance of the questions about his extramarital affairs or the judgment he exercised in handling his contractual obligations. Any other questions?" Judge Philips practically untied the noose Thomas had planned to fasten on Temileke's neck.

"No, my Lord," the defense counsel responded, downcast.

"In that case, and unless there are additional witnesses, the counsels must be ready to deliver their closing addresses a week from today. Case adjourned." And the gavel brought the day's proceedings to an end.

Chapter-62

The jury is out, but not for long

A WEEK LATER, THE three counsels gave their closing addresses. Both Williams and Stanley harped on the individual right to freedom of belief and man's constant dependence on God. "We are effectively surrounded by God and by forces totally loyal to Him. There is no escaping His Divine Presence or Power!" Williams had argued.

Thomas, by contrast, aimed his salvos at religion's inconsistency with reason, the lack of a precise definition of God, along with the conflict that such imprecision generates; the believers' hypocrisy, humbug, and affectation of moral superiority; and above all, religion's inability to correct human character flaws. Having called Temileke out for lying on oath, Thomas prayed the court to throw the book at the witness. He must be sent to jail for six months and fined one hundred thousand Dukyarian dollars, the government's legal counsel insisted.

The judge duly noted the counsels' submissions. He adjourned the hearing to allow him to draft his judgment.

Okoye returned to Utako, while Kamil headed straight to Hayat Hospital to check on Abdullah. Unknown to Kamil, government agents were hot on his heels. Sam's minions eventually got what they were after—the reason for Kamil's constant visit to Hayat. They promptly apprised their boss of their findings.

Chapter-63

And now, the kerfuffle in the church!

PASTOR EMMAN HAD ALSO planned to be at the High Court. However, since he was tied up in another case at the Wuse Magistrate Court, he would have to wait to be updated by the Dukyarian Television Service on how the Temileke case was resolved. In the meantime, he had to give the battle on the Wuse front his undivided attention.

Emman had expected that as General Overseer, he had the prerogative to hire and fire any church employee. To his surprise, Akin Mosefejo had filed a case at the lower court questioning this prerogative. The deputy had instituted a cause of action at the lower court challenging the decision to remove him as the second-in-command. What was worse, Akin had levied grave allegations against Emman, the head of the church. Emman had retaliated by excavating evidence of his deputy's misdeeds, ready to lay it bear at the opportune moment.

Whether by accident or design, the two cases had been listed for hearing the same day. As usual, the session at the Magistrate Court began at ten o'clock that morning, followed thirty minutes later by the High Court's commencement of hearing in the Temileke case.

For different reasons, the two cases sparked lively interest. Where the public was looking for illumination in the Temileke case, titillation of the senses would appear to be the sole object of the curiosity in the Mosafejo case's highs and lows. In other words, interest in the first case was basically meant to serve a higher purpose, notably, interrogating the legitimacy of the state's sovereign powers to freeze, inhibit, or otherwise reset, the spirit of the individual. By contrast, the average Dukyarian's fascination with scandal was behind the inquisitiveness about Mosafejo's lawsuit.

Although the procedure applied in trying cases at the lower court was more relaxed than that of the High Court, witnesses still had no choice but to swear "in the name of the WGO." Knowing that the WGO would not let perjury go unpunished, witnesses went overboard to check their words' veracity before uttering them.

As the plaintiff, Akin was the first to testify. Led in evidence by his lawyer, Ben Kolade, Akin told the packed court how he and Emman had met. "Unemployment brought the respondent and me together. We forged a strong bond after showing up at countless job interviews and always, or should I say, unfailingly, returning home unemployed."

"Whose idea was it to establish the Abounding Grace Ministries?" Kolade asked his client.

"The respondent's."

"How did you get involved?"

"He phoned to ask if I would be interested in working on a project with him. The project later turned out to be the Abounding Grace Ministries."

"Did you accept his invitation?"

"Yes, without hesitation!"

"What role did you play in the founding of the Ministries?"

"I came up with ideas of how to start small and grow big."

"You lost me there. Can you let this court know what you mean by starting small and growing big?"

"Certainly. The idea to start the church came from the respondent. That was about all he brought to the project. That is, if you forget his harebrained idea of starting with universities from the get-go!" The swipe at Emman's half-baked moneymaking idea drew laughter from the crowd. Akin had to pause until the magistrate's gavel restored calm to the chamber of justice.

"It was I who recommended starting with open air service, then erecting tents and scaffolding on vacant parcels of land, and, when we were able to put enough money aside, building permanent structures. The idea of headhunting real and counterfeit miracle makers was also mine. In other words, I am the brain behind the swelling crowds you see in the church and at revivals. Oh, I forgot, the business of dying was Emman's idea. Although I wasn't exactly crazy about funeral homes initially, I must give him credit for an idea which made the Abounding Grace Ministries a tidy sum within a short period. The funeral homes happened to be the fastest growing branch of our business."

"You said something about real and fake miracle workers. What exactly do you mean by that?" Kolade nudged his client.

"Emman and I knew from day one that if we were to succeed, we had to get individuals capable of making the impossible happen in the full view of the people. Dukyarians will believe anything as long as it is something that only a few could explain but none would understand." Akin's joke had the spectators in stitches.

Sam was the only exception. He cast a contemptuous glance at the crowd around him, wondering if they realized that they were the butt of Akin's joke. These sorry excuses for human beings! Can't they see that the so-called men of God are taking them for a ride? Can't these gullible, short-sighted Dukyarians engage their thinking faculties for once? In disgust, he quietly left the Magistrate Court and headed towards the High Court. One of his minions stayed behind to follow the proceedings and report to Sam later.

"Are you then saying that persons skilled in making or faking miracles are on the staff of the Abounding Grace Ministries?" Kolade continued his cross-examination.

"That's precisely what I am saying!" Akin replied, standing upright, his face looking stern. If he had to go down, he would take the entire church with him.

"What is the net worth of the Ministries?" Kolade asked his witness.

"The church accounts are never audited. However, my own independent research indicates that since we started operating, we have accumulated assets worth seventy-five billion Dukyarian dollars." Akin had done his homework.

"That's a whopping amount!" Kolade exclaimed. "Who are the signatories to the bank accounts?"

"The General Overseer and his Personal Assistant."

"That's interesting! If the Personal Assistant is a signatory, where does that leave you, the Deputy General Overseer?" Kolade prompted his client.

"That is a million-dollar question only the General Overseer can answer."

"But the General Overseer claims, in his counter affidavit, that you diverted and mismanaged church resources. How did you manage to do that without being a signatory to the church's accounts?" Kolade asked, casting a sideways and taunting glance in Emman's direction.

"That is one miracle the General Overseer will have to explain to this court." Akin again sent the spectators squeaking with laughter.

"If the respondent agrees to reinstate you to your former position, will you consider working with him again?"

"Highly unlikely. We have gone past kissing and making up. We have now reached a stage at which we should be thinking of splitting the church assets and going our separate ways." Akin was resolute.

"What percentage of the church's net worth do you consider rightly belongs to you?"

"Fifty. Fifty percent. No more, no less." Akin wouldn't settle for anything less than the clerical empire's two-way split, with one half going to the General Overseer and the other half ending up with him, the Deputy.

"I am through with the witness, my Lord." Kolade bowed and returned to his seat. It was now the respondent's turn to cross-examine the plaintiff.

"I am Hanbali Gidado. I am representing Mr. Emmanuel Kalu, the respondent in this case. Do I have my Lord's permission to cross-examine the first witness?"

"You do."

"Mr. Akin Mosafejo. That is your name, right?"

"Yes, that's my name."

"Akin Mosafejo is an Odu name. What does Akin mean?" Gidado continued his cross-examination.

"Akin means a man of valor. A brave, courageous, fearless man!"

"How about Mosafejo. What does it mean?"

"It means 'I run away from litigation or I avoid bickering and confrontation.'"

"Don't you see any contradiction in your name, and possibly in your personality? As implied in your name, yours is a split personality. One side of you is valiant, the other is spineless." Gidado wanted to unsettle the plaintiff.

"Anybody is entitled to his own opinion. I know who I am, and I know that spineless doesn't even come close to defining me." Akin foiled the destabilization plot with a confident response.

"Then it's your opinion against mine. I am happy to leave it at that. Let's now return to your testimony. So we understand each other, you agree that the idea to establish the Abounding Grace Ministries was entirely my client's. Yes or No."

"Yes."

"You agree that before my client invited you, he already decided to establish a church?"

"Yes."

"Do you know what is called intellectual property?" Gidado implicitly cast Akin as an uninformed and frivolous litigant.

"No, but I am sure you are going to tell me, a Business Administration graduate." Akin responded to Gidado's condescension with sarcasm.

"No, I won't tell you. This court will do that in the fullness of time. For now, let us continue answering the questions as they come. And the next one is: What specific role did you play in starting the church on a small scale and watching it grow into the billion-dollar entity it is today?"

"I already told this court. You want me to repeat?" Akin was getting prickly.

"If you don't mind." Gidado insisted on a proper response to his question.

"I came up with the ideas of open air service, the erection of tents on open spaces, and the construction of permanent structures."

"Do you agree that implementing your ideas costs money?"

"Sure."

"Do I take that to mean 'yes'?"

"Yes."

"How much exactly did you contribute when my client was raising the capital needed to move your ideas from the drawing board to reality?"

"I contributed nothing, but…"

"That's all I need," Gidado said, vetoing the witness's attempt to elucidate and expand his testimony. He instead followed up with another question. "Did you ask my client how he raised the capital?"

"No! Why should I?" Akin glared at the opposing counsel.

"You are asking me or this court? I take it that the answer to the question is: No, you did not ask my client how he raised the capital. I move that it be so reflected in the record, unless the plaintiff's counsel has any objection!" Gidado sought to pin Akin down to a specific response.

"No objection." Kolade saw no reason to make a case out of an inconsequential matter like how to interpret the word No.

"I thank my learned colleague. Now back to you, Mr. Akin Mosafejo. You told this court that you were the brain behind the real and the fake miracles performed under the auspices of the Abounding Grace Ministries—the miracles that pulled the crowds and brought lots of cash. Right?"

"Right!" He answered truthfully, aware of the consequences of mendacity.

"If I understand you well, you are the brain behind the miracle-making racket. Right?"

"I wouldn't exactly call it a racket...." Akin fidgeted

as he tried to get out of a linguistic trap he unwittingly set for himself.

"What would you call it then? Possibly, a swindle? A scam? Or a rip-off?" Gidado fired off his questions, a derisive expression on his face.

"No! What I mean is that the idea of using miracles to mobilize resources came from me."

"Do you consider yourself an honest person?"

"Certainly!"

"Even when you are the brain behind the plot to hoodwink unsuspecting individuals into parting with their hard-earned money?"

"Isn't that what evolution is all about—survival of the smartest?"

"Again, are you asking me or this court?"

"I am asking anybody who's ready to answer. This is the situation as I see it: the strong devour the weak, the Big Man walks all over the small, and those with power and money treat those without with contempt. In my own case, I spent years applying for jobs, but each time, only well-connected candidates got appointed. I don't see anything wrong in making the best of the only opportunity I had— which was to supply miracles on demand. Dukyarians love miracles. Woe betide a church that is unable to perform or fake them."

"I suppose that explains it…."

"Explains what? I don't understand where the question is going."

"In that case, wait until the question arrives at its destination before answering it. And here goes, do you think it is right to make hay while the sun shines?"

"The question is still vague."

"Do you think that evolutionary morality justifies defrauding your employer? Do you think that evolution is consistent with your doctrine, that of survival of the craftiest?" Gidado hit the nail on the head.

"I don't know what you are talking about. I don't know about any fraud or craftiness."

"How about the claims you submitted in respect of your recent visit to Laguna? Look at this voucher. It shows that you claimed hotel expenses for ten nights, whereas you and your girlfriend stayed at the church's guest house in Revival Village gratis, with full board and lodging. You also submitted bogus claims for 'out of pocket expenses' amounting to forty-five thousand Dukyarian dollars. Can you confirm if the signatures on the certified true copies of the payment advice are yours?"

"They are mine." Akin confirmed after checking the papers with squinted eyes.

"My Lord, defense requests permission to tender the payment slips as exhibits A, B, C, D, and E. We also have several other exhibits to support our contention that the plaintiff has been systematically defrauding the Abounding Grace Ministries and lodging the proceeds in his bank account at Area 8."

"Permission to tender exhibits granted."

The court clerk duly admitted the exhibits in evidence. Even though he sat too far from the scene of the day's bomb explosion to worry about his safety, the magistrate decided it was time to adjourn.

Chapter-64

Miracles to revive a dead business and wreck a marriage

WHEN THE MAGISTRATE COURT resumed its session, Kolade named two other witnesses for the plaintiff. The first, Cletus Daniel, a church elder, having duly sworn in WGO's name to tell the truth and nothing but the truth, testified that his ten-year, and largely blissful, marriage hit the rocks after the General Overseer put his wife in the family way. He had planned to institute civil proceedings for the dissolution of the marriage, but he was dissuaded by the Deputy General Overseer, who assured him that the church's prayer warriors would see to it that his floundering business picked up again. Unfortunately, the miracle he was promised never happened.

Rather than pick up, his dead business stayed dead. To make matters worse, when the bank repossessed his mansion, his wife deserted him. Mrs. Cletus Daniel moved to an apartment rented, furnished, and paid for by the General Overseer. At the time he gave his deposition, his wife was nursing the third child for the head of Abounding Grace Ministries. He had no choice but to pull out of the church.

The witness sent the spectators rollicking with laughter when he regretted ever going into the import and export business. "I should have started a church of my own! At least, I would not have had to worry about foreign exchange fluctuations, fiscal deficits, and macroeconomic instability. Instead of having to bribe officials to get my goods cleared at the wharf without paying custom duties, the officials would have lined up outside my door waiting to pay for paranormal acts, acts mostly contrived and cleverly choreographed by charlatans. Too bad. It is too late!" Cletus bit his right index finger. Signs of premature aging were visible on his face—a gaunt look, baggy eyelids, a sagging jaw, sunken cheeks, graying beard, and a skin waxen enough to require the attention of a qualified dermatologist. On top of it all, the twists of fate had left a permanent frown on the face.

Gidado wasn't buying Cletus's act—the act of an upstanding citizen victimized by heartless individuals. The respondent's counsel wouldn't let Cletus leave the witness stand without clearing up a few knotty issues. "According to your testimony, you were once a rich man. Yes?"

"Yes!"

"When you had the money, what proportion did you spend on your wife and children?" Gidado asked, turning his back to Cletus.

"How can you or anybody ask me how I run my home?" Cletus didn't see how what he spent or failed to spend on his household was anyone's business.

"My Lord, I request that the witness be made aware that I am the one that gets to ask the questions here. His is to answer."

"Mr. Cletus, simply answer the question." The magistrate was firm.

"I put food on the table. Didn't I?" Cletus responded defiantly.

"What else did you do besides putting food on the table?"

"I paid the school fees of one of the three children."

"That's interesting! How about the other two children? Who took care of their education?"

"My wife. She could afford to. She ran her own vehicle maintenance and lubricants workshop along the Airport Road."

"But weren't you the head of the house, the bread winner, the one that every member looked up to for the satisfaction of basic needs?"

"Yes, I was, but that does not mean they could dump all their worries on me?"

"You consider giving your children sound education a worry dumped on you?"

"That didn't come out right. What I meant to say is..."

"Let us park what you meant to say by the roadside. That way, it will be in plain view and passersby would be able to form their own judgment. Let us for now move to a simpler question. Would you consider buying your wife a car a worry dumped on you?"

"Certainly! She had a car of her own. She could afford…"

"That's ok, we don't want to saddle you with that onerous responsibility. How about purchasing a brand-new Thunderbird sports car for a girlfriend? Is that a worry dumped on you?"

"It would be if it were true!"

"Yes, Sir, it is true. You bought a brand-new Thunderbird for Miss Dorothy Anyanwu and registered it in her name at the Wuse Vehicle Registry three years ago. Here are the notarized copies of the sales invoice, the ownership booklet, and the receipt for the payment you made to renew the vehicle sticker last year." Gidado showed Cletus copies of the exhibits which the defendant intended to tender. "Do you agree that the transactions recorded on the papers actually took place? Remember that you are under oath."

"Yes."

"My Lord, defense requests permission to tender exhibits one, two and three in evidence."

"Granted."

The court clerk promptly admitted the new exhibits.

"We are done with this witness, my Lord."

Cletus stepped down.

Chapter-65

The plaintiff, the witness, and the character question

THE THIRD WITNESS FOR the plaintiff, Catherine Henshaw, stepped into the witness stand and took the oath.

"Ms. Catherine Henshaw, are you married or single?" Kolade started examining his witness.

"I am single."

"What is your relationship with the plaintiff?"

"We are friends."

"What is your relationship with the respondent?"

"We are friends."

"In other words, you know both the plaintiff and the respondent sufficiently well to testify about their character?"

"Yes. In fact, I have known the respondent longer than I have the plaintiff."

"That's interesting. How long have you known the respondent?"

"Eight years."

"Has he ever hit on you during that time?"

"Did you say 'ever'? He had his eyes on me from day one, and he did not stop trying his luck until he realized that he was wasting his time—and mine."

"What do you mean by that?"

"He did not leave me alone until he realized that it is the plaintiff, not him, whom I want to be with."

"Can you tell this court what you know about the plaintiff's character since you two became close friends?"

"He is a decent, polished, considerate, capable, and hardworking individual."

"How about the respondent?"

"He is the exact opposite."

"Can you please clarify?"

"The respondent thinks about none but himself. Believing that money could buy my love, he told me about the wealth he was sitting on and how it would be nice to share it with me."

"That still doesn't say much about his character. Is there any concrete evidence of his misdeed, as in financial recklessness?"

"Objection, my Lord. The leading question serves no purpose other than to coach the witness and literally lead her to a predetermined, or shall I say preferred, answer."

"Sustained. The Counsel will refrain from asking leading questions."

"As my Lord pleases. Question withdrawn. Now, Ms. Henshaw, what evidence do you have to support your contentions on the respondent's character?"

"He told me that the wealth he spoke about was under his absolute control. He could withdraw any amount he wished as he was the primary signatory to the church's accounts. The other signatory, his personal assistant, was just added as a formality."

"Objection! Hearsay! I move that the witness's testimony be ruled inadmissible."

"Sustained. That part of the witness's testimony should be deleted from the record. The witness should stick to what she knows for a fact, not what another person told her about a third party. Is that clear?"

"Clear, my Lord. The respondent rests its case." Kolade bowed and returned to his seat.

Gidado tugged at his right shoulder as if making sure that the gown stayed in place. He moved close to the plaintiff's witness. "Miss Catherine Henshaw! A fine name befitting a pretty woman. I am sure any man would do anything to get your attention. Right?"

Catherine blushed. She didn't know what to say. She said nothing.

"Ok, Ms. Henshaw, you told this court that you are single. Isn't 'searching' the fitting response to the question 'are you married or single'?"

"Searching for what? I don't recall taking an advert space in the newspapers letting the world know that I am searching for something. I have everything I need and want."

"Could one of this 'everything' be the hunky plaintiff sitting over there?"

"Objection! The question has no bearing on the case. After all, the witness is not on trial."

"Sustained. The Counsel should get to the point quickly. Time is of the essence. Get on with it!"

"As my Lord pleases. Now, Miss Henshaw, you described the plaintiff as, among other things, capable. Can you please tell this court how you arrived at this judgment? For instance, can you list the assignments you gave him and then rate his performance?"

"Objection!"

"Overruled! The witness will answer the question, more so as it came directly from her own testimony."

"Well, I can't think of any specific performance right now."

"How about his performance as regards one assignment called 'bedmatics'?"

"Objection! That is lewd, cheap, and downright offensive!" Kolade knew where Gidado was going. He had to stop him, no matter what.

"Sustained! The Counsel will not turn my court into a show of shame!"

"I apologize, my Lord." Gidado bowed towards the magistrate and then resumed his cross-examination. "You told this court that you and the plaintiff are friends. Is yours the platonic or the boy-meets-girl type of friendship?"

"Is the plaintiff my boyfriend? You bet. Am I his girlfriend? Oh yes, I am!"

"That means there is nothing you won't do or say on his behalf. Right?"

"Yes, especially, since I know…"

"Thank you." Gidado curtly stretched his right palm, signaling that Catherine had said enough. "Did you and the plaintiff ever travel to Laguna together?"

"Yes."

"Did you both stay at the Abounding Grace guest house at the Revival Village?"

"Yes."

"Did you know that your stay at the guest house was at the Abounding Grace Ministries' expense, that the plaintiff didn't pay a dime for your board, lodging, laundry, and phone calls?"

"Yes."

"Do you know that at the time you both stayed at the guest house free of charge, the plaintiff collected his usual allowances for the duration of your stay, that is, for nights ranging from seven to ten?"

"No, I didn't know."

"Do you know that the plaintiff billed the Abounding Grace Ministries for personal expenses by presenting them as 'out-of-pocket expenses'?"

"No. I didn't know."

"My Lord, the defense rests."

"The witness may step down and return to her seat." The magistrate directed and Catherine complied.

Chapter-66

The defendant becomes his own witness

"NOW THAT THE COURT has listened to the plaintiff and his witnesses, is the defense ready with its own witnesses?" the magistrate asked Gidado.

"Yes, my Lord. We have only one witness, the defendant himself." Gidado stood up and pointed at Emman.

"Call the defendant to the witness stand and swear him in," the magistrate ordered his clerk.

Emman promptly took the witness stand and, as expected, swore in the WGO's name to tell the truth and nothing but the truth.

"Can you let this court have your name in full?" Gidado began to interrogate his witness.

"I am Pastor Emmanuel Kalu."

"Is 'Pastor' not a religious title, and is retaining it as part of your name consistent with the Imperial Proclamation banning public display of religious affiliations and symbols?"

"Your observation is correct. However, since 'Pastor' is the name by which people know me, I decided to retain it, come hell or high water. It is like someone calling himself "Mr. White," "Mr. Black," "Mr. Wood," or something along those lines. It does not follow that Mr. White is a white man. And Mr. Black may be anything but black. After all, what's in a name? A name is simply that. Since there is no law forbidding one to answer to any name of his or her choosing, I settled for Pastor and assimilated it into my identity. I doubt that the Imperial Proclamation would have any objection to that. Anyway, the Proclamation doesn't dabble in something as pedestrian as christening." The Pastor had obviously given the matter a lot of thought.

"Pastor Emmanuel Kalu, you listened to the plaintiff's testimony, to wit, that although the idea of establishing the church came from you, it was he who proposed how to go about implementing it. Is that correct?"

"That is partly correct. As he himself acknowledged, I was not totally clueless regarding how to take the original idea forward."

"How much did it cost you to move from tents erected on open spaces at the initial stage to the permanent structures constructed thereafter?"

"Ten million two hundred and fifty thousand Dukyarian dollars."

"How much did the plaintiff contribute?"

"Nothing. Not a dime."

"Then, how did you raise the capital?"

"I took out a bank loan and pledged the land inherited from my late father as collateral."

"Did you and the plaintiff draw up any partnership agreement before, during, or after the establishment of the Abounding Grace Ministries?"

"No."

"Why?"

"Because there was no need to. He was not and has never been a partner."

"If he was not a partner, then exactly what was he?"

"An employee, like any other."

"But the person you call an employee is demanding the rights of a partner—specifically, a fifty percent slice of the Abounding Grace Ministries Inc. when carved up."

"He cannot be serious! He has no stake or share in the business. He took no risk. He bought no shares. He invested nothing, except, possibly, the working hours that he logged in like any other regular employee. He at no time asked for, neither was he paid, any dividends. He knew his place—the place of an employee on regular salary. Fortunately, no month ended without his salary being lodged in his bank account!" Emman had precise ideas about Akin's place in the church hierarchy.

"What was his net annual salary, that is, his salary after tax and other deductions?"

"Twelve million, eight hundred and fifty thousand Dukyarian dollars."

"Is he entitled to severance pay?"

"Yes, six months' salary, provided his separation is not due to misconduct warranting summary dismissal."

"So, are you saying that he forfeited that benefit because of his persistent act of indiscretion?"

"Yes."

"The defense rests."

It was now the plaintiff's turn to grill the defendant. Kolade instantly jumped to his feet and marched towards the witness box. "Are you sure that the plaintiff was just an employee?" Hints of mockery appearing on his face, Kolade looked intently at the respondent.

"Positive."

"Can you define an 'employee'?" The mordant expression on Kolade's face fleetingly unnerved the witness.

"An employee is one who is employed to carry out specific tasks and is paid either by the hour or by the quantity and quality of outputs produced." Emman quickly regained his composure.

"How then would you define a partner, one without any specified tasks and who takes no pay?" Kolade changed tactics, hoping to get the better of the opponent.

"The basic dictionary definition of a partner is one who participates with others in running a business. He or she has a stake, equal or unequal, in the running of a going concern." Emman must have known this question was coming. He was ready for it.

"Will you agree that someone who watched a business grow from nothing to a multi-billion-dollar enterprise has passed the 'stake' test and met the partnership threshold?" Kolade proceeded doggedly with his quest for disclosure.

"Staying with a business is a purely voluntary decision. An employee who decides to stay rather than bail out at any time has exercised his or her free will. Such an employee has no stake in the business and cannot carry or represent himself as a partner." Emman picked another hole in Kolade's partnership theory.

"Have you on many occasions publicly referred to the plaintiff as your 'right-hand man'?" Kolade looked for another opening.

"Yes."

"What is a right-hand man if not a partner?"

"I cannot prevent anyone from defining the term his own way. However, in the sense that I often use it, a 'right-hand man' is a man Friday, a minion, a lackey, a subordinate, a hired hand, an employee, at best, a mid-ranking one!" Emman blocked Kolade's new partnership crevice. The witness silently recalled but conveniently avoided mentioning the fact that without his deputy's ingenuity, the department responsible for fake miracles in the Abounding Grace Ministries would cease to function.

Emman's mind of course kept going back to the difficult road ahead. After all, the only person capable of performing genuine miracles was a voodoo priest, called Babalawo, whom Akin had brought from his village. If Akin pulled out, he was sure to take his Odu kinsman along with him. That would be the end of paranormal conceptions by barren women, the money potion eagerly sought by businessmen, and the amulets that assured politicians of blind following. With Akin's Babalawo gone, it would no longer be possible for jealous wives to reprogram their lascivious husbands' minds in their favor and against other women. Eunuchs whose horses would never kick without the Babalawo's virility herb would just have to keep popping Viagra and hope it worked.

Emman knew the risk he was running moving against his deputy. He was nonetheless ready for any eventuality. The man gave him no choice. It was either him or Mosafejo. He decided to safeguard his interest and let the troublemaker go.

All Emman would have to do was go to his village and return with his own miracle worker, a dibea known far and wide for his spellbinding ability to make the impossible happen.

"You said that after serving the Abounding Grace Ministries for years, your 'mid-ranking employee' is not entitled to the severance pay provided for in his terms and conditions of service. How is that?" Kolade brought the witness's wandering mind back to the courtroom.

"The terms and conditions of service which you referred to are clear on this: an employee found guilty of misconduct is liable not only to be dismissed without notice but also to forfeit his terminal benefits. We can let him retain the house he currently occupies. We shall also not repossess the SUV attached to his office. That is all we can do for him!"

"How nice and generous of you? Have you forgotten that, under our law, before a person is 'found guilty' of anything, he or she must be properly tried and given an opportunity to defend him- or her-self? Did you ever think of constituting a panel to try the plaintiff? Was he allowed to defend himself?" Kolade's rapid-fire questions further unsettled Emman's roaming mind.

"Well, you were here when your client admitted defrauding us. What other trial do you need?" Emman answered lamely. His mind was apparently still on what to do to rebuild the miracles department from the ground up after he and Akin had parted ways.

"I take that as an admission that my client was not given a fair hearing. He was found guilty before he had any opportunity to defend himself. I hope that the record will so reflect. We are done with the witness, my Lord." Kolade bowed and walked back to his seat next to Akin's. Despite the body blows delivered on his behalf by his counsel, Akin remained tense. Emman too stepped down and returned to his seat next to his counsel's. His countenance appeared less cheery than it was at the beginning of the trial.

The magistrate didn't look at anybody's face to decide who looked happy or crestfallen. Having listened to the two parties, he adjourned the hearing to give himself time to weigh the evidence tendered by both. He planned to draft his judgment thereafter.

Chapter-67

How's the war going?

SAM GOT TO HIS OFFICE early that morning. His secretary immediately passed on a message. He was to be at the Martial Law Administrator's office at exactly ten o'clock. The secretary had no idea why His Excellency wanted to see him. The message was terse and to the point: be at the MLA's office at exactly ten o'clock. That was all the secretary knew. That was all she told Sam.

How do you prepare for a meeting without an agenda? Sam asked himself. Or could it be the boss wanted an update on the Temileke case? That shouldn't prove difficult to handle. The case was proceeding apace, although nobody could yet predict the outcome. Yes, His Excellency must have been following the other case at the magistrate court. If he wanted Sam's opinion on how the government might turn the commotion in Emman's church to its own advantage, he should be able to come up with something. He hoped he wouldn't be asked any question on the swelling crowds sustaining Okoye's and Kamil's street protests. He also had no idea how to cage Abu Mamba. He kept staring at his wristwatch as he pondered responses to questions likely to be posed by the Administrator.

To be on safe side, he left his office early. He got to the third-floor venue of the impromptu meeting at ten minutes to ten. Kike politely led him to the waiting lounge and bade him sit on one of the vacant seats. Two or three minutes later, the Cabinet Secretary and Head of the Civil

Service leisurely strolled in. Sam instantly jumped to his feet. "Good morning, Sir."

"Good morning, Sam. Are you also here for the emergency meeting?" The Cabinet Secretary amiably responded.

"Yes, Sir. But to be frank, Sir, I have no clue what the meeting is about." Sam was hoping the Cabinet Secretary would give him a heads-up so he could send his brain on over-drive and line up answers to probable questions.

"Welcome to the club. I suppose our curiosity will soon be satisfied." The Cabinet Secretary's response added nothing to what his subordinate didn't know. Sam remained jittery.

His anxiety mounted when the Inspector-General of Police marched in, with the Director of Prisons in tow. No, he mused, these people aren't here to frog-march anyone, least of all me, to prison. Anyway, he could not remember committing any misdemeanor, much less a treasonable felony. And even if he stood accused of committing either, His Excellency would not go through the elaborate process of inviting these big wigs to his office to witness his apprehension. The government wouldn't even treat Dukyaria's Number One enemy, Mamba, that way. As the Cabinet Secretary said, our curiosity will soon be satisfied. Sam tried to calm himself.

At two minutes to ten, Kike walked into the lounge and ushered the high-ranking functionaries to His Excellency's presence. As Sam expected, the poker-faced Deputy was already in the room. The clone stood by Homkwap's side, his right hand on the throne. "Take your seats and make yourselves comfortable." That was Homkwap's way of welcoming his visitors.

The Administrator and his Deputy soon joined the others seated around the oval table, with Hompkwap in his usual seat at the head, and his cloned Deputy close by. The other attendees knew their places around the table. They promptly planted themselves in their seats.

"Gentlemen, I called this meeting to fill you in on the telephone conversation I had with the WGO's High Commissioner for Secularism, Professor Brad Cunningham last night. He told me that the Commissioner-General has expressed grave concern about the turn of events in Dukyaria. The Commissioner-General would have talked to me directly, but since he had to rush to India at short notice to mollify the restive leaders and members of a nationalist group, he directed Cunningham to hold a video conference with me and my lieutenants at four o'clock tomorrow afternoon, our time. The Commissioner-General's Chief of Staff, Ms. Evangelica Torres, will stand in for him at the conference. I also understand that the High Commissioner for Militarism, Marshall Popov, will participate in the video conference. Since the WGO side will ask direct, possibly, awkward, questions, my Deputy and I thought it fit to convene this emergency meeting to brainstorm our likely responses. Are you with me so far?" He looked round the table for hints of perplexity.

Homwkap saw no sign of incomprehension—except the blank expression on Sam's face. "Is anything in what I just said not clear to you, Sam?" The Administrator trained his eyes on the head of the Re-education Monitoring Agency.

331

"No, Your Excellency! Everything is clear." Sam responded truthfully. What he left out was the error that he spotted in the pronunciation of the Chief of Staff's first name. However, who was he to tell His Excellency that the correct name was 'Evangelista', not 'Evangelica'?

"In that case, lose that perplexed look! While you are at it, let us have an update on where we are regarding the fanatics in our midst. I am pretty certain that Professor Cunningham will ask hard questions on what we have done, or are doing, to obliterate religion from the people's hearts and to banish any of its manifestations in public places." Homkwap put Sam on the spot.

With so many things happening at the same time, which should he start with? Sam had to think fast and say something. "Your Excellency, we have made tremendous progress in spite of the formidable challenges we face." He replied from two sides of the mouth. He was glad that at least, he had something to say. He was not caught totally flat-footed. That must count for something. But he needed to say more. He needed to hype the 'progress' made on his watch and minimize the obstacles in his path. Progress. Progress. Progress. He quickly searched his memory for indicators of progress. Suddenly, it dawned on him to start with the most unlikely and least believable sign of headway in the war on religion. "Your Excellency, people will think that I am crazy, but our most reliable ally in the war on religion is Abu Mamba!" He paused for reactions.

"Preposterous! If you have nothing sensible to say, why not shut the hell up?" The usually unflappable Cabinet Secretary fired the first salvo.

"I too am shocked to realize that we have a mole in the government's nerve center. It's surprising that the terrorists' spokesman has been with us for so long without showing up on our radar." The Chief Commissioner of Police spoke next. He tapped his left palm with his wand, a sign that he was mad as hell.

"You humans are difficult to understand. You mean you secreted all these treacherous ideas in your head without once revealing yourself!" The cloned Deputy intervened, his face totally expressionless.

"Well, any time the Chief Commissioner of Police sends the criminal to us, we shall set him right," the Director of Prisons said, notifying those present of his readiness to clamp Sam in his jail. Every speaker wanted to curry Homkwap's favor at Sam's expense.

"That's enough. Let us hear him out. Let him show us how our Number One Enemy suddenly became our bosom friend." The Martial Law Administrator took effective control of the meeting. He told the others to shut up and allow the person who stirred up the hornet's nest to contain the fallout.

"Your Excellency, and Sirs, I would be less than candid if I were to say I didn't expect this type of reaction. I did expect to be misunderstood. That is why I came ready to defend what may at first appear an outlandish idea. My otherwise controversial view starts from a simple premise: if men and women of faith claim to be loyal to one and the same God, why would one sect need to massacre another in the same God's name? That of course is not where I am going, Your Excellency. If the WGO asks us what we are doing to rein in the terrorists, we can confidently say that we are fighting them on two fronts—the military, and the psychological fronts. As our special forces comb the Gashaka-Mambilla Plateau to ferret out Mamba and his band of terrorists, we are discreetly waging propaganda battles in newspapers, on television, on the radio, and on the internet. Even if we have not yet succeeded in capturing Mamba or in ending his insurgency, we are still succeeding in planting doubts about blind belief in the average Dukyarian mind. We are using Homo Haram's terrorism against Moslem fanatics in particular and against all manners of believers in general. In this regard, we must highlight the cooperation we have received from newspaper editors and a corps of dedicated current affairs analysts working in close collaboration with the Re-education Monitoring Agency. I don't know, Sirs, if I am making any sense."

"Go on! We are listening." Homkwap, an expressionless look on his face, asked Sam to continue.

Buoyed by the First Citizen's show of support, Sam proceeded with the rest of his report. "There is still a lot we can do. Depending on the outcome of the two cases pending at the High and the Magistrate Courts, we can take the psychological battle to the next level. For now, we are closely monitoring the movements of the dramatis personae. I refer in particular to Reverend Father Okoye and Sheikh Kamil, both of whom are leading the protests against the same-sex marriage law. The fact that Temileke brought a cause of action against the conversion of places of worship to re-education centers is by itself something to celebrate. It's an alarm signal. It is a sign of panic, a sign that our policy is working and that our inspectors are effectively supervising the evolution of the places of worship into re-education centers. Anyway, Temileke may yet live to regret his action. It will be a miracle if he does not go to jail. After all, he perjured himself and breached the key provisions of the new Civil Procedure Rules. The only person I pity is Pastor Emmanuel Kalu. He was never a threat to us. I was even counting on bringing him to our side and unleashing his forces on Okoye and Kamil. Too bad that he has a lot on his plate right now. He is locked in a tough legal battle with his deputy, Akin Mosafejo. Again, nobody knows how that case will end. We are keeping our eyes on it. As soon as the Magistrate rules one way or the other, we shall decide what to do. I wish to assure His Excellency that win or lose, Emman will be an asset in our war on religion. He is a pawn on our chess board. Your Excellency, Sirs, I think I should stop for now."

Homkwap liked the presentation. He was impressed with Sam's military strategic approach to the challenge on hand. Still, as the meeting's chair, he had to suspend judgment until the others had had a say.

"You seem to have under-estimated the military challenge posed by the footloose Homo Haram terrorists." The Cabinet Secretary picked holes in Sam's presentation.

"Let's leave purely military questions to professionals like my deputy and myself. We shall respond to those if and when they come up in the video conference. Let's, for now, focus on the broad legal and political questions alluded to in Sam's update." Homkwap came to Sam's rescue again. Something about the career civil servant must be appealing to the Administrator. It must be either the cold, conniving, constantly evolving Machiavellian character, or the ability to reduce knotty, multifaceted, seemingly impregnable challenges into a one-page memorandum.

"I think the report about covers the progress we have made in recent weeks. However, I am sure that New York will be interested in cold, hard facts, like the number of terrorists captured or killed, the number of troublemakers we have behind bars, and the number of places of worship effectively transformed into re-education centers," the Chief Commissioner of Police observed. He was determined to impress His Excellency. What better way was there than belittling the cocky Sam's contribution?

"You must have read my mind. I do have the number of terrorists captured or killed. However, you, as the head of the police, need to tell us how many fanatics you have arrested in the last three months, and the Director of Prisons will let us know how many are in his custody." Homkwap passed the question back to the Chief Commissioner of Police.

"Well, Your Excellency, I can't say right off the top of my head exactly how many we have arrested. However, I think we must have detained up to five thousand religious fanatics in the last three months. The exact figure should be ready before the video conference commences tomorrow." The Chief Commissioner of Police squirmed in his seat. He knew he should have such facts at his fingertips. He should be ready at any time—even when summoned in the middle of the night—to say precisely how many arrests had been made on his watch. He could read the contempt on Homkwap's face, and the gloating on Sam's as well.

"Does the Director of Prisons have anything to add? Or is he going to give us another excuse for ineptitude?" AZ, Homkwap's deputy, took a swipe at the Chief Commissioner of Police and readied another knockout blow in case the Prisons Director stumbled with the facts.

"We have four thousand three hundred seventy-seven inmates in our custody. I know this because I keep tabs on the number fed daily. I also have the number placed on half food rations as penalty for disorderly conduct. I am happy to report that the number on half ration is on the decline. The inmates know that the only way to survive is to be properly fed. And the only assurance anyone will be properly fed in my prison is to behave properly. You cannot challenge the authority of the state outside the penitentiary and expect to be given VIP treatment inside!" The Director of Prisons warded off the clone's killer blow with his mastery of facts. His loyalty to the government and uncompromising attitude towards the government's enemies got him what he craved most: Homkwap's approving nod.

"That's good. I hope you will remember to say that tomorrow when I ask for your progress report! Is there anything anybody wishes to add? Great! Since there is nothing to add, we can adjourn till tomorrow. The video conference is expected to start at ten o'clock New York time, which makes that four o'clock here. So, see you tomorrow at a quarter to four. And make sure you all have your facts ready."

Chapter-68

Don't tell me the losers are winning!

BY QUARTER TO four Dukyaria time, the officials had assembled in the waiting lounge. Sam spotted a face that was not at the previous meeting—Thomas's. Homkwap had decided at the last minute to ask the Legal Counsel to stand by in case the other side brought up questions with a legal angle. Thomas took a seat next to Sam, with both facing the Cabinet Secretary, the Chief Commissioner of Police, and the Director of Prisons ensconced on leather seats on the other side of the lounge.

Far away in New York, representatives of the WGO Commissioner-General made their way one by one to the Operations Room on the forty-seventh floor. By ten o'clock, they were ready to hold the long-distance conference with their interlocutors waiting in the Cabinet Room on the third floor of the Union Secretariat building.

The technicians on both sides immediately went to work, connecting the participants in the live conversation with the aid of Stream Control Transmission Protocol. Cunningham's was the first face to appear and the first voice to be heard. "How are you, General? It is morning here in New York, which makes it your own late afternoon. I must start by apologizing for the Commissioner-General's inability to join us. As I told you over the phone yesterday, he had to travel at short notice to clear up a slight misunderstanding in Delhi. As I speak, he is having a meeting with Swami Harelal Krishna and the leaders of the Hindu Vishwa Parishad. He is due to meet with the leaders of the other group, Rashtriya Swayamsevak Sangh, tomorrow. Happily, he left this video conference in competent hands. I have here with me the Commissioner-General's Chief of Staff, Ms. Evangelista Torres. Marshall Popov is also here to cover the military and para-military aspects of our discussion. Since the High Commissioner for Capitalism is also in India, he is represented at this video conference by his deputy, Hank Sandberg." The New York cameras captured and immediately transmitted the images as the participants on the WGO side were introduced by Cunningham. "The General can now introduce members of his own team."

On cue, the camera on the Dukyarian side started recording the faces of those assembled in the Cabinet Room and beaming the images across to New York, thousands of kilometers away. Homkwap did not need to introduce himself. He focused his attention instead on the others present: AZ, the Cabinet Secretary, the Chief Commissioner of Police, the Director of Prisons, the Legal Counsel, and the Executive Secretary, Re-education Monitoring Agency. As if visually but wordlessly parroting Homkwap, the camera matched each name with each face as it was introduced.

With the preliminaries out of the way, Cunningham got to the point on his mind. The Commissioner-General was, he began, gravely disturbed by the growing instability in Dukyaria. The Global Guidance Council and the Commissariat-General had expected that with the wheeling and dealing but largely incompetent Ugochukwu behind bars and the country firmly under military rule, there would be peace and quiet in that part of the Mali Empire. "Neither the GGC nor the Commissariat officials for one moment thought that those religious fanatics, those losers, would have the strength to threaten public order. How wrong we were down here! Abu Danja Mamba is all over

339

the place, blowing up armaments depots, butchering defenseless citizens, and thumping his nose at the WGO. Isn't it downright embarrassing that no one knows where he is? Then, you have the two clowns calling themselves clerics, Okoye and Kamil. They are out there leading street protests, some of which turn ugly, with the overzealous protesters going beyond the bounds of reason and attacking government and WGO facilities. Oh, and before I forget, there is also the case filed at your High Court challenging the decision to convert places of worship into re-education centers. Don't you ever think that we are not aware of everything going on over there! We know what is happening. What we don't know is exactly what the Martial Law Administrator is doing to deal with the situation firmly." Cunningham paused, in anticipation of Homkwap's reactions.

"That's quite perceptive, Professor Cunningham…."

"Let's make this as informal as we can. Ok? Feel free to call me Brad." It was very much unlike Cunningham to pass up the opportunity to brandish his academic laurels and titles. How many times had he silently ridiculed the WGO's hypocritical endorsement of egalitarianism!

"Ok, Brad. You are also free to call me Homkwap, if you don't consider it a mouthful. Now back to the situation in Dukyaria. I think that in recent months, we've made remarkable progress in our war on religion. Let me invite the Executive Secretary of our Re-education Monitoring Agency, Mr. Samuel Akerele, to bring you up to speed on our latest efforts to contain the religious pandemic. Over to you, Sam."

The camera swerved towards Sam, picking up not only the face but every word coming out of his mouth. As instructed, he catalogued the achievements made on

Homkwap's watch, paying particular attention to the number of places of worship that successfully "evolved" into re-education centers, the number sealed up for non-compliance with evolution orders, the range of crises fomented and regularly stoked by the government within, between, and among the various faith groups, and the psychological war energetically waged on the obdurate believers. The case which Temileke brought against the government was itself a sign that the policy on the conversation of places of worship into re-education was working. "Temileke would not have panicked if the policy had not hit close to home. They are running scared, and that is before the real hot pursuit begins!"

If Homkwap was wondering why he liked this man, Sam, he had just found one reason—the ability to close his argument with an unforgettable punch line. With the way Sam summed it all up, how would Cunningham not be convinced that we've come a long way.

Torres was hardly convinced. She listened patiently all the while. She reserved her comments until the others had read out their own report cards. Popov too said nothing. He kept his usual poker face. Sandberg had not been properly briefed about the meeting by his boss before the latter jetted to New Delhi. Sandberg was also not mandated by the Commissioner for Capitalism to make comments that might be mistaken as reflecting the position of the Capitalism Commissariat. The proxy dutifully stayed mute for as long as the video conference lasted.

"Lady and gentlemen, as you can see from the last presentation, we are on the offensive in the war on religion. Can I now call on the Chief Commissioner of Police to address Brad's concern on the troublemakers masquerading as street protesters?"

The Chief Commissioner of Police came prepared this time. He supplied precise data on the number detained in the previous three months, the number granted bail by the courts following legal proceedings instituted by Kamil and Okoye, the number actually standing trial, and the number so far convicted and sent to prison. He conveniently left out the number that broke out of prison and were still on the lam. To include that in his report was to raise the question what his men had done to track the fugitives down and send them back to prison.

Homkwap nodded approvingly. The Chief Commissioner of Police was relieved. Torres and Popov still said nothing. Sandberg knew better than to comment on a topic he had not yet studied. His and the two other faces remained expressionless. Brad's frequent grin was difficult to interpret. It could stand for approval or sarcasm. He kept mute, waiting for Homkwap's men to complete their presentations.

The Director of Prison was ready for the great event. He was determined to impress his boss with a superior performance. Ignoring the wife's come-to-bed pleas the previous night, he had spent the greater part of his sleeping hours preparing slides for the following day's power point presentation. With his laptop hooked to the projector in the Cabinet Room, he swiftly proceeded to flip the charts and the diagrams on felons in his custody. He was thrilled to report that without requesting a budget increase, he was able to cater for an increasing number of inmates. While his food budget was pegged at fifteen million Dukyarian dollars, he was able to cater for a total of four thousand seven hundred seventy-seven inmates, representing an increase of five hundred over the previous year. He was able to achieve this feat largely by saving on food rations, specifically, by placing misbehaving prisoners on reduced rations. "A hungry man won't have the stomach for troublemaking. Besides, you cannot challenge the authority of the WGO outside my gate and expect to be accorded VIP treatment inside. No way!" The Director of Prison pleased his boss by repeating the part of the presentation Homkwap liked most.

Homkwap next called on Thomas to update New York about the Temileke case.

Thomas's update soon froze the smile on Homkwap's face. "I am afraid it is premature to speculate on the outcome. The case may go one way or the other. All I can say for now is that we have raised cogent points of law to back the government's position. The rest is now up to the judge. The judge, Ganiyu Philips, is very well versed in the law. So, on balance, I would say we have a fifty-fifty chance of winning."

"That's most reassuring!" Cunningham sneered, thousands of kilometers away, and the Dukyarian television screen instantly showed both the sarcasm and the disdainful facial expression. "Are you done, or are there other fifty-fifty rolls of the dice?" Cunningham took a jibe at Homkwap and his team.

"I think that will be it for now. If you have any questions, we would be glad to answer them." Homkwap downplayed Thomas's reality check and Cunningham's scathing remark.

"You have told us nothing about the military response to the Homo Haram threat." Popov weighed in, his Russian accent as distinct as ever. "The military campaign is not going well," AZ, not yet properly schooled in the human art of lying, jumped in, head-first. He provided a truthful and precise update on the war on Homo Haram terrorists. Homkwap cast a sharp glance at his deputy.

"Are you telling me that even with the redesigned soldier clones we sent, the Homo Haram gangs are still giving you trouble?" Popov persisted.

"You want the truth? The new prototype fighters are no match for Mamba's fighting forces. Most of the soldier clones have been wiped out." AZ, himself a clone, did not mince words.

"How about the drones?"

"The drones? What drones? I still don't know how Mamba's men knew when to expect the drones and how to bring them down without sweat! 'Without sweat', isn't that how you humans say 'effortlessly'?" AZ had nothing but bad news for Popov and the WGO.

Popov was speechless. He let others have their say.

"General Homkwap, I listened with interest as you and your men took us through the efforts you are making to stabilize Dukyaria. While acknowledging the gravity of the challenges you inherited as well as the efforts that you have made to conquer these challenges, I cannot but wonder whether you have considered the long-term consequences of your actions. Your men kept telling us how many people they have apprehended, incarcerated, and even denied food rations. Aren't these your own people? Isn't there another way to approach the delicate situation?" Torres fired off her own questions.

"Like what?" Cunningham sharply cut in, irritation distorting the otherwise well-sculptured face.

"Excuse me! At least, you should let me make my point...." Torres snapped back, eyes dilated, the veins around her mouth taut, and the brow crinkled.

Chapter-69

Yet another family quarrel at Headquarters

ON TORRES'S INSTRUCTION, the New York technicians swiftly discontinued the transmission. The screen in Dukyaria's Cabinet Room hissed for a few seconds and then went blank. Apparently, the WGO bosses considered it inappropriate to wash their dirty laundry in the full view of their Dukyarian counterparts. Cunningham and his colleagues could not afford to make a spectacle of themselves in front of Homkwap.

The bickering in New York continued all the same, albeit unrecorded and un-transmitted for the titillation of the senses in faraway Dukyaria.

"Brad, I take strong exception to your rude behavior! At least, you should have allowed me to make my point!" Torres' effort to regain her composure was sabotaged by her acerbic tone and forbidding scowl.

"And precisely what point are you trying to make? Perhaps you are going to throw in my face this Biblical crap about turning the other cheek. Oh, I forgot, we should start cuddling the fanatics. Better still, we should go to them on bended knees and beg them to list their demands and the measures we should adopt to make them happy. There is no room for accommodation with deranged individuals."

Cunningham fumed, his eyes bloodshot, brow creased and hands flung wide.

"There you go again! I had hardly got in a word before you came up with your own interpretation. Alright, tell me what you have accomplished since the trouble started in Dukyaria? Remember that the Commissioner-General would not have rushed to India if you had not proceeded with unseemly haste to impose your secular view on a basically spiritual people. You may also not know this, but we have received reports from other parts of the India-Pacific Empire indicating that Buddhist monks have started immolating themselves in protest against an Imperial proclamation purporting to ban the tricivara. Emboldened by Kamil's and Okoye's tenacity, anti-WGO movements keep mushrooming in different parts of the globe. Mass protests have erupted in Makkah, Jerusalem, Turin, Rome, Naples, Thessaloniki, Bahia, Algiers, Tripoli, Niamey, Addis Ababa, and Mogadishu, to mention a few. I take it that you have a plan to clean up the mess!" Torres looked Cunningham straight in the eye.

"I don't have time for this crap!" Cunningham rose from his seat and stormed out of the operations room.

The video conference ended without agreeing on the way forward. It was left to Torres to fill her boss in on his return from New Delhi.

Back in Dukyaria, Homkwap asked his lieutenants what they thought of the inconclusive video conference. "Your Excellency, can I speak frankly?" It was the Cabinet Secretary.

"Of course!"

"I think we are on our own, at least, for now. Although I don't have any fact to back this up, my intuition tells me that what Cunningham described as a 'slight misunderstanding' in India is more serious than he cared to let on. After all, why would the Commissioner-General fly at short notice to New Delhi?" The Cabinet Secretary backed his observation with a question.

"I too have been wondering. Anyway, regardless of whether the misunderstanding was slight or huge, we should stay focused on our mission. Is that clear?" Hompkwap summed up before bringing the meeting to a close.

Chapter-70

And whatever you ask in prayer, you will receive, if you have faith

"HALLELUJAH!" EMMAN, BEAMING BROADLY and a copy of the Bible held aloft, whipped the cheering crowd into a state of frenzy. He stood on a makeshift platform, occasionally bending to shake his admirers' hands vigorously and embrace a few lucky ones standing close to the dais. "In Matthew 21:22," he continued, "the good Lord said, 'And whatever you ask in prayer, you will receive, if you have faith.'"

The adulating crowd went wild. Emman had earlier been carried shoulder high by his followers and admirers as soon as he stepped out of the Magistrate Court and flashed the victory sign. He and the crowd had every reason to celebrate. The court had duly considered the matter of Mosafejo versus Kalu and ruled in the latter's favor—well, not completely in his favor, as he still had to cough out one year's salary to compensate Akin Mosafejo for lost earnings and emotional distress. Still, what was twelve million Dukyarian dollars? He shrugged off the part of the judgment requiring payment of indemnity. The amount awarded to mollify Akin was measly compared with the fifty percent of the ecclesiastical empire that the "greedy bastard" had originally demanded.

"Strengthened by our faith in the good Lord, we prayed for victory. And the good Lord granted us victory. Victory! What did I say?" he asked.

"Victory!" the crowd chorused.

349

"You, our well-wishers, were highly disturbed when you heard about the misunderstanding in the church. We assured you that our Lord is very much on our side. Praise the Lord! We told you then and we are telling you now that the good Lord never forsakes one of His own."

"Hallelujah!" a voice in the crowd rang out.

"Hallelujah!" the rest eagerly repeated.

"My brothers and sisters, the victory that we have just won is not the end of our struggle. It is in fact the beginning of the ultimate struggle. It is the beginning of the triumph of truth over falsehood, of light over darkness, of candidness over deception. Hear what the holy book says in John 3:21: 'But whoever does what is true comes to the light, so that it may be clearly seen that his works have been carried out in God.'" Emman paused momentarily to gauge the impact of his delivery.

The crowd was ecstatic. "Hallelujah! Hallelujah! Hallelujah!"

Animated by the unceasing rounds of applause, he continued, "Many of you must have heard what our opponent said in open court. He claimed that all the miracles you witnessed were faked. Can you beat that? He owned up to willfully misleading our congregation! I personally know nothing about any fake miracles. All the miracles that took place on my watch were real. Glory be to God, the brains behind fake miracles are no longer with us. The good Lord has mercifully separated them from us and cast them into the wilderness. Hallelujah!"

"Hallelujah!" the crowd chorused again.

He was all-fired to resume his sermon when Amos walked to the platform, his right hand clutching the boss's cell phone. The personal assistant signaled with his left index finger that a call was waiting. He then handed over the phone.

"Yes, this is Pastor Emmanuel. Who's on the line?"

"Sam. Samuel Akerele. I just heard on the news that the magistrate ruled in your favor. Congratulations! I knew all along that you would triumph. But that is not why I am calling. I am calling because you have just recorded another victory." Sam wasn't particularly glad to relay the good news because, to him, the news was, from his standpoint, anything but good. He was merely looking for an opportunity to profit from the latest development, or specifically, to turn the government's humiliating rout at the lawcourt into victory. The plan was simple: set the believers against one another. Deepening the rift between Emman and the organizers of the street protests was part of the plan. The information that had just landed on Sam's desk would also prove useful in implementing the plan. Sam was determined to turn Kamil's frequent and harrowing journeys to Hayat to Homkwap's advantage.

"Victory? What victory? I need you to speak loudly because, with the crowd here in front of the Magistrate Court, I can hardly hear what you are saying," Emman told Sam.

351

"The High Court has just ruled that sending inspectors to houses of worship constitutes invasion of privacy. The decision, according to the judge, violates the key provisions of the Universal Declaration of Individual and Civil Rights. The government had hoped that Temileke would be sent to jail for lying on oath. To our dismay, the judge ruled that since the lie had no bearing on the case and would not have influenced the bench's decision one way or the other, the law did not support sending the plaintiff to jail. The facts adduced by the government legal counsel to back his plea for Temileke's imprisonment were, according to the judge, 'not material to the case.' Ganiyu Philips! I have never met a more temperamental and unpredictable judge in my life!" Sam added, trying desperately to dissipate a dark cloud that had settled on his face. The judgment was a personal setback for Sam. The abrupt embargo on "re-education" signaled the imminent retrenchment of inspectors and the shrinkage of his bureaucratic empire. Fortunately, Emman was too far away to see the disgust on Sam's face.

"It's nice of you to share the news with me, but since I was not a party to the suit, I don't see how its determination concerns me," Emman replied matter-of-factly.

"That is precisely my point. You were not a party to the suit, but that is what qualifies you to help the government, that is, help us turn the defeat to our own advantage."

"How?"

"We cannot discuss such matters over the phone. How about meeting in your villa later this evening? Around eight o'clock?"

"I am booked rock solid today. The church is organizing a special thanksgiving service followed by a victory dinner. Can we meet tomorrow? Same time?"

"Splendid. Tomorrow; same time. By the way, just as I treat your lack of interest in the Temileke case as our little secret, I trust you to exercise the utmost discretion regarding this phone conversation or anything you and I may discuss in the future. In fact, I would have invited myself to your dinner, but what will people say? 'The government's point man for secularism openly fraternizing with the divinely anointed!'" Sam tittered over the phone.

Either Emman didn't get the joke or considered it too expensive. He promptly switched off the phone and went back to working the crowd.

"My brothers and sisters, brace yourselves for the latest news! It is huge! Hold the hands next to yours and close your eyes. As you listen to the news that I am about to bring you, remember what I said about how the good Lord stands by the righteous. Hallelujah! Our Lord has answered another prayer of ours. He has granted us the victory that we craved by day and beseeched Him for all night long. Aren't you going to ask me what victory I am talking about?"

"Victory! Victory! Victory!" The crowd was ecstatic.

"I take that as a Yes. You want to know about the victory I am talking about!"

"Yes! Yes! Yes!" The crowd chorused uproariously.

"The victory that I speak of is the one we have long awaited. My brothers and sisters, as the Magistrate Court did a few minutes ago, the High Court has just ruled in our favor. The government, the Court emphatically states, has no business storming into houses of worship and peering under our pulpits to ferret out signs of devotion. From now on, we are free to worship the good Lord, the Lord of the heavens and earth! Hallelujah!" As mutually agreed, Emman's breaking news discreetly skipped Sam's name.

"Hallelujah! Hallelujah! Hallelujah!" The crowd, now totally entranced, screamed at the top of its voice.

Emman was not done. If the government intended to use him, there was no reason he too could not use the government and others. "Some of you must have picked a few words from my recent phone conversation. In order not to brag about the role our prayer warriors played in getting the courts on our side, I pretended that I knew nothing about the Temileke suit. Of course, the man who called me knew better. He could not be fooled. No matter how I humble myself or minimize my role, he fully appreciated our contributions. He knew that I was a party to the suit in the sense that matters most—in spirit. Tell me, which is more significant—spiritual or material support?" Emman asked rhetorically and waited for a response.

"Hallelujah!" The crowd concurred.

Emman was elated. He was not through with the crowd. Not yet. "My brothers and sisters, our gratitude to the good Lord will not be complete until we join the victory parade at the High Court. I am therefore appealing to each and every one to proceed immediately to Independence

Square. That is the venue of the multi-denominational gathering.

"Will you be one of the speakers at the gathering?" A voice asked.

"You bet!" Emman responded earnestly. He got off the platform and walked to his SUV, an ash-colored Mercedes. He took the right window seat at the back, while Amos sat on the left. Ossas, head of security, sat in the front, next to the driver.

With two motorcycles in front sounding the siren, the Mercedes and the convoy behind drove leisurely to Independence Square. Emman's admirers who had the means took taxis or perched on motorcycles doubling as taxis. The rest trotted closely behind.

Chapter-71

And the front stayed united long enough to trade blows!

THE SCENE AT THE Independence Square was surreal. The public was already used to Okoye and Kamil holding each other's hands aloft after addressing anti-same sex rallies. What it could not easily comprehend was the sight of Okoye eagerly embracing Emman or the latter reciprocating. No one ever suspected that the day would come when Emman would be caught being civil to the "Moslem fundamentalist," Kamil. But there they all were this late afternoon behaving as long-separated brothers finally reunited. The former antagonists laughed heartily at any joke no matter how bland, eagerly patted one another on the shoulders, and conveyed the impression that they thoroughly cherished one another's company.

Their followers instantly got the message. Today is love-and-peace-day. There would be no room for mutual recriminations. Everyone must keep up an appearance befitting the occasion—an appearance of solidarity and conviviality. As they were wont to, the Christians in the crowd repeatedly screamed "Thanks, Jesus!" but unlike in the past, their Muslim counterparts registered no protest. For their part, the Muslims rent the air with their chants of "Allahu Akbar," again, without anyone, least of all, Christians, objecting. If the polytheists had themselves agreed beforehand on a common deity, they too would have hailed him or her to their hearts' content and without fear that their act would be vetoed.

"Hallelujah!" Okoye intoned as he mounted the podium. "We thank you, Jesus! You stood by us when we needed you most. You have proven beyond doubt that your promise will never go unfulfilled. You promised us in Mathew 21:22 that whatever we ask in prayer, we will receive, if we have faith. We thank you, heavenly Father, for fortifying us with the faith we need to face a formidable opponent and, at the same time, remain optimistic of ultimate victory. We thank you for listening to our prayers. We thank you for removing a major obstacle in our path. Before I hand over the microphone, I wish to thank you, my brother, Salim Kamil, for your steadfastness."

Okoye nodded slightly in Kamil's direction before continuing. "I am particularly glad that we were able to set aside our doctrinal differences and work in unison to confront a major threat to freedom. I must also thank you, the good people of Dukyaria, for not losing faith even when losing faith was precisely what our opponents would have us do. At great personal risk, you supported us by turning up in large numbers at rallies and by contributing materially to the cause. Those among you with limited means made up for their handicap by standing in solidarity with us. We must of course realize that the struggle is not yet over. It has in fact only just begun. We hope we can count on your support and dedication in the months and years ahead. Thank you all!" Okoye stepped down from the rostrum to a thunderous applause. He handed over the microphone to Kamil after a brief introduction.

Kamil started by reciting the first surah in the Qur'an, Surah al-Fatihah. As soon as he finished, he rubbed his two hands on his face and then continued, "Allahu Akbar kabeeran, wal hamdulilahi katheeran! Allah is the greatest. We express our profound gratitude to Him. As my brother, Basil Okoye, remarked earlier, the victory that Allah has just granted us is the reward for our faith, patience, and forbearance. The promise that you have in the Bible also appears in the Qur'an, surah forty, ayah sixty as follows: 'And your Lord says: Call upon Me, I will answer you.' In ways familiar to each and every one of us, we prayed to the Almighty God for victory. The Almighty Allah, in His infinite mercy, heeded our prayers. We thank Him for strengthening our faith and for rewarding us with the victory that we earnestly beseeched Him for. As my brother, Basil, reminded us, we might have won this battle, but the war is far from over. The courts might have ruled in our favor today, but we should not for one moment think that our opponents have given up. We must keep our eyes open. We must be ready to defend our freedom. Above all, we must continue to stand shoulder to shoulder and foil every attempt to keep us at daggers drawn. Allahu Akbar!" Kamil descended the podium and the crowd cheered vociferously.

Following the protocol implicitly ratified by the impromptu assembly, Kamil, as the latest speaker, introduced the next, Emmanuel Kalu.

Emman had barely made it to the podium's edge when he was greeted by boos and catcalls. "Shameless hypocrite!" a voice in the crowd engineered the negative reaction.

"Go home!" Another heckler yelled.

"Let him speak!" One of Emman's groupies retorted in her tiny, squeaky voice.

"We want Emmanuel! We want Emmanuel! We want Emmanuel!" Amos, Emman's principal sidekick, orchestrated a song, hoping to whip up the church members' emotions.

Another detractor wouldn't let Amos have his way. The detractor came up with his own idea, a denigrating jingle: "Fake prophet! Fake miracles! Fake prophet! Fake miracles! Fake prophet! Fake miracles!"

Attempts by Okoye and Kamil to pacify the crowd ended in vain. Apparently, overlooking the salacious details of the Mosafejo case was not part of the peace deal that the anti-Emman crowd implicitly endorsed before the Abounding Grace Ministries' pastor stepped forward.

Within minutes, the mob at the Independence Square started dancing rowdily to the "Fake prophet, Fake miracle" song. To stave off further embarrassment, Emman quickly scurried towards his SUV, shielded by Amos, Ossas, and grim-looking security operatives. The pastor's supporters either stayed quiet or departed the Square quietly.

Chapter-72

Sowing seeds of discord on believers' soil

THE NEWS OF EMMAN's public humiliation filled Sam with joy, grotesque as that might sound. "This may not be trouble for our adversaries, but it sure as hell looks like it! I couldn't have planned it better!" He thought to himself, grinning cynically. He saw the nocturnal meeting he planned on holding with the pastor starting and ending well.

Sam had earlier watched with apprehension as staunch enemies appeared on television, all behaving as if nothing ever came between them. How could they have patched up their differences so soon? Even if someone had miraculously seized control of Judge Philips' mind to ensure that the scale of justice tilted towards Temileke and his collaborators, was that enough to turn implacable enemies into intimate, possibly, inseparable friends?

Sam might marvel all he wanted. The rapprochement between and among the bickering clerics was, or appeared, a done deal. This ran counter to Sam's plan. Harmony in the believers' corner was not part of the plan. The classified memorandum which he had submitted to the by now redesignated Governor-General Homkwap saw Okoye and Kamil constantly taking each other to task about the Trinity and Allah—not enjoying each other's company. Even on the off chance that neither the Trinity nor Allah succeeded in setting the two against each other, it should at least not be too difficult to pit both against their long-time adversary, Emman. Sam's memorandum to the Governor-General did not include or envisage the pastor associating with Okoye and Kamil, let alone sharing a moment of joy with both or either. But here they were on prime-time television, looking like newly inducted members of a reciprocal admiration fraternity!

To Sam's relief, the camaraderie was short-lived. Anti-Emman forces had gathered at the Independence Square and had told the pastor to leave their midst and go to hell. So, how could anything go wrong from then on? How could the meeting Sam planned with the pastor later in the night not go well? Go well it would. The meeting would enable Sam to assist the pastor reassess his options. It was at this meeting that he and the pastor would forge a formidable alliance against Okoye and Kamil.

While Sam was meditating on the plan that he would table at the night's meeting with Emman, the pastor was counting his loss and plotting the path to future gains. First and foremost, he needed a new miracle worker. Either he or Amos had to travel to the village and coax Dibea Nwogugu into shifting his operational base from Okigwe to the national capital. That shouldn't prove difficult—not when the sorcerer was promised a regular and substantial income in place of the occasional gifts of fowl that he received from the most generous of his clients. A house and a chauffeur-driven car would even be thrown in to sweeten the employment package. With Nwogugu on board, the Abounding Grace Ministries would no longer require the services of counterfeit psychics. Every miracle performed on Emman's watch would from then on be real. The only troubling aspect was Nwogugu's magic's dependence on rituals and fetishes.

Anyway, that was a bridge Emman would gladly cross when he got to it.

Although still smarting from the mortification he suffered at the Independence Square, the pastor did not rule out the possibility of reconciling with both Okoye and Kamil. In fact, mending fences with his former foes was the best assurance he had of isolating his latest adversary, Akin Mosafejo. After the court ruled against him, Mosafejo had resolved to establish his own church. Emman had to thwart any attempt by his former deputy to lure Abounding Grace worshippers to the new church, or to poach the Abounding Grace's major financiers. Above all, he had to make sure that Mosafejo neither joined nor was drafted into a tripartite, Okoye-Kamil-Mosafejo, gang-up against the Abounding Grace Ministries.

Meanwhile, Sam moved fast to perfect his own strategy. He sought and obtained Homkwap's authorization to negotiate a special deal with Emman. He was to give the pastor anything he asked for—so long as this included working closely with the government to sow seeds of discord in the believers' camp. Sam even had His Excellency's permission to invite Emman to be part of his entourage during the upcoming visit to America. Sam waited for the right moment to activate the Okoye-Kamil component of his plan.

Chapter-73

Let's go on pleasure pilgrimage

"BASIL, I JUST RECEIVED a 'funny' invitation." It was Kamil on the line.

"That's interesting. I was just planning to call you and tell you about mine. Since you beat me to it, you go first," Okoye responded.

"Your invitation wouldn't possibly be from the Governor-General's Office, would it?" Kamil asked, half expecting his suspicion to be confirmed.

"Yes. It is from the Governor-General, and it is dated Thursday, 30 November 2090...." Okoye wanted to continue, but his friend interrupted him.

"And the invitation letter is captioned, 'Invitation to Join Governor-General's Official Delegation to America,' right?" Kamil, anticipating Okoye's response to his earlier question, nodded slowly as he spoke.

"Right!"

"I take it then that you are going to frame the letter and hang it side by side with your college diplomas. I also assume that you have started buying your winter clothing and packing your bags! I understand that it is freezing out there in New York right now!" Kamil teased his friend.

"You must be joking. You think I have time for this kind of nonsense? The man is looking for ways to buy us over and compromise our integrity. I will never be part of the elaborate but meaningless charade!" Okoye responded derisively.

"The Governor-General won't like that one bit. He will take it as a slap in the face. They may even impound your passport, send you to jail, kill your cat, and marry you to a woman against your will!" Kamil screeched with laughter as he humorously warned his friend of the dire consequences of turning the Governor-General down flat.

"Who cares? At least, you, my brother, will visit me in jail. So, when will you begin packing your own bags? You will look ludicrously handsome when you squeeze your flowing babar riga into one of those winter jackets and trench coats!" It was Okoye's turn to crack a joke and hoot at the same time.

"Seriously, if I were not at home, and you were duly authorized to act on my behalf, how would you respond to such an invitation?" Kamil asked Okoye.

"I would eagerly accept lest you would be furious at my depriving you of such a golden opportunity. I would write back and say, 'Thank you, Sir, my brother can't wait to visit the Big Apple.' That will be your reply, won't it?" Okoye replied. Kamil could only imagine the chirpy expression at the other end. "I am sure you are kidding. You already know that going on a pleasure pilgrimage has never been, and will never be, on my agenda." Kamil was no longer joking. He did not see what would come out of visits to New York's Central Park; Disney World in Orlando, Florida; Las Vega's casinos and gambling dens, and other places listed on the invitation letter. As Kamil suspected, the tourist destinations built into the itinerary were for the pleasure of First Lady Ekineta. Kamil concluded that he was unlikely to find any satisfaction, real or vicarious, visiting any of those places.

"How about the passport you risk losing? The threat of a long prison sentence hanging over your head? Your cat that they may kill? And your beard! Yes, your beard! It will be the first to go! So, won't you reconsider your decision not to join the high-level entourage? Don't forget what you will be missing apart from the interesting sites! You will miss the warm clothing allowance and the stipends for nights spent away from home!" Okoye found a way to make his friend ease up.

A few minutes after the phone conversation ended, UPS delivered another official letter at Kamil's home. Signed by Sam, the letter commiserated with Kamil over the decline in his son's health. As fortuity would have it, the letter continued, Kamil would soon be in New York as a member of the Governor-General's delegation. This was a perfect opportunity to find a lasting solution to Abdullah's health crisis. "As a humanitarian gesture, the Governor-General has directed that, in addition to your good self, Abdullah and his mother be included as members of the official delegation to the United States. While in America, Abdullah will be cared for by specialists at the world-renowned Mayo Clinic. The Government has also agreed to bear Abdullah's medical expenses, including his mother's board and lodging for the entire duration of the treatment." The letter concluded tantalizingly.

Sam's letter put Kamil in a dilemma. If he turned down the Government's offer of assistance, he would be accused of being a callous and irresponsible father. And Amina, his wife, would never forgive him for allowing his pride or principle to stand in the way of Abdullah's convalescence and long-term wellbeing. The alternative was even unthinkable—swallow his pride, abandon his principle, and place Abdullah's health above the struggle for Dukyaria's freedom. How does the symbol of 'direct action' explain being the first to cave in to the adversary's pressure? How would he, Kamil, break it down in a language that Okoye would understand?

Kamil's immediate reaction was to fold the letter, insert it in the envelope, and keep it in his briefcase. Confronted with a question he could not answer logically, he did what his murshids had taught him to do when at a crossroad: turn to Allah for guidance. He washed his hands, face, and feet as he was wont to when performing the obligatory prayers. However, on this particular occasion, the ritual ablution was to purify him to complete salat al-istikhara, two rounds of supererogatory prayers. At the end of the prayers, he sought Allah's guidance on the matter before him. Later that evening, he instinctively decided to undertake a long-delayed journey. "Amina, we are withdrawing Abdullah from Hayat. You and I are taking him to Sheikh Awwal in Maiduguri."

Kamil called Okoye again to apprise him of the impromptu decision. He would brief Okoye about the purpose of the trip on his return.

Chapter-74

Hey Pastor! How 'bout our destabilization plot?

ALTHOUGH OKOYE AND KAMIL had decided not to accept the government's invitation to be part of the Governor-General's delegation to America, they waited for the right moment to communicate their decision. This was a blow to Sam, who had proceeded on the assumption that both would jump at the opportunity to mend fences with Homkwap. Anyway, it didn't matter if both clerics passed up the golden opportunity. It would matter a lot if Sam, now Permanent Secretary of the freshly re-named Faith Regulation Authority, failed in his mission to bring Pastor Emman to the government's side. Sam quickly dismissed the two uncompromising clerics from his mind and headed to Emman's villa.

"Mr. Akerele, long time no see! How are you and your family?" The pastor warmly welcomed Sam to his residence. He beamed as he shook hands with his guest.

"Thanks, Pastor. We are in good health. I could not believe what I saw on television three days ago. How could Kamil and Okoye stand by while those hoodlums attacked you? What a pity!" Sam looked the part of an individual scandalized by his fellow man's mortification. His inner feeling, the silent gloating, told a different story.

"Oh, that was nothing." It was Emman's turn to disguise his own feelings. He casually brushed off the ugly

367

episode. He bade his visitor sit on a soft leather sofa on his right. The broad smile was still on display.

"Pastor, you are the one saying this? Those vandals should not be living among civilized people. I was hoping that both Okoye and Kamil would set them right immediately. But what did they do instead? They ran all over the place waving their hands and virtually egging the ruffians on!" Sam wasted no time fueling the fire. His mission was to turn Emman against the arrowheads of resistance to the government and the WGO.

"In fairness to both Kamil and Okoye, the incident took everyone by surprise. They made every effort to calm the situation...." Emman wanted to forgive and forget.

Sam wouldn't let him. He cut in, "Took them by surprise, did you just say? If you believe that, it means you don't know the people you are dealing with. Anyway, let us leave that for now. His Excellency, the Governor-General, is proceeding on an official visit to America in a fortnight. He has asked me to deliver this letter of invitation to you personally. He wants you to be part of his delegation." Sam handed over a foolscap envelope with the Dukyarian government logo.

"Are you serious? Me on the Governor-General's delegation? I didn't realize that I am that important! Who knows Emman to consider him worthy of travelling to America with a whole head of government?" The pastor looked at him askance, acting surprised that someone that big knew someone like him, someone insignificant. He tossed the envelope on the coffee table, leaving it unopened.

"Don't underrate yourself. I know you. So does His Excellency himself. Need I add that all the members of the National Guidance Council know you very well? It is my hope that one of these days, you too will meet them," Sam pumped Emman's ego.

"What is the purpose of the visit, and where do I, a priest, fit in?"

"Why not open the letter and find out for yourself?" Sam responded with a smile.

Emman reached for the envelope, slipped his right index finger under it, and ripped the flap open. He pulled out the contents, a letter bearing the Dukyarian coat of arms and captioned "Invitation to Join Governor-General's Official Delegation to America." Emman's rapid-reading skill served him well. He got the substance of the letter within seconds. At the invitation of the WGO Commissioner-General, His Excellency, General Homkwap Hilary Homkwap, was proceeding on his first official visit to America. While in New York, the letter continued, the Governor-General and members of his delegation would pay courtesy calls on the President of the Global Guidance Council, the Chairperson of the Assembly of Nations, the WGO Commissioner-General, and his High Commissioners. They would also participate in a global colloquium on Faith and Public Order. The official visit would be rounded off with excursions to famous places in New York, Orlando, Las Vegas, and Hollywood. A day visit to the Grand Canyon was a possibility. The signatory, an obscure civil servant, was "pleased to inform you, that in recognition of your contributions to the development of Dukyaria, you have been nominated as a member of the delegation."

The letter ended by requesting the addressee to signify his acceptance of the invitation within a week so arrangements could be made for the procurement of a visa and for the expenses for warm clothing and daily subsistence allowances.

Emman took in the contents and quickly calculated the costs and the benefits of the New York visit. The honor from His Excellency certainly counted for something. And the monetary gain? That was also a plus. So was the opportunity to rub shoulders with the high and mighty at home and abroad. What of the risks? There weren't many that Emman could readily envisage. As a matter of fact, he could think of no problem except one: his public esteem that was rapidly going south. He was already battling to contain the fallout from the Mosafejo case. If his latest experience at the hands of the Independence Square mob was any indication, he faced an uphill task salvaging what was left of his reputation. His prestige would suffer irreparable damage if he was caught openly fraternizing with the Homkwap government, a government that was roundly condemned and utterly detested by Dukyarians. Besides, his miracles department, already incapacitated by Mosafejo's departure, needed to be reorganized and restarted. That meant that he needed to travel to Okigwe. He had to persuade Dibea Nwogugu to leave his clients in Okigwe and relocate to Abuja.

"Mr. Akerele, I have read the letter. Honestly, I don't know what to say...."

"Then, say Yes!" Sam didn't allow him to complete his sentence.

"I am afraid, I can't. The trip has come at a bad time. As you know, with my former deputy gone, I need a new right-hand man." He left out tiny details like the new right-hand

370

man's job description and the qualifications needed to fill the vacancy.

"Yah! The right-hand man can wait. This can't. You can get a thousand Mosafejos in the twinkling of an eye." Sam thought that Emman was seriously looking for a new deputy General Overseer. It never occurred to him that the experience with Mosafejo had taught Emman to proceed cautiously in filling the deputy's vacancy.

"I wish it was that simple! No, Mr. Akerele, I can't travel to New York now. That, of course, does not mean we can't work together in the future."

"What a shame. His Excellency will be sorely disappointed. Anyway, I shall find a way to pass on the message without upsetting him."

"Magnificent! I take it then that the matter is settled. If there is nothing else to discuss, can we have our long-delayed supper?"

"Not so fast, Pastor. There's still another small matter we need to thrash out. It is this matter of your relations with the two hotheads leading the street protests against the government. Can you give His Excellency your assurance that, rather than side with them, you will work with us to bring peace and stability to Dukyaria? Our country will forever be grateful to you."

"I don't see why the government and I cannot work together for the good of our country. But is it an either-or choice? Is working with the government inconsistent with working with Okoye and Kamil?"

"I really like your quick grasp of details. There is a wide gulf between the government, on the one hand, and Kamil and Okoye, on the other. We didn't create this gulf. They did. Whereas we want peace and stability in Dukyaria so we can regain our independence, the two extremists are interested in fomenting trouble for their personal gain. If you ask me, both of them have hidden agendas. Both have political ambitions. Both want to topple the Homkwap regime. However, neither has given any thought to the conflict that is bound to arise between them later. They will turn on each other when they have no other enemy to engage. Do you see the point I am trying to make?"

"Certainly. Since politics is up your alley, anyway, you are better placed than myself to discuss the subject intelligently. Still, for what it is worth, I shall take your views under advisement. I shall get back to you later with my and the church's decision. All I can say for now is that we are committed in principle to working with the government for Dukyaria's overall benefit."

That was how Emman got out of Sam's elaborately contrived situation. Homkwap and his entourage travelled to New York and all those fanciful places without the pastor. Ekineta, unaware of the background moves, enjoyed every minute of her visit. She smiled for the cameras. Newspapers at home and abroad fought for rights to splash images of her pretty face across their front and center pages.

Chapter-75

Bloody son of a test-tube! The clones revolt!

X300, A CLONED SOLDIER in Dukyaria, never had any cause to question his own identity. That is, at least not until he and Kevin set upon each other. He had earlier described Kevin, a regular but "upgraded" human soldier, as "an inferior species, an emotional human devoid of any capacity to reason." Kevin had in turn hit back by saying, "Thank Heavens, I am human. At least I came to this planet through a father and a mother. Where is your mother? Where is your father? You are fatherless, motherless, and to make matters worse, soulless. You are a branch without roots. You are worse off than what we regular humans call an 'orphan'! You hear that? Worse than an orphan! Bloody son of a test-tube! Just come to think of it, you are at par with machines invented by smart humans like me!"

That ought to get anyone angry. Not the emotionally detached clone. Kevin's insults got X300 thinking, not angry. Much as he detested Kevin's condescending attitude, the human had a point. As a clone, he was a motherless, fatherless, rootless, probably soulless being. It wasn't that his mother or father died. They simply did not exist. If they had existed, he would have known about them. And if he had known about them, they would have been part of his memory. He would also have mourned them if and when they died, as Kevin mourned a person he once called uncle.

X300 didn't even know what mourning meant or how it felt until he noticed the change in Kevin. He saw Kevin go about with a long, gaunt face, withdrawing to himself, refusing to interact with other soldiers for days, and very much unlike him, abstaining from the consumption of alcohol. The long face wearer's intake of food and water reduced considerably. Whatever Kevin's feeling was, X300 knew he was most unlikely to experience it.

That was not all that got X300 thinking; Kevin had a family of his own—a wife, and three children. The protocol governing the clone's "birth" and evolution did not leave any room for procreation or for the growing of family trees. The logic was understandable: family ties brought complications, such as the uncontrolled desire to keep up with, or even exceed, the Joneses, constant agitation for increased pay, impaired allegiance to the WGO cause, and clannishness or parochialism. X300 and his fellow clones were specifically manufactured to be totally loyal to the WGO, and not to engage in sexual activity, much less, get married, start their own families, or owe and bear private allegiances.

Regardless of how troubled he was about his identity, X300 managed to stay calm and to perform his tasks. After his tour of duty as a member of a task force sent to capture or kill Abu Mamba, he was assigned to purely civilian duties. The government needed individuals like him to keep a military eye on the street protests led by Okoye and Kamil. He and others with military training were to team up with the regular police to restore order if the protests turned violent, as they tended to in later months.

It was while participating in the joint military-police exercise that X300 caught Kamil's eye. Kamil had stood with the rest of the cheering crowd while Okoye spoke about the link between the same-sex law opposed by the majority of Dukyarians and the loss of the country's independence.

"We would not be in this mess if our politicians had exercised the highest sense of responsibility in managing our affairs. The WGO is able to treat us like minors because those claiming to represent us slept on the job. By the time they woke up, our sovereignty was gone. The next to follow was individual freedom. Our human and civil rights went up in smoke the instant our politicians bartered away our Deeds of Sovereignty for a bowl of gruel," Okoye had told the crowd.

Clones rarely showed any emotions. It was impossible to tell whether they were happy or sad. The lab technicians had frozen their emotional faculties and implanted order-obeying genes. However, X300 must have been an exception. Kamil noticed a change in X300's expression as soon as Okoye uttered the word "human." This particular day, the clone's brow furrowed, the nostrils dilated, the face darkened, and rage fleetingly darted across the eyes. What does this man mean by human rights? When will the orator get to clone rights? X300 thought to himself.

"What's with your man? He doesn't look happy to be in our midst!" Kamil teased another soldier, a regular human, standing close by. Kamil expected humor to melt the freeze and break the communication barrier.

"Why not ask him? After all, he is not too far from you!" The soldier spoke between clenched teeth. Kamil's attempt to break the ice had failed. The soldier remained frigid.

Kamil, in his typical derring-do style, walked across to X300. "I notice that you are upset. I hope we have not overstepped our bounds," he began cautiously.

X300 said nothing. He commended himself for finally being able to project an emotion that he had tried times without number to copy from Kevin: anger. He had at last discovered one mechanism that humans applied to get attention. He had to practice the facial act often. He also had to make sure that he conditioned his mind and brain to shift from the positive to the negative as the occasion demanded. That way, the facial act would match the inner feeling—and look real. The man standing before him had given him another opportunity to hone his emotion shaping skill. He contorted his face further. The result was different from the one he expected. Instead of recoiling from his presence, Kamil exploded into an uproarious laughter. X300's "anger" act looked more comical than convincing.

"I didn't know you have a sense of humor!" Kamil remarked, slowly recovering from the effect of the convulsive laughter.

"Get lost, you over-pampered human!" X300 did not have to contort his face to signify anger. He was and looked genuinely infuriated.

"Do you really mean what you've just said? Exactly how are we humans over-pampered?" Kamil looked for a window into the clone's mind.

"You figure that out yourself. Here is a clue: Anytime you think about human rights, think about others without rights. Now get lost!" X300 transferred the gun from his left shoulder to both hands. He levelled it in Kamil's face.

The window to X300's mind closed before Kamil saw what was inside. But then Kamil had got all he needed to figure out the paradoxes and the imponderables. For the first time, he saw a visibly angry clone. While the clone did not say what he was griping about, Kamil was certain it had to do with rights, notably, the gap between human and clone rights.

By the time Okoye ended his own pep talk and got off the dais, Kamil was ready with his own. He had earlier planned to hammer on the evils of same-sex liaisons—how same-sex couples were destined to rot in hell and all that. He immediately shelved the plan. Since the government had lately developed the habit of promoting discord within the ranks of believers, it was time to pay the government in its own coin. And in doing so, Kamil would hit where it hurt most. He would become an advocate of clone rights. He would let the clones know that the government had grossly and systematically trampled on their rights. He would tell them to join the ranks of those fighting for the emancipation of Dukyaria and for the preservation of human and clone rights.

Sam sat in his office wide-eyed as the Global Television Network transmitted Kamil's speech live. The cleric had delivered his speech extempore directly in front of the WGO office:

"Distinguished ladies and gentlemen, my brothers, my sisters, our mothers, and our fathers, I hope you listened attentively as my brother, Basil Okoye, eloquently told us how we got into our current situation. It is still not too late to get ourselves out. But aren't you going to ask me how?" Kamil relied on the interactive method to get his audience's attention.

"How? How? How?" As expected, the crowd asked loudly.

"The only way we can regain our freedom and reassert our dignity is to defend the rights of all Dukyarians with every bone in our bodies. We should proceed with determination to broaden and safeguard the rights of humans and of clones. Each clone must be told in no uncertain terms about his origin, who the father and the mother were, and how he ended up on this planet. Clones must have the right to enter into marital relations so long as they stay within the confines of Divine law, the law of duality, or what in Chinese philosophy comes out as yin and yang. They must have the right to start their own families and procreate so long as they respect the principle of differentiation. The right to paternity and maternity leave that is currently enjoyed by humans must be extended to them. They must, like their human counterparts, earn equal pay for equal work."

Sam, staring at his office's television screen, was not the only one who marveled at Kamil's audacity. His boss, Homkwap, placed an angry call to Sam, demanding explanations. As for Okoye and Emman, then standing directly in front of Kamil, neither of them could believe their ears as they heard the born-again advocate of clone rights spell out his new doctrine, the doctrine of inclusiveness.

Okoye had no objection whatsoever to the expansion of clone rights. After all, he had classified the clones among the "children of God" in his previous sermons. However, he felt blindsided by Kamil this particular day. At least, his comrade-in-arms should have had the courtesy to give him a prior warning of his intention to make a major pronouncement like that. Besides, he silently wondered if the clones would live to enjoy many of the rights Kamil canvassed on their behalf. To frustrate the clones' attempts to trace their roots, the authorities had directed that their DNA records be destroyed. The procreation right was equally meaningless, since the libido was the first thing that the lab technicians removed at the early stages of the cloning process. Unless the predominantly male clones stumbled on a prescription stronger than Viagra, their horses would neither gallop nor kick. Still, Okoye was prepared to listen and see how the crowd reacted.

Emman, by contrast, was in no mood for accommodation. He cast a sharp glance at Kamil, shook his head, and abruptly stormed out of the square. He took his supporters with him. The majority that stayed behind applauded as Emman's contingent withdrew. Kamil took the applause either as good riddance to bad rubbish or as a sign that he was on the right track. Either way, Kamil felt sufficiently emboldened and empowered to continue:

"Thank you, my distinguished listeners. Thank you for your patience and understanding. If I may continue with the rest of my speech, the time has come to take our struggle to the next level." Kamil cast a fleeting glance at Okoye. He saw apprehension in his friend's eyes. If he was not to alienate Okoye as he had done Emman, he had to tip-toe his way to the rest of his speech. He thenceforth had to weigh every word before uttering it:

"Please do not misunderstand me, my esteemed listeners. When I say take our struggle to the next level, I do not mean resorting to violence. I have never supported and shall never support recourse to violence. The Homo Haram terrorists do not speak for those of us at this gathering. Do they?"

"No!" The crowd responded emphatically.

"Thank you! Abu Mamba and his gang of terrorists do not speak for Dukyaria. They certainly do not speak for Islam, whose teachings they shamelessly distort to justify their criminal activities. And God Almighty has clearly disowned them. If anybody comes to you and says that God urges Muslims to kill Christians in particular, and non-Muslims in general, tell him or her it is a lie. Allah Himself unequivocally states in Surah Yunus, ayah ninety-nine, that none believes without His permission. He also warns our Prophet in Surah al-Isra, ayah fifty-four, against constituting himself into the supervisor or micromanager of other people's affairs. The Prophet's, and by implication, the average Muslim's, duty is simply to deliver the message. Whether to punish or to forgive is exclusively Allah's prerogative. That is the guidance we receive in Surah al-Ra'd, ayah forty, and Surah al-Ma'idah, ayah ninety-nine. Justice or fairness, as enjoined in Surah al-Mumtahanah, ayahs nine and ten, knows no religious boundary. It extends to all, regardless of their faith. So, where did they get this authority to kill in God's name and on God's behalf?

"I regret this diversion, but I consider it necessary to debunk Homo Haram's violence-oriented doctrine. The success of our struggle lies in the application of the intellect, not in the discharge of bullets or the detonation of bombs. Taking the struggle to the next level therefore rules out the use of force. It entails building bridges between and among diverse faith groups, between believers and non-believers, and between humans and clones. We cannot win this war without all of us working together." Kamil handed over the microphone, and the crowd went delirious.

The standing ovation continued long after Kamil had returned to his former place. Okoye was relieved. He shook his friend's hands energetically, thus prolonging the deafening applause. Even if the rights Kamil promised the clones eventually failed to materialize, Okoye was confident that his comrade had planted a seed in the clones' minds. They just had to wait and watch what would happen thereafter.

Meanwhile, at about the same time as X300 was wrestling with his identity crisis in Dukyaria, Jamie, the son of a lesbian couple, faced an equally agonizing question in Markham, a municipality in the independent Dominion of Canada. Jamie had no problem identifying his mother, Caitlin. Tired of parrying Jamie's questions on how he came to be in a same-sex household, his parents had told him that his birth mother was Caitlin. However, no matter the amount of pressure he exerted on his adopted parents, neither could tell him who his real father was or his whereabouts.

"We simply matched an anonymous male's sperm with Caitlin's. And to our eternal joy, we ended up with a fine specimen of a man, you." This was how Sarah, the head of the household, had handled and ended the paternity interrogation.

Jamie watched GTN's coverage of Kamil's address. He noted that the cleric championed the clones' interests. He could not understand why Kamil left out off springs of lesbians like himself. Why should he be penalized for being born to a single parent somewhere and raised by a same-sex couple elsewhere? This was most unfair. He too needed a man to call his father. If Caitlin didn't care what happened to her seeds, he, Jamie, wanted to know exactly who he was. Jamie took his self-doubt and frustrations to his regiment in Montreal. Considering himself a virtual or, at least, an associate, clone, he from then on deserted his human clan and started moving in clone circles.

Not long after, GTN brought news of mutinies in clone regiments in different parts of the world. The mutineers were either summarily decommissioned or placed in solitary confinement. Their human collaborators, like Jamie, were court-martialed and slapped with long prison sentences. The GTN promised to bring its viewers up to date on developments.

Chapter-76

You're now fully with us, Pastor? Wise decision!

"HELLO, MR. AKERELE. IT's me, Emman, Pastor Emmanuel Kalu." Emman held his phone close to the left ear.

"Pastor! It's nice hearing your voice. How is life treating you?" Sam was not surprised to receive the call. He was only surprised it took the pastor so long to place it.

"What is your program for the rest of the day?" Emman set protocol aside and went straight to the point on his mind.

"I have to be at an emergency meeting of the National Guidance Council starting at two thirty in the afternoon. From past experience, I don't see the meeting ending before midnight."

"Hey, are you a member of the Guidance Council now?"

"Not in a thousand years! The Governor-General directed that I make myself available in case Council members raise faith-related questions. Do you have anything on your mind, and can it wait till tomorrow, preferably, at the usual time in the night?"

"Sure! We can meet tomorrow. My house; at eight o'clock."

"Copied. See you tomorrow night!" Sam dropped the phone and went back to prepping himself for the Guidance Council meeting.

The meeting was not as eventful as Sam had expected it to be. The closest the meeting got to raising faith-related questions was when debating the strategy to apply to respond to Abu Mamba's latest threat. Troops under the terrorist's command had grabbed swaths of Dukyarian territory. They were poised to march on the national capital. Mamba said it in so many words in his video message relayed by the GTN: "When, not if, the Homo Haram forces seize control of the capital, we shall unilaterally declare Dukyaria an independent state, precisely, the Sovereign Caliphate of Dukyaria, SCD." Naturally, Abu Mamba would be the caliph, meaning the head of the new state.

Faced with the frightful scenario and bothered by the probability of its coming to pass, Homkwap's Guidance Council forgot about the anti-same-sex protests and focused instead on how to get Mamba out of its hairs. In effect, the Council deliberations shifted from matters of faith to the simulation of war and counter-insurgency strategies. Sam, a "bloody civilian," suddenly felt redundant.

Despite having virtually nothing to contribute to the scenario-testing discussions, Sam was obliged to sit through the Executive Council meeting. He did not reach his house until well after one o'clock the following morning. It was good he had not committed himself to an early morning meeting with Emman. He would have either missed the appointment or dozed off for the entire duration of the meeting.

Chapter-77

How should we fix the hotheads, Pastor?

BY THE TIME HE and Emman met at eight o'clock that evening, Sam had got back his strength, and with that, his concentration. He took his usual seat on his host's right.

"Bulus, get us something to drink! Red wine for me, and our esteemed guest's favorite, vodka! And tell Etuk to make sure dinner is ready in exactly thirty minutes," Emman bellowed his instructions to one of the domestic servants.

"You're probably wondering why I asked for this meeting." Emman opened the discussion, turning from Bulus to his guest.

"You are right. Ever since I got your call, I have been wondering why you wanted us to meet," Sam lied. He knew that the meeting had to do with Emman's unceremonious departure from the protest site in front of the WGO office.

"Did you watch the GTN coverage of the demonstrations in front of the WGO office two days ago?"

"I was tied up at one meeting or the other. You know how crazy the schedule is at the government nerve center," Sam lied again, this time, looking sideways to avoid his host's gaze. He took another sip of his vodka.

"Boy, you should have watched the live television coverage and listened to the filth coming out of Kamil's mouth. The Moslem fundamentalist suddenly became an advocate of clone rights! Clone rights! Can you beat that? While he may fool his audience, he cannot fool me. I know where he is going with all this. He wants to incite the clones against the humans and against the government," Emman said, refilling his glass.

"Is that so? Where did he get the obscene idea from? What then do you propose that we do about this?" Sam played his part well, that of one who was totally clueless about the topic of conversation.

"Should you be the one asking me? Shouldn't it be the other way around? Shouldn't I be the one asking you? Even if you are not yet in the Guidance Council, at least you are close to the seat of power. Someone even told me that you have the big man's ears. You yourself once told me that you do not need an appointment to see the Governor-General. So, don't ask me what you should do. Just tell me up front what you plan to do and how we could work together to stop the Moslem fundamentalist and his naïve comrade, Reverend Father Okoye." Emman paused and waited for his guest's reactions.

Sam was pleased that the idea of collaboration came from Emman this time. Instead of looking for ways to reach his host, his host was the one beating a path to his door. All he had to do was find a way to secure Emman's total commitment, his undivided loyalty, to the Homkwap's administration. "I see your point. I am not surprised by Kamil or his 'brother,' Okoye. I warned you about those two earlier. However, since I was under the impression that you and your religious buddies were joined at the hip, I decided there was nothing I could do to make you see them for what they are. Even if I wanted to separate you Siamese, or is it 'Triamese', twins, I don't have the necessary surgical skills! Anyway, from what you have just told me, my earlier impression of your undying love for Okoye and Kamil was mistaken. With the benefit of hindsight, I can now have the courage to go back to His Excellency, the Governor-General, and convince him of the necessity to work with you. How about that?"

"Super!"

"Of course, we would need to agree on the broad outline of our collaboration, a sort of memorandum of understanding. If you think that I am moving too fast, do not hesitate to tell me. I don't want to stampede you into any decision!" Sam continued cautiously.

"Don't worry. I know when to ask you to slow down. But yes, I agree with you. We need to sketch out the area of collaboration. For starters, we need to agree on what we mean by collaboration. What specific proposals do you have?" Emman prodded Sam for details.

"As I said earlier, I had no way of knowing that this topic would come up tonight. So, I had not really given it much thought. Still, if I am to think off the top of my head, I would place delinking Okoye from Kamil at the top of the to-do list." Sam presented his carefully thought out plan as random, off-the-cuff, musings.

"What do you mean by that?" Emman kept the dissembling game going. He asked a question to which he already knew the answer.

"May be separate or split is too strong a word to use in circumstances like this, but that is basically the essence of any effort we must make to delink one from the other." Sam, an amateur auto-suggestion practitioner, had specific ideas but would rather have Emman adopt them as his own.

"What is wrong with either? I have no problem whatsoever with the two words. There is nothing wrong with 'separate' or 'split'. I would even add 'divide', 'disunite', and 'drive a wedge or engineer a rift between'. I don't know what a Christian would have in common with a Moslem fundamentalist, anyway. I see no harm in tearing asunder what God the Father, the Son, and the Holy Spirit never once joined together." Emman was blunt.

"Alright, since those are your picks, I am cool with them also. Of course, it is not the choice of words that matters. It is the action behind each. So long as we are clear on what needs to be done, the rest is a question of semantics—one which needs not detain us."

"That's settled then. The next question is how we are going to proceed to translate the words into action. As you yourself said, action speaks louder than words. And action can't speak until money says it can! Action cannot speak unless money gives it voice! Do you see the point I am trying to make?"

"Since I have not had time to think this out myself, let alone discuss with the Governor-General, I can only, at this stage, indicate what we are likely to bring to the table. By 'we', I mean the government. First, provided I succeed in carrying His Excellency along, money will not be a problem.

We can dip into the security budget at any time without answering to anybody. I also have slush funds under my control. The funds are in a dedicated account to which His Excellency and I are the only signatories. That is not all. We have a propaganda department which would hype any statement you make, and insert well-timed op-eds in local and international newspapers. You will be frequently invited to the Dukyarian Television Service studio. You will be introduced to the GTN Bureau Chief in Dukyaria. That way, anytime the GTN needs a Dukyarian perspective on issues, you or your duly accredited representative will be the one to provide it. In return for all these privileges, you will do your utmost to, as you said, drive a wedge between Okoye and Kamil. You will see to it that those embarrassing street protests stop forthwith. One way to do that is to draw the crowd away from the protest sites and shepherd it to your church. You can also organize high-profile events on dates that clash with those marked for street demonstrations. You can think of other methods later. Finally, we shall need you to infiltrate the ranks of the Dukyarian Workers Association, the Teachers League, the Guild of Market Women, as well as the dreaded UTTTD, the Union of Truck, Tanker and Taxi Drivers. Once we have these formidable groups on our side, we can use them to neutralize Okoye, Kamil, and their street protests."

Emman marveled at the precision with which Sam mapped out the future. How did the man manage it? How could someone who had no forewarning of a topic appear so single-minded and coherent when commenting thereon? Still, Emman was ready to give Sam the benefit of the doubt. The man was probably telling the truth when he said he was totally blank about the topic his host had tabled for discussion. Sam was certainly quick on the uptake, but, for a top ranking civil servant, that was not totally unexpected. The man would not have lasted a day in the high-pressure environment of the Governor-General's office if he had not acquired and honed the capacity to think fast. The Governor-General wouldn't have him anywhere near if he was unable to proffer instant solutions to problems flooding in at short notice. Members of the Governor-General's inner circle must be ready with answers to questions coming from all directions, each question as thorny as, if not thornier than, any other. Even the conspiratorial turn Sam's plan somehow took could be explained by the type of company he kept or the experience he had acquired over the years. It was impossible to hang around the corridor of power that long and be a stranger to intrigue.

"Are you with me?" Sam noticed the distracted look on his host's face.

"Hundred percent!" It was the host's turn to bend the truth. Stirring in his seat as if jump-started by an invisible force, he snapped out of his reverie.

"What do you think of the plan? Will it work?" Sam asked.

"You bet!" With dollar signs and images of television appearances floating around in his head, Emman had no problem accepting the challenge.

Chapter-78

This's no way to say Merry Christmas!

"IS THIS HOMO HARAM's idea of Yuletide greetings? This is the season wherein we are supposed to pray for peace on earth and goodwill to all men and women. Instead of felicitating with us on the auspicious occasion, they blew up buildings at random and killed law-abiding citizens in cold blood. Look at how they separated heads from their bodies, how they ripped open human abdomens, how children as young as four were cut down before they reached their prime, how the terrorists are hell-bent on forcing their evil doctrine down our throats?" Emman looked indignant as the GTN and DTS cameras captured the gory spectacle, as well as his own reactions to the latest terrorist act. He had rushed to Gwagwalada the instant the major channels brought news of the violence perpetrated in the neighborhood. A television crew was at the scene recording the carnage.

"But, Sir, Homo Haram has yet to claim responsibility for the dastardly act. So is it not premature to lay the blame at their door?" The interviewer held the microphone close to Emman's mouth.

"When was this dastardly act perpetrated, if I may ask you?" Emman, the interviewee, traded places with the DTS interviewer.

"The report we got from the police indicates that the incident happened about an hour ago," the interviewer responded.

"So, if the incident happened an hour ago, did you expect Homo Haram to have started announcing two or three hours earlier that it was going to bomb this church? Oh, I forgot, Homo Haram is dumb. It will go on the air and say, 'Listen up folks! Sit tight wherever you are. We will be raining bombs on you one hour from now.' Don't you think Homo Haram would ensure that the deed is done before claiming ownership? Going by past experience, Mamba will not claim responsibility for this insanity until he sees us wailing and crying. Nothing pleases him more than to see or hear us wail and cry. As soon as he notices that his act has had the intended effect, he will gladly go on the air and say, 'Yes, I did it.' As we speak, he is asking himself, 'Who's your daddy?' And I bet with every penny in my pocket that his answer to his own question will be, 'I, Abu Danja Mamba, the one who can make you wail and cry. I am your daddy!'"

"Thank you, Pastor, for this incisive analysis. Now, back to the studio."

As the terrorists hoped and Emman expected, Dukyarians wailed and cried over the loss of the innocent souls. The mourners were particularly grieved that among the dead were two fine individuals who had set out on a noble mission—a mission to spread the word of God, and at the same time, touch the lives of their flock.

Chapter-79

RIP, Apostle of Love, Peace, and Hope!

AKIN MOSAFEJO HAD FINALLY decided to draw up and implement his own business plan. With the indemnity awarded by the magistrate court, he had started the Church of Latter Day Saints on a small scale in the hope that it would grow over time. He and Catherine had bought a partly completed building in Gwagwalada and had converted it into a church.

It was not easy at first attracting worshippers to fill up space in the new church. The church's awkward location proved a strong disincentive to would-be worshippers. Tucked in an overcrowded neighborhood far from the highway, the Church of Latter Day Saints was accessible only to those who did not mind trekking long distances, basically the poor. The rich never gave much thought to the celestial favors awaiting them at Mosafejo's church. What weighed heavily on the mind of the church's potential backbone were the deplorable condition of the only access road and the locality's high crime rate. The big men and their female equivalents simply stayed away rather than risk their life and possessions in such an unsafe neighborhood.

Akin, not one to give up easily, proceeded with messianic zeal to surmount the obstacles. To link his church with the highway, he dipped into his coffers and engaged the services of road maintenance contractors. Within three months of his arrival in Gwagwalada, the potholes on the road had been filled and the clouds of dust kicked up by passing vehicles had been banished by coatings of macadam.

Satisfied that he had got rid of one pretext to avoid his church, Akin proceeded to confront another challenge, 'civilizing' his environment. He was convinced that the location of his church in that remote part of Gwagwalada was not accidental. It was for a purpose. Helping the less privileged to advance in life was one way he might atone for his past misdeeds. He was thus determined to get his church's hostile neighbors to 'evolve' from barbarism to order, from nihilism to public spiritedness, and from paralyzing pessimism to a feeling of hope and empowerment.

To achieve his objective, Mosafejo started by identifying the neighborhood's gang leaders and inviting them for a meeting. Speaking in Kasaranci, he had asked if the gangs were willing to disband if he assured the leaders regular employment. So the followers would not feel betrayed, he had also pledged to slot gang members into vacancies as and when he knew of any.

"What is the catch?" Kyauta, the most vicious gang leader pointedly asked his self-appointed benefactor. He had been on the street for too long to be taken in by false promises. He had formed his gang nine years after his polytechnic degree in accounting failed to get him a job.

"You want the truth?" Akin answered Kyauta's question with his own.

"I thought that was already implied in my question." Kyauta wanted the truth and nothing but.

"I need you and your colleagues to bring the message to the people." Mosafejo was direct.

"What message?" Kyauta asked, a cynical expression on his face.

"The message of love, peace, and hope." Mosafejo ignored the skeptical face and announced his mission.

"Love, peace, and hope? Since you came here, have you seen any of those things? Have you even seen a single hint of love, peace, and hope around you? Consider yourself lucky that we have so far left you and your church alone. It wouldn't take us a second to descend on your congregation and chase you all from here!" The chary expression on Kyauta's face had disappeared, replaced by a grim and hostile one.

"That is precisely my point. You have power. You have influence. You have what it takes to change lives. Why not use what you have for the good of your people? Why 'descend' on innocent persons—persons who have done nothing to offend you?" Mosafejo placed special accent on 'descend'.

"You are not serious. I feel offended just looking at those you call my people. They know that everything is wrong with their life. Yet they go about with stupid smiles on their stupid faces. They convey the totally false impression that everything is going according to plan. Whose plan? The big men's? The politicians'? The local agents of the World Government? Well, if they are happy with their plans, we are not." Kyauta's eyes looked meaner than they had been at the onset of the conversation.

"I know where you are coming from," Mosafejo assured the increasingly agitated Kyauta.

"Do you?" Kyauta asked, looking Mosafejo intently in the eyes.

"Certainly. Sit down and let me tell you the story of my life." Akin sat Kyauta and his colleagues down. He narrated his experience growing up in a poor household and struggling through his adolescent to his school going years. As he told his listeners, when he eventually acquired a university degree, he thought that his problems were over. He believed that he was now ready to join the new middle class. He did not realize the obstacles "the System" had placed separating him from his dream. The upper class, that is the big men, were not keen on nurturing a strong middle class or addressing the concerns of the vast majority constituting the underclass. The upper class care for nobody except themselves.

Kyauta and his sidekicks sat wide-eyed as Akin ran them through his life history. The gang leader was particularly intrigued by what Akin had to say about his job search experience. "That in fact was how Pastor Emman and I first met. I am sure you know him. The now rich and famous Pastor Emmanuel Kalu. Well, as they say, the rest is history."

"Remarkable! I never thought that any life could be more wretched than mine. How about you, Habila?" Kyauta turned to Habila for comments, but the gang leader's second in command was only there in body. His mind was somewhere else.

Ignoring the absentminded Habila, Kyauta shifted his gaze back to Mosafejo and continued, "In fact, seeing you in your air-conditioned car, no one would ever believe that you once knew what we call poverty and destitution. But here you are, making us realize that you have seen it all. Maybe there is hope for the hopeless like us after all! Or what do you think Habila?" Kyauta looked sideways at his comrade again.

Habila still heard and said nothing. He was lost in thought. He was thinking of Nwoke, an Ndi merchant whose grocery they planned to rob later in the evening. Kyauta had designated him coordinator of the operation. He had to make sure that the raid was carried out with precision, and, above all, successfully. He didn't foresee any serious obstacle anyway. He had been told that the Ndis of the east were not only hardworking, but also very rich. What was more, they kept their money at home, not in the bank. Nwoke would be an easy target. His house also happened to be his grocery. All the merchant needed to do to start the day's business was walk from the back of the building and open the shutter in the front. Well, he might have saved himself rental money converting part of his property into a grocery. He would now have to pay the Kyauta gang the obligatory "protection" and miscellaneous fees.

"Habila! Are you deaf? Have you been listening to all we have been saying?" Kyauta yelled at his deputy.

"Sorry, what did you say?" Habila was clearly not listening.

"Forget it. What of you Gagara? Did you hear what the priest said? And did you listen to my response?" Kyauta turned from Habila to the next lackey.

"The priest said something about love, peace, and hope. And, as I understand you, you told him that those objects are alien to this environment. Then the priest told us the history of his life, and you wondered if it was possible that others had it rougher than us. That's all I heard." Gagara recapped as best as he could.

"Good. That's why I like you. You are very bright.

Now, let's hear you, Julius." Kyauta was pleased with Gagara.

He turned to Julius next.

"It's exactly as Gagara put it. I have nothing to add. The priest said something, you said another. Then when the priest told us about his struggles, you understood what he had said. That was how the two paths, yours and his, met." Julius got away with banalities.

"I can live with that summary as well. So, where do we go from here?" Kyauta's question was not directed at any one in particular.

"If you ask me, I would suggest that you and your men go back and think seriously about my proposal. I am not asking you to decide right away. Go and sleep over what I told you. You should ask yourselves what you need to do to change your life around and, with that, the life of the people around you. If you genuinely believe that my proposal makes no sense, feel free to reject it." Kyauta did not believe that the day would dawn when anyone would trust him with the capacity to decide for himself. Could this be a trick, or was it the empowerment which the man spoke about earlier? Kyauta instantly withdrew with his men. He promised to get back to the priest with their decision as soon as possible.

The first indication that Kyauta was forsaking his bad, old ways was his unilateral decision not to proceed with the raid on Nwoke's grocery. To Habila's utter disappointment, the boss revoked the plan. It was good the deputy thug reconsidered his decision to go behind Kyauta's back and carry out an operation clearly vetoed by the boss. He would have walked into Nwuke's trap and stared down the barrel of the Ndi merchant's revolver. Nwoke got his gun ready the minute he received an anonymous telephone call tipping him off about plans by hoodlums to invade his grocery.

That was how Kyauta and his men turned over a new leaf and became advocates of love, peace, and hope in their locality. In line with the Church of Later Day Saints' open-door policy, the former gangsters became apostles of tolerance. On Mosafejo's directive, they preached accommodation between and among rival faith and ethnic groups, between men and women, as well as between clones and regular humans. They extended protection to gays and lesbians so long as members of this minority group did not rub the public's face in their sexual preferences or force those preferences on the straight majority.

As head of church security, Kyauta saw to it that the flock and the shepherd came to no harm. In addition to performing neighborhood watch functions, Habila and other gang members nailed down regular jobs within the church. Mosafejo did not forget about Kyauta's other followers, the foot soldiers. He prevailed upon well-heeled members of his church to find the confused youth gainful employment in their organizations. Fortunately, the church had turned the corner. After a long struggle, it had started counting high-ranking government officials and captains of industry among its patrons. Considering the influence that the Okoye-Kamil partnership had on practices within his church, Mosafejo had looked forward to the day when his followers would reap the benefit of associating with the two clerics.

It seemed that disaster often struck any time Mosafejo saw hope on the horizon. When he thought that the future could not but be rosy, death denied him the chance to find out exactly what form that future would take. He and Catherine had organized a special thanksgiving service to mark the commissioning of a new clinic. The facility, constructed with church donations, was to save the locals the trouble of travelling long distances to obtain basic medical care. A beneficiary also did not have to give an arm and a leg to find a cure for common colds and other curable maladies. Unlike when they relied solely on government health care institutions, the sick did not have to wait hours in the outpatient lounge to see a doctor. The icing on the cake was not having to contend with the acerbic tongues and supercilious attitudes of the paramedical staff, especially, nurses.

The first bomb that tore through the church's entrance spared only a few. It took out many congregation members and the church elders who had taken their seats, as well as Mosafejo and Catherine, both standing close to the pulpit. Mosafejo, who had despised reform programs in his earlier days, died trying to reform his immediate community. The few that escaped the blast ran helter-skelter, thoroughly disoriented. The first explosion was followed by others, each exacting high casualties and wreaking incalculable damage.

Chapter-80

Arrest the fundamentalist and his Catholic pawn!

BACK IN HIS OWN villa, Emman sat on the living room sofa as DTS gave an account of the Gwagwalada incident on its nightly news program. He stiffened as Kamil's face appeared on the screen. The Muslim cleric had condemned the terrorist act "in the strongest possible terms." He repeated his by then familiar avowal that the terrorists did not speak for God or for Islam.

Emman was not impressed. He scoffed at Kamil's "lame condemnation." For all Emman knew, the man might have had inside knowledge of the terrorist act, from the planning to the execution stage. Kamil was a Moslem fundamentalist, wasn't he? He and his Homo Haram brothers were culpable. In fact, he would issue a press statement calling for Kamil's immediate arrest.

As Emman was mulling over what he would do to get Kamil out of the way, the DTS's channel flipped to the second interview on the same subject. Okoye's telegenic face stared at Emman. When he thought he had had his fill with Kamil, now this! Emman felt nauseated. His old feeling of envy mixed with animosity came welling up. He shifted in his seat, rolling his eyes disdainfully. He fleetingly considered spitting on the floor to show how much he detested the Catholic reverend. The tidy sum he recalled paying for the luxurious Persian carpet dissuaded Emman. He was down to only one option—stare dourly at the television set.

"You already know my position, Ben. I abhor violence. Violence solves nothing. Unfortunately, the message is not getting through to Abu Mamba and his gang. The Homo Haram terrorists have massacred innocent souls. They have destroyed valuable property. They have even got our attention, fleeting, I must add. Beyond that, what have they accomplished? Nothing! Absolutely nothing!" That was Okoye's response to Benjamin Uwujaren's first question.

"Are you sure, Reverend Father, that they have accomplished nothing? How about our territory which they are grabbing one city at a time?" The interviewer probed further.

"Do you think that Dukyarians will stand by and surrender themselves to the dictates of Mamba's Sharia law? I don't think so. There will be a solution to the Homo Haram problem sooner or later. Trust me!"

"We hope the solution comes sooner rather than later. Now, on this question of Sharia, aren't you aware that your best friend, Sheikh Salim Kamil, is an advocate of Sharia law? Some even call him a Moslem fundamentalist. Won't your continued association with him be interpreted as an endorsement of the Islamization of Dukyaria?" Ben finally got to the substantive topic. He asked the question handed to him by the Governor-General's office.

"Hallelujah! God bless you, Ben! You've nailed the bastard!" Emman was overjoyed at the last question. He waited to see how Okoye planned to get out of that one.

"Have you ever met Kamil? Do you know him personally? Has he ever once told you or anybody of his plan to introduce Sharia law across the length and breadth of

403

Dukyaria? And where did you get this story of Islamization from? Now let me tell you what you do not know about Kamil and his position on Islamization, the Sharia, and all that. I have pointedly asked what Kamil thought of Abu Mamba's intention to replace our legal code with Sharia law. Do you know what he said?" Okoye asked rhetorically.

"No, Reverend Father. I don't; if you would be so kind to tell our viewers." Ben cut in, requesting Okoye to do precisely what the reverend father had planned on doing anyway.

"He said anybody who plans to introduce Sharia law in Dukyaria must be insane, as that person would never succeed in subduing forces opposed to the law. You cannot be more realistic than that. Kamil's policy has always been 'to you your faith, to me mine.' He will not force you to come to his mosque so long as you do not force him to go to your church or shrine."

"And you believe him?"

"Implicitly! Do you have any reasons why I shouldn't?"

"Umm… but… I honestly don't know how to answer that question." The interviewer intermittently tilted his head left and right, at the same time turning his right fingers clock- and anti-clockwise. The comme ci, comme ça gestures were Ben's cynical answer to the question whether Okoye was right to continue trusting Kamil.

Chapter-81

A clash of street protests

EMMAN FINALLY HAD MORE than he could take of the media spotlight lavished on the anti-gay protests. It was bad enough that the protests were making his opponents increasingly popular and raising the political profile of Kamil and Okoye. It was totally unacceptable that the local and the world press would follow the troublemakers everywhere, blowing up everything Okoye and Kamil said or did. And where are those invitations that Emman had expected to come pouring in from the bureau chief of the GTN? The local representative of the global network hadn't yet gotten round to extending the invitations. As for the DTS, Emman fully understood the studio's standoffish attitude. As a local affiliate of the GTN, the DTS would not invite him for an interview without clearance from the New York head office of the parent company. Besides, both the GTN and the DTS kept their eyes on ratings. It would be commercially suicidal for them to leave personalities with a substantial following and run after the leader of a measly crowd. He wondered when Sam would start pulling the strings that he had promised earlier. Well, the senior official had probably been distracted by affairs of state.

As Emman fumed over the media coverage of the protests against same-sex marriage, he suddenly came up with an idea. Instead of remaining indignant under his roof, why couldn't he too get up and go? He should stop moaning at home. He should organize his own street protests and start milking the benefits. Okoye and Kamil were not the only ones capable of pulling large crowds. He too must be ready to get his own show on the road—literally and figuratively.

As it so happened, Okoye and Kamil had planned the next round of demonstrations for a Saturday, when turnout was likely to be highest. The venue remained unchanged: Independence Square with its wide, open space directly opposite the WGO office. Emman knew the time and place. He promptly announced that his own counter-demonstrations would be held on the same date and on the same spot chosen by Okoye and Kamil.

The Freedom of Assembly Law allowed any group of individuals to assemble "for the purpose of expressing support for or opposition to any policy or practice having direct or indirect bearing on public welfare." However, notice of intention to so assemble must be filed with the police at least a week in advance. The police lacked the authority to deny any applicant or group of applicants the permit to assemble unless it had reasons to believe that the proposed gathering "calls for the disbandment of the Union or directly threatens public order." To guard against risks to public order, the police had the discretion to block a date and a venue for a public assembly and deny any subsequent application to assemble on the same date and in the same venue. The police command was, however, not obligated to exercise this discretionary authority. It could approve or deny rival applications as it deemed fit.

Emman knew about the law authorizing public assemblies. The police register clearly indicated that the Saturday which the pastor picked for his own demonstrations was already blocked. Yet, Emman insisted on that Saturday, and the police obliged.

Sam was clearly not too distracted by affairs of state to pull the strings. He had peremptorily instructed the Chief

Commissioner of Police to see to it that Emman's application was approved.

"How about the other group? We already issued them a permit. If we cancel it, Okoye and Kamil will raise hell!" The Chief Commissioner of Police protested meekly.

"Who said anything about cancelling their permit? Let them go ahead with their plan. When you get to my office later this afternoon, I'll give you details of our own plan. For now, we must maintain radio silence." Sam sounded conspiratorial.

The Chief Commissioner of Police got the message. The matter was hush-hush from then on. He hung up and dialed the head of the Police's Public Security Department. "Go ahead. Issue the permit requested by the pastor."

"What of the permit we issued to Father Okoye and Sheikh Kamil? Shall I go ahead and cancel that?"

"No! Do no such thing! The two permits stay! You got that?"

"Yes, Sir!" The subordinate, holding the receiver close to his ear, stood up and dutifully saluted the absent commander. A newly recruited Assistant Police Lieutenant, a college graduate, watched as his immediate supervisor demeaned himself during the phone conversation. At least, if the head of the Public Security department wished to lick the

Chief Commissioner's boots, he should wait until the boss was there to watch. Why should a subordinate grovel before a superior who was not even there to see this definitive symbol of toadying?

Unmindful of the perplexed look on the rookie's face, the Public Security head deferred to authority as duty demanded. He expected his own subordinates to carry themselves the same way if they found themselves in the same situation. They would neither survive nor advance in the organization unless they were ready to outsmart rivals for the boss's approbation. No matter whether the subordinates stood directly in front of the boss or talked to him from remote locations, they were duty-bound to show him some respect and salute him properly.

Expecting the uninitiated lieutenant to learn the ropes fast, the Public Security Department's head shifted his attention back to Saturday. He began to wonder what would happen that day.

The Chief Commissioner knew what would happen. He and Sam subsequently agreed on the plan for Saturday. However, the police boss kept the plan close to his chest. He suspected many of his subordinates of divided loyalty. Some, the police boss feared, were ardent but clandestine supporters of Kamil and Okoye. A few others were on Emman's payroll. Even Abu Mamba had moles planted in the police. The only officer the Chief Commissioner trusted implicitly was the head of the anti-riot squad, Superintendent Maxwell Bawa. He called the superintendent over the intercom and invited him for a tête-à-tête. As soon as Bawa arrived, the boss whispered into his right ear. The mean, no, diabolical, look on the subordinate's face indicated that he got the message, loud and clear. Kamil was the first to notice the unusual police presence at the day's rally. Nudging Okoye by the elbow, he winked in the direction of trucks disgorging uniformed servicemen a few meters away. Within minutes, squads of constables in anti-riot gear hopped out of their vehicles and, on hitting the ground, took positions on straight lines. Each carried light arms, a gasmask, and teargas canisters.

"Left! Right! Left! Right! Left! Right!" A sergeant started drilling the troops, now in battle formation and combat mode.

Okoye ignored the display. He mounted the rostrum. The crowd cheered wildly. "We seem to have new well-wishers in our midst today. It appears the police has sent its own delegation to the people's conference!" Okoye swung his left hand towards the police. The crowd cheered even more wildly.

As soon as the commotion subsided, Okoye continued with the rest of his speech. He didn't plan to say much that day. He would rather hand the microphone to a new convert to the cause, Emman. The crowd was ecstatic. Emman and his supporters remained stolid.

"It is now my pleasure to introduce our next speaker, Pastor Emmanuel Kalu. Over to you, Pastor Kalu." As agreed with Kamil, Okoye got off the rostrum and handed the microphone over to Emman.

Emman's hitherto expressionless face looked stern as he walked up to the rostrum. Almost on cue, Amos marched into the square, followed by four men and three women. Amos's followers promptly started handing out their own placards—the ones sympathizing with gays and lesbians and berating opponents of same-sex unions. "GAY OR STRAIGHT, WE'RE ALL FROM GOD!" read one placard. "SINNERS CASTING THE FIRST STONE!" read another. "MY LIFE, MY CHOICE!" read yet another.

Okoye and Kamil were stunned. The original protesters, constituting the majority, glanced at one another, incredulous. Is this an act taken right out of a sitcom? Is it a joke? Are we dreaming? Will somebody tell us what is going on? An eerie silence suddenly enveloped the crowd.

Emman broke the silence. He was ready to tell his listeners about the madness that had gone on for far too long and what he planned to do to stop it: "Ladies and gentlemen, I have watched you troop out here day in day out to participate in what they call anti-same sex protests. Do you think that your protests can or will change anything? The ink on the Imperial Proclamation is dry and indelible. If anyone tells you that he can rewrite the law, tell him to dream on."

Emman's abrupt decision to hijack the protests infuriated Kamil. He walked across to the pastor to demand an explanation. "You have no right to do what you have just done. You are not supposed to be here if you are opposed to what we are doing."

"And where am I supposed to be?"

"Either in your home enjoying your millions or in Akerale's office begging for more money!"

Emman was stung by Kamil's remark. He did not expect that anyone knew that he and Sam had been meeting secretly at odd hours of the night, or that the little matter of money ever came up in their discussions.

"Where did you get the idea that I am asking anybody for money?" He put on a bold face.

"The person who farts is not the only one who knows what he has done. Those that are forced to hold their noses also know that someone is to blame for the foul stench in the air." Kamil thrust the knife deeper.

"You will rot in hell, Emman!" A voice shot out of the crowd like a bullet.

"And you call yourself a pastor? Barawo pastor!" Another protester lobbed his own verbal grenade, calling the pastor a thief.

"He even claims to be a prophet! Bloody hypocrite!"

"Pastor Counterfeit! Prophet Counterfeit! Pastor Counterfeit! Prophet Counterfeit! Pastor Counterfeit! Prophet Counterfeit!" The most inventive protester initiated a song-and-dance sequence. He had stumbled on a way to rid the gathering of the pastor and his followers.

"Pastor Counterfeit! Prophet Counterfeit!..." Another took up the refrain. One by one, the protesters joined the chorus. Before long, the song drowned out Emman's voice.

The dance was to cause greater havoc to the square's tranquility. The GTN and the DTS cameras had a field day, capturing the protesters as the anti-Emman forces ringed round the pastor and his supporters and accelerated the song-and-dance momentum. "Pastor Counterfeit! Prophet Counterfeit!…"

Kamil and Okoye tried to stabilize the situation. Both wished to release the placard-carrying intruders from the claws of the majority and whisk them off to safety. However, it was too late. Infuriated by the crowd's taunts, Emman had taken a swing at the man nearest to him. To his dismay, the young man's reflex was quick. The target of Emman's fury saw the punch coming and moved in the nick of time to duck it. The punch crashed instead on a slender lady's face. She collapsed instantly. It took spirited fanning by onlookers and buckets of cold water to resuscitate her.

Having brought the unintended recipient of Emman's blow back from the dead, the crowd set upon the intruders. It was now total bedlam at the square. Fists flew, bodies fell, and tattered strips of once pretty clothes scattered all over the place.

Chapter-82

The priests on the lam

X300 KNEW WHAT WAS coming next—his colleagues' application of deadly force to restore order. Taking advantage of the tumult, and relying on his statutory obligation to keep the peace, the clone left his post. He marched briskly towards Kamil and Okoye. "Follow me now, if you value your life." Kamil and Okoye did as the clone advised. X300 immediately got into the driver's seat of a waiting car. He asked Okoye to take the front passenger seat. Kamil's beard made him easily recognizable, even in a fast-moving car.

As they drove along the Outer Ring Road, X300 intimated his passengers about Sam Akerele's plan. Emman's presence at the protest ground was no accident. It was part of Sam's plan. The intention, X300 added, was to turn a peaceful assembly into a riotous one and then give the police the pretext they needed to carry out their shoot-on-sight order. The two arrowheads of the anti-WGO struggle, Kamil and Okoye, would be among the casualties. The police had it all figured out. It covered all its bases. The official explanation for the protest leaders' death would be 'accidental discharge'. The police would claim that Okoye and Kamil would still be alive if they had not interfered in the lawful performance of police duties. The two hotheads had not only attempted to evict police constables from the square but had also had the audacity to disarm them forcefully. Naturally, when two or more persons struggle for the possession of a gun, bullets are bound to fly. Since the protesters would have been blinded by teargas, none of them would be accepted as credible witnesses in an investigation. None would be able to contradict the official line on the cause of death—accidental discharge.

"So, where are we going now? I don't think that you know, but we've left my own house behind in Garki. Something also tells me that we are not headed in the direction of Reverend Father Okoye's vicarage in Utako either. So, if we are not going to my house, and we are not going to his, or to your barracks, where are we headed?" Kamil was sufficiently composed in his back-seat position to ask a question. He was glad that his wife and Abdullah had moved to Maiduguri. He was further calmed by the update he received a day earlier on his son's condition. Sheikh Awwal's medication and prayers were working.

"You are right. We are not going to your house or his. Neither of you will be safe until the dust settles and people start asking questions," X300 answered imprecisely.

"What do you mean by that? Is it that serious?" Kamil asked for clarification.

"It is more serious than you can ever imagine. Those who are after you won't give up until they are sure you are permanently silenced. However, if you lie low for a day and then resurface the following day, you can issue a statement asking why the police issued permits to two rival public assemblies. The questions which the public asks thereafter will compel those who want you dead to call off the assassins. They will know that the game is up. You catch my drift?" The clone borrowed a human slang.

"You have really evolved, haven't you? You have stayed with the humans long enough to know how their minds work. You are also speaking their language—especially, the language of deception." Okoye weighed in with his own observation.

"Let's just say that I am trying. If you humans don't know your inner selves, how can I claim to?"

"Another human trick, if you ask me! This's how the trick works: pretend to be clueless so your opponent will let his guard down! You sly fox!" Okoye was buying none of X300's modesty act.

"What does sly fox mean? Are you calling me a fox?" The clone was not acting.

"Certainly not! Sly fox is a term that humans use humorously. It is a funny way of complimenting someone for his ability to outwit others."

"Glad to be a sly fox, then. Maybe I should even adopt it as my name. X300 Sly Fox! How does that sound?"

"Beautiful!" Kamil and Okoye responded simultaneously.

"So, as I was saying, if the leaders of the protest movement were assassinated, that would be the end of the protests. And we, clones, wouldn't like that! We wouldn't like the protests to end until things change around here. We have grievances that the WGO will not consider once the only voice of dissent is silenced." Sly Fox's motive in rescuing Kamil and

Okoye was not entirely altruistic, after all. He and his fellow clones wanted to keep the pot boiling long enough for someone at the WGO headquarters to notice that not everyone was happy with the status quo.

"By the way, how did you come to know about the government's plan to disrupt our event and then take us out?" Kamil asked from his rear-seat position.

"Just let's say that we have friends in high and low places," Sly Fox responded tersely.

"Would those friends happen to be mid-ranking and low-echelon police officers?" Okoye was equally curious. Something told him that the head of Public Security Department—the one who passed up no opportunity to show his loyalty to his boss and to the government—was actually on the side of the protesters. So were the cops assigned the tasks of patrolling streets, controlling crime, and arresting criminals.

"No comment." Sly Fox refused to divulge the information sought by Okoye.

DTS soon suspended its regular program and focused instead on the ruckus at Independence Square. The studio repeatedly played back footage of the sudden invasion by placard-carrying supporters of same-sex union, the altercation between Kamil and Emman, and the song-and-dance act which led to the free-for-all fight. The news editor dutifully omitted Emman's incendiary comments—the comments that provoked the skirmish. DTS presented the pastor's battered face at close range along with the gory pictures of the wounded protesters as they were being rushed to hospital emergency wards.

The replay continued until it was interrupted by the studio to bring its viewers breaking news. "We have just learnt that both Reverend Basil Okoye and Sheikh Salim Kamil, the brains behind the mayhem at Independence Square, have been declared wanted by the police." The studio supplied the two clerics' mug shots. It went further to describe their physical features, including the height, weight, color and shape of the fugitives' eyes, texture of hair, and complexion. "Anyone who knows of their whereabouts is advised to alert the police immediately. The police further advise civilians against attempting to arrest the fugitives. Both are armed and dangerous."

"Armed and dangerous? These people are shameless liars! Anyway, even if I knew where they are, I wouldn't betray them for all the money in the world. Would you?" Kyauta asked Gagara.

"Never!" Gagara concurred with his former gang leader.

Kyauta's memory of his late benefactor, Mosafejo, nearly brought him to tears. "How I wish Pastor were here with us now! He would have told us what to do to help the two men of God. I miss him badly."

"Didn't they say that good people never die? The pastor may not be here with us physically, but his good deeds will never be forgotten," Gagara said, consoling Kyauta.

"You are right. Now that we remember the pastor, we must also remember our own brothers and sisters who perished in the church explosions—especially, Sister Catherine, Habila, Julius, Pascal, Mathias, and the others. May their souls rest in peace!"

"Amen!"

416

Chapter-83

Bring the criminals here right now, dead or barely alive!

"HOW DID THEY GET away? Didn't we agree that your men should surround the place and make sure that no person of interest got out alive?" The Chief Commissioner of Police paced his office, looking stern. He kept tapping his left palm with the baton in the right hand.

"It's all Pastor Kalu's fault, Sir. He created a crisis when we least expected it. Before we knew it, he struck a woman and enraged the crowd," Superintendent Bawa answered, his voice croaky, his eyes avoiding the commissioner's, and his hands fidgeting with the uniform.

"Are you listening to the nonsense coming out of your mouth? 'He struck a woman and enraged the crowd.'" The Chief Commissioner, tilting his head left and right, making a face, and gesticulating with both hands, mimicked Bawa. He quickly continued, "A crisis which we spent days planning and orchestrating caught you off-guard! Did you expect the pastor to announce to the whole world that he was privy to a plan to disrupt the gathering, and that the plan included decking a harmless, frail-looking woman? Didn't I tell you to swing into action at the slightest sign of trouble? Didn't I tell you to get rid of the two hotheads as soon as you noticed that the gathering's proceedings had been properly disrupted? What other smoke signal were you waiting for? And you call yourself an officer! Exactly where are the two trouble-makers now?"

the Chief Commissioner, still pacing the room and rapping his left palm with the baton, asked in a shrill, piercing voice.

"We don't know yet, Sir…"

"I can't believe this! Have you turned their houses upside down?" The Chief Commissioner, the baton still taking the frustrations out on the left palm, abruptly stopped pacing. He glared at the superintendent.

"We have, Sir. In fact, I was just coming to that, Sir. We opened every door, checked every room, and even peered under beds, tables, and, in Kamil's case, the children's cots. We found nothing, Sir. I instructed my men to stay behind and keep the two houses under surveillance. I have also detailed an officer to follow Kamil's driver, Lawan, wherever he goes. He may yet lead us to the high-prize target. I am confident that one way or the other, the criminals will walk into our trap."

"I wouldn't count on that. Neither will be stupid enough to return to their houses until they know that the coast is clear. You know what I want you to do?"

"No, Sir."

"I want you to send your crack team of plain-clothes detectives all over town. They should not come back unless they catch the two fugitives, dead or alive. You got that?"

"Yes, Sir!" Superintendent Bawa, stretching to his five-foot eleven-inch height, saluted the boss and quickly marched back to his own office.

To get the job done and restore his boss's faith in his competence, Superintendent Bawa pulled out the dossiers of sleuths under his command. He picked those that had proven themselves in the past—those that had not only cracked the most difficult cases but had also apprehended the most dangerous criminals, including sociopaths.

Bawa promptly dispatched the men and women to different parts of the city. Their mission was to collect data on strange faces and unusual movements recently noticed by the residents of each neighborhood. The faces were to be matched with the mug shots handed over to the various squads. The detectives had to follow every lead and record every minute detail.

The hunters promptly set out looking for their quarries. They stopped and searched vehicles on major highways, mixed freely with travelers at motor parks, peered under hospital beds, and stormed into private dwellings suspected of harboring the fugitives. They even combed amusement parks, forests, game reserves, hotel suites, mosques, churches, and school dormitories. They came up empty.

The detectives were on the point of giving up when luck finally smiled on them. The lead which they had been waiting for came when a boy, barely twelve years old, recognized seeing a man that resembled the one in the photo. "Yes, I saw the man with the beard." The boy was referring to Kamil. The cleric ought to have lost the beard the instant he was declared wanted. However, either he didn't believe or he didn't care that the police force was on his tail. Kamil had stubbornly kept his beard. That made him all but impossible to miss in a line-up.

"So, where are they now—the bearded man and his friend?" Dauda, the squad leader, pressed the boy for additional information.

"Over there!" The boy pointed to a house about three hundred meters away. The little informant smiled innocently. He had just acquired a new bragging right. His classmates would be extremely jealous when they heard that a small boy like himself had proved useful to "the government."

Dauda and his subordinates raced to the house, their guns at the ready. "You, you, and you, watch the back. Peter and Cosmas, stand guard in front and watch every movement. The rest of us will go in and smoke the criminals out." A moment later, the squad leader barked, "Now, John! Kick the door in!"

John did as he was instructed. His sturdy boot crashed into the knob and the door gave way. The security operatives quickly moved from the aisle to the living room. Two cups lay on the coffee table in the living room, empty. Judging by the tiny drops and the smell left behind, the cups must have contained strong, black coffee. Dauda was certain that those who left the cups in that state, the persons into whose stomachs the coffee had gone, were those they were after. And they could not be far away.

"The real search has just begun. We must turn every room upside down. Let's start with the one immediately on the right." Dauda instructed the men and the women on his team.

The detectives rummaged every room, angrily pulling out clothes, pots and pans, ripping pillows and mattresses, and yanking television cables from their sockets. By the time Dauda and his subordinates were done, the bedrooms had been thoroughly ransacked and the spacious lounge had been turned into one big junkyard.

Dauda was baffled. Where are the criminals? Surely, they could not have been tipped off so quickly. How could they have vanished into thin air that fast? And whose house was this anyway? How did they get there in the first place? Too many questions. Not a single answer. Something is not right here! Dauda thought to himself.

"Time to go, guys!" Dauda, realizing that he had exhausted his options, called off his hound dogs.

Chapter-84

Come and arrest us on live television!

BY THE TIME THE detectives reported back in the office, Kamil and Okoye had saved the government the trouble of agonizing over their whereabouts. Both fugitives had taken to the airwaves pointedly accusing the government of ordering their assassination.

Neither named X300 as the source of their intelligence. Neither provided any clue as to how the clone had led them out of the crowd and spirited them off to a safe house whose ownership remained a mystery. Both clerics were completely tight-lipped on how X300 had woken them up from sleep in the wee hours of the morning and led them from the safe house through largely deserted, zigzagging, reptile-infested foot paths back to the highway. One thing they did not forget to mention was Providence's support in their trying hour. "Were it not for Allah's mercy, we would not be here to relate our ordeal," Kamil, looking gaunt and exhausted on television, told the viewers, among them, Amina, then in Maiduguri, five hundred kilometers away.

"Thank you, Jesus, for keeping us safe!" Okoye concurred with Kamil the only way he knew.

"But what proof is there that the police are behind this? How are we even sure that you did not make it all up? How are we sure that you did not abscond from the crime scene, the crime the police accused you of masterminding?" Ben, the

424

DTS interviewer, did as he was tutored—discredit the clerics and cast doubt on their story. If Emman had been well enough to sit and watch the program, he would have been delighted by Ben's hostile line of questioning. Unfortunately, the pastor was still in the trauma wing of Hayat Hospital, his head draped in bandages, and his battered face stitched in many places. With one broken leg plastered and held suspended on his hospital bed, his immediate priority was getting back on his feet.

"I suggest that you direct your question to the police. Ask the police why it blocked a date for our rally, only to turn around and issue another permit to a group meeting on the same date and in the same venue, a group that was hell-bent on disrupting our rally." Okoye quickly cut in.

"How is that possible? How could the police issue permits to two rival gatherings knowing full-well that such an act would threaten public order?" Ben remained skeptical.

"But that is precisely what the police did. It created an atmosphere that was conducive to the breakdown of law and order. It authorized us, the opponents of same-sex law to assemble at Independence Square last Saturday. It later issued a permit authorizing Pastor Emman, a recent convert to the same-sex union's cause, to hold his own rally on the same date and at the same spot. Do you now see why the reverend father advised you to direct your questions to the police?" Kamil responded to Ben's question by exposing the duplicity on the police's side.

"That is not all. The police knew what they were doing. Since they were the brains behind the commotion, they knew that commotion was coming. They allowed us to meet last

Saturday and virtually escorted our opponents to Independence Square to start a riot. We must not forget that in anticipation of the pandemonium which they meticulously planned, the police had drafted an unprecedented number of heavily armed troops to the protest site. They were hoping to take Kamil and me out in the ensuing melee. Unfortunately for them, we knew about their plot. The good Lord foiled their plot. The good Lord helped us outsmart them," Okoye said, rubbing it in.

"Are you aware that you have both been declared wanted? In other words, you are fugitives from justice." Ben sought the fugitives' reaction.

"Yes, we know that. We also know that the police command is watching this program. We expect their men to wait outside and arrest us once the program is over. They are even free to come over to the studio and drag us to jail. We shall not resist arrest. If we don't see their agents before or after the program, we plan to drive from here straight to the nearest police station. Now that the world is aware of their treachery, they are welcome to arrest us. We hope that they are ready with their charges clearly framed." Kamil stared into the camera as he spoke, daring the police.

If that was a bluff, the police moved swiftly and called it. Their men were already waiting outside the DTS studio in Abaji by the time the interview ended. As soon as the two fugitives stepped out, Superintendent Bawa sprang into action. Handcuffed and treated like common criminals, the two clerics were driven to police headquarters for interrogation.

News of their arrest spread like wild fire. Within an hour, the police headquarters was besieged by a teeming crowd. The protesters carried placards demanding the immediate release of their leaders. One placard summed up the message as follows: RELEASE OKOYE AND KAMIL OR DETAIN US ALL!

Chapter-85

"The Government knows nothing about any assassination plot! Period!"

"WHAT IS THIS NONSENSE about the arrest of Okoye and Kamil?" It was Homkwap on the line.

"They are law-breakers, Your Excellency!" The Chief Commissioner of Police jumped to attention on hearing His Excellency's commanding voice.

"What law have they broken? Tell me, what law have they broken? Each time I try to patch up my differences with the two radicals, you people always find a way to sabotage my efforts! What kind of people are you?" Homkwap's rasping tone signified rage.

"Your Excellency, Sir, I was under the impression that..."

"What impression?"

"That the Executive Secretary of the Faith Regulatory Agency cleared this with ..."

"Cleared what?" Homkwap stopped the Chief Police Commissioner mid-sentence.

"Mr. Akerele and I met in his office and agreed on...."

"Agreed on what?" Homkwap kept guillotining the police boss's sentences.

"On how to fix the troublemakers, Your Excellency!" The Chief Commissioner finally succeeded in completing a sentence.

"Who told you to 'fix' them? And have you seen on television how 'fixing' them has helped? Are you in front of your television? Switch to any channel. The news is all about the people you tried to fix. I am not worried about the coverage on DTS. We can easily handle that. What we can't handle or 'fix' is the spotlight that the GTN has thrown on the crisis. Look at the pictures that the GTN is beaming to viewers in different parts of the world—pictures of Okoye's and Kamil's supporters willing to die to liberate their heroes. If Emperor Kambumba and the WGO Headquarters ask me to explain what is going on, as they are certain to do, how do you expect me to respond, you bumbling idiots?"

"I am sorry, Your Excellency." The Chief Commissioner of Police was all nerves. His job was on the line again. Last time, it was his lackadaisical response to the boss's questions on the number of criminals in his custody that nearly cost him his job. This time, his overzealousness would be his undoing. He should not have gone along with Sam's plan to add the two hotheads to the statistics of troublemakers captured or killed!

"It is too late to be sorry. What you should do is release both Kamil and Okoye immediately. I am sure your PR department will find the right face-saving language in communicating this embarrassing decision to the public. In the meantime, you are to proceed on leave immediately, in readiness for retirement. Your successor will take over from you first thing tomorrow morning. He has been ordered to clean the mess!" Homkwap hung up abruptly. He was glad to distance himself from an act which Sam had previously cleared with him.

"Yes, Your Excellency. Your Excellen…" The Chief Police Commissioner stared blankly at his telephone as the line went dead.

Chapter-86

At last, good news!

HOMKWAP COULD NOT BELIEVE his ears. "You have Mamba in custody? You mean, Abu Danja Mamba, the leader of the Homo Haram terrorists? The one who has slain hundreds of thousands in cold blood and given this administration a lot of headache? Are you sure it is him? Abu Danja Mamba?" He looked at AZ intently, his head bobbling as he spoke.

"Yes, H.H." Homkwap's deputy answered without any show of emotion. Finding Homkwap impossible to pronounce, he had settled for the initials when talking to or about the Governor-General.

"How did it happen?"

"It happened. Isn't that enough?"

"It certainly is. Who cares how the villain is captured so long as he stays captured and we have peace and quiet?"

AZ said nothing. He had other problems on his mind. That was strange, a clone ruminating like a regular human. Perhaps, like Sly Fox X300, this one too had stayed with the humans long enough to copy their ways, good and bad.

431

Homkwap was inwardly disturbed as well. It wasn't the blank expression on AZ's face that bothered him. After all, he was used to finding his deputy inscrutable. If Homkwap was worried this time, it was because he felt that something was off but didn't know precisely what it was. Call it intuition. Something told him that the poker face that stared at him from across his desk was pregnant with mysteries.

Whatever riddles lay buried in the clone's head, Homkwap quickly dismissed them from his own mind. This was no time to worry. It was time to celebrate. And celebrate in a big way he and Ekineta were going to do. He promptly instructed Kike to fetch the Chief of Protocol right away.

With AZ sitting across the desk and looking completely disinterested, Homkwap ordered the Chief of Protocol to organize an elaborate party to mark his administration's victory over the terrorists. He dismissed the Chief of Protocol and inwardly started to count his blessings. Mamba's capture was the jewel in the crown. Everything else was a bonus. Neither Emperor Kambumba nor the WGO's Cunningham was interested in the territory once lost but eventually recovered. The only news that would gladden their hearts was the termination of the terrorist king-pin's reign. That news would overshadow the PR disaster triggered by Okoye's and Kamil's arrest and the police's embarrassing but inevitable climb down.

The Governor-General was in the middle of his day-dream when he had an idea. He buzzed Kike. "Has Wanka left the premises?"

"No, Your Excellency. Mr Wanka is just about to step out." Kike, her eyes on the Chief of Protocol, informed her boss.

432

Wanka, his back to Ronke and his right hand on the door knob, paused, on hearing his name. Instead of exiting the ante-room, he let go of the door knob and turned to face the Secretary.

"Tell him to return immediately," Homkwap directed.

"Sir, His Excellency wants you back," Kike, with one hand holding the receiver and the other covering the speaker, relayed the message to the Chief of Protocol. "He is coming, Your Excellency."

Wanka hurried back as instructed. "I understand His Excellency wants to see me again."

"Yes. I know that you have a standard guest list. But this is an unusual get-together, which brings me to the question why I asked you back: Did I remember to impress upon you the necessity to ensure that the correspondents of local and international news organizations are fully represented at the banquet? You must leave no important name out. I want the whole world, especially, the WGO Commissariat to know that we have not been sitting on our hands. And who better than these pressmen and women to help get the message out?" Homkwap eyed the Chief of Protocol quizzically. He had to seize on any means available to launder his image, an image already soiled by the botched assassination attempt on Okoye and Kamil.

"I assure His Excellency that they will be on our guest list. I shall deliver the invitations to them personally and urge them to block the date on their calendars."

"Good. You do that!"

Chapter-87

Abu Mamba sends his regrets!

THE APPOINTED DATE FINALLY arrived. As expected, the party's guest list featured Dukyaria's high and mighty—the military top brass, cabinet ministers, high-ranking civil servants, film stars, writers, and representatives of the fifth estate. Arriving in the ascending order of importance, the guests waved energetically and beamed effusively as they promenaded around the spacious hall or headed unobtrusively to their pre-labelled seats. An assortment of background musical notes filled the air—from Kandia Kouyate's griot, through Yusuf Olatunji's sakara, Cardinal Rex Jim Lawson's highlife, and Joseph Kabasele's rhumba to Mamman Shatta's kalangu.

As the host, Homkwap arrived last. He was accompanied by the flamboyantly dressed and highly bejeweled Ekineta. To make the less-privileged green with envy, members of the Governor-General's large entourage trotted ostentatiously behind His Excellency, at the same time observing the palace etiquette requiring subjects to demean themselves in the king's presence.

The police band burst into the Dukyarian national anthem as soon as the band master sighted the Governor-General and his party. Everyone present jumped to his or her feet as a mark of respect. It wasn't clear who or what the object of veneration was—the Big Man who had just walked in majestically with his consort and accompanied by kowtowing subjects, the nation called Dukyaria, or the very anthem itself.

All the same, the world stood still while the ritual went on. The attendees gladly sank back into their seats once the formality was over and done with.

Then began the flow of beverages—vodka, whisky, champagne, red and white wine, and for the faint-hearted, club soda or, if that also proved too much, plain water. The menu afforded a wide choice. Only real connoisseurs could make sense of the variety of starters. Even Sam had a hard time choosing from among the items listed on the menu. He had a fair idea what potato chicken soup looked and tasted like. Even smoked salmon and shrimps didn't sound so strange. But what is 'Wild Mushroom Aranduni with Mozzarella'? And Griddled Seafood Salad? Scallops Provencal? Oysters with crab? Chilled cucumber soup? Like most of the guests, Sam fingered the starter he could easily recognize, pronounce, and above all, savor, chew, and swallow.

The main course was not much of a problem. The Dukyarians largely skipped exotic items like Vegetarian Meatloaf, Crockpot Lasagne, Burrito Casserole, Cajun Chicken Pasta, and Classic Baked Macaroni with Cheese. They instead went after familiar names like pounded yam with lamb or chicken stew, tuwon shinkafa, fufu, jollof rice, and edikang ikong. The majority dispensed with the use of the cutlery set on their tables, preferring to use their bare hands to toss in the foods and chew away voraciously.

The stewards performed their tasks diligently. They made sure no one lacked the food he or she ordered or the drink to wash it down. Duly waited upon, and soothed by the African classical music playing in the background, the host and his guests wined and dined to their hearts' content.

The Chief of Protocol, who had by then doubled as the Master of Ceremony, stepped forward for the umpteenth time. His latest brief, as he put it, was to introduce someone capable of performing a task greater than could be entrusted to a "small boy" like himself. And who might that person be? The individual was none other than AZ, the Governor-General's second-in-command. Wanka was right. It would have amounted to gross breach of protocol if a mere civil servant like him had taken it upon himself to introduce the evening's host and keynote speaker.

AZ dutifully accepted the weighty task. He of course dispensed with the formalities. He swiftly proceeded to introduce "a person who needs no introduction," Governor-General H.H., meaning, Homkwap. The clone was very economical with words. He did not say more than what the listeners already knew, to be precise, that H.H. was the Governor-General and the event's host. The humans, who constituted the majority at the gathering, were dumbfounded. They had eagerly waited for this occasion. They had come prepared to be bored by AZ with an elaborate introduction of the man of the hour. The rightful compere at such an event was expected to preface his introduction of the evening's star with recollections of the star's childhood pranks and the early signs of his future greatness. AZ was not supposed to stop until he had provided Homkwap's biographical details and filled in the blanks with flowery, sometimes exaggerated, accounts of the big man's exploits.

Well, the humans were free to expect all they wanted. AZ had said all there was to say about HH. He returned to his seat, his expressionless face intact. He did not look bothered that his skimpy introduction was greeted with an equally skimpy, nay, tepid, applause.

AZ's aberrant behavior and the gathering's lukewarm response did not bother Homkwap either. In fact, he couldn't have planned it better. The evening's glory was his. He alone had the right to bask in it. It was unthinkable that the adulation that was exclusively his would be shared with or squandered on his deputy, a mere clone.

Homkwap rose from his seat ready to address the august audience. The background music stopped. The police band instantly took over, ready to hail the WGO's highest ranking mouthpiece in Dukyaria. With the cymbals colliding, trumpets blaring, and the accordion humming and vibrating in tandem with other percussion instruments, the sound of martial music permeated the vast banquet hall.

When the musical interlude ended, the beaming Homkwap waved his right hand. The guests reciprocated with thunderous applause.

"And all this is before I opened my mouth and uttered a word! The demonstration of love and loyalty! The appreciation of our humble efforts to make this the greatest nation on earth! It's remarkable! The standing ovation and all! I am deeply moved by your kind gestures." Homkwap paused briefly. He glanced in Ekineta's direction and smiled when their eyes met. The First Lady blushed but managed to smile back.

"Deputy Governor-General, His Excellency, AZ; my lovely wife, Ekineta; Distinguished Members of the National Guidance Council; the Chairman and Members of the Joint

Chiefs of Staff; the WGO Representative; Cabinet Ministers and Ministers Without Portfolio; Secretary to the

Cabinet; Under-Secretaries and Heads of Department; Chairman and Members of the National Consultative Council; Chairman and Members, Caucus of Elected Traditional Rulers; the Very Last Chairman of the disbanded Council of Hereditary Rulers and now my Adviser on Cultural Reformation; the Union Chief Justice; the Dean of the Diplomatic Corps; Ambassadors Extraordinary and Envoys Plenipotentiary; Eminent Dukyarians; Invited Guests; Ladies and Gentlemen," Homkwap commenced his keynote speech, duly observing protocol and leaving no important name or office unacknowledged.

"You don't have to remind me that it is still night here in Dukyaria. That I know already. However, I hope you will try and understand if I call this the dawn of a new era. It may be dark out there now, but soon the light you see in here will radiate to every part of our country. The Union of Dukyaria, which has for years been plunged into darkness, will soon be illuminated with flashes of hope and joy. After all, our beloved country, which has been held hostage to Homo Haram terrorism, is finally at peace. Peace and security are no longer a dream but a reality. Abu Danja Mamba should have seen the handwriting on the wall. We extended an olive branch to him, and he thought we were spineless. We prevailed upon him to renounce violence, and he called us cowards. Then, when he exhausted our patience, we laid a trap for him. We spread our dragnet far and wide. And, as we expected him to, he walked right into it." Homkwap paused to gauge his audience's reaction. The clamorous applause was back. He wondered if anyone in the crowd knew that he had just made up the story of the trap and the dragnet. If truth be told, he didn't know a thing about how or exactly when the terrorist lynchpin was caught. AZ knew, but he wouldn't tell. That was AZ's business—whether he talked or kept sealed lips. Homkwap would proceed with his speech regardless.

"Mamba's downfall should serve as a lesson to other terrorists and nihilists. This government will not tolerate indiscipline in any form. We shall vigorously pursue and destroy any gang that threatens Dukyaria's peace and security. We shall match the troublemakers fire for fire."

Homkwap cast a quick glance at the Chairman of the Joint Chiefs of Staff and then continued, "Our armed forces have been placed on permanent alert. Where the police prove incapable of suppressing disorder, our gallant officers and men in the military will gladly step in to fill the void. Distinguished Ladies and Gentlemen, may I request you to stand and raise your glasses in a toast to the Dukyarian Armed Forces?"

The guests dutifully complied. Glasses clinked, and the Chairman of the Joint Chiefs of Staff, a Norwegian, acknowledged the honor with a bow. AZ looked about, disinterested.

The winning, dining, and speech-making over, the guests vacated their seats and trooped to Homkwap's corner. They elbowed one another aside to get the chief host's attention. The serial favor seekers were not so much interested in paying the customary homage as in making the most of the relaxed atmosphere to close long-anticipated deals. The career-minded among them earnestly hoped that

Homkwap would remember their names and their faces when prestigious positions fell vacant. For a few others, the photo op was too tempting to be passed up. They smiled self-consciously, hoping that the cameras would capture their best angles as they posed with the Governor-General and the First Lady. Government contractors observed due protocol by joining others waiting to genuflect before Homkwap and Ekineta. The contractors' target, of course, was the Minister of Finance, who was sitting to Homkwap's right. The Minister had to be prevailed upon to name the date when outstanding payments, less the usual "processing fees," would be released.

"Dance, dance, dance," was as Wanka announced, the next item on the grand event's program. The police band was equal to the challenge. It filled the hall with the sound of music, local and foreign, contemporary and classical.

Setting protocol aside, Homkwap held Ekineta's left hand and waltzed her to the dance floor. Other guests soon joined the First Couple, with each sashaying his partner close to the First Couple, expecting to be noticed by Homkwap, or failing that, by the flashing cameras.

The drinks or the caviar had to have made Homkwap horny. He couldn't wait to take Ekineta back to their bedroom, kiss her softly from the forehead, past the brow and the eyes, before moving to the lips and locking his tongue with hers. And that curvaceous body! He began to imagine what he would do to that body on their king-size bed later that night! Ekineta had seen the look in his eyes too many times not to recognize it. She was ready.

Homkwap decided he had imagined long enough. It was time for action. He snapped his fingers, and within seconds the Chief of Protocol came running. The event's host informed the master of ceremony that he was retiring for the night. Since the bar was still open, the others were free to continue. Homkwap, accompanied by Ekineta, promptly left the crowd. His courtiers followed closely behind. Having seen the Governor-General to his lodge, the courtiers knew better than to stick around. They took leave of him, and he gladly released them from any further obligation for the night.

Chapter-88

Any cure for clone clannishness?

KEVIN, WHO ONCE CALLED X300 a soul-less robot, had finally patched up his differences with the clone. As a peace offering, he agreed to tutor X300 on the inner workings of the human mind. "You see, we may put on a smile, but don't let that fool you. That we look happy does not mean we really are. It may in fact mean the exact opposite."

"How is that possible? How can you look but not feel happy?" X300 looked puzzled, genuinely puzzled.

"It is possible alright. We may look happy because we are too afraid to admit to ourselves that something is wrong, or too ashamed to let others know about the anomaly. Fear and shame are our inner demons that we don't like to face," Kevin explained.

"That is still odd. In fact, irrational."

"If you consider that odd or irrational, how about when we say something but don't mean it? Like, I say 'I am glad to see you' when in fact what I mean is 'the less of you I see the better'?"

"Now, why would anybody do that—say one thing but mean another?"

"Do you really want to know what it takes to be human or not?"

"Of course, I do."

"In that case, shut up and just listen."

"You got yourself a deal," X300 mimicked Kevin's way of signifying concurrence.

"Here then is the deal: We humans may praise you to high heavens in your presence but stab you in the back when you are gone."

"I am sorry, I have to stop you again. Did you just say, 'stab you in the back when you are gone'? How will you stab me in the back if I am not around? And if I am around, will stabbing me in the back not draw blood and cause pain?"

"You see what a simple tweak of language does to meaning? 'Stab in the back' does not mean plunge a knife into someone's back. It simply means doing behind somebody's back what you wouldn't dare do, would be too mortified to try to do, in his presence. It is all part of what we humans call figure of speech, metaphor, parable, proverb, allegory, or idiomatic expression. It is a way of communicating an idea by playing on, even blowing up, its easily memorable elements."

"Then, you humans are too complex," X300 observed.

"You can say that again. It is in that complexity that lies our true essence. We are made to be complex. We thrive on complexity. Sadly, we also go down with complexity."

"How can you thrive on complexity and fall with it?"

"Good question. It may at first sound paradoxical, but there is nothing paradoxical about it. It is the complex human mind that enables him to comprehend the mysteries and workings of the universe. Without such a mind, it would be well-nigh impossible to record advances in science and technology. However, the deeper we reach into the cosmos, the haughtier we become. Our complex mind which started us on a positive journey suddenly turns us ninety or one hundred and eighty degrees. Back to square one, our minds take us in a completely different direction—the direction in which we forget about our humble origins and begin to think godlike thoughts. That's how we end up becoming architects of our own downfall!" Kevin tried to explain the classic riddle—the riddle of a created being behaving like a creator in his own right.

"Isn't that the whole purpose of evolution—go as far as, and in any direction, your dream can take you?"

"I am afraid that 'evolution' does not accurately describe our condition. Evolution does not satisfactorily explain our progressive detachment from nature and unilateral declaration of autonomy. There is a word or phrase that accurately sums it up, but I can't readily recall it. I first heard it from that Moslem priest, Kamil. He mentioned it more than once at one of the rallies which he organized jointly with his Roman Catholic friend, Okoye."

"You mean 'inverse evolution'?" X300 responded calmly.

"That's it! That is the phrase!" Kevin snapped his right index finger, glowing with excitement. He continued, "Inverse evolution more or less sums up the human condition. Curious as that may sound, it is the human's idea of progress, the idea in whose name she or he has perfected the art of self-delusion and self-deception. Have you noticed that we humans have the capacity to project falsehood as truth—and in so doing, repudiate the very notion of conscience? What do you think is responsible for that? Inverse evolution's gravitational pull! That is what makes it possible for us to misrepresent falsehood as the truth effortlessly and without feeling any pang of guilt."

X300 smoked Kevin's peace pipe for some time before casting it aside. He stopped hanging out with Kevin the instant he decided that he had nothing more to learn from his guru. The friendship was doomed from the start anyway. The gulf between the humans and the clones was too wide to be bridged by peace pipes. The feeling of animosity was mutual and deep. Still, for as long as the friendship lasted, X300 learnt as much as he could about humans. He also shared the knowledge with his fellow clones, including the top clone, AZ. Communicating with one another was no problem. The transmitter wired into each clone's head allowed him to transmit data to other heads connected to the network.

Clones were not supposed to abuse their advantage, especially the high-tech advantage which they had over humans. They were specifically forbidden to transmit information which was not 'task-related' over the network. However, since those monitoring the facility's use were in faraway New York and had no means of verifying the purpose of the clones' online chatter, the line between official and unofficial communication tended to be blurred. Besides, the soldier clones deployed to Dukyaria took no chances; they encrypted sensitive messages transmitted through the network.

The technological edge proved deadly when combined with the 'psychological know-how', that is, the art and science of deception, which the clones learnt from their human counterparts. Not only were the clones able to communicate with one another on remote channels, they had, or had acquired, the capacity to put on a mirthful facade when angered and to move without being noticed by their adversaries.

Kevin's tribe, the humans, passed up no opportunity to provoke the clones. The urge to act out the human theory of duplicity became irresistible as the clones wrestled with human foibles. The clones had come to terms with the limitations imposed by their designers. They could live with the implant of desire-suppressing cells and the freezing of their sexual urges. What the clones found insufferable was the growing human habit of ganging up on the clone clan. Humans of the feminine gender would not interact with clones for fear of being impregnated by 'virtual robots' and giving birth to slimy, hideous looking aliens. It didn't matter that the robot slur hardly applied to the clones or that alien births were a figment of the human imagination. The myths were sufficiently encoded and perpetuated long enough to create a gulf between the clones and their human counterparts. Insensitive to the clones' feelings, humans of the masculine gender openly cavorted with their female partners, thus forcing the clones to watch every erotic move with palpable envy.

The humans too had their own grievances. The clones had become work ants ready to perform any task, from the menial to the top-paying. That, of course, was not the problem. The problem was the clones' willingness to undertake the tasks

446

almost gratis, thus depriving the humans of income-earning opportunities. The clones had not only taken over most of the non-skilled tasks but had also started eyeing middle- and high-level jobs coveted by the humans. Then there was the health and fitness gap. Designed to shun the frivolities of life, clones ended up living healthier lives. Instead of watching their diets and their weights, the disease-prone and rapidly aging humans envied the athletic clones. The humans might remain green with envy till eternity, that wouldn't assure them what they craved most, sound health and longevity.

Chapter-89

Jailed, shackled, and dangerous! That's Mamba, the terrorist!

MUTUAL JEALOUSIES SOON BRED personal antipathies. It was a matter of time before distrust took over. That time came when Mamba fell into the clones' hands. The Homo Haram leader's arrest blew the fissure between the humans and the clones wide open. This was ironic. Having the leader of the terrorist group under lock and key was every Dukyarian's dream. With him behind bars, it was reckoned, bombs would cease to go off at unexpected times and places. It was hoped that, with the Homo Haram franchise shut down, individuals that saw no point in living would thenceforth immolate none except themselves, and possibly others privy to their suicide pacts. In a nutshell, Dukyaria would be ushered into a new dawn, the dawn of peace. Everyone would live happily ever after—or at least, for some time.

As Abu Mamba sat in his tiny cell reflecting on his life's twists and turns, his former patrons, mostly humans, meditated his assassination or jail break. The attempt to take him out started the very day he, with his hands and feet manacled, staggered into his Snake Island cell. A prison steward had brought the high-profile prisoner's first meal. Unknown to the steward, the guards on duty had been firmly instructed by AZ to ensure that whoever brought any meal to the prisoner must be made to take the first bite.

"Hey, Mister! Come back! Take a mouthful of the rice! Now!" X750 called the steward who had hurried to the exit after dumping the plate in front of Mamba's cell.

"But the food is meant for him, not me. After all, I am a kitchen staff, not a prisoner!" Akpan protested, his frown accentuated by his wrinkled forehead.

"I am telling you for the last time: take a mouthful, or I shall force-feed you!" X750 was adamant.

"But I already had lunch!" Akpan stood his ground, the frown extending to the rest of his face and deepening.

"We will soon know how much lunch you had and how much more we have to force down that pot belly of yours." With his right hand training the gun on Akpan, X750 quickly reached for his cell phone with the left. "I need you here right away! We have a situation." He switched off the set, leaving the second hand free to level the gun on Akpan's brow.

"What is the problem?" X500 asked on arrival at the scene. His eyes darted from X750 to Akpan.

"This human brought the prisoner's meal. As we were directed, I told him to taste the food. He flatly refused."

"Is that so? Then what are we waiting for? I shall hold him down and empty the entire plate in his stomach," X500 volunteered to force-feed Akpan.

Now in full panic mode, Akpan's voice suddenly turned croaky. His mouth quivered nervously. Sweat dripped uncontrollably down his brow right to his bleary eyes. The game was up. He had to tell the guards why he had no appetite for his own food. He had been told that human life meant nothing to clones. Any dithering on his part was all but certain to cost him his life. "Sirs, I am ready to cooperate. I am ready to say all I know about this food." Not bothered that only a few iron bars separated him from the widely-feared prisoner, Akpan told the guards about plans to eliminate Abu Mamba ahead of his appearance before the ATT, the Anti-Terrorism Tribunal. "I have nothing to do with this palaver. It was my supervisor who handed me the tray and ordered me to bring the food here. He warned me against tasting the food as it is poisoned. I think they want the man dead." Akpan pointed towards Abu Mamba who stood there languidly, listening to every word.

The two guards were puzzled. They were curious about the identity of those who wanted their prisoner dead. Why have the mysterious characters decided to finish the accused person off before he has his day in court? What could he have done to personally tick them off? Unable to answer their own questions, both guards turned to AZ. At least the deputy Governor-General would, by virtue of his position, be in the know. He should be able to finger who authorized the extra-judicial execution of a prisoner in their custody. He might even be in the mood to share intimate state secrets such as why the fiendish and shadowy characters couldn't wait for the government's firing squad to finish the job. Why would anybody outsource the execution of Mamba to a low-level prison cafeteria steward?

Chapter-90

The terrorist with friends in high places

INDEED, AZ DID KNOW why some shadowy characters wanted Abu Mamba dead. The top clone was, however, not yet sure about their identities. The intelligence he had about the whys and the wherefores was not enough to draw firm conclusions about who wanted Mamba out of the way. Until he was able to unmask the faces behind the plot, he gave the guards three instructions, all to be carried out firmly and to the letter. First, no humans should be deployed as guards around Mamba's cell without AZ's approval. Second, the prisoner's videotaped interrogation must commence immediately. Finally, any food brought to the cell must continue to be pre-tasted by the steward assigned to the task. The last order nearly led to a breakdown in the kitchen chain of command, with a few stewards giving their supervisors one condition for obeying their wait-on-Mamba order—taste the food first, or be ready to serve the food yourself in the presence of the stern-looking guards.

AZ's interrogators moved swiftly to unravel the mystery surrounding Abu Mamba's would-be killers. Since Akpan had involuntarily divulged the plan to send Mamba to his early grave, the most dangerous criminal needed no pressure or incentive to sing like a canary. As he told his interrogators, Homkwap's government vilified his group by day but dined with it by night. He provided intimate details of the quid pro quo arrangement between top government functionaries and the Homo Haram high command. Specifically, high-ranking officials "scratched our back with sensitive information and decisions favorable to us, and we too scratched theirs with bribes regularly lodged in their secret offshore accounts in the Isle of Man."

When asked what he meant by "decisions favorable to us," Mamba cited the case of the huge catch of arms and ammunitions impounded at the Laguna seaport weeks before his capture. When one customs official tried to prove difficult, all it took to disarm him was one phone call from Mamba's Homo Haram hideout to the official's superiors. The heavy ammo was released without any hassle, thanks to "instructions from above."

Abu Mamba had not yet said anything of direct interest to the clones until he recounted how he was tipped off about impending attacks on his positions. The guards immediately knew how Mamba often managed to elude capture: the squads that he unfailingly outsmarted were led by, and predominantly made up of, clones. The humans never had the courage to go after Mamba. Yet, when they gave the job to clones, the double-dealing humans were the first to advise Mamba to lie low until the coast was clear! They, in their characteristic way, ran with the hares and hunted with the hounds.

"You haven't heard anything yet. All the soldier clones that walked into our trap were lured there by their human counterparts. At times, I often wondered if Dukyaria had two armies—one army fighting for the hegemony of the human race, and the other simply fighting for the clones' survival. It is ironic that the clone division of the army that I had earlier underrated would be one to bring me in. That shows that you, clones, have come a long way! You have mastered all our human tricks! Allah yai sa!" Mamba ended with a guffaw and a Kasaranci expression of shock. AZ was not sure at first what credence to give to Mamba's story. For all the head clone knew,

452

the terrorist might be up to one of his tricks. He might be looking for cracks between humans and clones through which to slither to get out of his tight spot. It was not until AZ ordered that another detainee, Ghazzalli, be interrogated that the veracity of Mamba's story was firmly established. Ghazzalli had risen to Mamba's second in command after Usman Darazo was shot dead in front of the Hausari Central Mosque. Ghazzali knew what his boss knew. Although held in a separate wing of the maximum-security prison, his testimony matched Mamba's in every significant detail. The only addition was his reference to the Treatise on Jinns which Mamba had filched before leaving Sule's sanctuary years earlier. "He never left home without this booklet. Your army wouldn't have stood a chance if the Khalifah had not misplaced the book the morning your forces and ours clashed. I suppose that was because you took us by surprise and we had to leave the base in a hurry." He referred to Abu Mamba by the title of Khalifah, or Caliph, which the leader of the terrorist group conferred upon himself.

Mamba and his immediate lieutenants clearly knew about another reciprocal arrangement—the one which Sam had concluded with Pastor Emmanuel Kalu. The clone interrogators sat wide-eyed as the prisoners provided intimate details of Homo Haram attacks carried out with the knowledge and acquiescence of the government and its Abounding Grace collaborator. It was Emman's idea to raze

Mosafejo's church to the ground. Getting the security agencies to look the other way while the deed was done was entirely Sam's call.

"Did Emman tell you why he wanted the Church of Latter Day Saints bombed?" X500 was curious.

"No, he didn't tell us, and we didn't care whether he did or not. We were glad to rid the world of one agent of Shaytan and even gladder to be held completely responsible for the deed! What was the church doing in Gwagwalada in the first place?" Mamba responded defiantly.

"How about Sam. What did he say?" X500 pressed on.

"He said something about personality clash and inter-church rivalry. As I said, we were not interested in who clashed with whom. We simply wanted to erase every trace of sacrilege. Even Kamil was in our sights. We wanted to eliminate him for preferring the company of the kuffar to that of his own Muslim brethren. It is still a mystery how he consistently managed to elude us. The same goes for Kamil's friend, Okoye. He too was always a step ahead of us! Funny! The apostles of peaceful protests didn't take their safety for granted. They paid attention to their personal and their followers' security. No rally started unless the site had been duly inspected for improvised explosive devices. And when a rally was under way, the security operatives often stayed alert, ready to fish out our suicide bombers and coax them into laying down their arms." Mamba recalled.

"Do you regret killing innocent persons and destroying valuable property?" X500 asked.

"Do you regret tracking me down and binding my hands and feet?" Mamba countered with his own question.

"Certainly not! We had a mission and we didn't stop until it was accomplished," X500 answered confidently.

"There is the answer to your question! My mission was accomplished the day I fell into your hands! Your own problem has just started. Your mission accomplished has just become a ticking time bomb." Mamba dashed X500's hope of extracting a mea culpa or even a mere hint of penitence from the terrorist.

Abu Mamba's reference to a ticking time bomb got X500's immediate attention, of course. The clone combed the holding area, expecting to find cartridges with explosives wired to a wall somewhere. Leaving nothing to chance, he sent X750 to search the premises and sniff out explosive devices that might have been concealed from naked eyes.

The clones were looking in the wrong places. Abu Mamba had been speaking figuratively. The bomb which he had in mind was not a real bomb. It was pointless searching for it since it was not planted within the vicinity. Even the ingredients needed for the metaphorical bomb were just popping up at different locations. They would first self-assemble, and then detonate and blow up in unsuspecting faces. Mamba was himself a critical component. He might have been taken out in the interim, but that by itself posed a new danger. At the very least, the sudden outbreak of peace removed the only pretext the government had for not moving the country forward. With Mamba in chains, the government had no other fall-guy on whose neck to hang the blame for its own failures.

Mamba's capture also meant that the "troublemakers" were now free to step up their street protests without being accused of endangering national security. Kamil, hitherto deemed guilty by association, was now off the hook. No terrorist label pinned on the "Moslem fundamentalist" would stick. What would remain indelible in the average Dukyarian's memory was not anyone's religious belief or affiliation, but the government's hand-in-glove dealings with the dreaded group. The public was also unlikely to forget or forgive the unholy alliance between Homkwap's state and Pastor Emman's church. Dukyarians would be up in arms once they knew about the dealings between the government and the "man of God." And on the off-chance that the government succeeded in killing the story or containing its fallout, it would find it well-nigh impossible bottling up another festering crisis: the crisis of confidence between the humans and the clones. As Dukyarians were soon to find out, the growing distrust between the two clans would be the most combustible and most cataclysmic of the elements making up Abu Mamba's metaphorical bomb.

Chapter-91

Clones' tutorial on crime and punishment

"SPEAKING HYPOTHETICALLY, HOW DO you humans handle wrongdoing between and among yourselves?" With Kamil on the rostrum addressing a gathering of same-sex union's opponents, X300 tried his charm on Okoye. The clone had been emboldened by a new government regulation allowing law enforcement agents to project a friendly image when dealing with members of the public. Homkwap was anxious to repair the damage caused by the police's collaboration with Pastor Emman to disrupt a penultimate rally organized by Okoye and Kamil.

"Can you be a little bit more specific? What kind of wrongdoing are we talking about here?" Okoye asked.

"Wrongdoing as in lying, cheating, treachery, deception, or absence of good faith. 'Duplicity' about captures it well," X300 clarified.

"Speaking hypothetically, but mind you, as a priest, I would recommend that the victim of duplicity continue to be open in his or her dealings with the two-faced friend."

"Even if doing that is clearly harmful to you or your loved ones?" "Yes. In Roman, 12:19, the Bible says, 'Beloved, never avenge yourselves, but leave it to the wrath of God. Vengeance is mine, says the Lord.'"

"I don't get it. How can God take offense when it is a human, not Him, who is directly offended?"

"Because God is the One that created the offense, the offender, and the directly offended. He is accepting responsibility for His actions, that is, for the exercise of His unique, unrivalled creative power."

"Ok, He is the Creator of the offense, the offender, and the offended. That automatically makes Him the Creator of the victim of attack, the defender, that is. If the Creator accepts responsibility for an offender's action, why would He not also accept responsibility if the victim of the offensive action defends him or herself? What is wrong with the injured party meeting his attacker's aggression with an equal and proportionate act?" X300 countered Okoye's Biblical injunction with cold logic.

"You must be familiar with the Mosaic Law!"

"Who is this mysterious Mosaic? Is he a famous scientist whose Law was not taught at our academy?"

"No, Mosaic is not a scientist. It is an adjective coined from a Jewish prophet's name, Moses. Mosaic Law basically stands for the principle of an eye for an eye. However, while that principle works perfectly in the state of nature, it is unacceptable in a modern society. I suppose that is why we humans surrender fractions of our freedoms to one form of government or the other. It is the duty of the government to intervene on behalf of injured parties and make sure that none takes the law into his or her own hands."

"Does that then make the government the substitute god, one that rewards good deeds, punishes wrongdoers, checks transgressions, and generally decides on right and wrong? But between this earthly god and your own, which one do you trust to intervene on your behalf promptly, justly, and impartially all the time?" X300, his own experience at the back of his mind, was curious about Okoye's God.

"You want the truth? God, the God of all creation, is forbearing and merciful. That is why humans, in the rush for instant justice, choose to bypass Him and rely on government, or failing that, their own devices. The earthly government, the government of humans, by humans, for humans, may first give the impression of earnestness and reliability. However, it is largely fickle. It intervenes only when it suits those running it."

X300 was impressed with Okoye's candor. He found the parallel between the human and the celestial notion of justice fascinating. His curiosity was, however, far from satisfied. "Then, don't you humans have a problem there? If the injury you are griping about is committed by the earthly god, the god you deem capricious, who else is there to consider your grievances? Or do I take it that what you humans say about the heavenly God applies to your earthly god as well, that is, 'God's judgment is final, and not subject to appeal'?"

"I am afraid that that is one question the human race has yet to answer. Try and get Kamil's perspective on this. He will soon be with you!" Okoye promptly walked to the rostrum to take over from Kamil.

Kamil's response to X300's relentless questions built on, and helped clarify, Okoye's views on retributive justice. As Kamil pointed out, it was the duty of anyone to interdict any act of wrongdoing brought to his attention. Kamil did not contest the affirmation that judgment of right and wrong lies with God. However, the human being still has an obligation to restore the balance in favor of right where wrong was palpable and had gone beyond bounds.

"Am I to conclude that, unlike Okoye's God, who does not delegate to humans, your own Allah allows you to decide right and wrong?"

"First, Okoye's God and mine, and yours, are One and the same…"

"Wait a minute! The god I am programed to obey is the WGO. Is that your god too?"

"The WGO is nobody's god—not mine, not yours, not anybody's! It may want to be accepted as such, but it is not!"

"That is a treasonable statement. However, in the spirit of the Governor-General's fraternization policy, I shall act as if I didn't hear that!"

"Fraternization! And you fell for that! You know better than that, X300! Have you forgotten that your Governor-General, the new advocate of fraternization, was behind the disruption of our rally? He suddenly found fraternization appealing when his aggressive policy stopped working, or should I say, backfired."

"That's enough!" X300's countenance suddenly froze. He stretched to his full six-foot four and held his head upright. He had to end the subversive conversation. Kevin was coming.

"What have you two been discussing?" Kevin had left his post and marched towards where X300 and Kamil were fraternizing.

"Has the fraternization policy been abrogated? We are just holding idle conversation on football. Anyway, you are free to join in. You've in fact come at the right time. Please answer this question: who won yesterday's match?" Kamil quickly invented a topic of discussion before the plain-talking clone gave the game away.

"I told him that the referee was wrong to disallow Brazil's goal, but your brother here thinks that the referee was right and that Honduras deserved to win. What do you think?" Kamil needed not worry. The clone had clearly mastered the human art of dissembling. Kamil was amazed. He kept a straight face, nonetheless.

"X300 is right! Brazil ought to have won by two goals to one!" Kevin corroborated a position that, unknown to him, was never affirmed or denied.

The rally ended shortly thereafter. The crowd dispersed. So did the regular and military policemen deployed to maintain order.

Having downloaded the conversations that X300 had with Okoye, Kamil, and subsequently, Kevin, AZ's secretary handed over the transcript to her boss. She promptly deleted the sensitive data from her hard drive.

Chapter-92

Smile, James Bond! You're on candid camera!

SAM HAD KNOWN FOR quite some time that something was off. The question he could not answer was exactly what that was. AZ's normally frigid countenance had lately taken a more forbidding, in fact, sinister, form. He had suddenly taken to casting sharp sideways glances at Homkwap anytime the latter said something at NGC meetings. Homkwap, too overwhelmed with pressing state matters, had no time to study anyone's face or notice the telltale signs.

"Your Excellency, is there any problem between you and your deputy?" Sam had had enough. Under the pretext of briefing the Governor-General on the progress made in containing faith and its spread, he had decided to broach the sensitive topic.

"None that I can think of. Why?" Homkwap answered casually, his eyes on the file before him.

"I can't really put my finger on it, Your Excellency. It's just the look on AZ's face. Granted that smiling doesn't come easy with him, he could still go about it without sending shivers down my spine!" Sam proceeded awkwardly.

"That's cryptic. Can you be any clearer?" Homkwap asked, without taking his eyes off the file.

"As a mere official, my seat is at the back of the NGC members. Nonetheless, since I am seated directly opposite Your Excellency and your deputy, I am well-placed to see and read the two faces, yours and his. If I am permitted to say this, Your Excellency's face clearly harbors no ill feeling. I can't say the same about your deputy's. I think something is eating him inside." Sam looked relaxed. He finally got the matter off his chest.

"So, what do you suggest?" Homkwap was now fully attentive. His eyes shifted from the file to Sam's perspiring face.

"I strongly recommend that we get the Director of Intelligence to look into the matter. We need to know what is bothering the man!"

"O.K. If that is what you want, sit down and let's get this out of the way quickly." As he was used to doing when faced with a delicate problem, Homkwap by-passed Kike and dialed Brigadier Anas-Adamu directly.

"Yes, Your Excellency, I am on my way." Anas-Adamu dropped the receiver and hurried to the Governor-General's suite. He had been transferred from the Directorate of National Security to the more powerful Directorate of Intelligence in the Governor-General's office. He was banking on replacing the Director-General of State Security on the incumbent's departure in a few months.

"We have a situation that we need you to look into immediately. Sam here thinks that AZ has something up his sleep. Your mission is to find out exactly what that is. I don't have to remind you that since this involves a clone, you may have to rely on your human subordinates. I trust you and your men to be discreet." Homkwap lost no time bringing Anas-Adamu up to speed.

"Consider it done, Your Excellency. We shall unearth whatever he might have buried in his office." Anas-Adamu assured the Governor-General.

AZ sat in his living room as Anas-Adamu's boys broke into his office. These humans are so predictable, he thought to himself. The secret service operatives hadn't realized that AZ had anticipated that his office would be ransacked and had taken the precaution to stash away sensitive material. The operatives also failed to sweep the office for hidden cameras. In the haste to get their hands on precious documents or information, they never considered the likelihood of AZ planting bugging devices in his own office. Homkwap's deputy watched with amusement as Anas-Adamu's boys ransacked his office. Unused to showing any emotion, he found himself laughing uproariously when one of the intruders asked their leader, "Sir, what exactly are we looking for?"

The leader's response further tickled the clone, "Anything unusual. Dossiers, orders of the day, incoming and outgoing e-mails. Anything. Anything that looks, smells, or feels suspicious."

That surely narrows it down! AZ mused, wondering how the burglars could have embarked on a mission without having any idea what the mission was. He left the intruders alone but taped every move they made and every word they uttered.

The mission ended without yielding any significant result, except, of course, minutes of the NGC meetings, with the NGC resolutions to be followed up by AZ duly highlighted in light orange. "We poked everywhere but found nothing, Your Excellency. The man is either clean or clever," Anas-Adamu reported.

"Or he's neither!" Sam interjected, not afraid that his grunt in the Governor-General's presence would be deemed unbecoming of an ordinary civil servant.

"What do you mean?" Homkwap snapped at Sam. He didn't know what the ambitious civil servant stood to gain, trying to stir up trouble between himself and his deputy.

"Your Excellency, if the snoop around the office turned up nothing, how about his residence? He might have anticipated a raid on his office and decided to shift all incriminating material to his house!"

"Are you suggesting that I authorize a raid on his house? What would I say I am looking for? Don't you consider that too risky? A search that produces nothing will not only be embarrassing but is sure to damage relations between AZ and myself."

"We certainly don't want to see anything come between you two, Your Excellency. I just feel something is not right, and we should act before it is too late!" Sam knew how to put the Governor-General on edge.

"What do you think, Anas?" Homkwap was taking no chances. He had to set wrong things right while he still could.

"I see Your Excellency's point. I can also understand why Mr. Akerele here is concerned. Maybe we can carry out a raid on AZ's house without really doing so."

"I'm afraid you've lost me there. What do you mean by 'carry out a raid without really doing so'?"

"Your Excellency normally briefs the High Commissioner for Secularism at least once a month. I was just thinking whether it is possible to invent a crisis which would compel the WGO headquarters to send its own inspectors to Dukyaria. The inspectors will not only search His Excellency's lodge but also the residence of each and every member of the NGC, AZ included. So long as the raid is not confined to AZ's house, he will not suspect anything."

"That's possible. The question is what crisis would bring the WGO inspectors to Dukyaria at short notice?" Homkwap wondered.

Anas-Adamu leaned slightly across the Governor-General's desk. Sam too adjusted his posture so as to catch every word muttered by the Director of Intelligence. The plan, as whispered by Anas-Adamu, was simple: The Governor-General would fabricate a report fingering subversive elements within the government. The report would show how some members of the NGC had become "sleepers," collaborating with anti-secular elements in the Dependent Territory, and feeding terrorists with critical intelligence. If that didn't get the needed attention, one or two members would be accused of providing technical advice to foreign guerrilla bands attacking WGO assets inside and outside Dukyaria. Since the details were still sketchy, the plan would end with a recommendation that the High Commissariat for Secularism send a team of investigators to work with the Directorate of Intelligence and reveal the traitors' identities. Homkwap nodded approvingly as Anas- Adamu ran the idea by him. Sam was equally delighted that the Governor-General shared his view that AZ posed a threat that should not be ignored.

Unfortunately for the three plotters, they were not alone in the room. AZ, or more precisely, his hidden cameras and listening devices, were there recording every word, gesture, and expression. The clone had trained his own bugging devices on Homkwap the day he caught the latter's goons poking around his own office.

The Governor-General, the snoop, was unaware that he was being snooped upon. He went ahead to implement Anas-Adamu's plan. Within a week, WGO investigators landed in Dukyaria, ready to work with the Directorate of Intelligence to fish out the traitors. The combined team of sleuths moved discreetly but swiftly, combing the NGC members' houses and offices, expecting to unearth subversive material.

The nearest the secret agents got to establishing a case of irregularity was the evidence downloaded from the desktop of the NGC member responsible for Public Works and Infrastructure Development. Apparently, the Minister, a member of the human tribe, had colluded with contractors to inflate contract costs and milk the government of billions of Dukyarian dollars. Believing that his office automatically conferred unlimited immunity on him, he had not bothered to erase highly sensitive details from his hard drive. Among the embarrassing titbits that he left undeleted were the amounts deposited into or withdrawn from his coded Swiss accounts on various dates, the names of the contractors making the deposits, and the beneficiaries of the minister's generosity, mostly girlfriends.

Homkwap promptly sacked the minister, making him the operation's only collateral damage. The primary target of the operation, AZ, came out of it smelling like a rose. The gumshoes found nothing incriminating in his office or his official residence. They could not have. AZ had moved all important files to a new safe house on Keffi road, far from prying eyes.

AZ waited for Homkwap to run out of tricks and ammunitions before rolling out his own guns. He had learnt of the friction between Cunningham on the one hand, and Torres and Marshall Popov, on the other. He had no business with Torres. Under the WGO chain and line of command, Popov was the one to whom he was to submit military-related reports. He duly placed a long-distance call to the High Commissioner for Militarism.

"Marshall, Sir, I need to come over to New York. There is a serious situation that I must discuss with you face to face. All I need right now is a directive asking me to report at your office in New York. If the Governor-General asks, you will tell him you need me for routine consultations."

"No problem! And you are sure you can't give me a hint what this situation is?"

"I am sure, Marshall, Sir."

Chapter-93

Permission to rebel, Sir!

AZ STAMPED HIS FEET on the doormat a few times before stepping into Popov's secretary's office on the 45th floor. He had to get rid of the slush which his boots had gathered as he trudged the snow-covered sidewalk from his Park Avenue hotel to the WGO Headquarters on First Avenue. The secretary, Padmini Kaul, was on hand to receive him. She promptly relieved him of his trench coat. He refused her offer to carry the heavy briefcase. The secretary led AZ to her boss's corner office.

"Welcome to New York and winter! Sorry for the disagreeable odor of the anti-virus spray. You can't be too careful these days!" Popov rose from his seat to embrace the august visitor. He instructed Padmini to leave the office door ajar. This was to let out the air which had by then been saturated with the acrid and suffocating smell of VirusOut, an insecticide targeting a new, highly malignant, strain of the West Nile Virus.

"Thanks, Marshall." AZ reciprocated. Popov was the closest he had to a father. It was his filial duty to address the Militarism High Commissioner respectfully, either as 'Marshall' or 'Sir'.

"Coffee or tea, Sir?" Popov's secretary, courteous, charming, and dutiful, extended office hospitality to AZ.

"Coffee. Hot! No sugar or milk, if you don't mind!"

"Just the way we like it in Russia! You know how we acquired that habit? The hard way! We skipped sugar and milk when the factories were unable to meet their production quotas. That was how we turned our economic adversity into a national beverage. And you know something? We haven't looked back since. We thoroughly like the aroma of pure coffee and its bitter, unadulterated taste! But that's not why you are here. We must get to that quickly. What is the situation that you could not discuss over the phone?" The thick Russian accent had mellowed slightly, coming back only when the letter r landed on his tongue.

AZ said nothing. He simply bent leftwards to reach for and open his briefcase. He brought out the contents one by one. First to be pulled out was a bulky dossier stacked with transcripts of the terrorists' interrogations. It was followed by a live DVD recording of the interrogations and the testimonies, another file containing the accused persons' signed affidavits, and a backup disk the size of a marker pen. These precious objects clearly survived Anas-Adamu's search-and-destroy missions.

"Marshall, I have served the WGO to the best of my ability. I have even risked my life defending the Organization's policies in Dukyaria. And believe me, Marshall, defending the WGO in Dukyaria is not an easy thing to do! Anyway, that is not my point. My point is that someone is trying not only to undermine the WGO but is also, for reasons known only to himself, anxious to get me out of the way. That someone is none other than HH, the Governor-General, himself." AZ cut to the chase. Popov sat stone-faced as AZ provided him a blow-by-blow account of the treachery in the war on Homo Haram, the plan to exterminate the clones, and the alliance that Homkwap's government had forged with the terrorist lynchpin and the renegade priest, Pastor Emmanuel Kalu.

471

"And you have all this on tape and on your hard drives?"

"Right down to the groans and the grunts! In fact, I am waiting for the technicians to get their equipment ready. As soon as the system is up and running, you will be able to decide what to believe."

As expected, Popov saw and believed the evidence of Homkwap's duplicity. The Marshall watched the footage of AZ's counter-espionage operation. Poor Homkwap! The amateur spies didn't realize they were saying "cheese" to their target's camera! Popov convulsed with laughter.

"I have seen enough. I am afraid, you have to postpone your departure. You cannot leave New York until you meet the Commissioner-General's Chief of Staff and possibly the Commissioner-General himself. If I had my way, you would even meet the President of the Assembly of Nations and appear before the Global Guidance Council." Popov craned his neck to be closer to AZ and to give the later a low-down on developments in the world. The Militarism Commissioner also cued AZ in on the tense atmosphere within the WGO itself.

"Look at this map." Popov subsequently rose from his seat and moved close to the wall map. "You see the flashing lights. Those red flashes are indications of trouble.

And as you can imagine, the flashpoints are spreading like wild fire." Popov took AZ into confidence on relations between and among the top echelons of the General

Commissariat. He strongly advised AZ to stay out of Cunningham's way.

Chapter-94

Permission granted!

AZ DUTIFULLY STAYED OUT of the Secularism Supremo's way while in New York. His subsequent meetings with Evangelista Torres convinced him that Popov knew what he was talking about and that he was right to heed the Russian's advice.

"Brad's impulsive decision to proceed full-blast with his secularization plan is largely behind the turbulence in today's world. The world would have been relatively stable if he had not moved impulsively and tactlessly to shove his atheism down the believers' throats. Now, we are running from one empire to another putting out fires. The way things are, the empires will soon be history. If care is not taken, the WGO and its props will be the next to go. It's absolutely necessary that you meet the Commissioner-General and the President of the Assembly of Nations before you return to Dukyaria. A change of leadership is necessary in Dukyaria, but only those two can make that happen. I shall arrange for you to see both of them tomorrow," Torres remarked after watching AZ's videos. Popov sat, nodding approvingly, as she made her point.

The following day, AZ met Commissioner-General Khaled bin-Sayed El-Maktoum. Both Torres and Popov were present at the meeting. In anticipation of the economic implications of the measures which the Commissioner-General planned to recommend to Madam Warioba, he invited the Commissioner for Capitalism to his own meeting. It was at this meeting that the Commissioner-General decided what to do to put out the Dukyarian fire. He firmly ordered AZ to return to Dukyaria and wait for further instructions. "You don't have to meet the President of the Assembly of Nations. Leave that to me. I know what to tell Her Excellency. Just leave the disks and other exhibits with my Chief of Staff. The Global Guidance Council may yet want to see them."

The meeting over, Torres, Popov, and AZ got up to leave El-Maktoum's office. They were about to exit when the Commissioner-General recalled Torres. "You stay behind. I need you to draft a memorandum to the Global Guidance Council. It will carry Madame Warioba's signature."

Chapter-95

The mother of all coups!

AZ'S LIMOUSINE ARRIVED at JFK Airport at about the same time Homkwap's flight departed Abuja airport. The Governor-General had received a terse message from Cunningham asking him to report in New York immediately.

"How the hell should I know? I haven't the slightest idea why the Commissioner-General wants to see you," Cunningham snapped when Homkwap placed a long-distance call to ask why he was required to be in New York at such a short notice. The message from the Commissioner-General gave Homkwap only twenty-four hours to make the meeting.

"Would this have anything to do with AZ's visit to New York?" Homkwap probed further.

"That's news to me! Was he here? When? To do what? To see whom? Goddamit! What the hell is going on 'round here?" Cunningham sounded even more exasperated than before.

"Anyway, whatever you people want from me, we will know when I get there tomorrow. I should be on the flight departing Abuja later tonight. Since I don't know what the trip is about, I am likely to travel alone."

Smart guy! Cunningham thought to himself. The Secularism Commissioner suddenly began to read ominous meanings into Homkwap's upcoming trip. Something told Cunningham that this wasn't going to be a pleasure pilgrimage. It was wise to leave Madam at home. Homkwap, an optimist to the last, saw nothing to worry about. He put the best construction on the abrupt summon; if they were going to fire him, they would give him due notice and allow him to prepare his handing-over notes. No, this must be one of those routine consultations requiring face time with the WGO high command.

However, try as he might, he could not take his mind off the unscheduled journey. His unease started as soon as he boarded the plane in Abuja. He could not stop wondering why he had to cancel several appointments just to show his face at the WGO headquarters. Could it be that Ugochukwu was pinning for his old job and had, from his cell, engineered a petition against him? Or perhaps the two clerics, Okoye and Kamil, were frustrated that their protests had not moved the Governor-General one bit, and had decided to take their case to New York? This couldn't have been AZ's doing. The raid on the clone's house and office had turned up nothing to suggest that he was aggrieved. But then, what was he doing in New York for so long, and why would the WGO bosses not wait for the deputy to return before ordering the Governor-General to come over? The questions continued to multiply, but comforting answers remained elusive.

Agitated, Homkwap was unable to sleep. He stayed awake as the aircraft zoomed along the runway and took off to cruising altitude. To relieve himself of boredom, he flipped through newspapers, glossy magazines, and other in-flight material generously supplied by the stewardesses. The escapist effort proved futile. Besides the photos of Ekineta splashed across the center pages of Dukyarian Diva, he found nothing of interest.

Six hours into the flight, Homkwap remained sleepless. He shifted and stretched in his first-class seat. He even tried the yoga exercise he'd just sighted in one of the magazines. Nothing worked. He decided he had had enough of the periodicals. He stuffed the pile into the compartment directly in front of him. Using the headphone and the video control panel under his arm-rest, he switched on the inflight entertainment system directly before him. As he expected, the classical music channel did calm his nerves. He thoroughly enjoyed the soft, silky, and heavenly sound coming out of Martha Argerich's superb rendition of Tchaikovsky's Piano Concerto No. 1, Swan Lake, Schumann's Piano Concerto Op 54, Beethoven's Piano Concerto No. 5, Op 73 in E-flat major, and Handel's Messiah. Soothing as the tunes were, they failed to send him to sleep.

It was time to flip to the movie channel. He found nothing worth viewing, not the contemporary drama flicks, not the box office hits, not the National Geographic channel's capture of the epic battle between a crocodile and a python, and certainly not the comedy.

Ruling out the possibility of being sedated, he fell back on distractions. He quickly switched to the interactive map channel. The map indicated that the plane was still over the Atlantic, but gradually approaching Labrador. Only a few hours to go, he reckoned.

He might as well listen to the news. The ubiquitous Global Television Network didn't disappoint. It brought interested passengers news of happenings around the world: The riotous demonstrations in New Delhi against the WGO; the GGC's decision to recall the Pope from exile and convey a special session of the Assembly of Nations to debate the merits of reopening the Basilica; the change of guard in Dukyaria; the World Bank's plan to reschedule Dukyaria's debt and return its DoS. Homkwap's mind raced backwards as the bulletin progressed. What was that again? The change of guard in Dukyaria? He rubbed his eyes with his left thumb and index finger to check if he was asleep or in a trance. He was neither. He was fully awake. He had also heard right. He had been deposed as Governor-General. Whatever doubt he might have about his removal was quickly dispelled by the object staring at him on the television screen—his own portrait, along with the object's unequivocal identification as the "former Governor-General of Dukyaria." The news anchor rounded up the Dukyarian scoop with details of the reception awaiting AZ on arrival in Abuja, including the guard of honor that had been mounted to welcome him back as Interim President.

Homkwap was totally devastated. His head swirled as worst-case scenarios raced through his mind. Although thousands of feet above the Atlantic, he felt as if he was right inside the ocean, lost and unsure in which direction to swim. His mind went to Ekineta, the pretty, classy, and adorable Ekineta. He imagined hands other than his groping that curvaceous body. His imagination ran wild, putting the First Lady in bed with the new chief of state. Homkwap was certain that the shrewd, go-getting woman would dump him in a heartbeat and throw herself at the new helmsman—what with the power and the riches out of the former strongman's reach! AZ might not know how to please a woman, but Homkwap wouldn't put it past Ekineta teaching the clone new tricks. The former Governor-General also had to say goodbye to those parties at which minions stumbled over one another to sing his praises! He could no longer count on sycophants running to him with stories of their closest friends' and immediate family members' disloyal acts or seditious utterances. AZ would now be the center of attention, and the one privileged to wave condescendingly to school children lining the street as his official limousine zoomed past.

The thoughts of what lay ahead were certainly dreadful and unnerving. Yet, they were nothing compared to Homkwap's feeling of absolute helplessness. Confined to his seat, and at that altitude, all he could do was moan his loss. He could do nothing to change the past, the present, or the future. If this had happened while he was still in Dukyaria, he could have mustered the support of loyal soldiers from the human tribe to foil the coup and keep him in office. Now he, or to be more specific, the plane carrying him, was thousands of feet above the Atlantic Ocean, in the middle of nowhere. He had no control over the flight or the crew. He could not order the pilot to turn around and head back to Abuja. In a matter of minutes, the aircraft would land in La Guardia, and he had not the slightest idea what kind of reception awaited him. He was of course certain that no brass band would be waiting and no red carpet would be rolled out.

Meanwhile, AZ was fast asleep on his Abuja-bound flight. He neither glanced at the inflight magazines nor tuned in to the news channels in the inflight entertainment system. He arrived in Abuja only to discover that a guard of honor— the type reserved for the head of state and government—had been mounted by a combined detachment of military and police personnel. He did not know he had been appointed

Interim President until the Chief of Défense Staff saluted him and then whispered into his left ear.

Chapter-96

A crisis-ridden government at home, turmoil abroad

AZ LOST NO TIME constituting his government. As he was soon to find out, the task was not as easy as he had imagined. Sheikh Kamil and Father Okoye flatly turned down his invitation to join the government. He called both on the phone, hoping to convince them to change their minds; he ran into a brick wall. Neither wanted to compromise the integrity of the freedom struggle. Kamil in any case preferred to spend more time with the now fully recovered Abdullah than "dabble in politics." Following his dad to the sites of anti-WGO protests, Abdullah had come to be viewed as a symbol of hope and a worthy successor to Kamil's freedom advancement legacy.

AZ wasn't giving up. He directed Sam to employ all the means necessary to bring the believers on board. Happy to be of service to the new regime, Sam travelled far and wide looking for candidates for ministerial offices. He succeeded, without trying, in winning Babalawo Kaka and Dibea Umezuruike over to the government's side. Both gladly agreed to serve. Emman would have been on top of Sam's list, but the pastor was still in critical condition at the Hayat Hospital. To fill the slots created by the prominent clerics' decision to stay out of the government, Sam recommended that AZ promulgate a decree granting closet Moslems and Christians in the civil service immunity from dismissal. As soon as AZ signed the decree, Sam compiled a fresh list. His name was at the top. It was followed by that of an ally who had never

481

renounced or concealed his Christian affiliation, Pastor Emman. Sam sat in front of his television screen at home waiting for news of his and other nominees' ministerial appointment. The news came alright, but Sam's name was conspicuously missing from the list of AZ's ministers. Also omitted was Pastor Emman's. AZ had not forgotten about either, though. He placed their names on another list, the list of individuals with cases to answer. Both and other accused persons were to be arrested and detained in the Snake Island prison.

To give AZ the breathing space he needed to function undisturbed, the WGO sent Homkwap into exile in Canada's Northwest Territories. The deposed Governor-General did not have to worry about his double taking over his connubial responsibilities. Ekineta's failure to separate official from domestic obligations had landed her in trouble, and eventually, in the women's wing of the Snake Island prison. Unless the lesbian inmates had been released by the time she checked in, the hands likely to grope that body would belong not to one or two, but to several female prisoners.

As a goodwill gesture, AZ tactfully filled prominent positions with men and women of human extraction. Even when he fired Homkwap's ministers, AZ made sure that their replacements were from the human clan. Also conceded to humans were the posts of Chief Commissioner of Police and Director-General of State Security. However, the interim President did not trust the humans sufficiently to leave them in charge of money and finance, defense, military intelligence, and the presidential guard. These make-or-break posts were given to clones.

Despite his best intentions and heroic efforts, AZ was unable to get a grip on Dukyaria. For one thing, the humans never stopped plotting against him and against one another.

He was also unable to curb the widespread and growing antipathy towards the WGO. The Organization had bent over backward to prevail upon the World Bank to grant debt repayment terms favorable to Dukyaria. The Dependent Territory would not only revert to its erstwhile sovereign status but would also be given more time to meet its debt obligations. It would of course continue to be part of the Mali Empire and answerable to the WGO. Its economy would be managed as directed by the Bank officials. The WGO's Capitalism Commissariat and the World Bank would second experts to the Dukyarian Central Bank, the Ministry of Finance, the Financial Records and Accountability Agency, and the Auditor-General's Office.

The external creditors' insistence on having a say in the management of the Dukyarian economy did not go down well with Okoye and Kamil. They did not see why their country's independence should be conditional upon external supervision and validation. They naturally stepped up their street protests.

The WGO faced opposition in other parts of the world. The Vishwa Hindu Parishad did not let up on its agitation for India's split from the Mongolian Empire and for autonomy from the WGO. The turmoil in the other Empires continued unabated. The world was enveloped in disorder— from the Greater America, through the Ottoman-Arab, the Mali, the New Europe, and the Russian, to the Mongolian Empire.

The WGO headquarters was itself a beehive of political intrigue and back-stabbing. Cunningham, increasingly marginalized by Torres and Popov, fought back by enlisting home support. Curiously, as he was about to convert that home support into victory over his internal WGO adversaries, the candidate of a rival political party won the latest presidential election with a landslide majority. Gary Landon, the candidate of the American Homeland Party/AHP, had fought the election by highlighting "the damage" which the American Progressive Party's policy had done to America's interest and to world peace. With the unrest in Dukyaria and other parts of the world at the back of his mind, Landon pledged to review America's position on the WGO and to restore order in an increasingly turbulent world.

As with all campaign promises, the new president's plan to "review" his predecessor's policy was vague. That notwithstanding, Okoye and Kamil were celebrated as heroes of the anti-WGO struggle. Were it not for their determination, nationalities and groups in different parts of the globe would not have rethought the notion of world government. Neither would their own country, Dukyaria, have regained its independence. Both Kamil and Okoye realized that the struggle for freedom was eternal. They knew that long after the WGO had been disbanded, the world would still need to look out for encroachments on individual and collective rights.

Interrogating threats to freedom in the post-WGO era is the specific remit of Dukyarian Rectangle II: Freedom Fiesta.

ACKNOWLEDGMENTS

"And He (Allah) taught Adam the names of all things. He then showed these same things to the angels and asked, 'Tell Me the names of these if you are truthful'. They (the angels) replied, 'Glory be to You, Allah; we have no knowledge except what you have taught us. Verily, it is You, the All-Knowing, the All-Wise." (Qur'an 2:31-32)

I would like to start by thanking Allah, Almighty, the First without a beginning and the Last without an end. Without His grace and mercy, I cannot be, let alone accomplish, anything. As the angels rightly noted, none has any knowledge except what he or she has been taught by Allah, the All-Knowing, the All-Wise, the indisputable Sovereign of the heavens and the earth. I humble myself before Him, and I acknowledge the guidance that I have received, and hope to continue to receive, from His inexhaustible store of knowledge. If I err, as I do from time to time, it is because of that twisted human gene in me, the gene that is already identified in the Qur'anic affirmation, in'nan'nafs la am'marah (Surah 12:53). If I make the right choices, all praise must go to Allah.

As one hadith of the Prophet (sallallahu aleihi wassalam) succinctly puts it, one who is ungrateful to his/her fellow humans cannot be truly grateful to Allah. It is for this reason that I wish to acknowledge the support which I received from a number of individuals. Names are too numerous to mention. However, I cannot but express my deepest appreciation for the assistance that was readily provided by the management and staff of Djarabi Kitabs Publishing.

I am particularly grateful to the Publisher, my esteemed sister, Papatia Feauxzar, not only for her faith in me, but also for providing editorial tips that helped move DUKYARIAN RECTANGLE along without stifling my creative impulses.

Someone once described Hend Hegazi as an amazingly brilliant content editor. My experience working with her confirms that this is a fitting characterization of her competence, professionalism, and attention to detail. I am of course not surprised. Djarabi Kitabs Publishing is home to consummate professionals. Its proofreaders and cover designers are easily among the best in the business. I did not meet them face to face, but I have seen the results of their efforts.

It will sound odd that a novel, which is not yet published, already has a following. Probably because of their familiarity with my previous works, my readers, who saw excerpts from DUKYARIAN RECTANGLE online, have expressed interest in the novel. No vote of confidence can be more resounding than this. The only way to react to such a leap of faith is by saying "Thank you all! In-sha Allah, DUKYARIAN RECTANGLE will not disappoint."

I thank, Allah (Subhanahu wa ta ala) again. I beseech Him to support this humble endeavor in every way that counts.

"There is no compulsion in matters of faith. Verily, the right path is clearly delineated from the wrong path. Whoever disbelieves false deities and believes in Allah, such a person has grasped the most trustworthy handhold that will never break. And Allah is All-Hearing and All-Knowing (Qur'an 2:256)

Glossary

Ajamyy: A non-Arab.

Almajir: Nomadic knowledge seeker.

Asr: Afternoon prayer; the third of the five obligatory daily prayers in Islam.

Ayah: Verse of the Qu'ran, sign.

Babar riga: Big gown. A laced African kaftan.

Barawo: Thief.

Dibea: Medicine man. A witch Doctor.

In-sha-Allah: Allah willing.

Iqamah: Second, small call to prayer, signaling that an obligatory prayer is about to begin.

Isha'a: Night prayer; the fifth of the five obligatory daily prayers in Islam.

Jahannam: Hell.

Khalifa: The heir apparent.

Kuffar: Non-believers.

Maghrib: Post-sunset prayer; the fourth of the five obligatory daily prayers in Islam.

Madrassa: A Muslim school.

Mallam: Teacher.

Markas: Learning center.

Sarauta: Local term for nobility.

Shaytan: Devil.

Shirk: Associating other gods with Allah.

Surah: Chapter in the Qur'an.

Tafsir: Exegesis, explanation, interpretation.

Talakawa: A low, peasant class family.

Tawhid: Pure monotheism; without associating any partners to Allah in any form of worship or belief in His Essence, Names, and Attributes.

Zanna bukar: A cap traditionally worn by the Kanuri people.

Zhur: Noon prayer; the second of the five daily prayers in Islam.